E.E. HORNBURG

THE NIGHT'S CHOSEN

THE CURSED QUEENS, BOOK ONE

THE NIGHT'S CHOSEN

E. E. HORNBURG

THE NIGHT'S CHOSEN
The Cursed Queens, Book 1

CITY OWL PRESS
www.cityowlpress.com

Digital and Paperback Cover Design by MiblArt. Hardback Cover Design by JV Arts. All stock photos licensed appropriately. Map Design by Cartographybird.

Edited by Tee Tate.

For information on subsidiary rights, please contact the publisher at info@cityowlpress.com.

Paperback Edition ISBN: 978-1-64898-018-3

Hardback Edition ISBN: 978-1-64898-426-6

Digital Edition ISBN: 978-1-64898-017-6

Printed in the United States of America

Praise for E. E. Hornburg

"*The Night's Chosen* is a fairytale-like fantasy romance about the burden of duty and following your heart. From the characters to the prose, the fairytale vibes are strong in this book. The world building pulls you in immediately. I look forward to reading the rest of the series!" – *Gabrielle Ash, author of The Family Cross and For the Murder*

"This stunning fantasy debut swept me away. *The Night's Chosen* offers up a delectable blend of intrigue, magic, and romance all wrapped up in fresh takes on fantasy tropes and themes. The author's vivid, lyrical writing is perfect for the story and brings to life a world of wonder in the most divine of ways to create an immersive experience sure to completely transport the reader. Hornburg's story is a total page turner that will keep you guessing through twists and surprises." – *Kat Turner, author of Hex, Love, and Rock and Roll*

"E. E. Hornburg has invented a world with several charming aspects. Her vision of a free-thinking society with fewer sexual hang ups is refreshing. Her pantheon of deities offers cultural variation, and her main character's devout nature is an admirable trait… The value in Ms. Hornburg's story-telling lies in the smaller touches which are sprinkled like stardust throughout the pages." – *InD'tale*

When I was 14, I wanted to write a book, but I didn't know what it would be about. My sister said I should write about Snow White.

For Natalie, who is the kindest, most loyal, and wonderful older sister anyone could ask for who always has my back.

THE KNOWN KINGDOMS

TOWN OF SLANIA

KINGDOM OF CRESIN

CITY OF MARALIS

TEMPLE LAKE

GALLIS HIGH TEMPLE

KINGDOM OF IMARE

UNCHARTED WESTERN SEAS

BELOVIAN ISLANDS

DIAR HIGH TEMPLE

LUANA'S CASTLE
PARAVIAN MOUNTAINS
THE DRAVIAN ISLANDS
COLMA HIGH TEMPLE
THE CEDYRA SEA
ERAL FOREST
SABRYL LAKE
GRANDMOTHER'S COTTAGE
FARREN CITY
EFARE HIGH TEMPLE
KINGDOM OF MARALI
THE LOTUS RIVER
NGDOM
OXARE
CITY OF CYRE
KAHDI
ESERT

Chapter One

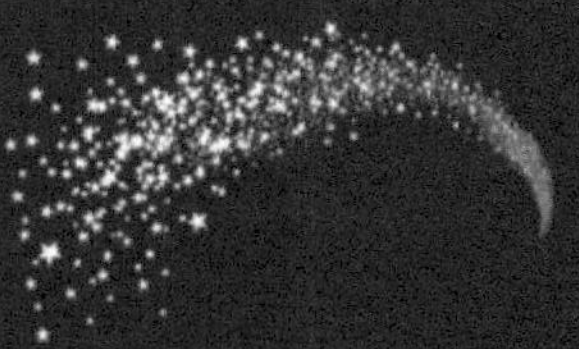

EIRA

Eira never dreaded sunset. Or the Moon Festival. Or returning home. Or seeing the Oxarian royal family. She had always looked forward to those things. But not today. If only she could stop time.

No, not stop time, exactly. If she stopped time, Eira would never become queen.

She'd spent her life, all twenty-odd years of it, preparing to reign. She wanted to stop the *wedding*, something she should have been as prepared for as ruling Cresin.

Eira twirled the betrothal band around her wrist. The wedding was going to happen, regardless of what she wanted. With a deep exhale, she closed her eyes and sang, hoping to ease the storm brewing inside and instead focus on the peaceful magic bestowed on her by Luana's priestesses.

The song ignited the crescent moon tattoo on her chest, and as it glowed, stars formed and sparkled around her head. Swirls of darkness poured out of her fingers and mingled with the betrothal band. The tune and words were meant to sooth and calm the soul, make the singer become one with Luana and be as peaceful as the night sky. Yet it did little to ease the darkness, ice, and stars warring underneath Eira's skin.

Luana grant me peace…grant me grace…

The wedding was this week. Tonight, she and Alvis were going to perform the opening ceremony for the Moon Festival, ushering in Luana's season, where the nights became longer than the day. This year, it would also signify the start of the wedding celebrations. As the Chosens of Luana and Ray, it was believed pieces of the souls of the god and goddess resided inside both she and Alvis, making them the closest to the deities their people would ever have. The two had been betrothed her entire life. Yet now the week arrived and she still wasn't ready.

A knock came at the door, breaking Eira's trance. With a wave of her arms, the stars and darkness vanished, and her tattoo faded. Taking a deep breath, she closed her robe and moved to the door, where the knocking was becoming incessant.

"Eira! Will you quit all your praying and let me in?" Rose's voice drifted from the other side of the door.

Her younger sister almost clubbed Eira in the eye with the velvet box she held as Eira pulled the door open.

"I'd imagine after a year of visiting temples, you'd have had enough of praying by now." Rose barreled into the room, leaning on her crutch, and dropped the box on the vanity with a thud.

"It was more necessary than usual today." Eira shut the door behind them and exhaled, pressing her lips together before placing her hands on her hips. "And maybe if I hadn't received dozens of letters from you and Father begging me to come home from those temples, I wouldn't need to pray so long this morning."

Rose waved Eira off. "It wasn't as though you hadn't planned on being home in time for the Moon Festival. We were simply reminding you."

She dropped her crutch and it clattered to the ground as she flopped onto the plush, deep blue bed, pale freckled arms outstretched. Her copper hair splayed out on the quilt like fiery waves.

Eira had only been home for a few days since her yearlong pilgrimage, and had a curious new fascination with Rose. In so many ways she was the same, but in spite of sending letters all year and seeing one another for the holy days, there was still something different Eira couldn't put her finger on. Rose had always been as fiery as her red hair and ready to speak her mind at any given chance. She never sat still for more than a moment. Yet now there was an air of unease and distance about her Eira didn't recognize. This was one of the reasons she was glad to be home, in spite of everything. She wanted to get to know her sister again.

"And it wasn't *dozens* of letters," Rose replied. "It's been a difficult year."

Eira crossed the room and sat on the bed next to Rose.

"I'm aware. It's not as though I was only sitting in temples praying the whole time. I went and visited as many of the villages that needed help as I could. They're recovering from the fires, but it's going to take a long time."

"I'm not only talking about the fire recovery." Rose propped herself on her elbows. "People have been…talking."

Eira shifted in her seat. "People talk often, Rose, whether I'm here or not."

"Last night after supper, Father and I overheard the Oxarian king and queen talking. It appears they have been concerned about your dedication to the betrothal."

"Oh?" Eira rubbed the band on her wrist again, as though it were squeezing her tighter with each moment.

"It's been five years since your original wedding date. While Father and Alvis have been more than happy to let you go off to university and travel the kingdoms, and your pilgrimage came at the perfect time after the forest fires so you could help the people while you traveled, King Rahim and Queen Shideh and other nobles from Oxare don't see it the same way."

They were smart. Of course they were. They'd raised Alvis, after all, and he was one of the most intelligent people she knew. Eira had been running for so long, and now there was nowhere else to go.

She straightened her shoulders and smiled. "Well, I'll have to prove them wrong, won't I? The whole opening ceremony for the Moon Festival is the commencement of the wedding celebrations. Once they see me there, they'll know I haven't changed my mind about the wedding."

Rose groaned and pushed into a sitting position. "It's not only them.

There're other people, too. They're wondering why you haven't been around."

"That's ridiculous," Eira said through a clenched jaw. "Royals travel through their kingdoms all the time. Father did before he became king, and still does. Besides, after I get married, I'm going to be in Oxare with Alvis for half the year anyway."

"I know."

Rose's touch on her arm sent a wave of warm comfort through her, and Eira felt her shoulders relax. A hint at the closeness they once had.

"But you know how people are. Normally I wouldn't worry about it, and I've been defending you, especially with the guard, and you have so many who are loyal to you…"

Of course Rose defended her. It's what she'd been doing for her their entire lives. What they both had done for each other. No matter how many months Eira was away, she knew she never had to doubt Rose. Even when Eira doubted herself, if Rose was there, she knew all would be fine.

"But?" Eira prodded.

The hesitation in Rose's voice was enough to make Eira's concerns heighten.

"But it's not only gossip. Some members of the council eventually listened, and talked too. So did Queen Amelia." Rose grimaced at the idea of their stepmother. "You know how she is, though. I don't suspect any of the priestesses have gossiped, but you know how close High Priestess Nyx is to some of the council members. I don't want to concern you, but I'd be lying if I said I wasn't relieved you were coming home. This ceremony could be the start of your gaining back their trust."

The new complication brought more to consider, and Eira rubbed her temples to ease the faint throbbing that had started, and slid off the bed. While she respected High Priestess Nyx as the leader of Luana's temple, the two of them often disagreed in matters of theology and politics.

With Nyx having the ears of many councilmen, planting seeds of doubt, Eira was sure all eyes would be on her even more during the ceremony and wedding celebrations. Regardless, whatever doubts Eira had about herself or this marriage, she couldn't—and shouldn't—let it interfere with ascending the throne someday. Her people needed to have complete confidence in her.

She may not have been ready to be married to Alvis, but her desire to be queen never faltered.

The remnants of an afternoon snack sat on the vanity next to the velvet box, and Eira took a piece of apple, popped it into her mouth, and gobbled it. When she opened the box to reveal a silver and blue diadem, the stardust sprinkled on the metal twisting around diamonds made it sparkle on its own without needing any light from the room. Eira lifted it out and perched it onto her long dark hair.

It was one of Cresin's oldest antiques and had been worn by Luana's Chosen for hundreds of years. Eira didn't wear it often, but when she did, she found herself sitting straighter, with her shoulders back and head held high. When she wore it, she could imagine herself being a woman worthy to have it on her head and to live up to the legacy she'd been born into.

She could do this.

She had to do this.

People always said she looked like Queen Isadore—the first Chosen of Luana—and Luana herself. Not as though she ever had anything to compare herself to, other than paintings that followers of Goddess Efare created of what they supposed Luana and Isadore looked like. Legend said all of Luana's Chosen through the generations looked like Luana, and all Eira's life people claimed she had the closest likeness since Isadore, with pale—almost translucent—skin, blood-red lips, dark hair, and sky-blue eyes.

Each of the firstborn heiresses of the Cresin throne were the daughters and Chosen of Luana, as the firstborn heirs of Oxare were the sons and Chosen of Ray.

Rose grabbed her crutch and limped over to Eira. They stood side by side in front of the mirror, opposites at first glance, with Eira's gentleness and Rose's wild nature. On further inspection, the two sisters were perfect compliments to one another.

Rose groaned. "You're not even dressed yet and you already look perfect. It's not fair."

"Perhaps it would help if you changed out of your training leathers."

Rose had a unique and free beauty about her, but usually she was too busy beating the other members of the guard on the training grounds for many to notice.

Or at least, for Rose to notice others noticing her.

Another knock came at the door. The familiar melodic voice of Priestess Cynth came from behind it.

"Your Highness? The opening ceremony is supposed to start soon. We need to prepare you."

Eira's heart sank. Once Priestess Cynth and the ladies-in-waiting came into her chamber, it would be nonstop preparations, celebrations, and being surrounded by people until she was at the altar and at Alvis's side for their wedding at the end of the week. She'd have no peace. No personal space. No chance of stopping the wedding.

Outside her window, past the white rose tree which bloomed and grew up the wall no matter what the season, the songs of Luana's priestesses floated in the air. Part of Eira wished to join them. They didn't know how lucky they were. Free to worship, to make friends, and even to take whoever they wanted to bed whenever they liked.

She could do it. Be one of the priestesses. She'd been bestowed with the same powers, and studied Luana's ways the way they had been—even more so as the Chosen. She'd trained and studied longer than most priestesses, and was given more power at her dedication ceremony as a young woman than the others. Traveling to all of Luana's temples over the past year had shown her this, especially when she'd been in the oldest temple in the Paravian Mountains and her magic awoke there.

Cynth's own mother, who was a priestess there, welcomed Eira with open arms, and when she'd left, promised there would always be a place for Eira.

The town was small, and the mountains dangerous, with strange winged creatures terrorizing them. But she'd still go back in a heartbeat.

And priestesses weren't required to marry.

Eira turned and glanced at herself in the vanity mirror, with the stardust circled around her hair, looking like the midnight sky. She was a queen. Or at least, was going to be.

Queen. This was what she should be focused on. Becoming queen was what was important here.

"Are you all right?"

Her sister's touch on her shoulder brought Eira back to reality.

She blinked and forced a bright smile. "Of course. Why wouldn't I be?"

Rose cocked her head, with a raised brow. "It's a big week, and we've barely talked for months. It's not an odd question."

Priestess Cynth knocked again. "I'm sorry to disturb, Your Highness, but we do need to prepare. Sunset will not wait for us."

No. It would not.

Luana bless it.

Eira took a couple deep breaths, touching her thumb to each of her fingertips to calm herself.

Her pulse slowed to normal, and her muscles relaxed.

"Yes, please come in."

A flurry of women entered the chamber with dresses and cosmetics overflowing in their arms and excited chatter pouring out of their mouths like a waterfall, drowning out the priestesses' songs from outside. Lady Evony at the back of the group held glasses in one hand and a bottle of wine in the other. As the women went to work at removing Eira's robe, Evony, court's unofficial patron of festivities, passed out the glasses and poured the wine with extravagant flourishes and twirls, without spilling a single drop.

Whatever calmness had resided in Eira vanished. Her nerves fired off, her senses overloaded at the ruckus surrounding her. She barely registered the weight of the drink in her hand.

The ladies cheered when Evony raised a glass over her curly head of hair, and they all followed suit.

"To our royal highness, Princess Eira," Evony said, "her betrothed Prince Alvis, and the coming of Luana's season. Gods know all the fun happens in the night, after all."

The stardust in the ceremony gown Priestess Cynth held glimmered in her eyes as she looked over her shoulder at Evony.

"I wasn't aware you had the patience to wait for night for your type of fun," Cynth said.

Rose chuckled when Evony placed a hand over her heart and dropped her jaw.

"It's not my fault people beg for my company, no matter the time of day," Evony said.

Rose cleared her throat. "Less drinking, more helping." She stretched her permanently twisted ankle in front of Evony and wiggled it in a circle. "I can never get my straps tight enough."

Evony sighed before she finished off her wine, then set the glass on the table with a thud and cocked her voluptuous hip.

"Out of all my talents," she said, "this is the one I'm asked to do. Whoever said coming to Farren Castle was going to be glamorous never mentioned this."

"Yes, I'm sure the fish in Slania are much more glamorous," Rose said.

"It took months to get the smell out of my clothes." Evony took the straps from the pile of Rose's ceremonial clothes, and winked.

Within minutes, the white leather-like straps were wrapped around Rose's ankle, straightening and smoothing the limb. It had been a gift from their grandmother, who served Kutlaous, the god of nature, in Eral Forest. The straps were enchanted with Fae magic to give Rose the strength she needed to walk without a crutch for short periods. Such as evening ceremonies and balls.

Or as Rose preferred, on the training grounds and while patrolling the castle.

The white of the straps faded until they were invisible, showing off Rose's tattoo, dedicated to Aros, the god of war and hunting. When unbound by the straps, the tattoo appeared to be thorny rose vines etched into Rose's warped and twisted skin. When straightened by the straps, it was the sword of Aros, with white and red roses wrapped around the blade, like the roses outside each of their bedchamber windows, planted after their mother died. A symbol of Rose's dedication not only to her god, but to their bond as sisters and princesses.

Something stirred inside Eira each time she saw it.

The time spent preparing went by in a blur of cloth and perfumes and stardust. The sparkling gown clung to Eira like a second skin once it was pulled over her head and down her body. The skirt swirled around her legs and ankles in a silver river. The neckline, like all of her ceremonial gowns, dipped low and wide to expose her tattoo. A symbol to be showed off and admired, proving she belonged to Luana. It was a fashion Eira had grown used to after she'd received her tattoo.

When she was younger and first growing into her body, she'd felt exposed and shy. Now she was proud to show her dedication to Luana and kingdom. She enjoyed the power mixed with sensuality in her costumes.

Where there wasn't fabric, there were crystals and stardust stuck and painted to her arms, legs, and bosom. This day, it was a gown she could hide in. In this gown, she not only belonged to Luana, but *was* Luana. Goddess of the night, darkness, and winter. In this gown, she was supposed to welcome the changing of the seasons, where the daytime was shortened to make way for longer nights.

She was also supposed to greet her lover, Ray, god of the sun.

Eira could only imagine what Alvis's ceremony attire would look like.

Perhaps Eira could at least pretend to be Luana if she was dressed for the part, and be separate from herself.

Time moved too quickly, and before she knew it she was being escorted by Priestess Cynth out of her bedchamber and toward the great hall. All the attendees were waiting for them there. Her father, stepmother, Alvis and his family, and all of the lords and ladies of the kingdom. Her kingdom. The one she'd spent months helping to regain its bearings after flash forest fires burned through the villages, leaving only ashes in their wake. The one she'd been born in, and who believed in her through every step of her life.

Until she'd started running away five years ago.

Now she returned, and people were talking. Eira's cheeks burned as shame washed over her. She'd been foolish and immature all this time. So many others had it far worse than she did, and Alvis was a good man. One of the best she'd ever known. He was the perfect person to bring the kingdoms of Cresin and Oxare together the way Isadore and Sanson did all those centuries ago, when they were at war with one another.

Rose was at her side when they approached the great hall's door, and squeezed Eira's hand. She was out of her training leathers and wore a simple silver gown which resembled a long jacket with short sleeves. It was shorter in the front, revealing tight leggings, and billowed out in the back like a cloak. If it weren't for Rose's usual playful smile, she'd look regal.

"You'll be wonderful," Rose said.

She gave her sister a warm hug, then walked away and into the great hall, leaving Eira and Priestess Cynth alone. Eira pushed her shoulders back and straightened her diadem, but despite that her heart sank as it begged her to turn and run.

No, it was time she behaved like the future queen and Chosen they all pictured her to be.

Chapter Two

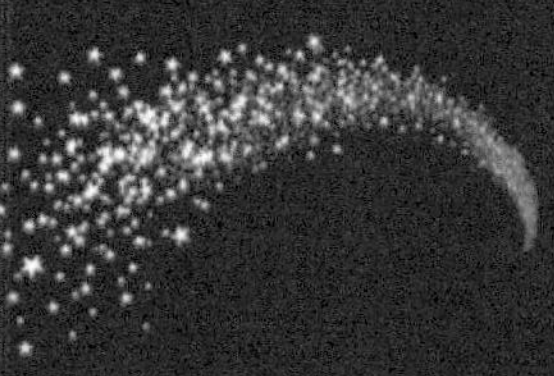

EIRA

As she entered the great hall, dread crept down Eira's spine to the tune of the flutists song, like a spider leaving a trail of silk. Her pace slowed, palms sweating, as she ascended onto a high platform. She tried to fixate her focus on the Efare priestess's tattooed fingers, which danced over the keys and glowed to create images of the notes that swirled around her deep purple robes—instead of how all those in attendance were focused on her.

Eira breathed in the gentle fragrance of the mums, and the beauty of the hydrangeas decorating the room, and could smell a hint of the decadent meal wafting in from the kitchens, waiting to be enjoyed once the ceremony was over. The grand hall was awash in deep autumnal colors of purples and oranges and yellows, celebrating the changing of the seasons when days grew shorter and night grew longer. This was when Eira should be connecting with her power and goddess the most, and embrace the cold and darkness. It was said that this time of year the love between Luana and Ray was the most powerful, which was why the colors of nature were so deep and vibrant. Why the wedding was held during season.

Eira closed her eyes and sighed. Finally, she allowed herself to glance over the crowd. All the council members were there—the lords and ladies of Cresin, nobles from Oxare and the other surrounding kingdoms were scattered through the room. Lady Evony, along with the other ladies-in-waiting, had their own table, and she raised a glass toward Eira.

Rose went to the huntsman Cal's side and adjusted the sword attached to her belt while muttering something to him, oblivious to how he looked at her.

Father and Queen Amelia were seated on the far side of the room, next to Alvis's parents. In past years, they would take turns performing the ceremonial dance to reenact the story of Luana and Ray's love. Not this year. They were passing the tradition onto Eira and Alvis now, so they stayed in the background.

Eira took comfort in Father's face beaming toward her, and decided not to focus on how the others would be watching her every move.

On the other side of the room stood Prince Cadeyrn, Alvis's younger brother. Eira attempted to unclench her jaw as he wrapped his muscular arm around a young woman. She wasn't sure if Cadeyrn would be there until the day of the wedding, as he often was away on some mission with his soldiers.

Or warming some woman's bed.

For a brief moment, he met Eira's gaze with his golden eyes, and winked. Her breath caught in her throat, but she couldn't help offering him a smile in return before looking away.

High Priestess Nyx stood on another platform above everyone's heads, and spoke over the music, her voice strong as she narrated the love story of Luana and Ray.

"Before there was the world, there was Luana and Ray. One in the dark, and one in the light. Yet each could see one another from afar. The bright light of the sun in the distance and the sparkling stars in the darkness."

The flute's music faded, and in its place a trumpet sounded as Eira and Alvis descended the stairs to meet one another in the center of the room. Her stomach sank as they moved toward one another, and she tried to let everything else in the room disappear so she could focus on Alvis.

He wore a sleeveless golden tunic with rich embroidery and sun crystals adorning the fabric. His tawny arms and face were painted gold the way Eira's were painted in silver. The swirls emphasized his dark brown eyes and the curves of his muscles like he'd been made from sparkling sand.

Next, high priest of Ray, Cyrus, spoke, strong and steady as though his words alone would convince Eira to continue on.

"Each day they watched after one another, and they would send messages across the space between them. The years went on, and the two fell in love. One day, they went out to finally see the face of their beloved."

Alvis's gaze roamed over Eira's face and over her body as he wrapped his arms around her before returning his gaze to hers. He gulped, his hand on the small of her back. Eira's own grip tightened to keep from shaking.

They danced in front of the floor-length windows, which displayed the setting sun, while the priestesses moved in on the sides as the dance went on, their lanterns filling with starlight. Priests came with torches, and together they made the room look as though it was bursting into flame, the way it had when Ray and Luana's love created the world. A reminder of what they were representing to their people, and Eira let herself get swept into the story.

They finished, and the emotion from the dance vanished as Alvis relaxed his shoulders and took a step back so only their hands were touching. The ever-formal and proper prince.

"I'm glad the dance is over," he whispered.

"As am I." Eira bit her lip.

Her mind began to race, and her stomach fluttered. Should they have been glad it was over, though? If they were to represent the greatest love story of all time, shouldn't they want any excuse to be near each other and express their passion?

"Yet their time together could only be short lived," Nyx continued. "The confines of the night and day meant they could never truly be together. As day turned into night, Ray was pulled further and further away from his love."

The priests circled Alvis, and they backed away off to the side of the grand hall. Alvis reached out as though he were trying to will himself back to Eira, and she also extended an arm out to him.

"Yet as Luana watched him leave and saw the new world they were creating," Cyrus said, "she vowed to find a way to be together."

Eira lowered her arm and stood tall. She shifted her focus across the room to her future mother- and father-in-law, and stared at them to dare them to doubt her intention to marry their son. In the costume, the makeup, the music, and the story, Eira let herself delve into the role of Luana, as they all saw.

Queen Shideh matched her stare and gifted Eira with a silent nod as the lights went out in the ballroom.

Within moments, the priestesses lit the space once again with starlit lanterns, making the room look as though it was the night sky. The spectators around the room broke into chatter, and an orchestra led by an Efare priest struck a bright tune while everyone prepared for the feast.

Rose appeared at her side and looped an arm through Eira's, and they strolled through the ballroom to the head table, where they would sit with their father and Queen Amelia.

"I believe any fears the Oxarian royal family had have been assuaged," Rose said. "At least a bit. Don't you agree?"

"I should hope so." Eira sat and avoided looking at anyone around her.

There was nothing else she could do now, save enjoy the meal.

The feast went by so fast, Eira didn't have time to get lost in her own worries. The moment their plates were cleared, the music started. Eira and Alvis led the dancing, along with their parents, and once it was done, they were separated to attend to the other nobles and guests.

Eira was able to escape one particularly awful dance partner, and tried to catch her breath. As much as she loved balls, the worst partners always seemed to find her. Either they were constantly stepping on her feet, or they were overly eager to be touching Luana's Chosen and couldn't resist the opportunity to let their hands wander, even though she would politely place said hands in a more appropriate location.

She sought out Alvis to dance with him again, but when she spotted him in the crowd, he was speaking with a group of Fae representing

Eral Forest in the stead of her grandmother, who was the god Kutlaous's minister in the forest, a permanent fixture to assist the dwellers there in whatever they needed. She wasn't their ruler or leader, as each group had their own codes and traditions, but aided in resolving disputes and offering shelter and healing.

As Kutlaous couldn't be there in all of his realms at once, a minister was anointed. The position bonded Grandmother to the forest, and she was unable to leave for longer than a day or two. Grandmother would join the festivities on the wedding day alone.

Alvis was in his element now, planning and negotiating, so Eira let him enjoy the moment before they needed to return to other Moon Festival duties.

Yet there wasn't anyone else to go to. Rose and Cal were dancing off to the side, Cal avoiding Rose's missteps. Evony and Cynth were in the corner, laughing and whispering. The other ladies had all found dance partners or were observing the crowd and bargaining with one another who they'd take to their beds that night. Meanwhile, Father was having his goblet filled with more wine, and wrapped his arm around the waist of the Marquis of Marallis, Phillip, his most recent lover.

Rose had written that the two of them had come together in the last several months, and they rarely left one another's side in the short time Eira had been home.

Part of Eira was glad for this. It was the worst-kept secret of their court, how King Brennan and Queen Amelia hadn't married for love, and it'd been years since they'd been faithful to one another. Eira couldn't remember the last time Father looked so happy and relaxed with someone.

She advanced through the ballroom, hearing bits and pieces of conversations. Most people were marveling at the ceremony, or about how towns were recovering from the fires the previous year.

"Well, you know it's doubtful an heir will come any time soon," said one tall noblewoman with slicked-back brown hair. "We all have been waiting for this wedding, of course, but once someone loses their first…"

The woman at her side gasped and clutched her breast. "You don't believe those rumors, no doubt spread by silly servants. That was years ago!"

Eira tried to catch her breath, and rushed past them before they noticed she'd been nearby. A small circle of space surrounded Eira as she wandered to a table full of food to get some refreshments to stop her trembling lips. People bowed and curtseyed as she passed, and she greeted them each with a smile and a nod. They all stepped to the side and cleared a path for her, but no one sought out conversation. Nor would they, unless Eira initiated it first.

They would talk about her, but never to her. As though the bits of gossip would never reach her ears.

Eira's mind raced. Where had those nobles heard such things about her? Were these the rumors Rose had been referring to?

"May I?"

Eira turned to see Cadeyrn standing before her with his hand outstretched. Her old friend looked dashing in his ornate red jacket, and with his long dark hair, which appeared as though he'd attempted to tame it for the festival. Cadeyrn's smile took up his entire face and could charm even the coldest of hearts.

Eira's face warmed. He'd always had impeccable timing.

She couldn't help but let her smile grow, and placed her hand in his to let him lead her out onto the dance floor. Her heart hammered against her ribcage as he twirled her around, faster than the song called for, until they were in the center and lost in the crowd, and Eira laughed, forgetting about the gossip.

"Cade, you're going to make me dizzy!" She patted his arm.

"If you fall, I'll catch you." He dipped Eira so low she nearly touched the ground, but his hands were strong and sure as he held her.

He brought his lips closer to her ear, and Eira's skin tingled.

"You were wonderful out there tonight," he said.

Heat crept up Eira's neck to her cheeks once again as Cadeyrn brought her upright. She'd been careful not to focus on who was in the audience, watching the passionate dance.

"Thank you," she replied. "I surely hope it was enough to convince your mother and father of my intentions."

Cadeyrn furrowed his brows and pulled her in closer. "Whatever do you mean?"

They turned in slow circles, and Eira also held Cadeyrn close while she willed her hands to stop shaking.

She took a deep breath to prepare herself for what she needed to say.

"I've been told there have been doubts about if I plan to marry your brother or not."

They now danced to the proper tempo and wore smiles so those around wouldn't suspect the nature of their conversation. But Eira couldn't help but notice how his pounding heartbeat matched hers.

"You wouldn't know anything about it, would you?" she said.

Cadeyrn swallowed hard and grimaced. "These days, I've been making more of a point to remain with my soldiers, or to be on my own lands and not in my family's palace. I am not privy to their private conversations, as I once was."

Whenever Eira met Alvis for an event where his family would be in attendance, Cadeyrn would be absent. He held a high ranking in their military and often was away. Otherwise, he spent time at his own estate. Even when Eira visited the kingdom on her pilgrimage a few months prior, and he'd been at the castle, they'd barely seen one another. She'd been hoping to speak with him, but each time they were in the same room he'd been occupied with the company of someone else, leaving Eira blinking back tears and wondering if he was also running away from something.

Eira searched the planes of Cadeyrn's face, as though she could find more answers, and found herself wetting her lips. She caught him doing the same.

"Perhaps not," she said. "But even as you traveled together to come here, you never spoke to them of me? Nothing which would make them doubt me? You haven't heard any rumors at all?"

Cadeyrn's smile faded, and a shadow fell over his gold eyes.

"No. I have not spoken to them about you."

Eira's breath caught, and she blinked a few times. After taking several calming breaths, she cleared her throat.

"Of course. I'm sure I'm worrying about nothing. I only hope your family knows I intend to keep my promise and marry Alvis, no matter what impression I may have given in the past."

A flash of surprise in his eyes, and Cadeyrn tightened his grip around her waist.

He clenched his jaw. "I never assumed otherwise. Neither did anyone else in my family, I'm sure."

Eira squeezed his hand. "There's no reason I wouldn't. We are both Chosen. It is the deities' will."

"Yes, and we all must do what they ask, mustn't we?" Cadeyrn pressed his lips together as he pulled Eira in even closer, as though he could keep them from falling apart.

Eira should have pulled away, but she didn't.

"And Alvis is your brother. He's going to be a great king one day, and a wonderful husband. He cares about me, and I care about him." The words came flooding out of Eira's lips as if a dam had broken.

If only she could've stopped them. But it was as though someone was forcing them out of her brain and into Cadeyrn's ears.

"He's never done or said anything that would cause me to not want to marry him. Besides, our alliance will be even stronger than it is now—"

Cadeyrn dropped his chin and rubbed her back in small circles, which no one else but Eira could detect.

"I know," he said.

Eira nodded and tried to let his touch comfort her. "Good."

"I'm glad everything is clear now. I'll be sure my family is aware."

He didn't stop rubbing her back, but the harshness in his voice cut through her.

Eira looked about the room as she and Cadeyrn danced. At least she'd made herself clear of what needed to happen. Yet it did little to calm her pounding heart.

She cleared her throat. "I'm surprised you're here before the wedding ceremony. I'd have thought you'd be out on campaign. You always are lately. There are many times I wished to speak to you."

Cadeyrn avoided her gaze and spun them around so they were lost in the middle of the dance floor again.

"Yes, it has been a long time since we've seen each other and spoken, hasn't it?"

"And when we have been in the same place, you've been too busy with other women."

He flashed a sly grin, which tugged at a corner of his mouth, curling his lip up, and Eira wasn't sure if she found it charming or worthy of a slap.

"Yes, they do keep me busy."

"Too busy to speak with an old friend?"

He finally looked at her again, his eyes narrowed. "If you've ever wished to see me, I never would have stopped you. Besides, you have been focused on your prayers, studies, and my brother."

Near a window leading to a balcony, Alvis stood sipping his wine and was still speaking with a tall Fae man, and for a brief moment their eyes met. A small grin came to his lips as he drank and watched her dance.

"I should go see Alvis, in fact. I've barely been able to see him since the ceremony, and this is part of our celebration, after all."

"Of course, it is what's right," Cadeyrn said, his voice almost a growl, then stepped away from her and bowed. "Thank you for the dance, *sister*."

"Thank you, Cadeyrn." Eira's voice cracked when she said his name. "I needed this."

He squeezed her hand one last time before turning to find a pair of young ladies who did not have dance partners. His smile appeared bright and charming, but it didn't reach his eyes. He said something to his new companions, making them laugh, then took one on each arm and spun them onto the dance floor. Their laughter echoed through the grand hall as Eira made her way to her betrothed, her own forced, bright smile plastered to her face.

"Pardon me for interrupting." Eira looped her arm through Alvis's and kissed his cheek. "But I've barely seen my betrothed all night, and I wish to have another dance."

The Fae bowed. "Please, enjoy yourself, Your Highness. And your grandmother passes on her best and says she wishes she could have been here sooner."

Eira nodded for him to rise. "Thank you. And it would be wonderful if she could've been here for the festival all week, but I'm grateful she can at least come for the wedding."

"Kutlaous's minister's life is never quiet. But it is my pleasure to be here in her stead. She likes for me to give reports on what is happening in Cresin, and I do enjoy a bit more of a refined setting periodically."

"Indeed, her life is not quiet in the least," Eira said. "And we are happy to host you whenever you wish."

She and Alvis excused themselves and returned to the dance floor. Alvis wasn't as smooth of a dancer as Cadeyrn, but still glided her around the room.

"It's good to have you back," Alvis said. "I'm glad you were able to do all you wanted. But I have to admit, I'm ready for our next chapter."

"You are?" Eira stumbled, but Alvis helped her regain balance.

"It's time, Eira. Why wouldn't I be?" He was as calm as he ever was, although she'd rarely heard him raise his voice. "This is what we've been preparing for, and it's our duty. Besides, it's a good time for me to get to know Cresin and help it more. I know a thing or two about fire, you know."

He raised his hand and let a few sparks dance from his fingertips. It was what Eira had been considering each time she visited a village. As Ray's Chosen, Alvis could manipulate and handle fire the way Eira could ice. He knew better than anyone how to recover from flames.

"You will be of great help to us in the coming months," Eira said. "And it is good to see you again."

Alvis pulled her closer, and they slowed the dance.

It wasn't a lie. Since returning home and preparing for the wedding, Eira did enjoy seeing Alvis again. He was a good friend, and always had been. She wondered if friendship was enough to carry on this marriage.

Eira brought herself in even closer, and whispered in his ear, "Should I come to you tonight?"

Alvis blinked a few times. "We only have a few days to wait."

The last time they'd been together and knew the next time would be the Moon Festival, they'd agreed to spend the nights in their own beds in the days leading to the wedding ceremony. Yet the nights they were alone together were the ones where Eira's doubts went away. At least, for a little while.

"I know," she replied. "But it's been so many months since we've seen each other, and I'd like to see you more on our own before the wedding. Just the two of us. Don't you want…"

"I'd be a fool not to."

"So tonight—"

A *clang!* echoed through the room, followed by a *thud!* that shook the floor. At the sound of Lady Evony's scream, Eira and Alvis turned. The crowd erupted in chatter and panic as Rose and Cal pushed through them, their swords bumping against tables and guests as they rushed to the scene.

"Make way! Move!" Cadeyrn followed them, gripping his own sword.

The crowd divided to give them a path, and Eira removed herself from Alvis to join them.

"We need an attendant!" Phillip yelled.

Eira fought the sensation in her chest and the dizziness swimming into her head before she hurried toward the noise as the others pushed through the crowd, to the center of dance floor, where a goblet lay on the ground with its red wine spilled across the marble tile, staining it like blood. Next to it, someone had fallen, their hand lying on the ground as though they had tried to throw the wine away from themselves but had lacked the strength before falling. The body was splayed across the floor in a lump, covered by a dark blue cloak, like a shroud.

Eira took a step into the clearing around the body. She didn't want to see who it was, even if deep down she already knew.

Cal knelt and lowered the cloak to reveal the victim, his head hung low as he did. Eira didn't need to see the face but couldn't tear her gaze away. A cry caught in her throat as air rushed from her lungs. Everything else in the room grew fuzzy, and her knees buckled just as Cadeyrn wrapped his arms around her waist to catch her before she collapsed.

Father.

Chapter Three

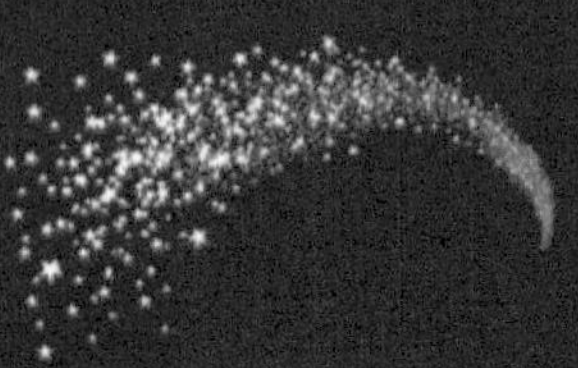

EIRA

Father wasn't dead—the one piece of comfort Eira clung to as she sagged in the chair at his side, Rose standing next to her. If only they could figure out what was wrong with him, why he wouldn't wake.

Eira's throat thickened as her gaze fell upon his chest and its shallow rise and fall.

"Are you sure there's nothing else we can do?" Alvis said to the attendant.

The attendant pushed up the sleeves of her blue robe and worked at dabbing oils into the king's head and feet. The tattoo of a chalice pouring a stream of water flowed around her wrist and glowed each time she administered an oil.

"There is nothing left now but to wait and pray to Gallis until we have more answers," she said.

Eira squeezed Father's hand and moved her stool closer to the bed. One would think he was merely asleep, but when one looked closely, his chest barely rose and fell to breathe.

She'd seen the dead before, and sat with grieving families when loved ones passed. Father's face hadn't lost any color. And hours after the poisoning, his limbs hadn't grown stiff, even if his skin was colder to the touch. Besides, when people died while their body was in the room, it was obvious the person's soul had already been taken away by the goddess Stula. Whoever was lying there in the room was only a body, not a person. But when Eira looked at the king, she saw her father.

The attendant had shown Eira where to find his pulse. It was so faint it took several minutes to notice the slight movement.

"You can administer oils if you like," the attendant said. "You don't need attendant magic for each round."

Rose scoffed. "Oils? That's all?"

Eira exhaled and shot her sister a glare. After hours of their stepmother yelling at every attendant who'd come into the king's chamber, and all the guards, before she'd finally stormed out for the night, Eira didn't need her sister to start the hostility all over.

"That would be wonderful, thank you," Eira said to the attendant, hoping her smile was apology enough for Rose's rudeness. "You can leave some on the table."

The woman bowed and left the room.

Alvis hunched over the bed's footboard, his knuckles white from grasping it. His brow was furrowed, as he'd been trying to find solutions all night.

"Do you think it could have been the marquis?" he said.

Phillip was the first person Queen Amelia questioned, claiming he was most likely the attempted assassin, since he was the closest to the king at the time. Eira didn't know the man well, but each time she had met him, he was kind and jovial. Yet he'd hardly left Father's side all night.

Thankfully, the questioning hadn't been fruitful, and Phillip was now in his chambers.

Eira leaned back in her seat, tapping the wooden arm rest. "It does seem out of character for the marquis. He might be able to answer more questions, though, once he's no longer in shock."

Rose rapped her crutch on the floor with a thud. She'd removed her straps to let their magic rest as the night wore on.

"He would never hurt Father," she said. "They are practically inseparable."

"I didn't know they'd become so close." Eira tilted her head.

Father had several lovers over the years, and it became the norm.

Queen Amelia had her own as well, and it didn't bother either one of them. They'd given up on having their own child years ago. It was rare for Father to keep with a single person for long.

Rose narrowed her eyes at Eira and tightened the grip around her crutch.

"His exploits have been fewer the last few years. The marquis and he have been close for some time now. I've told you about him in my letters, but you've been gone so much, there's some things you have to see for yourself. You've missed a lot."

Eira's jaw dropped. She had reasons for leaving, and intended to tell Rose about them. Eventually.

Through their letters over the last several months, Eira assumed Rose was fine, but apparently she wasn't.

Rose whispered, "I invited you to come as a guard and escort…and for company. You were the one who said no."

Before Eira had left for her pilgrimage, Rose told her she'd been running away from something, and Eira could still see the accusation in her sharp green eyes.

Rose bit the inside of her cheek and pushed her hair back. After a moment, her shoulders sagged and her face softened.

"It's in the past now. We can't change it." She tapped her fingers on the side of her thigh. "I can't sit here and wait any longer. I'm going to Captain Avarett to see if there's a way I can help." Rose kissed the top of Eira's head and gave a small nod to Alvis before leaving the room.

For the first time in months, Eira and Alvis were alone. He straightened his jacket and sat on a stool next to her. The paint on his body was still perfect, and hardly a wrinkle appeared on his clothing. He was calm and put-together, as though this were a simple misstep in a dance.

"I've sent messages to the best attendants in Oxare," he said, "and they'll be here as soon as possible. I'll also go to the library and see what sort of information I can find that could be of use. Is there anything else I can do to help?"

Something in Eira softened, and she felt guilty for how selfish she was being. He was such a good man. Many women had much worse matches.

"I wish I knew," she replied.

He reached out a stiff arm and held her hand in his. He spoke slowly, like he'd never done this before. In all the time Eira had known him, he always found solutions to whatever problems they faced.

"Do you want me to sit with you? Anything you wish to talk about? I know you're upset. You barely said a word through the council meeting when we discussed continuing on with the wedding if he doesn't awaken."

If he did awaken, they'd wait until he recovered. But the kingdom needed an heir.

Eira closed her eyes and willed the tears to disappear. Numerous times, she'd wanted to speak to Alvis about the wedding and her doubts, but never knew how. The problem was not with Alvis. Never Alvis. He'd been nothing but kind, considerate, and understanding. Eira's doubts lied with herself. But how could she ever explain this to him without hurting him? He was her friend, after all.

"I've barely had time to recover from my travels." Eira's voice quaked, and she tried to stop shaking. "When I came home, there was all of the wedding planning. And now this. It's all so overwhelming. I'm sure there are moments you feel the same way."

Alvis rubbed his short beard. "There are days the weight of what we're supposed to do and be for our people weighs on me more heavily than others. Then I remember how we've been preparing for it so long. The gifts the deities have given us. How I won't be going it alone…and it's what we're supposed to do. It's our duty to our kingdoms and deities. The Chosens have been doing this for a long time, and it works. The tradition is there for a reason. It helps."

Eira dropped her head and rubbed her temples. She wasn't sure what answer she wanted him to give, but that hadn't been it. The things that gave him comfort were what caused her dread.

Bells from the temple rang, and Eira and Alvis looked toward the window. Praise Luana, she was saved from having to give Alvis any more answers.

"Midnight prayers will be starting soon. I should go."

Eira escaped the king's chamber before Alvis could stop her.

Chapter Four

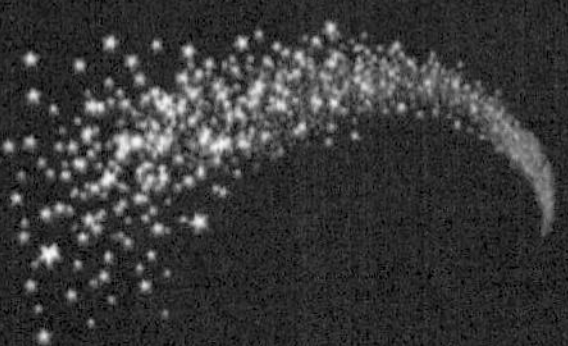

EIRA

The songs of the priestess and acolytes rose into the air, making the starlit lamps float and dance over the heads of the those seated on the benches. Priestess Cynth stood in front, her face and arms raised to the glass ceiling, and the swirling darkness in Eira calmed. She let it sooth her. The reflections of the moon and stars shining through the ceiling landed on Cynth's silver robes, making her glow in their light.

The midnight prayers were usually sparsely attended, save for a few devout followers and priestesses. It was why Eira loved it. This service was much more intimate than others, and the perfect time to clear her mind. This night, though, the benches were more filled than usual with all who wished to pray for king and kingdom.

It reminded her of the dedication ceremony. Hers, how the benches had been full then, and people stood in the back to watch. A porcelain pool, so large a person could swim in it, stood at the front, filled with black iced water. High Priestess Nyx dunked Eira underneath and pressed her hand against Eira's chest to form the tattoo. Eira wanted to scream from the pain as ice and darkness pierced through her skin and coursed through her veins. As Luana's Chosen, she was in the water longer than others who dedicate themselves to the goddess, giving the darkness and ice more time to seep into her body and give her more power. When she emerged, the whole temple erupted in applause as she stood before them, shivering, and skin blue as storm clouds. Alvis helped her out of the pool, and his skin was so hot against hers she thought her hand would burn. When the ceremony was over, Cadeyrn and Rose gave her warm blankets to wrap around herself. She'd spent the next several days in front of the fire, bundled in blankets, drinking hot tea until her body adjusted to the magic. Eira had only been twelve at the time—the first she'd felt the burden of being Luana's Chosen weigh on her shoulders.

As the service ended and the parishioners left the temple, Eira trudged to the front of the sanctuary and knelt before Priestess Cynth, basking in the gentle moonlight that shone on the crystals of her gown she still wore from the ball. It created a small ring of glittering stars on the marble floor around them. Cynth placed her palm on Eira's head and quietly chanted.

Sighs and syllables washed over Eira, and she tried to pull comfort from them. She clutched her hands to her chest as though she could stop the anxiety and sadness and the incessant need to escape for a little longer. Usually, the time with Luana helped to calm her mind, and granted clarity. But it failed her tonight. It was as though she'd been holding her breath all day, and in only a little while longer she could release it back in the comfort of her own chambers. Alone.

Eira knew she'd told the council she could go through with the wedding in spite of the circumstances, but it was a lie. She couldn't marry Alvis. Especially not without Father there at her side.

Yet she was the heir. She was Chosen. She needed to be strong for her kingdom.

Soft touches met Eira when she moved to her feet, entering Cynth's embrace.

"May Luana be with you during this time, Your Highness," she said. "If you need me, please do not hesitate. We have a priestess at your father's chambers now, praying over him for healing."

Eira offered a tight smile, but didn't speak. She hadn't spoken a word since arriving for the service. If she did, she would break.

After silently dismissing Cynth, and the temple emptied, Eira sat on a bench and looked at the altar and the wash of moonlight surrounding it. She tried to clear her mind and to release what was on her heart through silent prayers, but sensed the presence of someone else still in the temple. She knew who it was without having to look. He spoke with Cynth in muffled whispers behind her.

Eira poised her hands in prayer and focused. *Luana, give me grace.*

It was silent for a few moments save for his footsteps echoing as he approached her bench. Eira considered dismissing him, too, but couldn't find the strength. She blinked away the tears forming before he could notice.

Cadeyrn took a seat next to Eira, stretched his arms over the back of the bench, and they sat with only the sound of their breaths to fill the silence. He didn't touch or speak to her, but his presence was as loud as the trumpets from the ceremony earlier in the evening.

She was so tired. Of holding everything in all the time and denying what she wanted, and needing to be brave while feeling as though she had no one to turn to or to share the burden. In that moment, being alone would have been best. But she didn't want to be.

After a few moments, surprising even herself, when Eira knew they were alone, she slumped in her seat and her head landed on his shoulder. They were sitting closer together than she'd thought.

"What is this?" Cadeyrn wrapped his arm around her.

I should push him away. Someone could walk in at any moment.

She didn't want to, and didn't have the energy to care.

"Our Luana surely cannot be tired during her nightly reign?"

Eira sighed. "I am not Luana tonight. Nor any night. I could never be her."

Her voice lacked emotion and energy, as though the events of the day had sucked all of it out.

"That's not true." Cadeyrn tucked her in closer to his side and ran his fingers over her arm.

His touch was soft and mesmerizing, dulling enough that sleep was tempting. She need only close her eyes and she'd be asleep, right there in his arms.

"You can be anything," he said. "You're worried about your father. The attendants will find a cure, and all will be well. You'll see."

"Will they find a cure before I marry your brother at the end of the week?"

Cadeyrn hesitated, his breath catching in his throat. "I'm not sure."

Which was the truth of it. No one knew anything, and she was still going to have to get married. This was ridiculous. She needed to put her head on straight and stop behaving as though she were in some fantasy.

Eira sighed and sat upright again, pushing his arm away from her.

"I thought so."

Cadeyrn let out a heavy sigh and returned his arm to the back of the bench.

He outstretched his hands in surrender. "They're still asking you to proceed with the wedding?"

Eira rolled her neck and leaned against the bench once again, but refused to look at him.

"Yes, and the council raises a good point. If the worst were to happen, we need to ensure more heirs to the throne."

She sensed Cadeyrn tense at her side, and resisted the urge the place her hand on her stomach.

"Heirs. Of course."

A depiction of Luana and Ray stood at the center of the altar, their silver and gold statues intertwined as they reached for one another but never touched. Under their feet, they stood on the world they created.

Eira rubbed her betrothal band. "They're a large legacy to live up to."

Cadeyrn leaned forward and rested his elbows on his knees, looking at her, trying to catch her eye.

"If anyone can do it, it's you, Eira. You're going to be a wonderful wife and queen."

"Perhaps. But how do I know? How do you know?" She faced him.

He had such confidence in her that she didn't have for herself.

The casual and charming smile Cadeyrn usually wore was gone and didn't hide the concern in his gold eyes.

"Because it's who you are. This is what you're meant to do. It's what Alvis is meant to do, and I've never met anyone more suited."

Eira tightened her lips. What else could he say, though? Besides, it was what everyone thought. She must have been putting on an impressive show to convince them all—even those closest to her—that she was prepared to get married to Alvis.

"Besides, don't see it as marrying Alvis."

Eira furrowed her brows.

"See it as gaining a charming and handsome new brother." He delivered his most devastating smile and wagged his eyebrows.

Eira couldn't decide if she wanted to laugh or cry, but eventually released a chuckle. He smiled back, and her frozen heart began to thaw. He could simultaneously fix and break her with such a smile. They'd been several things to one another through the years. This was by far her favorite. Eira and Cadeyrn—no other labels or duties.

Eira moved closer to him and let her knee rest against his.

"Cade…what are you doing here? You don't come to midnight prayers often."

Cadeyrn mimicked her posture and held her hand. He paused and focused on their intertwined fingers as though he were choosing his words carefully.

"You are my friend, and will soon be my sister. I wanted to offer my assistance. Besides, this night has been distressing for all of us. We all could use some of Luana's peace."

Eira considered this for a moment as her heart sank. There was no other response he could give her. These were the facts, and Eira needed to accept it. Even if Luana's peace hadn't settled onto her the way it usually did.

Cadeyrn looked at her betrothal band and let go of their grasp on one another.

He grimaced. "Although, I do find it interesting your betrothed is not the one sitting at your side," he snarled. "I can't imagine Ray not being with Luana at a time when she needed comfort."

Eira rubbed her betrothal band and ran a finger around the sketches of Isadore and Sanson. Their love was said to be the most powerful since Luana and Ray.

Cadeyrn was right. She should have invited Alvis to join her for prayers. He was the one she should be receiving comfort from. She needed to leave.

"I needed some space, and I'm sure Alvis is tired." The words came out in a rush, fanning past her as she stood and moved away from the altar.

Cadeyrn stood with her, head shaking as he followed. They were so close she could feel his warm breath on her skin when he held her back. With gentle hands, he turned her around to face him again, but she couldn't will herself to raise her gaze to meet his.

"Eira, no matter what happens these next few days, or even beyond this week, I will always be here. However you need me. I am still here."

"I know."

He always had been. Ever since they were children. Eira's chin quivered at the reminder. In spite of it all, this knowledge was still a comfort.

He leaned forward and kissed her forehead, soft, tender. Tempting. It took her by surprise, but she leaned into it and released a small sigh.

No. She couldn't lean in.

Eira took a step back, her face flushed with heat. "I need to go."

"Eira—"

"Have a good night."

Before he could say a word in return, or notice how bright Eira's cheeks had become, she was gone.

Her footsteps echoed through the castle halls. Lanterns filled with starlight shone as she strode past, and dimmed once gone. She wrapped her arms around her stomach. The corridors of the castle rushed past in a blur of blue and stars. Eira didn't know where she was going. All she knew was that she needed to go somewhere, anywhere.

A choked sob escaped, and Eira leaned against a stone wall, unable to hold back the tears any longer. This wasn't how it was supposed to be. She'd had plenty of time to clear her head, and she needed to contain herself. If only she could speak to Father. Even after her mother died, he'd been able to be strong and continue leading his kingdom through his grief.

Eira wiped her eyes and took in a few deep breaths. She needed to see her betrothed. The future king of Cresin.

Assuming all the castle's inhabitants had gone to bed, Eira didn't bother to see if she was alone as she approached Alvis's door. After a few sharp raps, he answered.

"Eira." He sounded surprised, but not as though she'd woken him, even though he was in a thick, fur-lined robe.

He took a step back. Inside the room, a fire was blazing and an open book lay on a chair.

"What are you doing here? Has something happened?"

"No, I've come back from midnight prayers." Eira tucked a strand of hair behind her ear.

He shouldn't be wondering why she was there. Out of everyone, he should be the most natural person for her to go to. Shouldn't he?

"You never sent for me to come here tonight," she said. "But it is late. I wasn't sure if you would still be awake. I know how you like to be up early to greet the morning sun."

"I wasn't able to sleep, so I found as many books from the library as I could and tried to do some research." He scratched the back of his head and gestured to the book. "It hasn't done much good, though. I didn't send for you because I didn't think you would want company tonight."

Eira's shoulders relaxed. Stress was getting the best of her emotions, causing her to question Alvis, and there wasn't any reason for her to.

She stepped forward and placed her hand on his bicep. "You're my betrothed. Where else should I go for comfort on a night like this?"

His jaw dropped, and he looked into the room, towards the bed.

"Of course." He shook his head and blinked a few times, and his cheeks turned pale pink.

"Is this all right?"

"Yes, come in." He took her hand and led her into the chamber.

Once the door was closed, she stood on her toes and kissed him. After a moment, he kissed her back and walked her to the bed.

Chapter Five

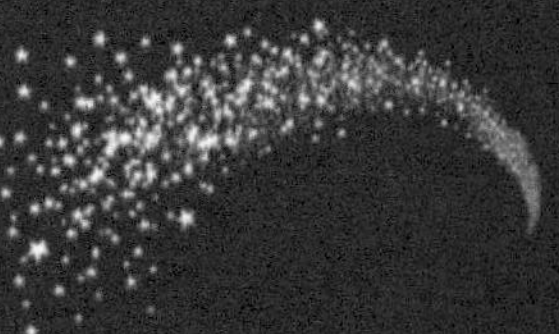

EIRA

Eira sank into a seat in Father's chamber the next morning as Rose handed her a steaming cup of coffee. It's heat was a welcome reprieve to the early autumn chill in the air, and with each sip her senses sprang to life. The previous night hadn't been a restful one, and not due to pleasant activities either. While Alvis slept soundly, she couldn't get herself to keep her eyes closed. Now, she and Rose were spending the morning watching over Father, and were waiting on another attendant in hopes of a new perspective.

By the looks of it, her sister was out of sorts too. Rose wasn't wearing her usual guard uniform, and instead had on a simple blue dress and flat shoes.

Eira took a sip of coffee from the porcelain cup and sighed.

"I wish Queen Amelia would let me help with questioning those who attended the ceremony last night."

In the past when Father was away, Queen Amelia acted as regent, and Eira would assist. Yet now, when Eira attempted to speak with her stepmother, she was turned away with the claim that she had other things to worry about, such as the wedding, and had been away too long to fully know how to help. A trail of shadows and ice followed Eira out of the grand hall, all the way to Father's chambers when she stormed away.

Rose didn't respond as she sat in the chair on the other side of Father's bed and focused on her needlework. It was one of the many hobbies her sister had learned as a young girl, before she had the straps to support her ankle, in an attempt to keep her still even for a few moments. At first, everyone in court had been pleased she'd found a suitable activity for a princess, until they saw the designs of battles and weapons in her stitchwork. On this day, she was working on a new dagger holder.

Rose stabbed at the fabric with her needle. "Apparently neither of us are needed with these matters. Captain Avarett won't let me near anything regarding the investigation. He claims that since I'm part of the royal family, I could also be threatened and need to stay out of danger."

The whole thing was ridiculous. Rose seemed to be having the same amount of luck. They were his daughters. Eira was the heir, and Rose second-in-command for the Guard, and should have a place in finding out what happened.

Eira let stardust float around her fingers and formed a dancing cloud to hover over Father's bed, giving a cheerful glow to the room. Yet the crescent moon tattoo on his forehead didn't glimmer in response the way it usually did when she performed magic in his presence.

The door opened and Amelia walked through, her blonde hair flying behind her. A tall man in a black robe accompanied her. The chill he brought made Eira rub the goosebumps on her arms. He wore a hood so large she couldn't see the face underneath.

Amelia held her hands over her heart. "No changes?"

"No, nothing." Eira guided the stardust into formations to look like the different star constellations.

Aros's sword floated next to Gallis's chalice. Above it shone one of Kutlaous's bears, with Diar's rose. They circled and danced around one another, letting their starlight glimmer against the stone walls like they were part of Luana's sky, watching over them, while the hooded man hovered over the king and put his hands on his chest.

"Well, I'm hoping a Stulan priest can give us some answers." Amelia closed the door behind her and glanced around the room before returning her focus to Eira. "You look as tired as you were this morning when I saw you. Did you not get much sleep? I didn't see you go to your chambers last night. How nice it must be to still be able to distract yourself with such…pleasurable…nighttime activities at a time such as this. Why, I was so wrecked with worry I wore myself out and went right to sleep."

Eira's cheeks heated, and she wiped away the stardust. No matter how old Eira was, Amelia still found ways to make her feel as though she were a silly young girl.

Eira pressed her lips into a thin line as she gritted her teeth. The queen had no place to comment on what Eira did in the bedroom, with all the men who'd gone in and out of her own chambers.

Rose set the needlework onto her lap and stared at the Stulan priest. Her glare was as harsh as a winter's icicle formed from one on the castle's pillars, which could kill a man if it fell hard enough.

After several long moments, the priest removed his hands and stood straight.

"This is an ancient magic we no longer use." His voice was so deep it made the room rumble, and Eira flinched. "The king stands in a place somewhere between life and death, unable to go in either direction. He needs to decide which way to go."

"And how does he decide?" Rose said.

"It is a magic we no longer use."

In her travels and studies, Eira had heard about old magic and ancient potions and spells such as this. She'd put her main focus on Luana and the tradition of the Chosens, but whenever she had the opportunity to learn about the other deities, she did. Stula's followers were the most mysterious, and no matter where she looked, there wasn't any concrete information about them. Most libraries had children's resources to learn the basics of the deities, and other texts only mentioned Stula in passing, or had a short chapter on her.

Centuries ago, sects of Stula's followers misused the ways of death, bringing people to the brink of it, then brought them back. Even resurrecting those who'd been buried already. Those groups had long since passed on. The current followers of Stula renounced those practices, and any of those ancient texts regarding such practices were gone.

Eira continued to rub her arms. Usually the cold didn't bother her much, but the sense this priest brought into the room was different than Luana's cool wind.

Rose sneered. "You already said that."

"Rose, I know you want what's best," Amelia said, "but you cannot speak to him in such a way. We had to pay a hefty offering for him to come answer our questions." She bowed her head toward the priest apologetically.

She may as well not have bothered with the apology, as he stood still, with his hands hidden inside the sleeves of his robe, his head still aimed down at the king, and Eira wished she could see the expression on his face.

As Rose approached the priest, her crutch thunked across the floor, and she stood before him. It didn't matter that he was a head taller. She lifted her head to gaze into is face and squared her shoulders. The constant protector of their family, regardless of clothing or what others thought or told her to do.

"You can't say he's caught and not tell us how we can help him get back to the land of the living."

If she could see into the hood, Eira would have said the priest stared into Rose's eyes.

"It's an ancient evil magic, and it goes against the ways of Stula. We have nothing to do with it any longer. This type of poison hasn't been made in centuries. No one should even be able to conjure it. I'm sorry. There's not more I can do for you."

Amelia stepped between them, wearing her most charming smile.

"And we are grateful to have even a hint at an answer. What are we to do in the meantime?"

The priest opened his hands to her and closed them. "You must wait. The king is the only one who can decide where to go now."

Eira's heart sank. They'd already been waiting.

She rubbed the betrothal band and let it spin around her wrist. How long were they supposed to go on like this? Father could stay in this dead-like slumber for weeks. Possibly even years.

Amelia touched a hand to her heart. "I see. Well, thank you for your time. I'll see you out."

The room felt cold and had gone silent, with only Eira and Rose to contemplate the situation alone.

Rose tapped her fingers against the wood of her crutch. "Wait? How long are we supposed to wait? It's the most ridiculous thing I've ever heard." She flopped into a chair.

"It's unlikely *none* of Stula's servants know about the poison. Surely there's someone who can tell us more. Or another solution. Or a place we can go." Eira slouched in her seat and strummed her fingers on the armrest, trying to remember the tales of Stula she'd heard in her travels.

Rose leaned forward and watched the hall, her face scrunched in concentration, biting her lower lip.

She cocked her head and looked to Eira. "Where do Stula's servants go?"

Eira glanced toward the hall and back to Rose. "What do you mean?"

Rose aimed her crutch at where the priest and Amelia had gone.

"All the other priests and priestesses have a place they go to learn and reside. Temples. Stula doesn't have them. So where do people go to find her servants?"

Eira rolled her neck and massaged the back of it. "It's what I've been trying to think of. Usually they're summoned by magic or a message."

Rose's gaze was focused on the door leading to the hall, as though she was still staring down the priest.

She stood. "They have to come from somewhere, don't they?"

Eira jumped up out of her chair and followed as her sister left the chamber, her heart beating faster.

"Where are you going?"

"I'm following the priest."

Eira darted her gaze around the castle corridors to be sure no one was paying attention as they spoke. Her chest tightened and swallowed past the lump in her throat.

"Should we get your straps?"

The glow of Rose's tattoo peeked through the fabric of her dress, and silver shimmered from her eyes. A faint hum from her ears filled the space around them. With her magic from Aros, she was strengthening her senses to track the priest better.

"Not enough time. I can get enough of a sense of him now, but if we wait much longer, I'll lose it."

Rose continued to track the priest through the castle and to a back entrance not many people used. Eira and her sister grabbed a couple discarded cloaks and headed out into the chilly autumn day. The priest's trail ran into Eral Forest, whose edge was close to the city walls, so it did not take long to enter.

The grass was soft beneath their feet as Eira and her sister searched for any sign of the priest. Eral Forest was beautiful this time of year, as the leaves were beginning to change their color. Bright reds and oranges peeked through the branches, which were still filled with green in anticipation, as though they were children eagerly waiting their turn to join a game. The forest dwellers stayed hidden when new visitors arrived, but Eira could sense them hiding away to spy on the princesses snooping about.

Eira followed her sister in silence, not wanting to distract her concentration. Periodically, Rose would pause and glance at a patch of forest as though something had caught her eye, but she didn't stay still for long. Eira offered her arm for support in the more treacherous terrains, and prayed they would find the information they needed.

She rubbed a sore spot on her back from walking the uneven ground for so long, and was tempted to remove her cloak, for in spite of the autumn weather, perspiration was seeping through her clothes.

Rose's pace was slowing, and her limp was becoming more pronounced, but she didn't complain of being tired or attempt to rest.

After much exertion, and not being any closer to finding the priest, Eira gave an exaggerated groan and stretched her arms.

"Rose, may we sit for a while? I don't think I can go much further."

Rose paused and strummed her fingers on the crutch, sighing. She may have been hesitant to stop, but there was a glimmer of relief in her eyes.

"Fine. I can still sense the priest, but we'll only rest for a moment so I don't lose track."

Rose groaned as Eira helped her to sit and stretch her leg out in front of her. They were both tired from all of the walking and from the stress of the last couple days. It was tempting to offer to massage her sister's leg, as she was sure it was aching, but knew it would only frustrate her. Instead, Eira decided to enjoy their surroundings and try not to let her thoughts venture into dangerous circles of what was to happen in the coming days. There was no use in it, and they needed to focus on this next step.

"So are you ever going to tell me what's the matter been?" Rose still glanced around at their surroundings with sharp eyes, but her voice was dry, as though she were bored by the whole situation.

Eira flinched at the question, which seemed to come out of nowhere. The words hung in the air like an early autumn day's fog, blocking the view.

She cleared her throat. "Whatever do you mean?"

Her sister cocked her head, her unkempt red braid hanging over her shoulder and lose pieces falling into her glassy stare.

"I know something has been bothering you, even before Father was poisoned. You didn't want to go to the ceremony last night. I could tell."

Eira tightened her cloak around her, not from the cold, which didn't bother her, but from needing something to do with her hands as she tried to think of how to answer what she'd been avoiding for too long. She'd always told Rose everything—except this. The one thing Eira could never tell anyone, but it pained her every day to not talk to Rose about it. It wasn't as though Rose wasn't trustworthy, but if she told anyone, she would have to face the truth.

Perhaps the time had come.

"If Alvis has done anything—"

Eira shook her head. "He hasn't. Alvis has done nothing wrong. He's been wonderful."

"Yet you still seem to find a way to run away from the wedding at each opportunity."

The forest grew darker with each moment, and a chilly breeze wound through Eira's hair while she debated how to tell Rose. It was difficult for even herself to comprehend.

She closed her eyes and breathed deeply while rubbing her betrothal band.

"I don't love Alvis. I don't know if I can marry him."

Eira opened her eyes to see Rose blink and let out a small breath—like a laugh.

"Well, to be honest, not being in love with your betrothed is not the most tragic thing to happen. Plenty of political marriages aren't made from love. It's not ideal, but once you have heirs, if Alvis feels the same way, surely you can have your own lovers. Everyone knows Father and Amelia do, and no one cares."

Eira was surprised at how calm Rose took her announcement. Perhaps she hadn't been clear as to how dire the situation was.

"Father and Amelia's marriage isn't supposed to be based on Luana and Ray, the greatest love story of our faith. Everything Alvis and I represent is supposed to embody the love they have for each other and for our people. If Alvis and I were to take other lovers, it would be a mockery to all we're supposed to be."

Through all her travels and schooling, Eira had poured over every text she could find on the matter. The marriage of the Chosens was not only about maintaining peace, but to show the people of their kingdoms what true and everlasting love was. They valued health, beauty, desire, and peace, of course. But love was always celebrated and honored the most.

Rose bumped Eira with her shoulder. "I know, but surely you don't believe that out of all of the Chosens through the years, one of them never had a single affair or weren't truly in love?"

"There was one." Eira continued to rub her band and traced over the engraving of Luana. "A few centuries ago. Her name was Malle. The Chosen of Ray was…not a good man. He abused her, and in time she fell in love with someone else. It did not end well."

Eira shivered thinking about the moment she'd read the story while studying in the temple of the Paravian Mountains. Malle had her magic stripped, was excommunicated and exiled from the kingdom. Her lover was also exiled, but before the couple could leave for another kingdom, the people of Cresin were so angry the lover was killed by a mob, and no one ever heard from Malle again. The Oxarian royal family cut off all ties with Cresin, and not until the next Chosens were born several generations later were they were able to rebuild the alliance between the two kingdoms.

Rose took a deep breath and must have sensed the darkness in Eira's tone, for she didn't press for the details.

"Surely being with Alvis will not be so terrible."

Eira groaned and looked down at her feet. "There's someone else."

Rose straightened her back, and her jaw dropped. "Someone else? Who?"

Eira closed her eyes, shaking her head. She couldn't keep the secret any longer.

Her voice shook. "Do you remember about a year before my original wedding date? The time when you found me in my room…and the blood…"

Rose gulped. "The baby didn't belong to Alvis?"

Eira shook her head.

She'd only known for a few weeks that she'd been with child. So early it was possible there hadn't even been a child, even though she'd missed a cycle. She woke one morning in pain, and there was blood all over the bed. She'd banned anyone from entering her chambers until Rose barreled in. Her sister never asked any questions, only helped Eira clean, and sat with her while she cried the rest of the day. It'd been one of the worst days of her life, and it took all of Eira's control to not cry while speaking of it.

"It was Cadeyrn's."

Rose dropped her crutch to the ground with a thud. "Shit!

"But…it was so long ago. Surely you aren't holding onto a short-lived affair from so many years ago. Unless it's continued…"

Eira shook her head and hid her face in her hands. "It's hasn't. He and I have never spoken of it. He doesn't even know about the baby." She rubbed her eyes and could still picture their time together as though it had only been days ago instead of years. "It isn't only about our short affair, though. I'd always cared about him for as long as I can remember, and tried not to, but it was as though we've always been drawn to one another. When he and I were together, it was only for about a week, but it felt like it was how things had always been. The way they were supposed to be. I've tried to remove him from my mind, but I can't."

Losing the child alone had been devastating enough. It was also the loss of the life Eira had imagined she'd have. She'd dreamed of the whole conversation she'd have with Cadeyrn when she told him about the baby, and how they'd make plans to be together. When she woke up in the morning surrounded by blood, the reality of how her silly girlish daydreams would never come true had only deepened the loss.

Rose nearly collapsed back against the tree trunk. "I didn't expect that."

Eira laughed. "I'm full of surprises, I suppose."

Rose shook her head as though she were marveling at the announcement.

"In fact, I'm a bit—"

A stick cracked close to where they were sitting. Both women looked toward the sound, and Rose reached for her dagger. Eira shivered at the growl of a creature hiding among the trees.

They scrambled to their feet and hurried away. Rose hobbled along with her crutch, and Eira stretched an arm to the vines along the ground, willing them to gather around Rose's ankle. With so much focus on her gifts from Luana, Eira's practice of the forest magic from Grandmother's Fae bloodline was weak, but she knew a few things she could do with it. The vines weren't the same as the enchanted straps, but they were better than nothing.

No footsteps followed them, but the growl hummed as though it were right behind Eira's ear. Yet nothing in sight.

The forest ground turned gray and crunched beneath their feet. The deep brown of the tree bark and green of the pine trees faded to more shades of gray. The leaves still had color, but faded as though someone cast a shadow over them. While they hadn't intended to leave Eral Forest, Eira had the sinking feeling they'd done so anyway.

"I fear we're nearing the end of Kutlaous's realm."

"The whole forest is his realm. How could we be nearing the end?" Rose panted and slowed as her limp deepened, in spite of the vines Eira had wrapped around her ankle.

"I'm not sure," Eira said.

She was not as intimately familiar with Eral as Grandmother, but as it lay in the kingdom of Cresin, she knew where its borders were. Never had she seen or heard of any patch of land or forest like this one.

A shiver ran through her, and she pulled her cloak tight. No sound to be heard, or any creature nearby, but she couldn't shake the feeling that someone was still hunting them.

A dark cave appeared. Whether they hadn't noticed it through their fear, or it formed out of nothing, Eira wasn't sure.

Once inside, she waved her shaking hand, and an array of starlight lit the cave. She waved another hand over the entrance, and a dark mist covered it to conceal their presence. The growling faded, but they stood against the cave wall and peered out, unsure if an appearance of some forest creature would be good or bad.

"Someone is watching us." Rose looked out the cave mouth.

Eira looked about as she tried to calm her staggering breath.

"I was wondering," she said, "but I never saw anything. Have you?"

A shimmer of fear sparked in Rose's eyes. "I didn't tell you before, but earlier I saw these yellow eyes staring at me. I didn't think it was anything, but they keep appearing."

Eira bit her lip. "Did the eyes look dangerous or angry?"

Rose shook her head. "I'm not sure. I don't think so. Curious, maybe?"

"Perhaps Kutlaous is protecting us." Eira's voice wavered as she realized how little she knew about Eral, in spite of her heritage. "Keep a weapon at the ready, though, just in case."

The starlight sparkled against the cave walls, and a splash of color caught Eira's eye. She stepped forward and guided the starlight along with her so she could examine it more closely.

"Something is painted here."

They weren't crude drawings of ancient cave dwellers, but extravagant illustrations. Once, they may have been vibrant and glowing, but the colors were now faded.

Eira stood and wondered at the wall, and Rose followed, taking in the images—depictions of the deities and their stories sprawled before them. Luana and Ray in a warm embrace, Diar naked and dancing in a field of flowers, Aros with his sword, Colma commanding the ocean.

The images went on, all blending into a magnificent mural. Thorny rose vines weaved through the mural, and petals were scatted around the deities.

Further off, away from the bright-colored images, the paint turned darker, with deep reds and purples, and Stula, goddess of death stood to the side. Watching. Waiting. One of *them*, but still separate. Dark swirls surrounded her, and she held her hands out toward the front of the image as though she were welcoming whoever was looking at the painting. The swirls led further and deeper into the dark cave.

Through the darkness, something else was in the distance, as if the swirls came to life and beckoned Eira forward. A chill ran through her, and she stopped.

Something odd about this cave and portion of the forest. Yet it was undeniably touched by the deities.

"They led us here, Rose. We must be on the correct path."

Rose's heavy sigh echoed off the cave walls, and soon the click of her crutch on the ground followed. Eira slowed her steps until Rose could catch up, and they walked side by side, the air around them growing colder and darker until they could see breath escaping their lips in small clouds. Wasn't like the cold of winter Eira was used to, which her Luana-given magic let her body adapt to so she could withstand the frigid temperatures. Rather, it stuck to her skin like a clammy outer layer she couldn't shake off.

A growl echoed around them, and they paused. Perhaps Rose was correct in being hesitant to go exploring.

Rose bent forward to find her dagger. "Eira, take my sword."

Eira unsheathed the blade from its holder on Rose's belt. A wind blew through the cave, whipping her hair around her head and swirling the stardust about in a sparkling blur. It calmed, and before them stood a tall young man with dark hair and yellow eyes.

Eira grasped her sister's wrist, which was tense around the handle of the dagger. The young man eyed them like a cat examining a frightened mouse, and wore a smile which looked as though he was keeping a secret.

"Follow me." He tilted his head.

Rose pointed her dagger and glared at him. "Who are you? Why should we?"

The young man performed a sweeping bow. The leaves that made up his clothing rustled and blew around his thin frame from the motion.

"Rafe at your service. And it is Stula's wish for you to follow me."

Eira's breath caught in her throat. "Why does she wish to see us?"

Rafe smiled once again. "And you don't have any questions for her?"

Rose pulled Eira aside. "How do know we can trust him?"

"Isn't the possibility of finding how to wake Father worth the risk?" Eira sheathed the sword and stepped toward Rafe.

This had been Rose's idea, after all, and Eira was as fed up with waiting for answers as she was.

"Take me to her. Rose can do what she pleases."

As Rafe walked further through the cave, Rose followed. The walls grew tighter around the trio, and before long they needed to walk in a single line, with Rafe in front, until they reached what appeared to be the end of the path. Rafe held his palms against a black stone wall, and on his arm glowed a tattoo of a rose intertwined with a skull, and the wall turned into a dark mist and vanished to open to a large cavern.

The cavern was a mixture of darkness and light, with red, purple, orange, and gold reflecting throughout the walls without an indication of where the colors or light came from. The air turned crisp and smelled of bonfire, and dried leaves wafted around them. In the center stood a large pool with still, black water. Rafe knelt before the pool and drew symbols in the water that Eira didn't recognize. He howled, and the water rippled at the sound. As he stood, the ripples grew into larger waves, and the center of the pool hollowed out. A wind blew through the cavern, and Eira and Rose huddled closer together to protect themselves from the chill.

From the hole that formed in the center, a dark hooded figure rose and glided across the pond toward them. The figure looked similar to the priest they'd met at the castle, but this person was thinner, and the sight filled Eira with a sense of dread she didn't have before.

The wind calmed when it reached the edge of the pond to greet them, the water parting at their bare feet. Eira took a step back. This couldn't be Stula, could it?

The figure removed the hood, revealing a man with long braided hair and black paint across his equally dark eyes.

"You brought me princesses?" His voice was thin and cold, and didn't shake the walls the way the other priest's did, but Eira's blood still froze.

"They were seeking the cave," Rafe said. "They wish to find answers from Stula, and her wish is for them to be here."

The priest's eyes were blank as he observed Rose and Eira.

"The goddess did show me that someone wanted to speak to me. She has a great desire for this."

Rafe turned to Rose and Eira. "Do you have your offering?"

"Offering?" Rose said. "What kind of offering? I thought we were seeing Stula."

Eira bit her lip. They should have gotten something as they traveled through the forest. Rose could have hunted a piece of game, or they could have brought something from the castle.

"All those who wish to inquire of Stula must give an acceptable offering for change, sickness, maturity, or death," said the man from the pond. "And I am one of her priests, here in her stead. She doesn't see audiences personally unless it is of extreme importance."

There must be something they could give to receive some answers.

Eira twisted her betrothal band as she tried to think of something, and held out her wrist.

"My band. I am to be married in a few days, and regardless of the results from this conversation."

"Clever little princess." The priest held Eira's wrist in his gray bony hand and twisted it back and forth.

His touch was cold and clammy, and it took everything for her to not pull her hand away.

A burning pain shot through her wrist, and before she could cry out, the band was gone and the pain vanished.

The priest let go of her. "What is it you wish to know from Stula?"

Eira stared at her wrist, empty and cold. She shouldn't have felt relief, but she did.

"Our father has been poisoned and remains between life and death, unsure of where to go. We want to guide him back to the land of the living."

The priest cocked his head, and a glimmer of amusement appeared in his eyes.

"If your father requires healing, perhaps you should seek Gallis."

"Attendants from all over the kingdoms have seen to him," Rose said. "But none know what to do, and death is Stula's realm. Surely she has some way to sway his spirit."

The priest turned his back to them and knelt beside the pool of water. He waved a hand over it, and the water turned still as black glass. When neither Eira and Rose moved, he beckoned them, and the pair walked to the water and knelt at his side. Within moments, the water cleared and the silhouette of a man walking along a road appeared and stopped when he met a sorceress. She handed him something to drink, and he took it and continued on until he came to a crossroad. One path was filled with light. The other was darkness. He stood there for a long time, looking between the two, and each time it appeared he was ready to take a step, he was unable to, until finally he went to his knees in prayer.

The moon rose over the image, and Luana floated lower to join him and filled the darkness with light. When she left, the sun rose and Ray came into the scene with flames in his wake, filling the whole space, and helped the man rise to his feet. Next was the horned and hoofed Kutlaous, and the man doubled over as though in pain, but stood again as red and white filled the space. Finally, Gallis in her pure blue robes came into the scene, carrying a large silver chalice. She gathered everything the other deities had left and placed them all inside the cup. The final deity was Stula, who formed a black pond. She took the cup and filled it with water and handed it back to the man. Once they had all left, the man drank from the cup. He took a step forward, and the scene went blank.

Eira blinked, trying to make sense of what they'd watched. It was clearly a tale of the deities, but one she'd never heard before. The crossroads must have been where the spirit of the man was deciding between life and death, and what he drank from the chalice at the end cured him. But what was it? What were the ingredients the deities gave him?

The priest stood, turned back around, and walked across the pond to where it opened once again in the center.

"There's nothing else?" Rose used her crutch to push herself back to her feet. "You're going to show us some strange story and leave? We didn't even see which direction the man went! What did he decide? Life or death?"

He acted as though he didn't hear Rose's cries of protest, and continued to the center.

"Damn!" Rose said.

Eira looked back and forth between the water and the priest. Rose was right. This couldn't have been all he would give them.

Eira clenched her fist and stood. She pushed past Rose and strode into the water. It didn't hold her up the way it did for the priest, or spread open to reveal solid ground, and she advanced until she was thigh deep. It was freezing and made her shiver in a way winter never could, but she took in a deep breath and withstood it.

"You cannot leave us without any other answers."

The priest paused and slowly turned to her. "You said you wanted to know about your father. I showed you a tale detailing the cure. What else do you need?"

Eira stretched out her arms in exasperation. "What were the ingredients the deities gave him? This can't be all Stula wished to share with us! Why did she bring us here?"

The priest moved to Eira and studied her. His eyes were endless pits of darkness, and not the comforting kind of Luana's nighttime. She wanted to look away, but forced herself to maintain his gaze.

"You asked the wrong question. If you wish to maintain your throne, and peace in your kingdom, there are other matters you need to be focusing on. The poison which was used is evil and betrays the ways of Stula. You should be dealing with the one who administered the poison before anyone else is harmed." The priest looked over his shoulder. "Rafe, take them away."

Rafe offered a deep nod, and the priest continued his journey across the pond to the center, where it opened and he sank back to where he came from.

Eira shook as she watched him go. The story was all he was going to tell them. They were led to this horrid cave, she was wet and freezing, and they still had no answers.

She slapped the water and screamed, the sound echoing off the walls. What was she supposed to do? The damned deities and their cryptic answers.

"Eira, we should go," Rose said.

She trudged to the edge of the pond, the cold water making each step heavier than the last. It wasn't until she collapsed to her knees that she realized tears were streaming down her face. She had been pretending she was strong and confident, when she didn't know anything. This was outside of her realm, and she was powerless here.

Eira's sobs poured out from her as she buried her face in her arms, not caring that her clothes were soaked through. All of it could be gone, and she had no way to bring it back.

Rose knelt at Eira's side. "We'll find a way."

As though it was so simple.

"Sitting in a wet cave isn't going to solve anything, Eira."

No. No it wasn't, was it?

Finally, Eira nodded and wiped her eyes, which didn't do much, considering her arms were as wet as her face. The cavern faded, and they were back outside in the forest where it was warmer.

Rafe leaned against a tree, relaxed as though nothing out of the ordinary were happening, and still smirking.

"Are we ready?" he said. "No more weeping and moaning?"

"It's been a long day," Rose snarled. "Let her have a minute."

He pushed off the tree and crossed his arms. "And your day will be even worse if we are still traveling by nightfall." He jerked his chin toward another part of the forest. "This way. I'll take you back to the city."

Within a moment, Rafe had shifted into a midnight-black wolf tall enough to where his nose reached Eira's chest. The transition was so seamless she couldn't tell when he stopped being a man and was a wolf.

"Hop on my back. It'll be faster."

Eira bit her lip and contemplated going with him.

She pulled Rose aside. "You think we can trust him?

"Maybe? He might be the one who's been watching me."

"I wondered the same thing."

"If only I knew if it was a good or bad thing." Rose patted the hilt of her sword. "Well, if he betrays us, I'll be sure we have two warm wolf-skin cloaks this winter."

Eira chuckled.

"I can hear you," Rafe said over his shoulder.

"At least a cloak wouldn't eavesdrop," Rose called back.

"Nor would it lead you to your destination." Rafe winked at her.

"I suppose the destination is worth the risk." Rose crutched over to the wolf and climbed on his back.

Eira followed and wrapped her arms around Rose's waist.

Chapter Six

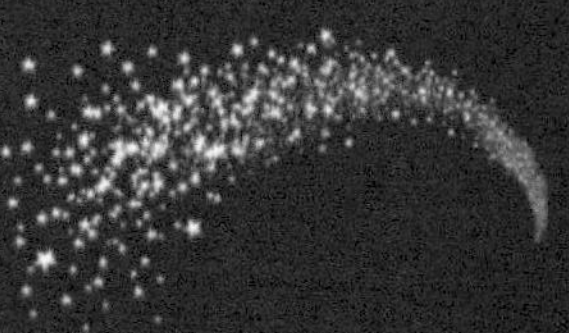

EIRA

Eral forest was nothing but a sea of color as Rafe ran. Eira squeezed Rose's waist and buried her face in Rose's shoulder to stop the wind from burning her eyes. Her mind raced as quickly as Rafe's feet, with the little she'd learned from the priest. Of course she was concerned about who the assassin was, but Father needed to be the priority.

She nearly fell off when the wolf skidded to a halt. Over the horizon, the sun was setting and the city of Farren was preparing for the evening's festivities. Eira slid off his back and helped Rose balance as she followed, and handed her the crutch.

"Thank you for your help," Eira said.

Rafe shifted back to his human form and bowed, still wearing the same mischievous grin.

"It is my pleasure to serve."

Rose barely gave Rafe a second glance before moving towards the castle.

"We'll be fine from here," she said.

Eira wanted to ask Rafe more about the cave and the priest, but with the blink of an eye he vanished, so she had no other choice but to follow her sister and wonder what the objects from the story meant.

For the first time, Eira was eager to see Alvis again. Once she told him the story the priest shared, surely he would have an idea of what it meant. He was the most well-read and curious person she knew. If anyone could find the information they needed, it was him.

Rose was still ahead of her, so Eira quickened her steps. They would make a plan. After, they would deal with whoever had poisoned Father.

The first thing was the cup. There was an old legend about Gallis's chalice, which would make the most sense, but it was only a legend which claimed that with the proper ingredients it could heal any ailment. Even bring the dead back to life. None of the sacred texts spoke of it directly, so Eira had never taken the rumors seriously. The image of the chalice in the story the priest showed them looked like the one Eira had heard about. As much as she wanted to deny it, she didn't have any other ideas of what it would be. The water must have been the pond in the cave. The rest of it didn't make any sense.

A scream threatened to escape Eira's throat when she was jerked back by her tunic and her back hit someone's chest with a thud. A bolt of panic shot through her like lightning, and she tried to break away, but he wrapped his muscular arms tighter around her and covered her mouth.

Rose. Where's Rose? Who's doing this? Eira's heart thudded as though it were a bird trying to be set free from its cage.

"Don't make this harder than it already is." The attacker pressed his lips against the side of her head, and his breath was hot against her skin. The point of a blade poked her in the stomach. But the voice was familiar.

"Cal?" Her voice was muffled against his palm.

It couldn't be. He was her friend. Rose's closest friend.

Where is she?

Rose was still ahead. Eira could see the corner of her cloak waving in the wind.

"Eira, don't—"

She elbowed him and removed his hand to scream. Rose turned, and her face became bright red. Cal pressed his dagger harder against Eira's stomach as Rose ran toward them. She crouched so her fingers grazed the grass, and vines sprung from the ground, wrapping around her ankle. The tattoo on her leg glowed through the fabric of her dress, and she sprinted to Eira's side, unsheathing her sword and casting the crutch aside.

"Let go of her." Rose sneered.

"You're next." His voice quaked as he continued to pressed the knife against Eira's stomach, and his body trembled behind her.

"No, she's not," Eira said. "You don't have to do this, Cal. We're you're friends."

Rose's knuckles turned white around the hilt of the sword.

"If you wanted to kill me," Eira said, "you would have already done it before I had the chance to scream."

Cal's throat bobbed, and his hand trembled, but he still held the knife against her body.

"Traitor!" Rose pointed the sword at him like a spear.

Cal released Eira and raised an arm in defense.

Eira tumbled to the ground, gasping. Through his sleeve, his tattoo shone, raising a glowing shield around him, and pushed Rose away long enough for Cal to put away the knife and draw his own sword.

Rose charged again, and their swords clashed while Eira crawled away.

The priest had been right. They should have been focusing on the one who had attempted the assassination, not only the cure.

But Cal? Didn't make sense. He hadn't even been in the room when their father collapsed. He'd been with Rose, outside.

Something was missing here.

"You don't understand." Cal fought off Rose.

"I understand perfectly. You aren't our friend."

"You don't know what she can do."

She. Eira gasped.

He only took orders from one person—aside from Rose.

Eira stood and turned in time to see Rose's sword meet his again, and she pushed it out of his hand, causing him to lose balance. With a thud, he landed on his knees in surrender, and Rose kept the tip of her sword pointed at his back. His white hawk, Kudo, cawed overhead and watched from a perch.

Cal gripped the brown grass. He spoke only a few words in a low voice. As though it were a plea or perhaps a prayer.

"She's going to kill her," he whispered.

Silence. Not even the wind whispered to the trees, as though the forest itself was holding its breath in anticipation.

The silence lasted a lifetime as Rose kept him on the ground, waiting for Eira to give her the command of what to do with Cal. As the one who'd been attacked, and Rose's superior, it was Eira's choice. One Eira hoped she'd never have to make, especially against someone they'd considered to be a loyal friend. What scared her the most was how willing Rose was to carry it out.

"Who is she going to kill?" Eira said.

"Myra." His voice strained and battled against him. "She said if I don't kill you both, she'd murder Myra. I had no choice."

His sister. Eira didn't know the young servant well, but was familiar with how loyal Cal was to her. It made sense. He was too good of a friend to them to have been willing to go to such extremes for anyone else.

Rose nudged his back with the tip of her sword. "There's always a choice."

Eira glared at Rose, who released her stance by a hair.

"Who gave the order?" Rose said.

Cal panted and gulped while Kudo hooted as though he were giving permission to share the information.

"Who else do I take orders from? I'm Queen Amelia's huntsman. She was the one who sent me. She's the one who had the king poisoned. I didn't know it was her until last night after it happened, when she told me her plans and wanted me to be sure you were taken care of. You have no idea the work she has me do. She's done…things. She's made *me* do things. In turn, she makes sure Myra is cared for."

The revelation struck Eira like another bolt of lightning, and all she could do was stare at Cal, trying to process the information.

Queen Amelia never did anything harmful to their family before. No, she and the king did not have the most dedicated of marriages, but it was something they'd decided on mutually. Even when she acted as regent, there was never an indication of treachery, or even jealousy. She had a well-known temper, but Eira had never considered deceit such as this.

Yet…her stepmother had been oddly reluctant to let Eira assist in finding the perpetrator. Rose had warned her how Amelia was whispering in the ears of the nobles about her when she was gone. She must have been plotting this for some time. All of the interactions they'd ever had were now in a new light, and a knot formed in Eira's stomach. She'd been foolish and naive to not see all the hate before now.

Cal lowered his head, and his shoulders shook. The once tall and strong man knelt on the ground before them. Eira should have hated him. Instead, she sat by his side and touched his shoulder.

Rose dropped the sword to her side and released her stance. "Tell us everything."

He shook his head. "The queen will—"

"It'll be nothing compared to what I'll do to you if you don't tell me why you were going to kill us." Rose started to raise her sword again.

Eira held out an arm to stop her, and Rose lowered it once more with a sigh.

Eira looked back to Cal. "We need to know we can trust you."

Cal sank back so he was no longer kneeling, but sitting on the grass the way Eira was. He was silent for a few moments and looked out towards the castle.

"Our family has been in service to Queen Amelia as long as I can remember," he said.

"We've always been poor. We made do, but my father likes the coin. Too much. My mother tried to help him, but…he was always losing whatever it was we brought into our home. Myra came to us when she was a young girl. Won, to be truthful. The only good thing to have come from Father's gambling."

"Won her?" Eira said. "But the selling of people is outlawed in most of the kingdoms, including the Dravian Islands. Ever since they became part of Cresin territory."

She'd always known Myra wasn't blood-related to Cal, but he'd never treated her otherwise. They always assumed she was adopted.

"It being outlawed doesn't mean it doesn't happen," Rose said.

"Father won her in a bet. She'd come from Oxare, and her family sold her off. Myra never told us the whole story. One of the few bets Father had won where his opponent didn't have the money, so he gave him Myra instead. We couldn't afford to support her, but Mother refused to sell her off to someone else, so…she stayed. There wasn't a way we could formally adopt her into the family, but Mother and I treated her as though we had. A couple years later, Myra and I had gone out, and when we returned, the cottage was in shambles. Blood was everywhere, and only pieces of my parents were left."

Eira closed her eyes and willed her face not to show the shock that poured through her. When she opened them again, Rose's face had paled.

"But there were footprints." Cal stared at the ground. "I took my father's axe and found the creature. Myra begged me not to go, but nothing could stop me. I was blind with rage. The footsteps led me to a small camp of Fae. Apparently, Father owed them debts. They didn't see me coming. Outside of hunting, I'd never killed before then. I was thirteen."

"Aros curse it." Rose wiped a hand over her face.

Cal still wouldn't look at them. "That was when Queen Amelia found me. Lady Amelia, at the time. I thought she was going to have me arrested, but instead she took us in, saying I was exactly what she needed. At first we were grateful to her. She gave us a place to stay, work to do, and she helped me to get training with the best priests of Aros that the Dravian Islands offered. She sent me off on different tasks, and each time I returned she rewarded Myra and me. But the older I became, the more sinister my tasks were. I tried to refuse her, but she'd remind me of all she'd done for us and what would happen if she weren't there. One day, I didn't do what she asked…Myra paid for it."

Silence enveloped the woods, and tears burned Eira's eyes. She'd known Cal and Myra had served Amelia since childhood, but had no idea how twisted it was. All this happened right under their noses.

Finally, Cal lifted his head. "I didn't want to do this. You know my loyalty to the crown as a servant and as a friend. I tried to fight back when Amelia told me what she wanted, but she hurt Myra. I couldn't let anything happen to her after all we'd gone through. I wanted to find a way out of it, I promise. If I hadn't gone with her the day my parents died, or searched for the Fae—"

A blaze roared in Rose's eyes as she locked gazes with Cal.

She knelt in front of him. "You were a child. What were you supposed to do? Where is she now?"

"I don't know."

"Do you know why Amelia is doing this?"

Cal's gaze never left Rose, and he took a deep breath as though he were gaining strength from her finally acknowledging him.

"She's always held animosity against you. Her family forced her to marry your father for political advancement. Over the years it has grown, and I saw how much she grew to love the power. I'd foolishly thought the resentment she had toward your family had been pushed to the side. I never knew it would come to this, I swear."

Eira gazed back at the castle. All these years and they'd never known.

Well, they knew now, and they could do something about it. But if Amelia was as dangerous as Cal was making her out to be, they couldn't waltz back into the castle and remove Amelia from the throne without putting themselves, or Cal and Myra, in danger. There would be no use in them getting hurt, or worse. They would need to find another way.

"Do you know how to get to the dungeons?" Eira said.

Rose and Cal broke their gaze.

He blinked a few times. "There's a hidden back entrance from the outside, but it hasn't been used in years."

"We need to get inside. It can be where we hide while we decide what to do next." Eira stood and straightened her tunic.

"We're going to hide?" Rose said. "You can't be serious."

She struggled to get to her feet, so Eira extended a hand to help her.

"Only for the time being. Cal can't go back empty-handed, and he needs to convince Amelia we're dead. She must want evidence, right?"

Cal stood with them. "Your hearts and livers."

Eira swallowed. She hadn't expected their *organs* as an answer, but perhaps nothing should surprise her anymore.

"Right," she said. "So you'll need a couple animals to kill. Perhaps some bloodied clothes to convince the court we're dead. Meanwhile, Rose and I will hide in the dungeons while we form a plan." She went to work tearing off pieces of her tunic.

"A plan for what, exactly?" Rose said.

Eira looked at them. "We're going to remove Amelia."

Chapter Seven

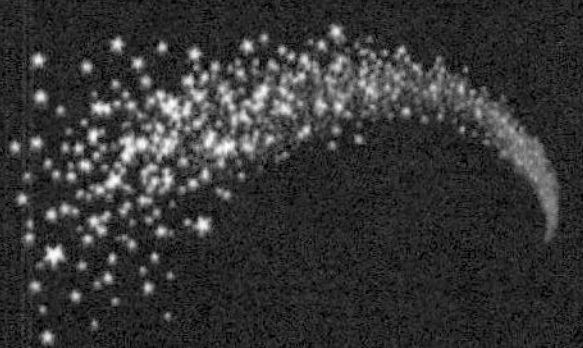

AMELIA

Amelia couldn't sit still as she waited for Cal. Half her lunch sat untouched on the table, and she paced around her chamber. The stream of water circling around the bed lapped to the beat of her footsteps.

She'd done it. After all this time, she'd finally done it.

It had taken everything in her to not dance around the grand hall only minutes before Cal had burst inside, tears streaming, with his declaration of how the princesses had been attacked and all he had left of them was pieces of bloody torn clothing. If only she'd been there to witness the gruesome scene. The screams and looks of terror they must have had when Cal attacked with his dagger.

Eira would have been no trouble at all. A slash, and her pale skin would be painted in red. Rose had surely put up a fight, but Cal was stronger. Amelia's only other regret was how she wouldn't see the king's face at the news of his daughters being killed.

What a glorious sight it would have been.

Ah, well. What was done was done, and she couldn't change the plan now.

Now, when she sat in the great hall before the court, no one else would be on a throne next to her. All eyes would be on her, Queen Amelia, even if it was only as regent for the time being.

In the beginning, she didn't want to be queen. But the king came to her home all those years ago, when she was barely into adulthood, to court her. The Dravian Islands being part of the Cresin territory was still new, and the nobles, along with her own mother, made her marry him, even if she had promised herself to someone else. It was for the good of the land, she was told. She'd done everything she could to avoid marrying him, but what the king wanted the king got.

Now, King Brennan no longer had choices, either. He'd taken everything away from Amelia, and it was her turn to do the same.

At first, she didn't want to sit on the throne. But as the years went on, she found the power exhilarating. Whenever she walked into a room, she was the center of attention. Men and women alike wanted to hear what she had to say. They wanted to be in her bed. They envied her clothing and status. She'd had a taste of such things in the manor she grew up in, of course. But as queen, it was entirely different.

If she couldn't have the life she wanted on the Dravian Islands, she would have King Brennan and his daughters' lives instead. All she needed was the evidence that Cal was bringing to her. After seeing the hearts and livers, she would know for sure the deed was complete.

A knock came to the door. "Your majesty."

Finally. Took him long enough.

The water halted without a drop slushing over the edge of the stream as Amelia rushed to the door, and opened it to find Cal standing before her, clutching a box. She grabbed the burly young man by his shirt sleeve to pull him inside, and shut the door behind him.

"Do you have them?" Amelia snatched the box out of his hand.

She trembled as she opened the lid, and sitting inside was the most glorious sight—two hearts and two livers, fresh and bloody.

"You did it. I doubted you, but you did it."

Cal offered a deep bow. "I do your bidding."

Amelia opened the door again and shoved the box into one of her guard's arms.

"Take this to the kitchen. I'll be having it for supper this evening, in my chambers."

Amelia stalked toward Cal once the door had clicked shut. His blue eyes were still red from the performance he gave in the grand hall. This had been the most difficult part of it all—being sure Cal carried out his role. He spent so much time with them, especially Rose, seeds of doubt were planted in Amelia's mind that Cal may not be dedicated to her at all. But she didn't need to worry about it any longer. Rose was gone, as was Eira.

"Now I know you are truly dedicated to me."

"And my sister?"

Usually, it was easy to get Cal to do what she wanted. Granting a gift or a position for his younger sister, or a small threat, and Cal would go running. This time it had taken more convincing.

The young girl was fine. Bruised, but fine.

"No harm will come to her now that I know you will do what I say."

"And the king's child?"

Oh. She'd almost forgotten.

Amelia touched her belly, the key to all this, and she cursed the thing for having to be so integral to the plan. Daily, she prayed to the deity Yla for the child to look even remotely like King Brennan so it could pass for his. Amelia couldn't stay on as queen regent forever. But if she carried the king's child…she could be in the center of it until the child was old enough to take the throne. Even then, she would have their ear and as much influence as she wanted. Everyone would look to her and want her. The beloved and beautiful queen mother.

She hadn't intended to tell Cal about the baby. Not yet. But he'd needed a little more convincing to complete his task.

"I never said who the baby belonged to. Why do you have such concern for it?"

The truth was, she didn't know who the father was, and didn't care. The last thing she needed was some man to come barging in and claiming the thing for their own. She'd had so many men in and out of her chambers these past several months, she couldn't keep track any more. At last, one of them finally took.

Cal tightened his fists and loosed them again. "Regardless of who the father is, you do not plan to harm yourself or the baby, do you?"

Something twisted inside of Amelia. She'd gone to a few extreme measures to properly scare Cal, and it had taken some time with an attendant to remove the self-inflicted bruises afterwards. Yet she wasn't sure if he cared about her well-being, or only the baby's.

At least he'd done it. If he only cared about the child, perhaps she could still use it to her advantage.

Amelia smiled sweetly at him. "Of course not. Now I know that no matter what, you're here for me and me alone. There's nothing to worry about. Please celebrate with me."

She offered him a glass of wine and sipped her own. He took the glass but didn't drink, and looked out the window toward Eral Forest, instead of at her, the one who gave him everything. The one who could take everything away. His beautiful queen. It was as though he were thinking of someone else.

Must have been Rose.

Maybe Eira.

Even in death, those damned girls still followed her.

Rose wasn't even attractive. Too many freckles and the silly limp of hers. Maybe if she'd attempted to dress more like her sister instead of playing at a guard, she'd be tolerable.

Everyone saw the way Cal looked at her, even if Rose didn't, and it made Amelia want to wring her hands around that pale freckled neck.

Not as though she wanted two versions of Eira, either. Her ultimate competition for attention and love. Eira's pilgrimage had been a blessing so she could finally get into the ears of the nobles. They all had such an odd attachment to her.

But they were gone now. Amelia never needed to worry about them again.

"Your mind is somewhere else," Amelia cooed. "Is your queen not enough to keep you occupied?"

Cal looked back at her and smiled, but it didn't reach his eyes.

She'd lost him. When had that happened?

"You're more than enough, Your Majesty."

Cal would never dare lie to her. He knew what she could do to him and to his family. Besides, he wouldn't be here now if it weren't for her. Amelia's eyes must have been playing tricks on her with his smile. He'd completed the task, after all.

Well, any whims Cal had of leaving her would be erased from his mind soon enough. Everyone's would.

The kingdom would have its time of mourning, of course. What sort of queen would Amelia be if she didn't understand their pain? In time, everyone would see how much more suited Amelia was for the throne, and how the royal family didn't deserve their place. Then her child would be on the throne, and the Dravian Islands would have their say.

It was time for change in Cresin, and Amelia was going to lead them there.

Chapter Eight

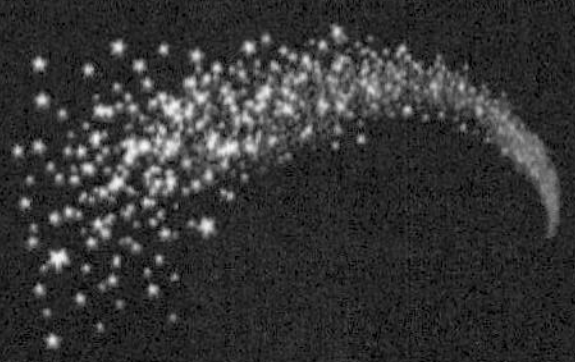

ROSE

TWO DAYS THEY WAITED. TWO DAYS OF SITTING IN THE COLD ABANDONED dungeon cell while they planned, and enough time passed so Amelia believed they were dead. Then Cal and Myra were safe.

Myra was finally released from wherever Amelia had kept her prisoner, and found her way to the dungeons a couple times a day to bring food, extra clothing, and Rose's straps and weapons. Her normally warm brown face was now bruised and discolored, and under her sleeve were cuts along her arm. She refused to say anything about them, no matter how much Eira asked. Instead, she shared news of what was happening in the castle and how Amelia led in mourning the lost princesses and praying for the king.

On the third day, Rose awoke calm. It had been years since she let nervousness overtake her on a mission. The anticipation of knowing you were about to kill someone could easily distract you—and therefore cause you to fail. But Rose had trained herself to push the doubts and fears aside and focus on the task at hand.

She and Eira dressed in tight-fitting trousers and loose shirts. Eira helped Rose wrap her straps so she could have her full abilities, and Rose assisted Eira in hiding daggers in her boots and belt. They prayed

Eira wouldn't need to use them and Rose could get the deed done quickly.

With each task, Rose reminded herself they were doing the right thing. That this was going to protect their family and their kingdom.

She had to do that each time she needed to kill. It was the only way to live with herself.

Eira's tattoo glowed as she gathered the shadows lingering in the dungeon and shrouded herself and Rose so while walking through corridors they could hide in the darkness. The trick was to stay close and among other objects where they could blend in. Otherwise, they would be two blobs of shadows moving around.

While Rose was the one who would perform the assassination, Eira needed to be nearby to be sure she was still hidden. She could control the shadows from a short distance, but if she was too far away, Rose would be discovered.

Everything was quiet in the castle corridors. All wedding decorations were replaced with black drapes of mourning, with the occasional blue and green banner of Colma hanging in a window. Little by little, Amelia was erasing the symbols of Luana and replacing them with her own god. Before, they'd been side by side and intermingled with one another as a sign of partnership. Now, it only showed someone else came to reign.

People didn't pay the princesses any notice as they crept to Amelia's chambers. Sea salt filled the air, and a light breeze wafted through Rose's hair. She gripped the dagger around her belt as she approached the entrance where Cal stood guard, his blue uniform sharp, with the buttons shining in the lamplight. Rose prayed he hadn't been lying and wouldn't betray them again.

Eira extended her hand, and swirling shadows with a hint of stardust floated across the floor. The only indication that Cal noticed was a blink and a nod.

Rose tiptoed forward and met Cal at the door, with her sister close behind. She continued to wave her hands, controlling the shadows concealing Rose.

She paused and took a deep breath before entering. She was close enough now where Cal could see her, and he grasped her wrist—a gentle touch for someone so strong and foreboding. She looked into his blue eyes, and he gave her a silent nod. Rose gulped.

Eira trusted him, and Rose wanted to. She desperately wanted to, but she couldn't get the image of him holding Eira captive out of her mind. No one threatened her sister—not even her best friend. Yet she wanted his dedication to them to be true.

Today would confirm if her wish was to be granted.

Rose tore her gaze from his and entered. It was more difficult to remain concealed here, as the floor was as pale as sand, and a faint blue glow filled the space.

Queen Amelia stood with her back to the door, looking into a floor-length mirror. With silent steps, Rose hid behind a chaise in time for Amelia to glance at the door, then return her focus back to the mirror. There was something strange about the queen Rose hadn't noticed before, but she couldn't determine what it was.

Amelia stood with strong shoulders and a back of iron. "You'll be free soon. We must wait until the time of mourning is done. Then I can continue. You would like that, wouldn't you?"

Who is she speaking to?

Rose gripped her dagger again. There were two reflections in the mirror, but she could only see a vague outline of one, as they were being hidden by another. Someone Rose had never seen, and who was not standing in the room. Next to the hidden figure stood someone who looked like the queen, but had light blue-and-green scaled skin, long blonde hair, and silver eyes, as if the queen herself was in another form.

"Sorceress," Rose whispered.

Queen Amelia was not only a young noblewoman from the Dravian Islands, she was also a sorceress. One born with magic and who did not need a dedication ceremony to be blessed by the god's gifts.

Rose had never met anyone who'd been able to kill a sorceress without magic. Her mouth went dry. She needed a new plan.

Only, there was no time.

She had to try anyway.

Amelia whipped her head around, and the image in the mirror went blank and reflected only what was visible in the room.

"Who's there?"

The door opened, and Cal stepped forward and bowed.

"It was only me, Your Majesty."

"What are you doing? You know I don't like to be disturbed at this time."

With good reason. This must have been why she took her midday meal alone. If word spread that she was not a woman but a sorceress, it would be the end of her.

"I heard something and wanted to be sure you were all right," Cal replied.

"Of course I'm fine. Why wouldn't I be fine?" Amelia strode to a chair across the room and sat with an elegant cross of her legs.

"One can never be too careful these days. The people are wary, and I want to be sure no harm comes to you."

Amelia chuckled as she poured herself a glass of water. "I can't shake some of the nobles. They are too wary. But no one would be able to enter my chambers without your knowing it."

Rose tiptoed around the furniture, hiding in their shadows until she was behind Amelia's chair, and prayed Eira's hold on her concealment would last. She placed a finger on her lips to shush Cal, and lifted her dagger.

Rose's hand shook as waves of adrenaline ran through her. One fatal cut in the right place, and they would have their vengeance. Eira would take back the kingdom. Amelia would pay for what she'd done to their family and to Cal and Myra, and together they'd find a cure for Father.

As Rose raised her arm, the shadows concealing her faded.

She furrowed her brow. *No. Eira shouldn't be far enough away for it to affect the shadows.*

From outside of the room came a muffled male voice. "It can't be…"

Damn! What's Cadeyrn doing outside Amelia's chamber door?

"Eira?" Cadeyrn's voice cracked.

As Amelia jumped up from the chair, Rose wrapped her arm around the queen's neck, with the blade pressed against her throat, and prayed to Aros it would work. The queen gasped as a bead of blood escaped her neck.

"For my father," Rose hissed in her ear.

She pressed the dagger against Amelia's neck, but fell against the chair when Amelia vanished, and water poured from where the queen had been sitting.

Amelia appeared before Cal, body void of water. "You said she was dead!"

"Your Majesty—"

"Where's the other one?"

From outside the room, voices argued, but their words were muffled, until a rumble came from the hall, which made the floor shake. It was as though the world had stopped, and all Rose saw was Amelia rotating toward her with slow and powerful movements, her eyes turning a mix of blue, white, and green like roaring waves.

"I'll have to finish you myself." She extended her hands and water poured out from them toward Rose.

It hit her like a wall, and she gasped and sputtered. She gripped her sword and tried to rush toward the queen, but water kept coming, and she crashed to the ground.

"Rose!" Cal cried.

Crash! The chamber door collapsed, followed by a deep roar.

No, not a roar—a growl.

Standing in their presence was a brown bear with golden eyes, and Eira stood at its side, a dagger in each hand. The bear's broad shoulders filled the doorway, and it nearly didn't fit inside. It breathed hard and bared its teeth as though it could kill with a mere glance.

With a shriek, water exploded all around them, and the bear charged toward Amelia, with Eira close behind. Rose attempted to stand once again, but when another wave flew out of the queen's hands, she collapsed and her straps unraveled. The water poured out from the queen, creating a river that ran out the door, carrying Rose along with it.

Well, this wasn't part of the plan.

She coughed and pushed her head above the rising water before being pulled under again. Water filled her vision as she searched about for her straps, but they were nowhere to be found. She flailed her arms and legs in a poor attempt to regain footing and swim back to where the others were.

The bear and Eira were fighting against the waves, and thin lines of ice escaped from Eira's hands, freezing the water. Rose gasped from the cold.

"You'll freeze it all!" she yelled.

Water filled her mouth, and the last thing she saw before closing her eyes was the glow of Cal's tattoo. He cried out as she collapsed to the ground. He grabbed her with his strong arms as water continued to crash around them. She blinked, and a purple glow surrounded her and Cal as he forced through the crashing waves. He placed her against something large and furry.

It was the bear, and Eira, sopping wet, was sitting on his back. Rose grasped her sister's extended hand and did her best to climb onto it's back.

"Get back to your grandmother's home," Cal said. "Stay safe."

Another wave crashed and Cal lifted an arm, blocking the water from hitting them. Rose wrapped her arms around Eira's waist, and the bear ran out the chamber door and down the hall. But Amelia followed, sending a roaring river in her wake.

"Come," Rose gasped. "Come with us."

"Rose—"

She looked behind only to see waves crashing around Cal and dragging him under.

"Cal!" His name tore out of Rose's mouth as she watched the scene unfold.

"We have to go," the bear said.

His voice was deep and familiar. Were the surprises of today never going to end? First, Amelia being a sorceress. And now…

"Cadeyrn?" Rose said. "But…how…"

Eira shook her head. "No time to explain, but he's right. We need to leave."

Sure enough, guards were running through the halls, and Amelia was yelling after them.

"Murderers! I'll have their heads!"

Cadeyrn bared his teeth and growled as they barreled through the castle. Water splashed all around as he charged, and the sisters drew their daggers. They slashed any guard who managed to catch up to them.

Rose hoped Eira blocked out the faces of anyone they may have known. She'd never killed before, and if she put too much thought into what she was doing, Rose knew she'd never be able to live with herself. There was a reason Rose was part of the Guard, and not Eira.

People screamed and cried as they passed. There were no friendly faces wanting to help, only those in shock, or people who'd already heard that the princesses were alive—and assassins.

They should have been trying to help them, but Rose decided to ignore their betrayal. It was all she could do now.

News spread quickly in the castle. Especially when the whole place was turning into a roaring ocean.

Rose tried to grip Eira's waist with her free arm, but they were both so wet she kept slipping. Eira grasped her hand and held on, but almost lost her balance and had to let go to hold onto Cadeyrn's fur instead. Streams of water shot out at them and crashed into Rose's shoulders, tossing her back and forth.

Something grabbed Rose around the waist. Impossibly strong wet arms squeezed as though they intended to crush the life out of her.

The water. Amelia had turned it into arms.

Rose tried to hold onto her sister, but it was too late. She was pulled off Cadeyrn's back, and fell back into the waves. She gasped and sputtered as she attempted to rise back to the surface and swim to them.

Eira turned and yelled Rose's name, but it only sounded like a muffled cry. Waves made of arms shot out again, towards Eira, but Cadeyrn ran faster. He barreled outside, and Kudo cawed overhead. He swooped and circled around them, then shot off toward Eral.

"Rose!"

Eira's scream was the last thing Rose heard before someone grabbed her tunic and pulled her out of the waves.

Chapter Nine

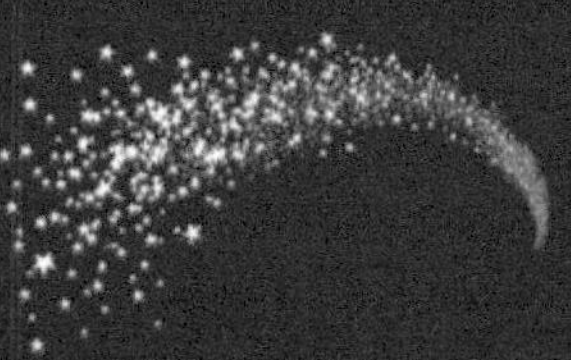

AMELIA

Cal sputtered and coughed as the water dripped off of him. He would have collapsed to his knees if it weren't for the chains which held him against the wall.

Amelia raised her hand as streams of water twisted around her fingers while her skin remained bone dry.

"Where is she?"

Cal strained against the chains and pulled himself to stand once again, but stayed silent, as he'd been since the guards had him dragged to the dungeon. It was usually easy to get him to share information or to do her favors. Now, he was a stone wall.

Amelia curled her lip and tilted her head, examining his face as though he were a stranger who'd walked into the castle. This wasn't the obedient boy she'd taken into her care all those years ago.

What had changed?

Or even worse, had he been lying to her all this time? What other secrets were in his mind? How long had Cal been betraying her?

No one betrayed her. Ever.

"Answer me!" Amelia shoved her hand forward.

Nothing seemed to happen at first, until Cal coughed and his eyes bulged while water dribbled from the corners of his mouth and out his ears and nose. When he opened his mouth, water gushed out of him as he tried to gasp for air. Unlike humans, who needed a dedication ceremony and a tattoo to gain their magic, as a sorceress, Amelia had her own. Her wave tattoo on her foot was more symbolic and to keep up pretenses to appear human. Her magic was stronger, and she didn't need to use water nearby or the magic bestowed on her and injected in her veins. Water was her essence. Her being. She could command it wherever and however she wanted.

She lowered her arm, and it all stopped. Cal gasped for air and sagged against the chains, not even bothering to stand again. He'd tried to resist her at first, the tattoo on his arm glowing and fading as each moment passed. But her power was too strong for even him.

"Where is Princess Eira?" Amelia let water twirl around her fingers and arm as she stood in front of where he knelt, shaking and trembling.

The dungeon hadn't been used in years, and it was cold, dark, and damp. It didn't bother Amelia, but even the guards who'd stayed dry had bumps on their arms as they grew more chilled.

It was a perfect time to put it to use.

She crouched before Cal, and he didn't avoid her face. He knew what she could do to him. To his precious little sister. He'd seen it happen to others. He was either incredibly brave, or incredibly stupid.

He couldn't be silent forever. He never had been able to resist her. Sooner or later, she would find what would make him break.

"You look tired, Cal. This isn't like you at all. Usually so big and strong. It's what I liked about you, after all. In fact, I don't enjoy doing this." Amelia ran her fingers through his sopping wet hair as she held his chin.

She forced her voice to remain calm and soft. Let him think she cared.

"I knew you were someone to be trusted. Someone I could ensure that I, and in return, the kingdom, would be safe with. Was I wrong? I would hate to be wrong about such a thing. We had such a good time together, didn't we? Haven't I helped you and your sister all these years?"

Cal didn't flinch at her touch, or even dare to blink away from her face. She stroked his scruffy cheek before slapping him with the force of water behind it. It hit him so hard he fell to the side and gasped, leaving a red print across his face.

Amelia stood once again and let the water fade. "Put him in the cell. Perhaps a night or two will make him want to talk."

She followed as the guards unlatched the chains from the wall and dragged Cal into the cell. It took all their strength to move the muscular man, who did nothing to assist them. He collapsed to the ground once thrown in, and did not fight.

Pathetic.

How all people were when you stripped them to their essence. Weak, and not worth her time.

Amelia grasped a bar on the cell door. After shutting and locking it, she closed her eyes.

A ripple ran through the dungeon, and the bars were cool to the touch. Moisture hung in the air. A chill would always be present in the dungeon, one which would sink into the body and lungs.

When she opened her eyes, Cal was staring at her. He rubbed his chest and coughed.

"Can't be too comfortable, now can you?" She strolled away, but stopped and looked back over her shoulder. "Perhaps if I made my hair red you would love me again. It is all I ever wanted, you know." She turned to the guards. "He's a danger to me and to the kingdom, and he's to be watched at all times. Alert me when he's ready to talk."

"And if he doesn't?" one of them said.

Amelia gave a flippant wave of her hand. "Then he'll stay here. Have Captain Avarett meet me in my chambers."

If Cal wasn't going to be loyal to her, he couldn't be loyal to anyone. Let him rot away in there, for all she cared. Anyone who betrayed her deserved worse. The only reason she was being generous by letting him live was because she needed to know where Eira was.

Amelia sauntered to her chamber while the servants all around knelt as they soaked up the water which was left behind during her battle against Rose. She took a deep breath, and the water gathered and moved toward her as though it had no other will than to be a part of the queen. It was the servants' job to dry the floors, but Amelia was feeling generous. Besides, she couldn't track Eira while people were slipping and sliding all over the place.

Everyone she passed bowed and curtsied before her, but not daring to speak unless she said anything to them first. She smiled, though, reassuring their worried glances. A smile which said yes, indeed, she was fine. Their queen was still on two feet and would continue to lead. There was nothing to fear.

Except, with Eira still alive, all of this could slip through Amelia's hands and vanish, like Eira's dark magic. Why this kingdom placed such focus on the night was ridiculous. The night was unreliable, secretive, and dangerous. Water was much more logical. Water was strong and powerful, elegant and beautiful, and it gave life to everything in the world. Without water, they would all be nothing.

Amelia needed to be rid of Eira as soon as possible, but at least Rose was taken care of for the meantime. She could have killed Rose, but determined she could be useful later, so Amelia hid her away. Everyone had seen Rose fall into the water, and they mourned the loss of the princess again.

For the time being, Eira was the focus. Once she was taken care of, Amelia could truly take the throne.

Captain Avarett met Amelia upstairs at her chamber door, and she let him inside after her. The stream running through the room awakened at her presence, and its soft waves were music to her ears.

He knelt to one knee once inside the room. "What are my orders, Your Majesty?"

A plate of fruit sat on a table, and Amelia took an apple before sitting in a chair and crossing one leg over the other, then motioned for him to rise.

"Did you know the princesses are both still alive?"

Captain Avarett hesitated and had a wary look in his eye. "It was a surprise when I saw them riding a bear through the castle, as I'm sure it was for everyone. Although, Rose had fallen off, and I'd been unable to save her in time, I'm sad to say. But why were you fighting against them, my queen? I thought they were dead. Did Cal lie to us about them?"

"It was Rose. All of this was Rose and Eira." Amelia stood, and the streams of water silenced as she drifted to the window.

She looked out at the autumn day, toward Eral Forest.

Eira must have been going to her grandmother's home. The minister's cottage was guarded by magic for those who sought to harm its inhabitants. But if her guards were to catch her before she arrived there, this could all be done. Even if they didn't, she couldn't stay there forever.

Amelia rested her hands on the sill and took a deep breath.

"The princesses have always been bitter towards me for marrying their father. The three of us never got along, and over the years they became so hostile that, in time, their hatred filtered over to their father. Eira must have become impatient waiting for the throne, and wanted to be rid of her father and myself. Rose…you know she'll do anything Eira asks of her. It appears as though they also got Cal and Prince Cadeyrn involved. You know what a rogue *he* is."

"They have always been so close to their father. I never heard them mention—"

Amelia spun on her heel to face the captain. "But it all comes together, doesn't it? How convenient that Rose had found a way to be out of the ballroom at the time her father was poisoned. When she and Eira were supposedly attacked by an animal, Rose wasn't able to defend them? We all know what a fierce fighter she is and how in the past she was so quick to defend Eira. This one time when it mattered most, she fails? Today confirmed everything. When she and Eira returned to the castle to murder me…we cannot deny the threat the Rose and Eira are to the kingdom."

"The events *have* been strange these past days," Captain Avarett said.

Amelia stood and clapped. "So we are agreed. Send all of your best men. Spread the word throughout the kingdom that Princess Eira, Princess Rose, and Prince Cadeyrn are traitors to the royal family and have committed high treason. They will be captured and brought to me, and whoever does the deed will have the highest of rewards. But bring them to me alive. I have my own plans on how to deal with them."

Amelia wasn't trusting anyone else with the task of killing Eira now. Being rid of Prince Cadeyrn would be a complication, but undoubtedly fun.

"If it is what you wish—"

"It is what I wish," Amelia said. "All I have done since the ball is take care of this kingdom and this family, and I have no intention of stopping. I will not let King Brennan's memory to be tarnished by some petty and jealous girls. Besides, don't you want to be sure the next heir is healthy and safe?"

Amelia placed her hands on her stomach, not large enough to show much of a baby belly, but she still achieved the desired reaction.

The captain stared at her. "You're…"

"Indeed." Amelia patted her stomach like the proud mother they all needed to think she would be. "I wanted to wait to share the joyous news when the king was awake once again, but alas, it is possible that this little one will have to be raised without a father. We will find them, and I will have their heads. Now go."

"Yes, Your Majesty, and congratulations." Captain Avarett bowed one last time and left the room.

Amelia sighed. This was turning out to be an exhausting day. She took the plate of fruit from the table and approached the floor-length mirror on the far wall. She put her hand on the glass, and when it turned liquid, she circled her finger in the water and made a design in it.

"Soon. Soon all of this will be ours."

She stepped through the mirror.

Chapter Ten

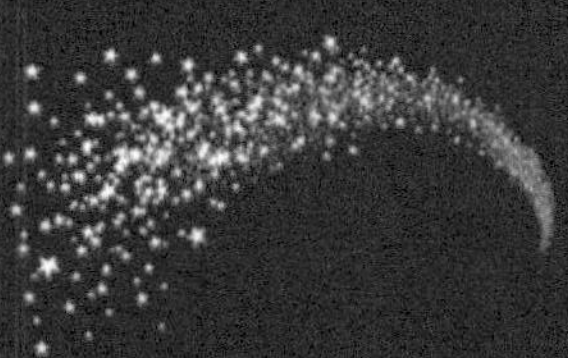

EIRA

With Eira on his back, Cadeyrn ran through the trees even faster than Rafe had. Echoes of guards calling their names bounced among the tree trunks. They weren't worried shouts the way they had been when Eira and Rose had wandered off in search of flowers as children. These were angry, with the guards' swords at the ready, as the princesses were now traitors and outlaws.

No other outcome when one betrayed the queen.

The guards' voices kept coming closer in spite of the speed Cadeyrn was going. Eira looked behind them to see the glimmer of torches in the distance. Her stomach tightened and her mouth went dry. Rose was still there.

"We need to go back."

"We need to find a place to hide before they catch us," Cadeyrn said over his shoulder, and kept running.

Eira tightened her grip on his fur and bit her lip. They'd come so close escaping together.

A pit of despair had settled in Eira's stomach when Rose lost her grip and fell into the water. Anything could have happened to her. She could be captured by Amelia. She could be…

Eira shook the thought out of her mind. She couldn't go there.

They were soaked to the bone, and the autumn air wasn't helping to dry them off, which didn't bother Eira much, thanks to her powers from Luana, which gave her a higher tolerance for cold. And Cadeyrn's fur coat should protect him.

He slowed to a halt when they found a group of trees to hide and rest in for a while. Eira concealed them in shadows and touched the tree bark so the branches moved to hide their presence even more. She slid off Cadeyrn's back and took a few deep breaths to calm herself, but her mind kept replaying the image of Rose being pulled into the water. Eira never should have left her there. Rose wouldn't have.

Eira was shoved to the side, and her back hit a tree. She almost yelled at Cadeyrn for pushing her, but heard the queen's guards nearby. Cadeyrn's body hid her deeper in the shadows she'd created. As the horses raced past, dirt and leaves shot out from beneath their hooves and scattered through the air. One paused near where they hid and looked around the area with narrow eyes. Cadeyrn's snout was next to her head, and she looked into his golden eyes, so familiar even on an animal's face. They breathed silently until the guard gave up his investigation and moved on with the rest of the group.

When the coast was clear, Eira pushed Cadeyrn's massive shoulder. He barely moved.

"Take me back. Now."

He didn't budge, so she stepped to the side to go around him.

He moved and blocked her path. "You're not going back."

Eira pointed toward the castle. "Rose is still there. My sister! Who knows what the queen has done to her?"

"You don't have a choice."

Eira tugged on her hair and bit back a scream. She kicked the ground and buried her face in her arms. Some things she didn't have a choice about. But saving her sister? Letting her kingdom and crown fall into the hands of Amelia?

Eira stepped forward, eyes narrowed as she pushed him again.

"My sister is being held captive, perhaps drowned, and my kingdom is being taken away from me. Get out of my way."

Cadeyrn took a step closer, glaring, and bared his teeth, which were as long as her hand. He could rip those teeth into her and tear her apart with ease. Not as if he would. But it still didn't make him any less terrifying.

She swallowed past the lump in her throat and shook her head. She couldn't let him bully her. Couldn't let fear make her submit to his will. Not at a time like this.

Eira straightened her spine and pulled her shoulders back.

"I said, get out of my way."

"And what are you going to do when you go back? What's your plan to rescue your sister and your kingdom? Storm the castle? What weapons do you have? I wasn't aware you'd had combat training in the time you'd been away."

Eira fumed and balled her fists. "I know how to wield a sword."

"Better than Rose can? Even with all her training, she still wasn't able to get out. You can do better than her?"

"Amelia has my sister!" The words blasted out of her, making her throat burn.

"And my brother is there too!" His voice roared over hers, and Eira had to take a step back.

He moved forward so his nose touched hers and she could see each hair on his head.

"Don't make the mistake in thinking my dedication for my brother is less than what you have for your sister," he rumbled, making Eira tremble.

They all were in danger now because she'd been so reckless in wanting revenge.

Eira gulped. She wanted to both run far away from Cadeyrn, and also wrap her arms around him and bury herself in his thick fur.

Cadeyrn's eyes softened. "We'll save Rose. I promise. But it won't do her any good for you to get killed barging into the castle. I wouldn't be surprised if Amelia had a warrant out for our heads right now."

Eira slumped her shoulders and bit her trembling lip. The plan had failed, and now she might lose another family member. The person who meant more to her than anything.

"What if we don't get to them in time?"

"We will. I promise. Besides, Rose can take care of herself. She always has. I wouldn't be surprised if by tomorrow she had the whole castle flipped upside down." Cadeyrn sighed and sat on his hind legs, his front paws in front of him. "What were the two of you planning to do once you got away?"

Eira unclenched her fists and paced. It sounded silly now, but their options were severely limited.

"We were going to go to our grandmother's house."

"Kutlaous's minister?"

"As his representative in Eral, we'll have his protection there. It's the safest place to go. Besides, she'll know more about the cure for Father, or have an idea of where we can go." Eira rubbed her eyes, the remainder of her tears fading.

If they hoped to reach Grandmother's cottage without being caught, Eira needed to have her head on straight.

Cadeyrn cocked his head. "You know how to cure him?"

Eira groaned. "Yes and no. It's complicated. I'll explain when we get there."

Cadeyrn shifted his paws and stood. "We should go, then. If anything, we can rest and regroup as we decide on another plan. You know where it is?"

Eira let his anticipation and confidence pass onto her, and smoothed her hair. She looked deep into the forest as though it would reveal a path to them.

"In the heart of Eral. No one knows the exact location, though. Eral guides those who need the minister to her cottage."

A place of peace and solitude in Kutlaous's realm. Where the forest dwellers could seek guidance, healing, and shelter when they needed the forest god. Kutlaous did not dwell among those in Eral, but instead let his minister speak and act on his behalf. Eral was contained inside Cresin, but was not ruled by the royal family. The minister was the closest to a ruler they had, but they were mostly left to their own devices. Grandmother's home was the one place that centered them all.

Eira climbed onto Cadeyrn's back once again. They didn't run at the fast pace as before, so they could see more of the sights. The purple and red leaves crunched under their feet, and there were moments Eira could see the shimmer of a pixie fly by.

Their enjoyment didn't last long. The winds shifted, and a cool breeze blew through Eira's hair. The farther they traveled, the more clouds covered the sky and drops of rain fell on her face. With each step, the rain fell harder, and thunder roared overhead. They traveled until everything was as dark as midnight, and Eira had to create stardust to light the way. She couldn't tell if it was truly nightfall or if the forest itself had merely grown darker.

Hours later, out of nowhere, a path of red gravel and dirt formed beneath their feet the way Stula's cave had. This time she wasn't frightened.

Eira took a breath as trees moved out of their way and rocks lined the edge of the path. To their left was a large pond and a small peninsula with small trees, a bright autumn garden, and a tall and narrow stone cottage. There seemed to be a second floor with a single room and a balcony outside the window.

Eira knew better than to believe the small size of the cottage. Inside, it was much larger and had several bedrooms and floors that climbed up around the tree branches behind the building. The cottage always made sure there was a place for those who needed somewhere safe. Smoke came out from the chimney on top of the pointed rooftop.

As they inched closer, the front door opened and Grandmother walked out. She crossed her arms, the blue sleeves of her simple dress rising enough to show off the green vine tattoos etched on her skin.

"Well, it's about time you arrived. I was beginning to worry." She cocked her head toward the inside of the cottage, her long gray hair waving across her shoulders. "In, both of you. I have tea brewing."

Eira wasn't sure if she wanted to laugh or cry when Grandmother ushered them inside the small and cluttered, but cozy, cottage. She was greeted with the scents of spices and the burning wood of the fireplace. Cadeyrn had to duck around stalks of herbs hanging from the ceiling.

"How did you know we were coming?" Eira said.

Grandmother handed a blanket to Cadeyrn, who'd turned back into a man. A naked man.

Eira flushed. This was not the way she'd imagined seeing Cadeyrn without clothes on.

Again.

Not as though she imagined him without clothes.

Well, not often, at least.

This was ridiculous. She was a grown woman and had other things to be worrying about.

"I knew something was amiss," Grandmother replied. "I knew about all that was happening with your father. I'm so sorry. I wanted to be there, but couldn't leave until the day of the wedding."

She lay another pile of blankets on a worn and patched-up couch by the fire, then paused as though she were searching for the words.

"Today, something changed. I always know when someone enters Eral, and there were so many emotions behind it. Fear, anger, desperation…" She placed a hand on her heart. "I knew it was about my girls. So I waited here for you. But where's Rose? I assumed she would be traveling with you."

Eira bit her lip and once again willed herself to not cry. Tears weren't going to save Rose or any of them.

"I don't know," she said.

Grandmother's breath caught, and she closed her eyes. When she opened them, she offered a weak smile and hugged Eira.

"Well, let's get the two of you settled. A warm bath is already prepared for you, and I have new clothes. When you're finished, you can tell me what happened, and we'll decide what to do."

They each took turns, Eira going first. It wasn't a large porcelain tub like the one Eira had at home, but a smaller wooden one tucked away in one of the many hidden rooms of the cottage. The water was still warm, though, and a lavender-smelling bar of soap was there to use. The small indulgence was a comfort.

When she was done, she changed into the simple green cotton dress and thick tights provided on a stool near the tub, along with a fluffy knitted shawl she wrapped around her shoulders.

When Cadeyrn took his turn in the bath, Eira curled up in a cushy armchair and snuggled in a billowing green blanket to watch the fire. The flames were like the ones Alvis would make. Who knew what became of him after their battle with Amelia? Now that they were safe, Eira had nothing else to do but let all the events of the last couple days settle as she sipped her tea.

She lowered her gaze to focus on the clay mug. The tea had a mixture of herbs Eira wasn't familiar with, and a light purple steam rose from it. No matter how long she held it, the drink never cooled, and little by little her sore muscles relaxed.

By the stars, Eira was truly out of her element. Only a few days ago, she was worried about marrying Alvis, and now she was hiding for her life from the queen. She needed to find a cure for father and reveal that it was Amelia behind the attack so she could regain the throne for her family. And save Rose from whatever fate had befallen her.

Eira turned to watch Grandmother as she bustled about the cluttered cottage, getting their wet and dirty clothing in the wash and preparing more tea. She couldn't find any rhyme or reason for why Grandmother put one herb in one jar and another in a cabinet. Yet there was a surety about her steps which showed that Grandmother knew her system—even if no one else did.

Eira breathed a sigh of relief and let herself relax into the soft chair. If she wanted to keep her sanity, she needed to appreciate the reprieve from the disaster which had befallen her and the kingdom. Grandmother's cottage had always been a place of peace and comfort for her, and she basked in it's warm and calm atmosphere.

Cadeyrn emerged from his bath, fully clothed. He met Eira's gaze, and they shared a smile. He ran a hand through his long hair, then accepted a mug of tea from Grandmother and took a seat next to Eira.

Grandmother sat in her own chair by the fire and leaned forward, elbows resting on her knees. Her silver hair glimmered in the fire, her years weighing lightly on her strong shoulders.

"Now tell me, what brings you to my door?"

There was so much explain, including why Cadeyrn was there and why he could turn into a bear. It was laughable that Cadeyrn being able to shapeshift was the least of her concerns.

Eira did owe him an explanation, though, if he was to be an outlaw along with her. Him appearing outside Amelia's chamber was not something Eira had planned on. Covered in shadows, Eira was difficult to see, but not invisible.

"Queen Amelia is the one who poisoned our father."

She slumped further into the chair as she told the tale from the moment Father was poisoned to seeking out the Stulan priest, her wonder about Gallis's chalice, all the way to arriving at Grandmother's doorstep. Cadeyrn watched her the whole time, his gold eyes intent on her face. She hadn't had the chance to tell him much before he transformed into a bear and stormed into the chamber. All she'd said was that they were in danger, and then there were cries from inside the room and water pouring out from underneath the door. That was all Cadeyrn had needed to launch into action.

"I'm sorry we weren't able to get them," Cadeyrn said. "All of them. Rose, Cal, Myra, Alvis…" He hung his head. "But Cal is one of the strongest warriors I know. If anyone can take care of himself and everyone else, it's him. We'll find a way to be sure they're safe."

Grandmother stood and paced in front of the hearth. "I should have found a way to leave Eral the moment I heard about your father. And I never liked Amelia. I'd heard rumors she was opposed to the marriage, but it was years ago. Why would she wait until now to do something about it?"

Eira couldn't remember much about the short time when Father was betrothed to Amelia. It all happened so quickly. For most of their childhood, he had several relationships and never stuck with a single one. When Eira was thirteen, he was encouraged into this marriage to have a stronger alliance with the Dravian Islands. He went and visited once to form the betrothal. A year later, he went back, and when he returned home, he and Amelia got married. The marriage started off strong, but as time passed, they went on to have their own affairs. Many nobles in arranged marriages such as theirs behaved the same way, so they never thought anything of it. Eira even sympathized with Amelia, as she wanted to avoid her own arranged marriage. But she would never fathom doing something like this because of it.

A soft thudding formed in her head, and Eira rubbed her temple.

"And now she's the one ruling my kingdom."

"I'll rip her throat out," Cadeyrn growled, making the floor tremble.

He'd sat silent and tense while Eira told her story. During certain moments, his hands shook, and claws emerged out of his fingertips.

"What about you?" Grandmother pointed to his hands.

Cadeyrn stretched his fingers, and whatever was rumbling beneath his skin calmed.

A sly smile crept across his face. "You want to see more of me in action?"

"I want to know how you're a bear."

"It isn't important right now."

"I still want to know. You're dedicated to Aros, not Kutlaous. It's Kutlaous's followers who usually have those sorts of skills, and it's rare unless you have some other sort of blood. Can your brother do it too? Am I to expect little bear cubs roaming about when Eira and Alvis have children?"

Eira's felt her face grow warm.

Cadeyrn shifted in his seat and glanced over to Eira. "Do you want to know, too?"

Eira set her mug on the table. It was the least of their worries at the moment, but it had come as a surprise.

"I'm curious, of course. But we don't need to discuss it now."

He sighed. "I'm not what everyone thinks I am. I'm only Alvis's half-brother. My father was a shapeshifter. But the king and queen raised me as though I was born of both of them so my mother wouldn't have to be part of a scandal."

Eira swallowed a gasp. "But people have affairs often—"

"They don't get pregnant, though."

No. They didn't.

Eira's shoulders sagged, and she averted her gaze from his. She resisted the urge to touch her stomach as she so often did when the subject of children and affairs arose.

"They also wanted to be sure there was another heir in line. Alvis will inherit the throne, but in case anything was to happen, it was good to have me there."

Grandmother snapped her fingers and crossed the room to a bookshelf full of books and papers threatening to tumble off. She stood against the wall and thumbed through some of the volumes.

"Scandalous or not, it is a gift which could be useful in your task."

The old woman paged through one of the books and held it open for them. Eira left her seat and met Grandmother there by the shelf. She took the book and looked at the page with an illustration of a silver goblet.

"We at least know of one ingredient," Grandmother said. "The chalice is not a legend, as many would think. There are many of us—several of your attendants, I'm sure—who believe it still exists."

Eira cocked her head as she remembered the day after Father was poisoned. The attendant who'd helped Father had a tattoo of a chalice on her wrist. She should have asked her about it.

"Even if it were true," she said, "it's been missing for centuries. Besides, how would his being a bear help with a legendary cup?"

Cadeyrn stretched in his seat, flexing his muscular arms. "I am bit of a legend myself."

Eira gave him a look, catching his sly smile.

Grandmother cleared her throat. "According to the legend, Gallis's chalice was hidden away by Luana. She took it far away to the mountains for it to be guarded by one of her most trusted servants, an ice dragon."

Eira continued to turn the pages, which showed more illustrations of Luana and Gallis, who were lifetime friends. She didn't try to read all the words, but was able to gather enough from the pictures. There were tall mountains, with one of the ancient temples of Luana, and a dragon flew in the background.

Her eyes lit up. "These are the Paravian Mountains."

There had been rumors of a winged creature who terrorized the village. At night, sometimes Eira could her the beating of wings in the sky, but always convinced herself it was just the wind.

"They are," Grandmother replied. "I don't know about you, but I would imagine having a powerful bear at your side when confronting a dragon would be helpful. Regardless of how you do it and who goes with, the Paravian Mountains should be your next stop if you plan to find the cure for your father."

With a glimmer of hope stirring within, Eira went to the bookshelves and searched for ones with maps.

"You're right," she said. "And surely the priestesses there will be able to give us some guidance. Do you have any idea what the other ingredients are?"

Grandmother pulled out another book and handed it to Eira. "I don't. It's a story I've never heard before. We can research, though."

Cadeyrn stood and joined them at the shelves to hold the books Eira couldn't keep in her arms anymore.

"What about Amelia and the others?" he said.

Eira paused her searching. Once again, the words from the priest rang through her mind. She was focusing on the wrong thing. But it had been days ago, and things had already changed. They couldn't ignore Amelia, by any means. But if they could save Father, perhaps they could take care of Amelia at the same time.

"I have some of Kutlaous's followers at the castle," Grandmother replied. "They were there in my stead for the moon festival, and when I knew something was amiss, I instructed them to stay. I'll be sure they're looking for Rose and will do whatever they can to save her and the others."

Rose wasn't alone. A small wave of relief washed over Eira. Not even a wave, but a stream of hope. She could survive off a stream.

Eira nodded. "Nevertheless, we don't have time to waste. We'll leave first thing in the morning."

After scouring the books for more information, they eventually decided that getting rest was the best thing they could do to prepare for the long journey ahead.

Several series of stairs throughout the cottage lead to the various rooms. The first level was an average cottage, but additional rooms and spaces were tucked inside the trees in a haphazard manner, with dozens of stairs and halls leading to them all.

Eira paused before she reached her destination, another room whose wooden door was painted with white and red roses. They matched the ones that grew outside of Eira and Rose's rooms at home. She pushed the door open to find a cozy bedroom filled with paintings of flowers, and a bed with a plush green quilt on the top.

She gulped. This had been Mother's room.

Eira walked through the space, arms wrapped around herself, and let her mind wallow about not having a mother. She didn't allow herself to dwell on it often.

Hanging on a hook on the wall next to the door was a blood-red cloak, waiting for its owner to take it on a stroll through the forest.

Mother left it all behind when she fell in love with the king. Including her inheritance of being the next minister of Kutlaous.

Eira took the cloak off the hook and swung it over her shoulders, then examined herself in the full-length mirror on the far wall. The cloak was warmer than anything she'd ever worn before, but it was as light as a feather.

People said Rose resembled their mother, while Eira looked more like her father. She was too young when Mother died to have any memories of her, but had seen paintings and sketches. She tried to imagine was it must have been like to grow up here.

"You said you were going to bed."

In the mirror, Eira could see Grandmother enter the room.

"It's my mother's chamber. I couldn't simply walk past it."

Grandmother sat on the edge of the bed and sighed as she looked around the space.

"Is it too foolish and sentimental for an old woman to have never changed anything in here?"

Eira stroked the edge of the hood. "I'm glad you didn't."

"For so long I dreamed she would come back someday. Selfish as it was. But she knew what she wanted, and it was your father. No matter how much I protested."

Eira's heart sank hearing the sorrow in Grandmother's voice. Her daughter was never able to return and live in Eral. The wounds of her death still clung to the air like dust in the sunrays coming through a windowpane. Always there, but never seen until you shone a light on it.

"Are you still angry she went against your wishes and plans for her?" Eira joined her on the bed.

"No, of course not, my darling. I wish things had turned out differently, but you should have seen how your mother and father were together. Even I couldn't deny how happy they were. Also, it brought me you and Rose." Grandmother stroked Eira's cheek and smiled. "I wish I could see you more often. But Eral needs me. It's my duty to stay. My hope now is to find the proper replacement. As much as I wish I could be minister forever, even I must go someday."

"Please, no more talk of such things. I've had enough discussions of death these past few days."

"So you would prefer to talk about your young man?" Grandmother raised a brow. "Or should I say, young bear?"

Eira guffawed and blushed. "Grandmother! I don't know what you're speaking of."

Grandmother chuckled. "You're young, Eira, and he's handsome. If you were drawn to him, I wouldn't blame you. Only…be careful. You'll be alone with him as you travel."

Eira raised her brows. "Are you sure you should be suggesting such things?"

Grandmother laughed. "I only ask for you to be careful."

"I will."

Grandmother pushed off the bed and stood. "Take the cloak with you. It was made for your mother, enchanted by Fae to protect you from danger, and it keeps you warm on the coldest of nights. I know you have your Luana gifts for that, but you aren't completely immune, and the mountains get cold."

She'd never had something that belonged to her mother. Save for borrowing a tiara on a rare occasion.

"I'll be bringing it back in one piece. I promise."

Grandmother leaned forward and kissed Eira's forehead.

"Get some rest. You have a long journey ahead of you."

Chapter Eleven

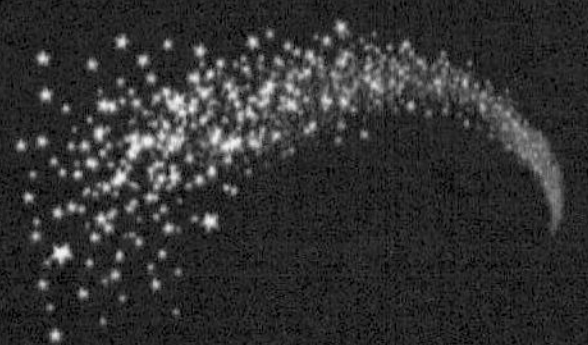

EIRA

Hints of sunlight trickled through the tree branches the next morning, without any trace of the rain from the day before. Eira decided it was a sign of good fortune from Ray for their journey.

She embraced Grandmother in a warm hug, and the small amount of forest magic inside Eira stirred at the contact. A small blessing and reminder that it was not only Luana who was a part of her.

"May the deities guide your steps. I will pray to Kutlaous every day to help you."

A part of Eira wished her visit with Grandmother didn't have to be so short, but she knew they would see each other again soon.

Cadeyrn waited for Eira outside, no longer in his palace finery, but simple black trousers and a loose white shirt. His brown hooded cloak swayed in the breeze, and Eral Forest loomed behind him. The autumn colors were starting to come into full bloom, welcoming the season and beckoning Eira forward.

A smile played on Cadeyrn's lips as though he went on missions such as this every day. Which, perhaps, he did in Oxare.

What lay beyond Eral forest, Eira did not know. The moment she stepped beyond the cottage threshold, there was no going back. Even though returning to the castle and resuming how it had been was their goal, as she looked at Cadeyrn waiting for her to join him, she knew things were going to be different. The realization didn't frighten her as much as she imagined it would but created the opposite effect. It was freeing.

Dust swirled around Cadeyrn, and in a few moments he'd transformed into a bear, with his clothes in a pile on the ground. Eira gathered them into her travel sack and harnessed the rest of their supplies on his back.

"Are you ready?" Cadeyrn said.

Eira straightened her shoulders. "Yes, I am."

Thanks to her own travel clothes, a pair of tight-fitting trousers and a long tunic beneath her mother's red cloak, she was able to climb on his back with ease.

She patted the top of his head. "Do I need to be asking you the same question?"

"Whatever lies ahead, and whatever you need me to be, I'm here."

It was an uneventful first day, but Eira was too busy enjoying Eral to be bored. None of the forest dwellers bothered them, even though she periodically spied the swish of a tail around a tree, or heard the scurrying of little feet through the bushes.

They stopped to rest a couple times and ate the rations Grandmother had provided. Cadeyrn never switched back to his human form, and Eira had to resist the urge to stare, for she still wasn't used to this new side of him. It was harder still to not giggle, watching him attempt to eat berries with his large claws.

Their breaks didn't last long, though, and they continued on. Cadeyrn was unusually quiet the whole day, but she enjoyed the peaceful company.

She had never gone so deep into Eral before, and they didn't find the edge until the sky turned pink as the sun set.

The day was over, and they were hardly any closer to their goal. Yet as she stood at the edge of the forest and waited for Cadeyrn to return from being sure the coast was clear, the Paravian Mountains towered in the distance. She'd been there towards the end of her pilgrimage only a month or so ago, but they'd never looked so big before.

Cadeyrn bounded toward her when he returned from the village with pieces of paper in between his teeth. Dirt flew as his massive paws slid through the trees and went deeper in and remained hidden. Eira chased after him and stopped when he dropped the papers.

"We shouldn't go outside of the forest." Cadeyrn sat, but his eyes didn't stop moving as he examined the area.

"We'll have to, eventually. Why shouldn't we leave?" Eira gathered the papers, and her eyes went wide at the sight.

A small rip tore into them from her tight grip. Sketches of her and Cadeyrn stared back at her, with messages of being wanted. Queen Amelia hadn't wasted any time.

"And that's not all." Cadeyrn looked over his shoulder as though someone could be watching them. "There's soldiers all over. They're patrolling the roads and are stationed outside the town gates. We'll be caught in a matter of minutes."

Eira tore apart the wanted posters and threw them to the side. With a tap of her foot, they froze, and once she stomped on them, they shattered into bits.

It did put a damper in their plans. They could travel a great distance north in the forest, but Eral didn't stretch all the way to the mountains. They'd have to leave the protection of Kutlaous eventually.

Eira pushed her hair to the side to calm herself. "Let's rest for now and begin again tonight when it's darker. I can help guide our way with star charts. The priestesses in the temple are only awake during the night, anyway, so it won't do us any good to arrive there in broad daylight. At some point, we'll need to adjust to sleeping during the day. Might as well be now. We'll be tired for a bit, but we'll get used to it."

Cadeyrn glanced at the shattered sketches. "Let's find somewhere to sleep."

They wandered further away from the forest's edge and found a group of trees with fallen limbs to hide in, with enough branches and bushes for Eira to manipulate into creating a covering for the two of them. She wrapped their spot in shadows for good measure.

She unloaded their supplies and lay on her bedroll. It was still early in the evening, but Eira forced herself to close her eyes. The air was growing colder, and while she tolerated it more than others, especially with her mother's cloak, a chill still kept her awake. She tossed and turned, and sleep didn't deign to woo her.

"You can sleep by me." Cadeyrn yawned.

Eira pulled the cloak tighter around her. "I'm fine."

"My fur is warm, I promise. I'm only thinking of your comfort."

The invitation was tempting in more ways than she cared to admit. But he was a bear at the moment, not the man she was familiar with. In a way, it wouldn't be any different than the times Rose had spent nights in the stables with the horses.

Sort of.

A cool wind blew, and Eira shivered.

"Make room." She crossed the space and rolled her bed mat to Cadeyrn's side.

It indeed was warmer next to his hulking mass. His fur caressed her arm, and Eira shivered again, but not from the cold. They were silent a few moments, and Cadeyrn's breathing slowed enough to where she assumed he'd fallen asleep.

"I'm sorry if I was harsh yesterday. I know leaving Rose behind is difficult for you." His breath tickled Eira's neck, and his chest rumbled with each word.

Eira rolled onto her side and faced him. Odd how easily she accepted him as a bear. It was the eyes, she concluded. They were still the dazzling gold she'd always known.

"I needed it," she said. "I wouldn't be able to free Rose in the state I was in. Even now, I'd be putting everyone in more danger than anything else. I'm useless, Cadeyrn."

He nudged her cheek with his nose. "That's not what I meant yesterday, and you know it. You're not useless."

Eira propped up onto her elbow. "Aren't I? I couldn't save my father, couldn't save Rose, and now each moment the kingdom falls further into the hands of Amelia."

"You are going to save your father, your kingdom, and Rose. Why else are we doing all this?"

He scooted a hair closer, and Eira felt small next to him. Even when relaxing, he radiated strength and power.

"You're the one who's going to eventually get the chalice, not me." Eira rolled onto her back.

Through the shadows she'd made to hide them, and the trees overhead, she could barely see the stars. They were dull specks far away in the darkness.

Cadeyrn rubbed his furry arm against her smooth one.

"I'm here to help *you*. You're incredible, Eira. Always have been. If anyone can save Cresin from Amelia, it's you."

THEY WOKE IN THE MIDDLE OF THE NIGHT TO CONTINUE ON TO THE mountains. Eira made a star chart to navigate and created a cloud of stardust to light their path. The journey wasn't long compared to those Eira had taken with a horse and carriage. With Cadeyrn bounding through the forest, and not needing to worry about a caravan of people joining them, they rode through the rest of the night and most of the morning. They ran as long and as hard as they could. Eira clung to Cadeyrn's fur with white knuckles, and her legs ached from trying to stay on his back.

"When we wake your father, Amelia will get what's coming to her. Your people will have justice, I promise."

Cadeyrn, now in his human form, sat under a tree and ate the last of the bread and cheese Grandmother had provided. He grimaced at how quickly they'd gone through their food.

"I should find some game for us. At least for before we sleep this afternoon. We can't rely on these rations any longer."

Eira picked at her last piece of bread with a frown. Her stomach was already groaning at how little they'd been eating in an attempt to stretch their food out.

"It would save us some time later," he said. "We can stop as soon as we're tired and hungry, and eat right away when we make camp."

When they finished, Cadeyrn went off in search of their next meal. Eira leaned against the tree trunk to conjure stars and map out the night sky so she could determine the direction to go. They'd traveled mostly in silence thus far, and conversation wasn't as natural as it normally was between the two of them. Granted, it had been years since they'd had so much time alone. Not since…

Eira shook her head and tried to focus on the stars again. She couldn't go back to those days so many years ago. Surely Cadeyrn hardly gave any attention to it. He'd had so many women before and after, she must have been only a single unmemorable moment. Repeatedly over the years, he'd proven he was her friend.

Only her friend.

Which was what he needed to be.

A crunch of leaves made Eira pause. She grasped for her sword with one hand and cloaked herself in shadows with the other, and blended into the dark portions of the forest.

Maybe it was only Cadeyrn returning with game.

The pit in her stomach made her think otherwise.

A man emerged from the shrubbery, and Eira's breath caught in her throat. He searched the area with his sunken eyes, no doubt noticing any remnants of food and supplies Eira hadn't been able to hide in her haste.

She held still as he tiptoed about, boots crunching on the leaves, and prayed he wouldn't notice her. His clothes were the sturdy cotton and wool of those who resided in the local villages, instead of leaves and branches. Not a forest-dweller. He also made far too much sound. Those familiar with Eral Forest were much quieter. Which Eira hadn't learned such tricks yet either, so an attempt to sneak away and hide would be unsuccessful.

"I've come to take you home, Princess."

He threw a dagger, and she gasped as it whirred past her head and sank into the tree behind her.

"There you are."

Eira swung her leg out and around his ankle. He tripped and fell on his back, which gave her time to stand and draw her sword. At least she'd learned a few things from Father and Rose.

"Oh, no need to throw a fit now." He crawled back to his feet and drew his own sword. "The queen wants you back to the castle alive and well."

"I have no doubt." Eira lunged at him with the blade, and he blocked her.

"And I had heard it was the redhead cripple who knew how to fight."

Eira yelled and lunged at him. He blocked her again but nearly missed. He wasn't talented, and neither was she, which made them evenly matched.

They sparred, neither making much progress, until Cadeyrn came running toward them, sword raised over his head. Eira's heart jumped at the sight of him.

She dared to watch as he attacked, sprinting in a blur. The bow and arrow tattoo on his triceps blazed through his sleeve, and his cape billowed out behind him.

The man swung his blade toward her, and she tried to block, but was thrown to the ground. She landed on her side and slid across the forest ground. Rocks and dirt scratched her, and she cried out. Cadeyrn jumped in front of Eira and stood guard over her.

"The queen wants you, too. Two for the price of one. I'm sure I'll have a large reward from both royal families now."

The man swung his blade with awkward moves, none landing a strike, and Eira could hear Rose chuckling in her mind about how un-difficult the said tricks truly were.

He was trying to distract them, but Cadeyrn didn't fall for it. A snap of his wrist, and Cadeyrn's sword met his, stopping its movement. The man tried another swing, and Cadeyrn stopped it again.

The attempted kidnapper was out of his league.

Eira crawled backwards into the trees as Cadeyrn fought, his powers from Aros increasing, his muscles growing larger and stronger, and each movement coming faster than the previous. It was a mesmerizing dance as he swung and sidestepped and blocked the man's blows.

Eira could have sworn claws were itching to pry out of his fingertips, and fur grew on his arms, but they were gone as quickly as they came. She became entranced by the scene, her vision glued to each of Cadeyrn's movements.

With a strong blow from Cadeyrn, their attacker lost his balance and fell. The man swiped at Cadeyrn's legs. Cade grunted as he kicked the sword out of his hand. He sneered as he looked at the man and grabbed the weapon for himself.

"Pathetic."

The attacker pushed up onto his hands and knees, and crawled to Cadeyrn. He didn't have a weapon, but Eira could tell he wasn't going to quit, and she wanted to leave. Especially before any other people hunting them came across their path. There had to be something she could do to help.

Cadeyrn kicked him again and slashed the swords at him. The man rolled back and forth, dodging the weapons. He swung his leg, tripping Cadeyrn. The second sword flew out of his hand and landed with a thud. The two men lunged toward the weapon, and Eira threw out an arm across the man's path. A dagger of ice flew from her palm and shot through the man's shoulder.

They all froze, and Eira gaped at what she'd done. She only intended for the ice to distract him, not impale him.

The man looked at his shoulder, panting and yelling.

Cadeyrn backed away with wide eyes. "Eira, do that again."

Eira clambered to her feet and stared at her hands. She wasn't sure if she could do it again. But she stomped on the ground, and ice spread over the grass and toward the man. It extended over his ankles so he stood frozen in place.

The ice would thaw.

Eventually.

But it gave them time.

Cadeyrn grabbed Eira's hand, and they ran.

Starlight scattered across the dark stone steps leading to the dungeon. Rumors had spread all through the castle about what happened the day Cadeyrn ran away. Alvis hadn't seen anything himself but heard enough. Eira and Rose were not dead but tried to kill Queen Amelia, and Cadeyrn was an accomplice. It couldn't be true. Rose and Cadeyrn he could imagine for pulling a stunt like this—even if it were in the outer range of possibilities. But Eira? She didn't have a violent bone in her body.

On top of it all, Amelia's hunter, Cal, was locked away. It'd been ages since the dungeon was even used. Alvis had to see for himself if it was true. Everyone was focused on capturing the others, so as one of the few who didn't believe the stories, he was on his own to find out their whereabouts, and Cal was his greatest possibility of finding answers.

Alvis was exhausted from not being able to help. As many volumes from the library as he could find were in his chambers, but none revealed any new information about the king's affliction. Learning more about Eira, Cadeyrn, and Rose was the next thing he would focus on.

It was damp, dark, and quiet underneath the castle. Mildew infiltrated Alvis's nostrils, and he tried not to breathe it in. As children,

Cadeyrn, Rose, Eira, and he would all dare one another to go into the dungeons to see who was the bravest. They heard stories about how it had been haunted. Cadeyrn went once and told wild stories about the spirits who spoke to him. Alvis no longer believed these tales, but a shiver ran down his spine as he neared the entrance, and the memories haunted him.

He'd never had any cause to anger the guards in the past, but he was greeted by one with a steely gaze at the dungeon entrance.

Alvis squared his shoulders and approached the hulking man.

"Let me see him."

"The queen has requested the prisoner has no visitors." The guard tightened his grip on the sword at his side.

Alvis didn't enjoy abusing his rank to get what he wanted but knew there were times it was necessary.

"I am the Crown Prince of Oxare. I will see him if I wish."

"With all due respect, Your Highness, you are no longer the future king of Cresin, and your station has no power here."

Alvis summoned the light and fire dwelling within him, and let sparks fly out of his fingertips, only enough to remind the guard of the power he had.

"Perhaps not. But Queen Amelia is merely the regent, and when King Brennan awakes I will be sure he knows of your hospitality toward me."

The guard eyed the sparks. "Only a few minutes."

"It's all I ask."

He nodded once and let Alvis through.

It wasn't difficult to determine where Cal's cell was, as all the others were empty. Not even a single soul for him to commiserate with. The only hint of the outside world were the small windows in each cell, but they barely gave enough light to see in front of you.

Cal sat with his back against a stone wall near the cell door, eyes closed.

"Cal."

The hunter's eyes popped open, and he furrowed his brow at the sight of Alvis.

"Your Highness? Am I…?"

Alvis knelt in front of the cell and placed the lamp on the ground. It illuminated the dark dungeon, and he could see Cal's face more clearly. Light stubble was growing on his chin, and his usual blond hair was ragged and dirty.

"I'm afraid not," Alvis said. "I heard the news and had to see for myself. What happened? Why were you brought here?"

Cal bent his knees and rested his arms on them with fragile movements. Bruises covered his face and neck, and a long scratch ran over his arm. They were healing over, thanks to his gifts from Aros, but he moved as though there were more serious injures elsewhere on his body.

"I betrayed the queen and didn't do the dark deed she requested. I assisted in the assassination attempt against her. She tried to drown me, and she beat me, and now I'm here." He shifted and groaned. "She cracked my rib, too."

Alvis sank onto his heels and rubbed his chin. Under normal circumstances, those would be plausible reasons to be locked away. Even in his own kingdom, if someone had betrayed the royal family in such a way, he would have made sure discipline had been served.

The pieces didn't add up, though. And by the way Cal avoided his gaze, Alvis knew there was more he wasn't being told.

"But how? What did Eira, Rose, and Cadeyrn have to do with any of this? Why here in the dungeon? Even criminals…King Brennan sent them to another jail."

"The queen wants to punish me," Cal said in a monotone voice, as though he'd accepted his fate. "I'm sure she's simply holding me here until she decides the proper way to do so."

"What did you do to betray her? It's unlike you."

Cal stared straight ahead at the wall in front of him and not at Alvis.

"I cannot say."

Alvis shivered. He never did enjoy the cold and missed the heat of the Oxarian sun. Spending half the year in the Cresin winter was going to take some getting used to. If they were to use the dungeons again, they at least needed to be sure its inhabitants didn't die from hypothermia.

Alvis summoned his fire again and formed a ball of fire in his palm. He reached through the cell door bars and let it float in front of Cal a few feet away to give heat and additional light. The hunter leaned into the warmth and sighed.

"Eira, Rose, and Cadeyrn were in your confidence, weren't they?" Alvis whispered.

Cal didn't say anything, but for the first time looked toward him and nodded.

Alvis grasped the cell bars. "What about them? What has happened? You must tell me."

Cal shook his head again. "I swear to you I cannot. It would only put you and your family in danger, for anyone could hear us. The queen could have ears everywhere. Who knows who else could be harmed? I do know your brother had nothing to do with it, though, and was only caught in the crossfire. He saw that Eira and Rose were in danger, and protected them."

Alvis loosened his grip. So Cal did know more than he had been letting on. Trouble was afoot, and Alvis, along with all the courtiers and nobles, had been blind to it. All this time, he thought he was prepared for whatever would come his way, and now this. How was he supposed to be a good ruler if he could not even sense something this large was amiss?

"Where are they?"

"I wish I knew."

Alvis sighed. "And you are dedicated to them?"

"With my life."

Alvis tightened his jaw and strummed his fingers against the cell bar. Cadeyrn and Eira had always been honest with him, and it hurt to know they were keeping a secret. Yet if Cal was as dedicated to them as he claimed, Alvis was grateful.

Soft footsteps approached them. A girl—no—a young woman who seemed to be near Eira or Rose's age, stood before them with a meager tray of food. He could tell she had the light brown complexion of someone from Oxare underneath the grime, and her clothes were dirty and tattered. Her hair was in such disarray, Alvis could not even tell what color it was.

He stared for a moment. All the servants here were well taken care of and had suitable clothing and were given proper tools for hygiene. This was not right.

The young woman gasped when she saw Alvis and dipped in a courtesy.

"My apologies for intruding, Your Highness. Rations for the prisoner, and the guard says you need to be leaving. He did not tell me who was visiting."

Cal extended his hand to the woman. "Alvis, this is my sister, Myra. Adopted sister."

Alvis nodded toward her but furrowed his brow. He'd known Cal had a sister, but never met her. She was nothing like he imagined.

"It's a pleasure to meet you," he said.

Myra bit her lip as she looked back at the dungeon door, where the guard was stationed.

"The pleasure is mine, Your Highness. However, the guard says you've been here too long."

"I will handle him. I'll only be another moment."

She bit her lip and passed the food between the cell bars. She let off the impression of a timid servant girl, but the way she held her shoulders straight and head tall told him she was more than she appeared.

Cal's meal consisted of some small pieces of stale bread and cheese. Even for a criminal, it was an insulting amount of food. Alvis was going to have some words for Captain Avarett. This was not how King Brennan's castle was to be run.

Myra curtsied again and scampered away.

Cal didn't touch his food and lowered his voice so low, Alvis had to strain to listen.

"There's a mirror. One the queen has in her chambers. I'm not sure what it does exactly, but I have a hunch that we may find what we need with it, and you'll see the queen's true nature and intentions."

Something in his tone made Alvis's stomach turn. It all went back to Queen Amelia. He'd not spoken it out loud, but suspected as much. He didn't claim to be an expert on Eira and her motivations, or Rose's, but they wouldn't attack the queen without good reason.

"A mirror?" Alvis said. "What sort of mirror?"

"Tall, old, magic. I hear her speaking to it from time to time, and sometimes when I'm in her chambers, she has me move it away. She won't let me see what it does, though."

"And it's important?"

"It's a place to start."

Alvis extended a hand through the bars and shook Cal's hand. "I'll search for the mirror, and I'll find a way to get you out of here."

"The mirror first. And the moment I have the opportunity to tell you more, I will."

Alvis left the floating ball of fire for Cal to keep. He returned to the castle proper, mixed with disappointment at not learning more about the situation but also with a shred of hope.

If he could find this mirror, he may find answers.

ALVIS SIPPED HIS WINE AND TRIED TO AVOID THE PENETRATING STARE OF Queen Amelia from across the table. Servants were clearing their places of the dinner they'd completed, and Alvis braced himself for what needed to be done.

Dinners at Farren Castle used to be joyous occasions, with music and dancing after. Now, without King Brennan, Eira, Rose, or Cade, their table was bare, and the courtiers were not in the mood for dancing. Even Lady Evony hadn't thrown one of her infamous gatherings since the Moon Festival. Amelia was as kind and generous as she had ever been, playing the role of the dutiful ruler and doting wife. Yet Cal's words stuck in Alvis's mind, and he noticed a tightness in her smile and bitterness to her words he hadn't before.

Queen Amelia smiled at him and raised her goblet in a toast.

"I admire your dedication to staying here during this difficult time."

Alvis raised his goblet in return. "Of course. Cresin is like a second home to me, and you have always treated me like family. I will stay as long as possible to help find a cure for King Brennan."

"Even if Cresin will no longer be yours to rule someday?" Her voice was light and conversational, but he caught a hint of a challenge in her sharp blue eyes.

Alvis hid a grimace and took another sip of wine. The loss of the kingdom was difficult to bear, almost as much as the loss of those he cared about. But not because he wanted the power of ruling Cresin and Oxare. What he'd said to Amelia was true—Cresin was a second home to him.

"I want to help as much as I can," he replied.

"I'm glad to hear it." The queen walked toward his seat at the table and extended an arm to him. "I need to attend to the king and check on the attendants. Will you escort me?"

To his side, Evony attempted to hide a smirk, and Cynth nudged her with her elbow. Alvis gave her a warning glance before returning his attention to the queen.

He smiled. "Of course, Your Majesty."

Alvis stood, offered his arm to Amelia, and together they exited the room.

"I was surprised to hear about your huntsman being locked away," he said as they traveled through the castle hall.

Amelia sighed—a bit too dramatic if Alvis had a say.

"His betrayal was a shock. I took Cal and his sister in when he was only a boy, and he's always been so dedicated to me."

Alvis kept his face neutral but concerned. He needed her to trust him if he was going to learn anything.

"May I ask what happened?"

"I have suspicions he may have been involved with Eira and Rose's plot against me. He was the one who brought us the news, and it all seems highly unlikely they were attacked by a beast. Don't you agree?" Amelia looked at him through her lashes.

Alvis chose his words carefully, and avoided eye contact, but found he didn't like the curious glances of the servants and courtiers roaming the halls, either, when they saw the two of them together. He decided to keep his gaze straight ahead, instead.

Besides, if the queen had eyes and ears everywhere, then any of them could as well. It was unsettling not knowing who he could trust in a place he considered a second home.

"It was a mysterious event," he said. "However, he truly appeared to be mourning their loss. Can one be such a good performer to mourn so convincingly?"

Amelia squeezed his arm. "You would be surprised, Your Highness."

They walked in silence for a few moments, and when they arrived at the king's chambers, Amelia turned to face Alvis.

"May I tell you a secret?"

"Of course, Your Majesty."

"The attendants are unsure how long we can wait for the king to awake. They are worried about it, as am I." She closed her eyes and wet her lips before looking at Alvis again. "I am happy to act as regent and guide the kingdom. But if the king never awakes or takes a turn for the worse, I do not know what Cresin will decide to do. I am only queen by marriage, and sadly the king and I have never had an heir. I do not know who will take the throne next." She ran a hand over Alvis's arm, and he tried not to cringe. "Perhaps the two of us can find a way out of this situation. Together."

Alvis removed her hand from his arm. "Your Majesty, I am honored you trust me. However, I'm not sure if I understand what you're implying."

He'd been flirted with by dozens of women, in spite of his engagement to Eira, and he knew what it looked like. Never by the queen, though. She had plenty of other lovers, and therefore no need of him. It was better for him to act as though he didn't understand and not give her, or anyone, reason to think he was plotting with her.

Amelia smirked. "Don't act so innocent. Betrothed to the same woman your entire life, and the two of you never lay together?"

Alvis opened his mouth to argue, but she waved him off.

"Yes, I know of the tradition of Luana and Ray to remain virgins, but do you honestly expect that anyone believed you would stay away from one another until the wedding day? It's natural and normal, Your Highness, nothing to be ashamed of. Now Eira has sadly betrayed us all. You no longer need to keep pretenses and can pick any companion you want. If I happen to become with child, who is to say it wasn't conceived before the king fell ill?"

Alvis crossed his arms. It was all he could do to prevent himself from spitting in her face, or worse.

"You have had many men in and out of your bed over the years. I'm sure any one of them would be willing to donate their services."

"But none of them were supposed to rule Cresin and had it snatched away from them. In name, the child would be known as King Brennan's own. But what if their actual father were the one to raise them?"

Alvis furrowed his brows. "You want me to marry you?"

Amelia tipped a shoulder and gave a flippant wave of her hand.

"I was young when I married the king and am not much older than you are. I'm not even forty yet. It would be natural for the two of us to come together in comfort during this difficult time. Cresin would have an heir. You and I would act as regents until they are of age. Once it happens, we can do as we please."

Alvis's skin crawled at her proposition. She wanted the throne for herself. Maybe even his throne in Oxare.

"I simply want what's best for the kingdom," she said. "You already care about Cresin and are prepared to rule it. It's natural you would be here in our time of need, isn't it?"

"I believe you said you need to attend to the king. I will leave you to it." Alvis bowed. "Have a good night, Your Majesty."

Alvis turned on his heel and walked away before Amelia had the opportunity to say anything more. While he desperately wanted a bath now, he instead decided to head to Amelia's chambers. A set of footsteps followed him, and someone tapped him on the shoulder.

Evony appeared at his side and matched his stride. "You aren't seriously considering the queen's proposition, are you?"

Alvis looked at her out of the corner of his eye. Nothing ever got past her.

"You should be careful what conversations you overhear."

She examined her nails and grinned. "I was walking by, and it is not my fault if voices echo against the stone walls. And you didn't answer my question."

Alvis raised his brows. "I find her proposition suspicious and on the brink of treason."

The idea of marrying Amelia made him sick. But if he could act as regent, perhaps he would still be able to protect Cresin.

Then he remembered what Cal told him.

"Would you like to help me with a couple things?" he said. "I think you have the precise expertise I need."

Evony's face lit up like a sunrise. "Of course."

They hurried through the halls to Amelia's chambers.

"I spoke with Cal in the dungeon. While I was there, I met a young woman. A servant. She didn't look well cared for. Her clothes were dirty and torn, not like the other servants here, and the food she served Cal was meager, at best. I have a hunch she is given similar rations. Would you be able to find a way to deliver new clothing and food for her?"

"It would be my pleasure," Evony whispered. "I can ask Cynth to assist. I know they keep extra clothes and rations at the temple for those in need."

Alvis clapped her shoulder when they arrived at Amelia's chamber.

"Good. Now one more thing. Keep watch for me. I don't know how long the queen will be *attending to the king*."

Evony's jaw dropped as she stared at the door.

"Is this her…"

"Yes."

"You're going in?"

"Yes."

"Why?"

"It's for the princesses, and I need you to trust me."

Evony nodded, but her face was still scrunched in confusion.

"Of course."

Alvis opened the door and stepped inside. He'd never been inside the queen's chambers before. He was never the one to go on adventures and spy on people. Cadeyrn did. The prospect was both thrilling and terrifying.

Being in the queen's room was as though he'd stepped onto a sandy beach. In spite of the autumn season, the room was warm with a gentle breeze. Alvis swore he smelled salt in the air. The room was draped in blue, green, and white cloth, and the floor was the same color as the ocean shore. If one could have embraced the spirit of

Colma in a single space, this was how to do it. A bubbling fountain stood next to a full-length mirror, and a stream sloshed around the bed.

The mirror itself must not have been a secret but have some other significance. Most people had a mirror in their chambers. Why was Cal concerned with this one?

Alvis examined it. The glass was dark and seemed to have waves on the surface. Not surprising for someone dedicated to Colma.

He grazed the silver frame, which was carved with images of waves and sea creatures swimming about. Perhaps there was a secret button that activated something. Or maybe he needed to find an incantation carved into the frame.

Something moved under the surface of the glass from the corner of his eye. At first it appeared to be his own reflection, but nothing else in the room reflected in the glass.

He saw it again. A strand of curly blonde hair.

He placed a palm on the glass. "Hello? Is someone there?"

A faint silhouette appeared in the darkness. Someone small, with long curly hair overtaking their body. So long it seemed to go out past the mirror. Alvis wanted to look behind it to see where all the hair went.

"It's all right." Alvis removed his hand. "I'm a friend."

He hoped they were a friend as well.

"Whose friend are you?" Her voice was small and light, like the morning's first gentle wave cresting on the shore.

"Cal sent me." He prayed it was the right answer.

"Who is Cal? I think I know the name. But so many men come in here."

No doubt. "Big, tall, has a hawk."

"You know the kind hunter?" Her voice raised into a hopeful squeak, and the dark glass made waves, with clamoring in the background.

Through them, her silhouette grew larger and clearer. No longer a shadow, but a full person. She was young and on the edge of ending childhood. She wore a simple white dress without any shoes, and had warm golden-brown skin. Yet it was her hair which drew the eye. Brown and blonde curls rolled over her shoulder all the way to the floor and trailed her, filling the endless space in the mirror. Alvis tried to not let his jaw drop at how much of it there was.

"Yes, Cal, the hunter. He sent me."

He'd never mentioned a girl, though. Alvis doubted Cal was as familiar with her as she was with him.

"Do you know him?" he said.

"Yes!" The girl smiled but looked at the floor bashfully. "He doesn't know me, though. I see him when he visits Mother, and he seems kind. Mother never lets me meet anyone. She keeps me hidden."

Alvis knelt to one knee so he could look at her more closely at her level.

"She doesn't? Have you spoken to anyone?"

The girl shook her head. "Only Mother. You are the first person. Does Cal know who I am?"

Alvis hesitated, not wanting to dash her hopes, but decided honesty was the best choice.

"I do not believe so. But he told me your mirror is special."

"It's my home."

"How long have you lived here?"

"My whole life."

Alvis couldn't imagine life inside of a piece of glass. Was there more? Was there a whole world where she lived? Who was Mother?

He was most afraid to know the answer to the last question.

"How old are you?"

"Eleven."

Queen Amelia had been living at the castle for ten years. This girl was here the entire time, and no one knew.

"Eleven is a good age. You're almost a lady." He smiled. "My name is Alvis. What's yours?"

"Nell. And you're the prince," she blurted out. "I've never seen you, but Mother speaks of you. She speaks of everyone! You, Princess Eira, Princess Rose, Prince Cadeyrn…"

Incredible. He wanted to press her for more information to see what she'd been told about all of them. She seemed friendly and happy for the company, but if she was who he thought she was, he may need to gain her trust. And she needed to gain his.

"It's good to meet you, Nell."

She looked at Alvis with a shy grin, and something in him softened. This was no place for a child to be raised.

A knock came at the door, and both Alvis and Nell looked toward the chamber entrance. Evony poked her head in, and her gaze landed on Nell in the mirror. She stared for a moment before snapping herself out of her surprise.

"Someone is coming. We need to leave."

It hadn't been nearly enough time, but at least he found what made the mirror so interesting.

He faced Nell again. "May I visit you again?"

"That would be lovely."

"But you mustn't tell your mother or anyone how I, or my friend, were here. Can you promise?"

Nell hesitated. It was a large favor he was asking of a child he'd just met. Queen Amelia was the only person she spoke to, and to keep a secret from her would surely be a challenge.

She glanced behind her and looked at Alvis again, to where a shadow moved, and opened her mouth as though to say something.

Was there someone else inside the mirror?

"I don't want to rush you, Your Highness, but we do need to be going." Evony kept looking back and forth between Alvis and the hall.

Nell nodded.

"Who's there with you?" Alvis said.

How many people was Queen Amelia holding captive?

Nell paled. "No one. It's only me. I've been here alone my whole life."

"Prince Alvis, please. We need to go…"

He wasn't going to get any more information out her. Not before they were caught.

"I'll return. I promise."

Alvis stood and waved goodbye to Nell. She waved back, and Alvis hated to close the door, but he had to before Amelia caught them.

Alvis and Evony hurried away, and when they were a safe distance from the chamber, Evony asked the question burning on her tongue.

"Who was that?"

It was a revelation he could barely admit to himself. Yet it was the only logical conclusion.

"I think it was Queen Amelia's daughter."

Chapter Thirteen

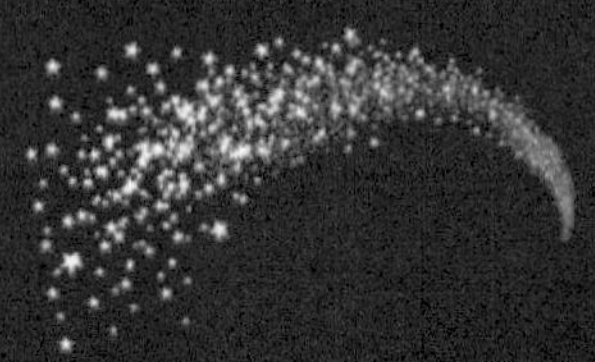

EIRA

Branches slapped Eira's legs and arms, but she didn't care. She had no idea where they were going or if their enemies still pursued, but this journey told her one thing—danger came with each step.

Grandmother promised she would be safe in Eral, for the forest was in her blood. But what about people and things who weren't part of the forest or under the canopy of Kutlaous?

Eira's side ached, and her calves felt lit from within. She trailed Cadeyrn until she had to pause.

"Cade, please, I need a rest."

He slowed enough to turn back to her. "Are you hurt?"

Eira panted and held her side. "I'm fine. I'm not used to running like this. I need to catch my breath. Where are we heading?"

He scanned the area while rubbing Eira's back. "I'm not sure. I only wanted to get you away from there. You sure you're not injured?"

Eira stretched and twisted at the waist. "Yes, I'm sure. I was able to hold him off enough until you got there."

Cadeyrn shifted his weight to his right leg. Eira stopped stretching and looked at his pant leg.

"You're bleeding."

Cadeyrn twisted his leg and grimaced. "Oh. He must have scratched me. It'll be fine."

Eira knelt and pinched her eyebrows as she examined the wound. Blood seeped through the pant leg. He flinched when she placed her hand on it.

"Cade, I'm not the only one who needs to rest."

"I'll be fine." He moved his leg out of her grasp. "Give it a couple hours and the wound will heal."

His tattoo was glowing to help his body heal itself. Still, rest would speed the process along.

Eira placed her hands on her hips. "We're going to find a place to rest. We both need it, and I'm not going to run until we do."

There didn't appear to be any sign of people hunting them anymore, so she continued to seek out a place for them to relax a while. Behind her, Cadeyrn let out a heavy sigh but followed. They walked side by side for a while, his limp growing more noticeable as they went on, until they came to a cave. She had to resist asking how he was feeling every few minutes and was glad to find the shelter.

Cadeyrn looked inside first, and when he saw it was empty, they sat and unloaded their supplies. He groaned as he lowered himself and leaned against the wall.

Eira wrinkled her brow and waved her hand so clusters of stardust filled the area to give them light. It was small and damp, nothing like the one she'd found with Stula's priest, but it fulfilled their need.

"Your leg still hurts, doesn't it?"

He waved her off and closed his eyes. Such a stubborn man.

"I'm fine. As I said, give it a few hours."

Eira knew how quickly those dedicated to Aros healed, and it was usually faster than this, unless it was a severe wound. There may not be much she could do, but it didn't mean they were helpless. She dug around in her pack until she found one of the satchels of herbs Grandmother had prepared for them.

"I'm going to find some water so we can get this patched. I saw a stream not too far away."

"I'll go with you." Cadeyrn pushed against the wall to stand, but his leg gave out on him.

His groan made Eira's stomach tie in knots.

"I'll be right back. Stay there."

Before he could argue, she left the cave. The stream was only a couple minutes' walk, and if either of them cried out, the other would still be able to hear them. She paused every few steps in case he called after her. She needed to calm herself, though. No use in worrying.

Eira tried to let the cool water calm her nerves as she mixed the herbs Grandmother had provided, on a strip of fabric she'd ripped from one of her spare pieces clothing. She'd always liked water and spending time with Colma's followers. They had a sense of freedom and relaxation Eira found she often lacked. A shame Amelia's actions had put such a taint on it. Would she ever be able to look at a body of water without thinking of her stepmother now?

Her hands shook as she rubbed the cloth together, mixing the herbs until sparks of white flew out of the cloth. It wouldn't heal wounds, but could diminish swelling and pain. At least, she hoped.

Eira took a deep breath before returning to the cave, where Cadeyrn remained sitting against the wall, a cluster of stardust hovering as the only light, and he'd already gotten his bed mat out.

"I thought maybe you'd left me for dead," he said when Eira approached, a smile tugging on his lips.

"I wasn't gone long." Eira knelt and pushed his pant leg to reveal the scratch.

She bit back a gasp at the sight. The wound was red, with something black oozing from it. His skin was working to close over the opening, thanks to his magic, but it was a slow process.

"Shouldn't this have closed over by now?"

Cadeyrn angled his leg so he could see better, and frowned.

"Some wounds take longer than others."

A hint of uncertainty in his voice made Eira believe worry was creeping into his usually confident attitude.

She placed a sliver of cloth on the scratch, and Cadeyrn yelped. His leg twitched and sprang to life as tough it had been hit by lightning.

"What are you doing? Trying to kill me?"

She sat back on her heels. "Oh, please. I barely touched you."

"It stung."

"You're a soldier, for Aros's sake. Surely you've endured more than a simple herbal remedy. It might sting for a moment, but if you hold still, it'll help, I promise."

He pressed his lips together in a thin line and clenched his jaw. He held his leg back at first, before laying it on the ground to let Eira work. This time she was gentler, and he only flinched a tiny bit. The muscles in his calf relaxed as she spread the cloth over the wound. With a sigh of relief, she rubbed it, and the cloth adhered to Cadeyrn like a second skin.

The tension in his shoulders eased as he rotated his leg side to side.

"Did one of the attendants at the castle teach you?"

Eira scooted across the cave floor and leaned against the wall opposite him, letting herself relax for the first time since the attack. It was a small space, and her extended feet still almost reached his.

"My grandmother did. It's nothing special. You don't need magic to make it work. She always wanted us to be prepared for anything."

"Smart woman."

"She is."

They sat in a comfortable silence, and Eira darkened the shadows covering the cave entrance. Couldn't be too careful. It hadn't even been a couple days of travel, and already things had gone terribly wrong.

She hugged her knees to her chest. "Where do you suppose we should go next?"

Cadeyrn slouched, with only a small wince at the movement of his leg, and held his hands behind his head.

"My first instinct is to go deeper into Eral. We know now that there are scouts looking for us here, but your average hired man who isn't familiar with the forest won't want to venture far."

"Aren't we already deep into the forest?"

"I thought we were. At least, deeper than I've ever been. Who knows how far it truly goes? Its enchantments could deceive us and not appear on our maps."

Eira waved her hand, and the floating stardust formed constellations for her to examine and determine which way to go next.

"I can't decide if we should travel at night or during the day. I don't want us to get attacked while we sleep during the day, but it's easier to stay hidden at night."

"We can try during the day. I'll be able to stay awake better. How about we begin tomorrow? I'm already wiped."

It was a relief to hear him admit to being tired. Especially since Eira was, too.

She spread her mat out and lay on her side to face him. Her hip twinged from a bruise she must have gotten from her fall earlier, and she adjusted so her weight wasn't lying on it.

"We should get some rest. We can be gone before the sun rises and take a break during the day so we can travel longer at night."

Cadeyrn hissed when he moved to lie on his mat. When Eira extended a hand to help, he shook his head. Still stubborn.

They made themselves comfortable, and Eira dimmed the stardust so it was only a glimmer. It sparkled against the walls, and Cadeyrn's gold eyes shone through the dark.

Eira couldn't look away as he yawned. "Thank you for coming so quickly. I'm not sure how long I could have held my own against him."

"Of course. Thank you for the ice. I didn't know it was something your magic was capable of."

"Neither did I," Eira whispered.

She'd always been more comfortable with shadows and stars, so she'd never expected her ice to behave so powerfully—or violently. She couldn't let Cadeyrn fight alone, though. As much as it frightened her, she didn't regret how it assisted their escape.

Cadeyrn stretched his arms over his head and laid them at his sides.

"Well, it helped," he said. "At least maybe we'll be able to evade him now. We make a good team."

Their mats were so close together, it wouldn't take much for her to cross the gap and touch his hand.

Eira's gaze darted to their hands lying on the ground, and she was tempted to hold his.

"We do," she replied.

They lay on their sides, looking at each other for a long moment. Things they'd never said weighed in the air like a blanket threatening to smother Eira. She bit her lip and knew it would come out in time. Maybe they'd talk about their affair.

Cadeyrn blinked a few times. "What is it?"

Eira shook her head and lowered her gaze. She'd been staring at him too long.

But he'd been starting at her, too, hadn't he?

"Nothing," she said. "We should get some sleep."

"Right." Cadeyrn tried to turn into a more comfortable position, groaning at the effort.

Glimmers of the remaining stardust reflected in his messy dark hair.

Eira swallowed. No, this wasn't the proper time to discuss such things. He was wounded, and they needed to keep their focus. Besides, it had been years ago. Surely he'd had countless women by now, and she was only a glimmer of a memory.

She cleared her throat. "Good night, Cadeyrn."

"Good night, Eira."

THEY ROSE BEFORE THE SUN BUT AFTER THE STARS HAD FADED, AND WENT out on their journey once again, gathering berries from various plants to eat for their morning meal, since Cadeyrn hadn't been able to hunt the previous day. Their pace was slower than before as he limped along.

When they took a midday break, Eira removed the cloth to wash it and inspect the wound. She was grateful to not have much in her stomach, as she may have retched it up. The swelling had lessened, with some evidence of healing, but parts of the wound remained open, while the rest turned black.

Eira replenished the herbs and returned the cloth back to its place.

"You sure you're all right?" She forced her voice to remain neutral, as Grandmother or an attendant would have.

"Of course. I'm walking, aren't I?" Cadeyrn tossed a handful of berries into his mouth.

"Walking and being all right are two different things."

Eira knew as much from Rose. More times than not, Rose continued to walk and use her leg when it was obvious she was in pain. Her sister and Cadeyrn were alike in that sense. Too stubborn for their own good, causing Eira to worry for the both of them.

Rose.

Eira had been praying to every deity she could think of during the quiet moments of the day, in hopes she was still alive. Alive and well.

She blinked away tears and sank back, sitting on her feet. Rose would have been able to talk sense into Cadeyrn, or give Eira some insight into how Aros's magic helped heal different types of wounds. Eira could only hope Rose's own powers were healing whatever wounds she'd received at the castle.

Eira shook her head as though she could toss the thoughts from her mind. Rose should have been there with them. And they couldn't rescue her until Cadeyrn was healed.

"You can't keep ignoring it if something is wrong," Eira said.

Cadeyrn waved her off. "Weren't you the one yesterday who said I've probably endured worse? Which I have. It will pass over in time. You'll see."

But it didn't pass over. By their second day of travel, they were walking slower and taking more breaks. Each time they sat to rest, Eira removed the cloth, washed it out, and replenished the herbs. She was running low, and the wound didn't appear to be getting any better. The skin was closing over it, but the color remained odd, and Cadeyrn's limp was more noticeable with each step. Thankfully, they hadn't run into any more potential kidnappers along the way. Perhaps the last one was the only who dared go so deep into Eral.

On the third afternoon, Eira frantically consulted a star chart while Cadeyrn took a nap, which was happening more frequently. As much as she tried to remain calm, Eira knew Cadeyrn wasn't going to heal anytime soon. They needed a new plan.

When Cadeyrn stirred, one eye opening, Eira wiped away the star chart before he could see which direction she intended for them go. He'd never agree.

His eyes were glassy, but a lazy smile tugged at the corners of his mouth. He gazed up at her, and the smile broadened.

"Didn't mean to fall asleep."

"You're fine." Eira stood and pointed west while securing the cloak around her neck. "We're going to head that direction next. The chart said it would be best."

Cadeyrn stretched, his muscles flexing to pull his shirt tight. At least nothing else in his body had been affected by the injury.

"Isn't this a different path than we've been taking?"

"Yes, but it'll be more efficient."

A partial truth. The path in that direction was longer, but it would get them to a village and an attendant sooner. The small detour would help them travel more quickly in the long run.

"You're the granddaughter of Kutlaous's minister, so the gods will guide you through Eral. I trust your judgement."

Eira helped Cadeyrn to his feet. She considered suggesting going into his bear form if it would be easier, but wasn't sure what the repercussions of his injury would be.

They continued on, even if it was slow. At times, Eira had to support him by having his arm wrapped around her shoulders. For being as fit and slim as he was, the man was heavy. But she didn't mind if it kept him upright and awake.

Eira squeezed him closer, and he leaned into her as they hobbled along.

Cadeyrn straightened and looked at their surroundings, which were illuminated by stardust.

He stopped. "This isn't right."

Eira tripped. "What do you mean?" Her cheeks flushed.

He was more alert than he appeared.

Cadeyrn broke away from her and turned his head back, then further up the path, scanning the area.

"We're going west, not north. How is this a more direct path to the mountains?"

Eira looked to the ground. "It's not."

"Eira, where are we going?"

"We're going to find a town." She continued walking while Cadeyrn attempted to catch up.

If Eira estimated correctly, there was a village not far from one of the northwestern edges of the forest. They could arrive there in a day or two, possibly less.

"It's too dangerous. The closer we get to the edge, and even to a village, the more likely we are to run into someone sent from Amelia."

Cadeyrn paused to catch his breath and leaned against a tree, trying to keep his face neutral, but there was no denying the pain in his eyes.

A pang of guilt ran through Eira. She'd been pushing him too hard and making him walk further.

"And I can't risk you not healing." Eira stopped walking so he could rest.

She offered him her arm so he could sit, but he pushed her away.

"I'm fine."

"No. You're not." Eira went to rub her betrothal band, which wasn't there anymore—an old habit.

Instead, she tugged her sleeves over her bare wrists.

The man was impossible. Surely he had to see how much his injury was slowing them down.

"You said you would be whatever I needed. I need you to be healed and able to travel, and if necessary, defend. We've already lost time because of your stubbornness to receive help. We'll disguise ourselves and find an attendant before going to the mountains."

"We can find an attendant at the temple, I'm sure."

The pain must have been too much, and he struggled to sit again. He tried to ease himself to the ground so he didn't fall, but his leg shook.

Eira sat with him, holding his hand. "I don't think you'll make it that far."

Cadeyrn linked their fingers and looked to the ground. "I've already failed you. I was supposed to be helpful, not a hinderance."

She squeezed his hand tighter. She'd never seen him this badly hurt before, and he always was able to overcome whatever befell him. Either of them. He'd always been there for her and made her feel strong, and now she needed to do the same for him.

"You haven't failed. If you hadn't come, he would have taken me back to Amelia, and who knows where I'd be now. Doesn't mean you can't have help at times. Right now, the best way to help me is to find an attendant."

Cadeyrn ran his thumb along the back of Eira's hand, and she shivered.

He finally met her gaze. "Fine. But at the first sign of danger, we go back to our original route."

"Agreed."

Eira stood and searched for a fallen branch. When she found one, she brought it back and handed it to him. Cadeyrn grunted in response and tried to stand on his own, but only landed on the ground again.

Eira put a hand on her hip and thrust the stick back at him.

"If a crutch is good enough for Rose, it's good enough for you. It'll help."

His shoulders slumped. "That was low."

"I know. But it's true."

Cadeyrn chuckled and took the branch. "First, you freeze a man, and now you aren't afraid to hit me where it hurts. This is a whole new side to you."

Eira grinned. "Having your father poisoned and your kingdom taken away from you by your stepmother will do that to a person."

He used the branch to stand, and their walk was still slow, but far more productive. It took a majority of the evening, but whatever had been hanging the air between them over the last few days had now vanished, and they talked and joked like the old friends they were. He told her about when he had to fight the sand serpent in the Black Desert while on a mission to find supplies during a drought a few years before. Eira shared stories of her pilgrimage over the previous year. He laughed when she told him about the time she attempted to fend off a raccoon who wanted a group of orphans' food in a poor village. Her feeble fighting skills, aided by her pity for the animal, didn't give her the same success as Cadeyrn's sand serpent battle.

As the sun set and they got closer to Eral's edge, she could finally see the day turning into night and enjoy the bright pinks and reds of sunset as Luana and Ray greeted each other. At least they were getting closer, but without a map, Eira wasn't sure where the nearest town or village was, and once they were out of the protection of the forest, there wouldn't be many places for them to take shelter.

Twin yawns came more frequently, and their conversation grew fragmented. Even with the help of the stick, Cadeyrn's walking became slower with each moment.

They took a rest, and Eira inspected his leg. The cloth was covered in blackened dried blood, and his leg was turning the same color. The scratch had finally closed, but infection had spread.

Eira's stomach turned. Something must have been on the blade, which prevented Cadeyrn's magic from healing him. Eira didn't know much about the art of restoration, but this couldn't have been good.

"How is it?" Cadeyrn's voice was hoarse, and he panted.

As she tried to decide the best answer to give, Eira tore off a new strip of cloth and disposed of the old one. All the dirt and grime of the forest didn't help the situation, and it was impossible to keep the infected area clean. She didn't have any herbs left, but she could at least cover the wound.

"It's gotten worse."

Cadeyrn groaned.

The strumming of drums sounded, along with the whispering of a flute. Voices chattered and sang along.

Hope soared through Eira. *People!* Someone who could possibly help.

"I'll be right back." She stood and jogged ahead to find the source of the sounds.

A caravan was preparing their camp to end a day of travel. A few horses stood to the side while a tall Fae woman placed saddles on their backs. A child laughed and danced to the tune a dwarf played on his flute, and others bustled about, singing and tapping drums as they unpacked their things from a large cart. Along the side of the cart were painted swirls and music notes in bright shades of purple. They were servants of Efare, bards who traveled from village to village, sharing the stories of the deities.

Praise Luana and Kutlaous. They'd guided them to help.

With newfound energy, Eira ran back to where she'd left Cadeyrn and scooped up handfuls of dirt. She landed on her knees next to him and waved shadows over his face to disguise his features, and did the same to herself. With the dirt and the shadows from the trees blended with her shadows, she prayed it would be enough to disguise their faces enough where they wouldn't be recognizable.

Cadeyrn coughed and shook his head as dust and dirt flew in his face.

"What are you doing?"

"There's a caravan of bards. If we disguise ourselves, perhaps we can convince them to let us travel with them."

Eira gathered dirt and smeared bits of it on her face to make it appear as though they were poor travelers—which wasn't far from the truth—and raised the hood of her cloak.

Cadeyrn followed her lead, and she helped him to his feet. Using the branch and Eira's shoulders, Cadeyrn limped along with her to where the caravan was still unpacking their things for the night.

"Hello!" Eira called out as they approached.

The dwarf who had been playing the flute lowered his instrument and turned to look at the pair. Taking it as an invitation, Eira led Cadeyrn to him.

"I'm Zeno. How may I help you?" With his dark hand, he moved his long gray beard over his shoulder, as it nearly touched the ground.

"We've been traveling all night, and when I heard your music I had to come. You see, my…" Eira glanced over at Cadeyrn, "…husband…"

Cadeyrn gave a few startled blinks.

"…was wounded. We were attacked, and the wound is getting worse. Are you heading to town tomorrow?"

Zeno pocketed the flute into his robes and stepped forward to look more closely. Eira cursed herself for not being able to conceal their faces more, but if she did anything more her tattoo would glow through her clothing and their cover would be gone.

"How long have you been traveling?" he said.

"Only a few days." Cadeyrn hugged Eira to his side. "We were married not long ago. She's part Fae, and I'm human, but she wanted our ceremony to be blessed by the minister. She's so sentimental when it comes to her heritage. But we were traveling to the Paravian Mountains to have some time together." He squeezed Eira's side, and she giggled.

"But we were attacked by someone. He mistook me for the princess. But now my husband is hurt, and it's becoming infected. We need an attendant as soon as possible."

The dwarf gestured for them to follow. He led them into the now completed camp, and they sat on a log.

"Come on in and have a seat. We can discuss the matter. We don't usually take fellow travelers along with us."

"But you are going to a nearby village, aren't you?" Eira helped Cadeyrn extend his leg, and propped it on a rock.

"We are."

"We don't have much money, but we can assist with whatever you need in payment." Cadeyrn's eyes fluttered, and he shook his head. "Sorry…a tad dizzy."

Eira rubbed his back and supported him as he nearly fell over. That was new.

She touched his head and snapped her hand back. He was burning up.

Eira looked to the dwarf again. "Please. We'll do anything. When I saw your caravan, I knew the deities must have led us to you."

Zeno whistled and waved over the tall Fae woman with long blue braids. She joined them and crouched to eye level with them.

"Priestess Kier, this couple seems to have run into trouble and wish to travel with us. He's been wounded by one of those who are searching for the princesses."

The Fae looked over them with sharp purple eyes. "We would need an offering."

Cadeyrn's weight was growing heavier on Eira's shoulder as she tried to hold him upright on the log. He could barely keep himself sitting now.

She held him tighter. "Of course. Whatever you like."

"Stories," the priestess said. "Tell us whatever stories you have, and we'll grant you passage to the next village. Your man can sleep in the cart, and you can care for him there."

Eira bowed deeply while still sitting. "Thank you, Priestess. May Efare bless you."

Priestess Kier called over two more bards, and they helped to carry Cadeyrn to the cart and lay him on a bed of hay. Eira climbed in after him. The bards also provided some blankets and pillows.

Eira could have cried from gratitude.

"I cannot thank you enough." She found a place to sit near Cadeyrn.

"You're welcome." Zeno spread a blanket out for them. "I didn't catch your names."

Names. Yes, they needed names, didn't they?

"Lennox," Eira replied, her mother's name being the only one she could conjure of on such short notice. "And…"

"Darius," Cadeyrn said.

As one of the legendary warriors of Oxare, many men were named after him.

Eira's shoulders relaxed, and she smiled at Cadeyrn while pushing his tangled hair away from his eyes. At least he'd been coherent enough to think of a name for himself.

"Yes. Darius."

Zeno eyed her but eventually nodded. "If you need something, call for me."

"We will."

The cart jostled as Zeno climbed off, and Cadeyrn groaned again. Beads of sweat poured over his face, leaving wet streaks which washed away the dirt used to cover his identity. Eira dug in her bag for another piece of cloth and wiped his brow with it.

"We'll find help soon. You'll see. You'll be well again."

Cadeyrn's head rocked, and his eyes slowly opened and closed.

"I'm here with you. Of course I'll be well, darling."

Eira continued to dab his forehead and rolled her eyes.

"No one is listening. You don't have to keep acting any longer."

Cadeyrn closed his eyes again and sighed.

"Whatever you need."

Chapter Fourteen

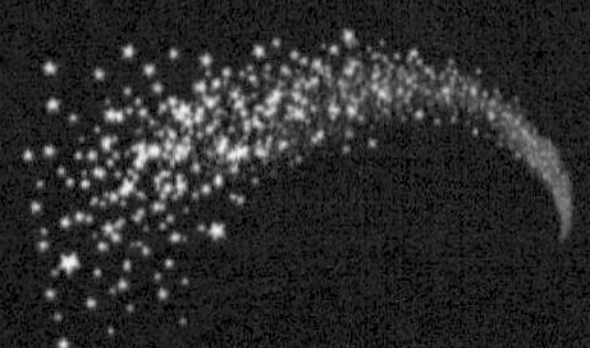

EIRA

Cadeyrn slept the whole night and napped on and off all day as the caravan traveled out of Eral Forest. When it seemed as though he was in a deep sleep, Eira lay next to Cadeyrn and covered them both with one of the blankets, then allowed herself close her eyes, letting the songs of the troupe and a sweet yet smoky smell from Zeno's pipe lull her to sleep.

His breathing was labored, and when she pulled herself closer to keep up pretenses of being a newly married couple, she noticed his skin was scorching, but he still shivered. He murmured at her touch and leaned his head against her. He came along on this quest with the intention of taking care of her, but it turned out to be the opposite.

If he didn't heal…

Not an option. Cadeyrn was going to see this through, and he was going to be by her side when they arrived in the mountains.

Eira woke when the cart jerked to a stop, while Cadeyrn only stirred and then fell back asleep. The sun was setting, and the troupe of bards worked to build their camp for the night.

They were well out of Eral Forest now and in a field with only a few scattered trees. In the distance, the Paravian Mountains loomed. Now she could see the tree line at the base, and the sunset dazzled with vibrant purples and pinks illuminating the sky. Each time she saw a hint of sun or the colors of it setting, or if the stars were bright, she saw it as a sign of Ray and Luana looking down on her.

They were still a few days away, but at least they were a little closer. Once Cadeyrn was healed, they would be able to make up for lost time.

Cadeyrn stirred again. "Are we there yet?"

"No." She wiped his brow and pushed his hair back. "We're only stopping for the night."

"Oh, good. I'm exhausted." Cadeyrn stretched and faced her, his glassy gaze meeting hers. "You're good at this doting wife thing, you know."

She chuckled, stretching as she stood. If only they'd been pretending under better circumstances. If he only knew how close they could have become for this to have been their reality. If only…

How often she thought those words and imagined the scenario they were in now.

She looked at him, at the once strong man who now lay in bed, pale and weak, and rubbed the center of her chest to chase away the ache.

"You need to sleep some more, and I'll help the troupe get prepared. Now that I've had some rest, I can help them in exchange for their hospitality. I'll bring you something to eat."

The troupe was a cacophony of joyous sound, like what the the days of the Moon Festival in the town square would have been if things hadn't taken the turn they did. Songs and chatter and laughter mingled in the air, along with the constant smoke of Zeno's pipe. It was a comfort to see how there was still some joy to be had in such dark times.

Priestess Kier recruited Eira to assist in preparing fruit baskets from one of the carts while the bonfire was being built. They spread Eira's red cloak over their laps like a blanket and sat on a log to cut apples and clean off pumpkin seeds to roast. It didn't take long until fire illuminated the camp and a rabbit was being cooked over the flames.

Kier was good company and chatted about life in a caravan and how she taught painting and sculpting to people in the villages they visited. It was good to have another woman to talk with, and Eira let herself get lost in the story of her fake marriage to Cadeyrn, finding the fib easy to play into. At first, the Fae priestess seemed tough like the stone she carved images out of. But she was much more like the soft and bright paints splattered across her tunic and pants. Eira imagined she and Rose would make a vivacious pair. She hoped they could be introduced someday.

As the evening journeyed into night, Eira's stomach became happier than it had been in days. With Cadeyrn unable to hunt, their meals were meager at best. The roasted pumpkin seeds left a subtle sweet taste in her mouth, and she made sure to leave some for Cadeyrn...if he could stay awake long enough to eat them.

The flames' reflections danced across everyone's faces, mimicking the stories and songs the bards shared. Most of them were ones Eira knew, and she sang along. For a moment, she let herself forget about her worries and enjoy the evening. Music and stories always helped to sooth her. Perhaps in another life she could have been a follower of Efare.

It was such a different life they led than Eira's. Even when she traveled from town to town the way they did, evenings were much quieter, and she had an elaborate tent to sleep in on the rare nights they were unable to find quarters.

They were so jovial and relaxed. Even when they'd spend the entire day singing and dancing for the people they met, they didn't tire of it and wanted to continue deep into the night.

Eira may have traveled around the kingdoms and interacted with the citizens, but she'd never been a part of them like this before. They didn't put on a show for her, or try to bend her ear about policies, or ask for favors—other than her paying her part in sharing stories.

The young acolyte danced around the fire. The ribbons in her hands made streams of color float through the air and illuminated the night in radiant hues. There was no sign of fear or worry in the girl, similar to how Eira and Rose would have been at her age. All she wanted to do was enjoy the night and honor Efare.

Eira forced a thin smile, jealous of the simplicity of her life.

She glanced back at the cart where Cadeyrn slept, and something in her chest ached. Their child would have been a few years younger than this girl, but it wasn't difficult to imagine what it may have looked like. How perhaps it would have danced around the fire.

Eira shook her head. It'd been ages since she'd given more than a passing thought about the child she lost. Cadeyrn would have been a good father, and she could picture him playing with their child and teaching them how to use a sword.

She rubbed her temples. There were too many things she shouldn't be thinking about. This wasn't the time or place.

"Now it is your turn, Lennox." Priestess Kier passed Eira a wooden tankard, which she was grateful to take.

Any reprieve from all that weighed on her was welcome.

Eira took a sip, and her eyes fluttered closed when spiced cider hit her tongue. She couldn't remember the last time she'd indulged in the heavenly drink. And right now she didn't mind the alcohol that spiked it, even if it burned her throat, as long as it helped ease her nerves.

She took a big gulp, but coughed and handed it back to the priestess. It was much stronger than what they served at home.

Priestess Kier laughed. "You get used to it. But you should take smaller sips. Now you promised a story. Or perhaps a song?"

Everything turned silent—even the fire—as the troupe looked at her, ready for a tale, and Eira rubbed her hands on her trousers. She'd seen new acolytes and members of troupes have to give a performance or deliver a piece of art to become a member or fulfill their vows. She'd been invited to several such ceremonies, and while this was much less official or grand, the intent was similar. They were testing her to see if she was worthy of their trust and assistance. It was exciting to have to prove herself without the context of her station.

She'd been thinking about what she would share with them. While she was a fine singer, it wasn't her strongest quality. Most of the dances she knew, she needed a partner, and Cadeyrn was indisposed. Even if she wasn't abysmal with a paint brush, she didn't have supplies to paint something. It would have to be a story.

All day she'd rehearsed in her mind the tale of the man at the crossroads, and hoped it would be satisfactory. If it was as uncommon as she thought, it would be one they hadn't heard before, which would make her stand out from others who'd tried to join them in the past. Not only could she impress them to have protection and passage to a village, but also spark discussion on the story and gain some insight.

As long as she performed well.

Eira stood the way she'd seen the other members of the troupe do when they had something to share. Maybe it had been the spiked cider flowing through her which gave her confidence, but she didn't care.

She gazed into the dancing firelight and made her voice low to reflect the mysteriousness of the story she'd seen enacted in those dark waters.

"Once, there was a man walking through the wilderness…"

In the flames formed the silhouette of a man walking down a path, which urged Eira to make the story come to life.

"Along the road, the traveler grew thirsty, and soon came across a woman." She lowered her voice even more. "A sorceress."

Eira didn't know if the woman had been a sorceress, but Amelia was one, and that was good enough for her to include this piece of intrigue in the narration.

Sure enough, a sorceress appeared in the flames. Out of the corner of her eye, the young acolyte leaned forward and rested her arms on her tucked in knees.

"She offered him something to drink, and he accepted, not caring who or where the liquid came from, as long as it quenched his throat, which had become as dry as bones lying in a desert."

As she told the tale, the images in the flames acted it out. It was the quietest the camp had been since Eira had joined them, with only her voice to reach the troupe's ears. She let it slow, then quicken with urgency when the man fell into his enchanted sleep, then lightened her tone and slowed her pace as the deities granted him their gifts. When she spoke of Luana, she let a river of stardust fall onto the heads of those around the campfire, and they smiled in delight. Yet they never made a sound to interrupt her. The longer she spoke, the more confident she grew and no longer needed to fix her focus on the flames, but instead on the faces of those surrounding her. The fire danced in the reflections of their fixated eyes as they listened.

"The traveler raised the chalice to his lips and gulped the concoction down his throat, the smooth liquid coating it like sweet honey."

Eira tilted her head back and pantomimed in unison with the images in the flames as though she were drinking the potion herself.

"When he opened his eyes, he found he was no longer frozen in place, and took a step forward."

She lowered her hands and set her head upright once again. It was an abrupt ending, but she hadn't been told which path the man had chosen. While there were some elements of the story she'd embellished, it felt wrong to do so with the ending.

The applause that erupted was enough to tell her she'd made the correct choice. With a flourish, she grasped her tunic like a gown and gave a deep curtsey.

Zeno leaned back in his seat and stroked his beard as he smoked from his pipe. Large circles floated into the air and changed into musical instruments.

He stared at her, his head tilted. "Where did you hear that story, young woman?"

Eira fumbled around, rubbing the edge of her green tunic. She might have said too much. If any of them knew the story and looked too closely at her face and recognized her…they could start putting pieces together.

She sat back on the log and wished Kier would pass the tankard of cider again.

"I only heard it recently. Something in passing. I've always considered myself well-versed in the stories, but had never heard of it. Is it significant?"

The acolyte looked toward Zeno. "It's not one I've ever heard."

Outlines of musical notes sketched along the side of her face, framing it. They were only drawings enchanted to not wash off, and not full tattoos, as she was still in training.

"Do you know it?" she said.

Zeno puffed his pipe, and the smoke circles took the form of mountains. For a brief moment, Eira swore she saw wings flying over the top.

"Not many these days know this tale. The story you told speaks of an evil poison. One which is no longer taught, and it betrays the ways of Stula. Whoever told it to you must have been an old Stulan servant."

"I suppose they were old."

Eira wished she hadn't finished her plate so quickly so she'd have something to look at or fill her mouth with. Instead, she merely stared and fumbled for words.

They were discussing the tale, though, which was what she wanted.

"But they didn't tell what items the deities gave the man," she said. "My husband and I have talked about it in great detail, and we're baffled."

Zeno rested his elbows on his knees and leaned forward.

"Why do you want to know?"

Priestess Kier took another swig from her tankard and offered it to Eira once again.

"Stop grilling the poor thing. It's not as though *she's* poisoned someone."

Eira accepted the drink and took a large gulp. She was going to need more to get through this conversation.

"The gift from Gallis is obvious." The priestess took the tankard back, and with a stick, drew an image of a chalice in the dirt. "It's her chalice. It has been lost for centuries, though. Humans took advantage of its power and betrayed the way of the world. Life and death are natural, and to prevent it from happening is against the ways of the deities. So Gallis gave the cup to Luana, who hid it away for her."

Eira listened with wide eyes as though all of this was new information. Let them continue thinking she was the naive and innocent young bride.

Priestess Kier drew the moon and stars. "Supposedly, the other ingredients are more symbolic. But with the proper magic, they could be physical items. Luana's gift, for example, I would imagine is light in the darkness. Which could be nearly anything. The flame of a candle, starlight or stardust, a ray of light from the moon. You understand?"

"Ah, yes. That makes sense."

Eira had gathered as much on her own, and with her magic it would be easy enough.

When the priestess drew flames next to the moon and stars, Eira tapped her chin.

"Perhaps Ray's ingredient was walking through the flames," she said. "Something about enduring hardship?"

Priestess Kier pointed the stick at her. "Exactly." Then she turned to the young acolyte. "What would you suggest for such an item?"

A common practice among the bards was to help train their acolytes. They couldn't merely know the stories, but had to learn how to interpret and translate them. Bring the tales to life.

The acolyte was sitting on the ground near the fire, and pulled her knees to her chest.

"I'd seek out a phoenix and retrieve their ashes, or a feather. They burn at the end of their lives and bring new life out of the ashes."

Zeno puffed his pipe again, and the smoke circles turned into a cawing bird that flew toward the acolyte and vanished as it hit her face. Her and Zeno's boisterous laughter rose into the night.

"A phoenix would have been my choice, too," he said.

They spoke of Kutlaous next, who appeared to give beauty in pain. Eira suggested a possible ingredient—a rose like the ones growing outside the castle. The flowers were beautiful, but the thorns were painful.

The final ingredient was the water from Stula. Dark and beautiful and dangerous water. Once again, Eira sat wide-eyed and smiling as though she'd never heard of such a pond.

When they were finished, Eira took a cup of broth and some pumpkin seeds to the cart, and climbed inside, where Cadeyrn was still lying on the straw. His eyes were open, though, even if they had an odd haze about them.

"I missed you," he said.

Eira put the cup on the cart next him and pressed her hand to his forehead again. Still as hot as before.

"The fever is truly getting to you."

Cadeyrn's head rocked back and forth. "You were gone for so long."

Eira put a hand behind his back to help guide him into a sitting position.

"It wasn't long. And you need to eat something."

Cadeyrn obliged and sat as best as he could. Eira brought the cup to his mouth, and he tried to drink. It was a slow process, but at least he was getting something in his stomach and wasn't only napping.

"I found out more about what we need to find for the cure." Eira told him all about the conversation around the campfire.

But halfway through, Cadeyrn lowered the broth and lay back against the straw, his eyes fluttering closed. Eira helped him change his position so he wouldn't become sore from lying on his back for too long. Something attendants had once told her during her own travels.

She sat next to him until he was asleep. Most likely she'd have to repeat what she'd learned once he was better.

Her own eyelids grew heavy, and her limbs ached. Their journey had taken more out of her than she'd anticipated. She could use the extra rest, even it was on a bed of straw in a hard-floored cart.

She gathered blankets and pillows and piled them around her and Cadeyrn to make it more comfortable, and propped his leg on one of them. She curled next to him and faced him. The nights were getting chillier, and now she was grateful for his warmth.

Almost.

Cadeyrn being healthy and strong was far more preferable.

"You take such good care of me, Eira."

His words slurred so much she had to ask him to repeat what he said.

He grimaced and scrunched his face in frustration. "You're there… all the time…and we never talk…"

Eira scooted closer to him and ran a hand over his arm. "We always talk. You're my friend."

Cadeyrn groaned and twisted where he lay. "We never talk about…*that.* You were so beautiful and perfect. But you never talked about it after. You acted like it never happened, but it did. It happened, and I had to pretend… I'm tired of pretending, Eira."

Each muscle in Eira tensed, and her eyes widened. She pulled back her hand. He couldn't be talking about their intimate encounters. And never once had he acted as though he wanted to.

Eira swallowed hard. "Cade…"

"I'm tired, Eira." His voice cracked as though he were about to cry. "I'm so tired…"

A second later his eyes closed, and he fell asleep. Eira blinked back tears and rolled onto her back.

The fever. That's all it was. The pain was going to his head.

But her heart thrummed fast, and her mind raced. Lying next to Cadeyrn only made it worse. So she left the cart and wandered away from the caravan. The moment she was far from prying eyes, she formed a dagger of ice out of her hand and threw it. It soared, hit a tree trunk and shattered into thousands of pieces in a satisfying crash. She did it again. And again. And again. Until the space became an icy garden of shards lying about like flowers.

Someone cleared their throat, and Eira spun around. Zeno leaned against a tree and smoked his pipe. Smoke clouds, like a glittering crown, rose into the air, and its sweet scent soothed her spirit.

"How is your *husband*, Princess Eira?"

Eira lowered her hands, and the ice melted into the grass. She should deny it. Pretend she was someone else. But there was a certainty in his voice which told her that if she continued in her charade, he still wouldn't believe her.

"How did you know?"

"Other than your grand icy temper tantrum?"

Eira groaned, and the glow of her tattoo faded. "Yes, other than that."

"Your *husband* spoke your name in his sleep. Many times. Your real name. You're also a terrible liar, and you never look at any of us in the eye when you lie. Who is he? I'm assuming his name isn't Darius."

"Prince Cadeyrn of Oxare. My betrothed's brother."

"Ah, yes. He's also outlawed. I should have recognized him from the posters, but he's not as recognizable in these parts as you are." Zeno puffed his pipe, it's smoke turning into a bear and roaming around their heads before fading.

Curious how he seemed to know so much about them. He knew what the risks were when he offered them assistance.

Or he could want to betray them.

Eira stepped around the ice as she melted the remainder of it, aiming herself away from him but not letting her gaze stray from his.

"You knew who I was, but you still kept me here? It could put you and your whole troupe in danger."

Zeno removed the pipe and pointed it at her, with his other hand in his pocket.

"The story you told tonight. It's the poison the king is under, isn't it? You're searching for the cure, aren't you?"

She wiped away the rest of the ice with a swoop of her hand but didn't say anything.

He paced around her in a circle, still puffing his pipe, the smoke swirling around Eira's head. This time it was a dragon, but she could smell a hint of ice coming from the smoke. They sized one another up to get a sense if one could trust the other. She kept her shoulders straight and strong like the ice she conjured.

Zeno paused and chuckled. "You aren't telling me because you know I'm right, but you don't want to trust me. You have one powerful enemy, Your Highness, but you have more allies than you know. You may travel with us, and we'll take you where you need to go. We'll get the prince healed. If you need to stay with us longer, along the way you'll keep the pretense of your marriage and tell stories with our troupe."

For the first time in days, a flutter of hope stirred in her chest.

"You'd help us? Even though we're outlawed?"

"As long as you find a way to get rid of the queen, I'll take you wherever you want."

Chapter Fifteen

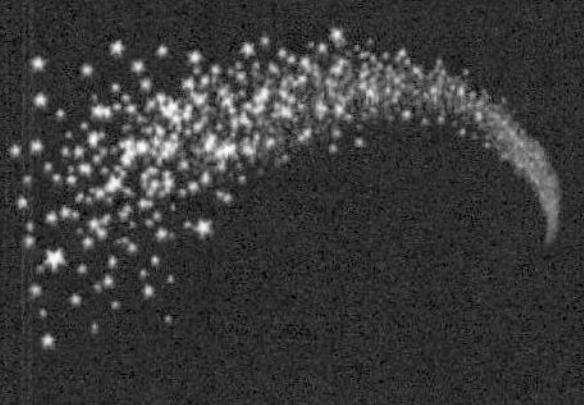

EIRA

They arrived at the next village the next afternoon, and Eira paced in front of the cart where Cadeyrn was taking another nap as she waited for Priestess Kier and her acolyte to bring an attendant out to examine him.

Eira had been here before. It wasn't a wealthy place, and she'd always visited with her family before the winter months to be sure they had adequate supplies to survive the cold. They had always been welcomed there. But now she was waiting outside because if she entered it was a danger not only to herself and Cadeyrn, but also to the people. All the more reason to be *rid of the queen*, as Zeno had stated the night before.

Priestess Kier and the acolyte returned with an attendant in blue robes, who followed with a large satchel looped over his shoulder. The flutter of hope in Eira's chest returned, and she went to meet them, but Zeno blocked her path.

"You should stay back."

"But I know how it happened and the details of the injury."

Eira tried to step around him, but he only blocked her path again.

"And I'm sure the attendant will recognize you, and we don't know what would happen when they do."

Her heart sank. He was right. So Eira did as she was told and went away from the caravan to hide in a tree nearby. She cloaked herself in the shadows of the golden leaves and sat on a low branch. It was too far away to see or hear anything, but at least the cart was still in her line of vision.

The minutes dragged on while she waited, and with each one the flutter of hope in her chest turned into a churn of worry. She rubbed her wrist as though her betrothal band was still there, and recited old prayers and stories to distract herself.

It was of no use. The only thing on her mind was the well-being of Cadeyrn.

When she saw Zeno approach the tree, Eira jumped to meet him, fallen leaves crunching beneath her feet.

"Can they heal him? Is he going to be all right?"

Zeno raised his hand to calm her. "He can help Cadeyrn but needs to bring him into the village to the Restoration House. They need more power and more supplies."

A few of the bards were already preparing to transfer the prince. Eira nodded and moved to head toward the caravan.

"So we'll go into town," she said. "Whatever needs to be done."

Zeno caught her wrist before she could get far.

"Eira, you can't go with them. It's too dangerous. We're already risking enough having him go inside the village."

Eira clenched her fists and pulled away from the dwarf in a huff. As if she wasn't aware of the danger. She knew Zeno meant well and wanted to help, but she was going.

"I will not sit out here and wait around for answers."

Cadeyrn wouldn't let her go alone if he was in her place. He promised to be whatever she needed, and now she needed to make the same promise. So she raised the red cloak over her head and blended her face into its shadows. Keeping a safe distance away, Eira followed the group carrying Cadeyrn into the village, through a back pathway to avoid people noticing. Yet she remained close enough to manipulate the shadows of those helping to mask his face when the cart was inspected by the guards who stood near each entrance. She tilted the hood to cover her face more, and kept a slow pace. They hardly paid her any mind, but she shivered at the sight. She'd never seen the village guarded so heavily before.

On the star lanterns, posters with images of Eira and Cadeyrn's faces were plastered on them. They were wanted by the queen for high treason. Those who turned them in would be heavily rewarded, and anyone who sheltered them would be killed.

Eira took a step back and gulped after reading it.

Killed.

In a stone building ahead, with a blue sign, Cadeyrn was carried in on a long mat, and Eira followed. When all was clear, she crept inside after them. Even there, she didn't dare to lower her hood or remove the shadows from her face.

She walked through the shadows of the Restoration House, and a cry echoed through the halls. Her heart dropped at the sound. In spite of it, she moved faster and searched for the room where Cadeyrn was being cared for. Attendants in blue robes stepped aside in smooth strides, and the white stone walls were a blur as Eira rushed past them. It may have been dangerous for all who were there, but if she were in his position, she'd want someone she knew at her side.

She recognized Cadeyrn's voice as she passed a room towards the end of the hall. He told them what happened to his leg. The stone wall was cool as she leaned against it and listened in on the conversation.

"It's good you arrived when you did," and attendant said, "or else we may not have been able to save the leg. Or maybe anything else. We'll need to do more rounds of treatments. Are you ready?"

"Do what you need to." Cadeyrn's voice was hoarse, but steady, before another cry ripped out of his throat.

Eira closed her eyes and sank to the ground. She should have made him seek help sooner. Or maybe she could have fended off the attacker better. But they were here now. As awful as it was. She sat there and listened for as long as she could focus, sending prayers to Gallis for him to heal.

"Your Highness?"

Eira lifted her head. The hall was darker now, and there weren't as many attendants wandering about. It must have been hours later, but the cries had stopped, and the attendant who'd come out to the caravan stood before her. Now that she was close to him, she could see he had soft brown eyes, and tattoos of herbs wound around his tan neck and disappeared beneath his blue robes.

She'd fallen asleep. She was also terrible at hiding her identity.

"How did you know?"

With an outstretched hand, he helped Eira to her feet and bowed.

"Your shadows have vanished, Your Highness."

Eira raised her hood again. They all must know she was there.

"I should go."

The attendant didn't move to block her path the way Zeno had earlier, but his gentle voice was enough to give her pause.

"You don't want to see the prince? He's doing well, now that he's resting."

There it was, the flutter of hope.

She clasped her hands near her mouth. "His leg is—"

"It's healing, and the infection has been washed away, yes. You did a wonderful job controlling it as long as you did."

Eira choked back tears. "I don't want to endanger you any longer, Attendant."

"My name is Hugo." Another wave of hope and peace washed over her at the touch of his hand on her shoulder. "And we are all loyal to the true crown here, Your Highness. You are welcome in these halls, no matter the risk."

Zeno had assured her she had more allies than she realized. Perhaps it was true.

Hugo opened the door to Cadeyrn's room and ushered Eira inside. It was simple and clean, but bright with blue lanterns lining the light-colored walls. Cadeyrn lay on a soft bed, his face relaxed for the first time in days, and the color had returned to his cheeks. The tension building in Eira's shoulders released.

"I'll let you have a moment. If you are in need of anything, please call." Hugo bowed deeply and closed the door behind him, dark blue robes fluttering in his wake.

Eira sank into a chair next to the bed and grasped his hand as though it was the only thing to convince her all this was real. She had been sitting next to sick beds far too often these days, and it needed to stop.

Tears prickled at her eyes and she wiped them away.

"So dramatic. But I suppose I would be upset, too, if someone as handsome as I am had almost died." Cadeyrn's eyes were open, and the smile she was so familiar with was back.

He squeezed her hand.

Eira wiped her tears again and chuckled. "You almost lost your leg, not almost died. I'm not the one being dramatic."

He sighed and pushed upright so he was sitting. "You're always dramatic. Rose had a cold once, and you cried for a week."

Eira scoffed. "I did not! And she didn't only have a cold. She was also vomiting. Besides, I was a child and didn't know it was a common illness that would be fine in only a few days."

"You absolutely did, and the only way you were able to get calm was when I had to take dance lessons and I made you watch as I stepped on my instructor's toes." His words were playful, but there was a deeper tone to his voice, filled with a lifetime of memories they both shared of their years growing up together.

Eira laughed at the memory. He'd always done such things when they were children. He knew exactly what would make her smile. She couldn't help but run her fingers through his and over his hand. It was as though she could memorize him through touch alone.

Cadeyrn took his hand from hers and cupped her face. "Thank you for everything, Eira."

She leaned into the touch as his fingers tangled into her hair. His skin smelled of the fresh herbs they'd used in his treatment.

"Thank you for being here with me," she said.

If it weren't for him, they may not have even made it out of the castle and to Grandmother's house.

"There's nowhere else I'd rather be," he said.

Cadeyrn remained in the Restoration House for another day to be sure the infection didn't return. As much as they needed to keep moving, it wouldn't do them any good if he was injured and sick again.

Eira spent most of her time outside the town, with the caravan, to avoid bringing any attention to herself, and helped tell stories and sing songs. But she decided to visit Cadeyrn for a least a couple hours. He'd returned to his usual spirit, and they sat side by side on his bed. He draped his arm over her shoulder, and she relaxed against his chest while he told her about when he and Alvis once brought home a baby manticore and tried to keep it a secret from their nannies. It was almost like how it had been…before.

Their laughter calmed, and Cadeyrn rested his chin on top of Eira's head. He ran his fingers across her arm, almost lulling Eira to sleep.

"What was it like during my fever? It's all a blur to me."

Eira adjusted her position so her other arm wasn't caught between them.

She shook her head and sighed. "Terrifying. You could barely even sit on your own, and your leg was turning black. I worried we wouldn't make it to an attendant in time."

Cadeyrn continued to rub her arm, but moved even slower and cleared his throat.

"Did I…did I say anything unusual? I know I spoke a little. I remember bits and pieces, but I couldn't tell when I was dreaming and when I was awake."

Eira tossed her hair behind her shoulder. Cadeyrn's breath stilled at her side.

Did he remember mentioning their affair? It was in the middle of the worst of it all, and he couldn't have known what he was saying. As tempting as it was, she couldn't hold him to anything he said during that time.

"I remember something about you saying you were the most handsome of all of the bears and should be a bear king."

Cadeyrn laughed, and it bounced off the walls, filling the whole space.

"I don't remember, but I don't doubt saying it."

She couldn't contain her sigh of relief, and relaxed against him again. At least she'd evaded the topic for the time being. She wasn't sure how long she would last, though, not speaking of it while they were traveling together. Already they were toeing a dangerous line.

She should move so they weren't holding each other like this, but she couldn't bring herself to. Maybe this was a small gift she could savor before the inevitable happened.

Cadeyrn slid his arm lower so it was around her waist, but his free hand strummed against his thigh.

"I…I remember something else. Perhaps it was a dream. It's silly."

Each strum of his fingers was like the pulse of a heartbeat.

She shouldn't. She couldn't. But…

"What's silly?"

She felt him stiffen, and he looked at the ceiling.

"I saw you often in my dreams. I remembered…that night. All of those nights."

Eira swallowed. "Oh."

Cadeyrn adjusted his position and sat forward so she couldn't rest against him anymore. His absence, even if it was only a few inches, felt like miles.

"I dream about it a lot, in all honesty."

He did? The blood drained out of Eira's face, and she was dizzy.

"Oh."

Cadeyrn looked at the blue quilt and back to her again, this time latching his gaze to her.

"I know we never talked about it, and perhaps it was the right thing." He shook his head and set his jaw. "No, it *was* the right thing. It never should have happened. But I think about it. Often. More than I should."

Eira swallowed the lump forming in her throat again. She must be dreaming.

Cadeyrn cleared his throat and pushed far enough away where their bodies weren't touching any longer. Eira's skin shivered from the cool air.

"I'm sorry," he said. "I shouldn't have said anything. You have never discussed our time together or initiated anything more, and it's clearly what you want. Please forget I mentioned it."

Eira's pounding heart threatened to break through her ribs at his words. Blinking, she searched for how to respond. Only in her dreams had she ever imaged Cadeyrn telling her this. If there ever was a time to be honest about what she wanted, this was it. What she wanted now more than anything was him. Cadeyrn was all she ever wanted. If she'd learned anything from their journey so far and seeing how close she came to losing him, it was how much she loved him. She'd never been able to let him go in the past, and she never would.

She rubbed her eyes and tried to calm herself.

"Cade—"

Screams erupted from outside. The walls shuddered, and the floor trembled, making the bed shake. Cadeyrn grabbed her shoulder, and she covered his hand with hers. The pounding against the walls was like thunder, and Eira and Cadeyrn jumped from the bed and ran in search of Hugo.

Hugo must have had the same thought, because they almost ran into him in the hall, and he thrust a sack into Cadeyrn's arms.

"You must go, now."

"What's happening?" Cadeyrn said.

"It's a raid. They came to our village once already a few days ago, but they must know you're here. There's more herbs and bandages and some food in the bag."

Eira tied her cloak around her neck, and Cadeyrn slung the sack around his shoulder. From the front of the house, there were a series of crashes and clangs and cries, which sent a shiver down Eira's spine.

Cadeyrn unsheathed his sword and grasped Eira's arm, his hand and his voice tight with urgency.

"We'll go out the back."

Hugo opened his mouth, but instead of words coming out, he gasped and groaned, and blood trickled from his lips, down his chin. He collapsed at their feet and blood seeped across the white floor, and an armored man with the Cresin crest blazoned across his chest stepped over it with sword drawn.

Eira froze as she stared at Hugo's body. Cadeyrn crossed in front of her, and she woke out of her trance and stepped aside as Cadeyrn's sword clashed with the soldier's. They fought, backing through the hall, avoiding being tangled with the other soldiers and victims. Eira tried to remain hidden, drawing the shadows around her, too stunned to do anything else as Cadeyrn blocked each blow, his tattoo shining, and with each hit his reactions grew stronger. One by one, more soldiers appeared and charged after them.

"Go! Use your ice!" Cadeyrn said over his shoulder.

Remembering what she'd been able to do in Eral with their attacker, Eira shot shards of ice toward the soldiers, avoiding bystanders and Cadeyrn as he fought their way out. The soldiers slipped and slid along the corridor, making it easier for Cadeyrn to focus on one man at a time.

Two came at him on either side. He swung his sword and hit the man on the left, who fell with a thud, and spun to slice the man on the right.

"Eira, get out of here."

"But—"

"I'll meet you out there. Go!"

A soldier hit his blade, and he blocked it while kicking away someone aiming for his newly healed leg.

She didn't want to leave him to fend for himself, but Cadeyrn was one of the best warriors of Oxare. While Eira had some skill with a sword, if she stayed, she'd only be a distraction.

With a nod and bite of her lip, she sprinted off, and in her wake shot ice from her hands to leave various spots on the ground, making the terrain more difficult to navigate. She gathered shadows around her and hid inside them, ducking and dodging soldiers along the way, with Cadeyrn's shouts echoing behind her. The soldiers she shot with ice froze mid-step.

She made it out of the village, but when she stopped at the gate, the ground trembled. A large brown bear barreled through the village, his mouth stained with blood, and his paws left red prints in their wake. He thrashed his head and knocked the soldiers pursuing him off their feet, and the satchel Hugo gave them hung around his neck. He slid to a stop in front of Eira, and dirt flew all around them.

"Get on my back."

She climbed onto him, and they bolted away from the crumbling village.

They ran as far as Cadeyrn could, until the soldiers were no longer in sight, then stopped by a small wooded area with a babbling stream, and Eira slid off. With a thud that shook the ground, Cadeyrn flopped onto his belly, enormous paws and legs splayed.

Eira lay in the grass and attempted to catch her breath. It'd been close. Too close. Now those they'd helped had been harmed.

She slammed her fists into the ground. She'd gotten too comfortable with her joy from Cadeyrn being healed and the assistance of the bards and attendants. Even if she had allies, it didn't make her enemies disappear.

She sat up and crawled over to Cadeyrn. He'd been fighting so soon after his injury, and there was blood all over his fur. He lay there panting as she took the edge of her tunic and dabbed at the blood.

"Is the blood yours?"

He shook his furry head. "No."

"Good."

Although, Eira didn't like the idea of another person's blood being all over him either, even if it was necessary for their escape.

He propped up onto his feet and padded over to the stream. He dipped his front paws in the water and let the blood wash away. Eira set the weapons she carried aside with shaky hands and followed his lead. In the satchel were some extra cloths, and she used them to help scrub away the grime on both of them.

"I'll stay like this for a while," Cadeyrn said as he shook out one paw. "I know it'll bring us more attention, but if you ride on my back, we'll get to the temple sooner."

They'd planned to travel with the troupe of bards to Paravia, which may have taken longer, but at least they would have had extra protection. Now speed was more important.

Eira dipped the cloth in the water and set to work on wiping the blood off his mouth. She paused when she took a good look at his teeth, which were as long as her hand.

"I don't bite, I promise." The familiar glint in Cadeyrn's eyes returned. "At least, not without asking first."

Eira blinked, and a burst of laughter escaped from her mouth as she swatted at him with the cloth. He chuckled, a rumbling she could feel all the way to her bones.

"How can you joke about such things right now?"

"It made you smile, didn't it?" Cadeyrn jumped into the stream.

He rolled around in the water and shook his fur, splattering Eira, who shrieked and tried to shield herself.

"Sometimes you need to laugh," he said. "Especially after a battle. It's the only way you can live with yourself surviving it."

They finished washing, and Cadeyrn carried branches and sticks over in his mouth to create a fire with. They dried off and settled in to get rest. He'd been able to save some of the supplies, but many were lost during the fight, including bed rolls.

"Come over and sleep by me," Cadeyrn said. "I've gotten used to it now."

Eira's face warmed, and she hoped it was too dark for Cadeyrn to notice. She wrapped the red cloak tighter around herself and lay on the grass next to Cadeyrn. The ground was hard, but it was more comfortable at his side. She stroked the soft fur around his ear, and he leaned into it. She kissed his cheek.

"Eira…" His voice rumbled against her neck.

At least for the moment, they were both all right. As much as she wanted to savor it and return to the conversation they'd been having before the raid, there was still another day of travel ahead. If they spoke of it, she feared they'd never get sleep. Perhaps it was for the best she hadn't been able to respond to his confession.

Eira patted his paw. "We should get some rest if we want to arrive at the temple tomorrow."

Chapter Sixteen

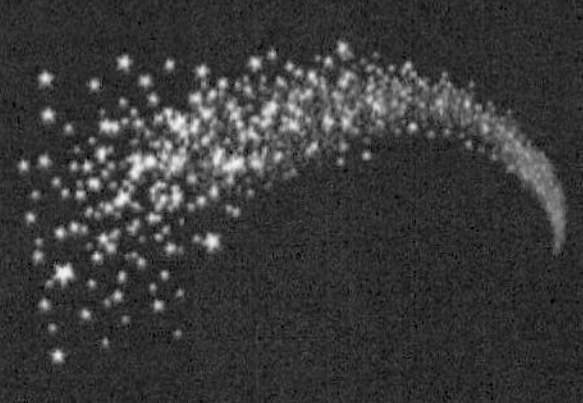

EIRA

THE MOUNTAINS LOOMED AHEAD, TALL AND MAGNIFICENT. IF ONE looked close enough, they could see the ancient glass spires of Luana's temple shining among the peaks. Centuries ago, the priestesses of Luana had it built, for they said the mountains could almost touch the night sky, and it snowed at the tops year-round. For generations, it was Luana's high temple. When the capital was relocated to Farren, a newer and larger high temple was built there. But Luana's followers still worshipped in this location, and young acolytes trained there before moving to the high temple to fulfill their vows.

They arrived late in the night, cold and exhausted. The tall blue-glass doors opened on their own as Eira and Cadeyrn entered the foyer. She slid off his back, onto the crystal floor.

The temple at Farren Castle was stunning, but the ice and darkness in Eira's veins swirled when they sensed the ancient magic which lay within these crystal, glass, and ice walls. The ceiling shimmered with starlight, and bands of galaxies glowed overhead.

Cadeyrn hid in a dark corner and shifted back into human form before dressing. While he did, a priestess in a silver robe greeted them and bowed. The silver crescent moon amulet on her brow sparkled in the starlight.

"Welcome, Your Highness."

Eira's hands shot to her face, and she covered her cheeks. She must have forgotten to shadow her appearance. While the incidents they'd had with those hunting her were awful, it was a miracle there hadn't been more.

"Do not fear, Princess. Your disguise is clever, but like calls to like. We sensed your presence hours ago, and it didn't take long for us to put the pieces together. Your secrets are safe with us." The priestess lowered her hood to reveal a smiling and familiar face.

Priestess Cynth's mother, who had always welcomed Eira with open arms each time she'd come to visit.

"Priestess Corvina." Eira hugged the woman, grateful to be with someone she knew and trusted. "I wasn't sure if you would be able to give us shelter. But I'd hoped."

Cadeyrn emerged from the corner, fully dressed, and bowed to the priestess.

"We thank you for your help."

Corvina bowed back and beckoned them to go with her further into the temple.

"Come. It's time for our midnight meal, and we would love to have you join us. Unless you would prefer to retire to your chambers."

"Food sounds wonderful," Eira said. "Thank you."

While the food they'd scavenged and were given at the Restoration House was satisfactory, her stomach still turned with emptiness, and she was sure Cadeyrn was feeling the same way.

They followed Priestess Corvina though the temple and marveled at the glass mosaics covering the walls, depicting Luana in her finest moments—painting the night sky, guiding lost ones as they tried to find their way home. Meeting Ray. There was even an image of the moon shining over a crossroads, like in the story Stula's priest showed her.

The aroma of meat and fresh fruit greeted them as they entered the dining hall. It was alive with chatter of the priestesses who'd gathered for the midnight meal, around small circular tables. Starlit lanterns floated over them and twinkled their greeting. It was a nightly tradition that all the Luana temples maintained, to have their main meal after midnight prayers, as the priestesses slept during the day.

Two places were set at the front table, decorated with a silver cloth and glass place settings for Eira and Cadeyrn, and Corvina sat beside them. At the front of the room stood High Priestess Atti to lead a blessing for the meal. She was a small woman and needed to stand on a stool so they all could see her. Her large, angled eyes were deep violet, and if one looked close enough, it was as though galaxies lived inside them.

Those in the hall hushed to a reverent silence as she prayed, her arms raised to the skies. When she was done, she stepped off the stool with the assistance of another priestess and sat at the last open seat at the front table.

Atti's smile was warm toward Eira and Cadeyrn. "Your Highness, it is good to have you back. It's not often we get to have royalty dine with us, particularly on visits so close together. How long has it been? A couple months?"

A priestess arrived at the table with a tray of apple cider soup with delicate cheese puffs floating on top, and placed a glass bowl in front of each person. All of the priestesses took turns preparing and serving the meals each night.

Eira breathed in the spices and let the warmth from the steam waft over her.

"Something along those lines," Eira replied.

This temple had been one of her last stops on her pilgrimage.

"And it is our honor to be seated at your table," Eira said. "Especially considering the dangerous circumstances it puts you in."

Cadeyrn swallowed a spoonful of soup. "As wonderful as your hospitality is, High Priestess, we do have business we need to attend to while here. Urgent business."

Atti raised her glass to him. "I assumed as such. We will be happy to help in any way we can, as we have swiftly come into dark times. Rumors of how towns are being raided and neglected are not hidden from our eyes. Am I safe in assuming your business here will be to help correct the wrongs being done?"

"Yes." Eira blew on her spoon to cool off the soup, and took a sip. "I have reason to believe Queen Amelia is not as dedicated to our family as she claimed."

Eira and Cadeyrn went on to share their tale, and the priestesses seated with them listened closely as they ate. When they finished, Atti leaned forward and rested her elbows on the table.

"So you've come here to find Gallis's chalice. And you are aware of the dragon who guards it?"

Cadeyrn leaned back in his seat and stretched his legs. "So the chalice and the dragon are real?"

"As real as I am." Atti outstretched her hands. "The dragon is bold and fierce. None have retrieved the chalice since it has been hidden in the mountain, though many have tried. Some are wounded and return to us after only a few hours. Most we never see again."

Cadeyrn gulped, and Eira patted his hand with false confidence.

"Well, Cadeyrn here is one of Aros's finest warriors. And in his bear form, he is even stronger. I am Luana's Chosen. Perhaps it is what it will take for us to succeed where others have not."

Corvina stirred her soup, and the spoon clank against the bowl.

"If what Cynth has told me about the princesses of Cresin is true, once you have your mind to something, there is no going back. We will assist you in any way we can."

"In the meantime," Atti said, "enjoy your night with us and get some rest."

Before long, Eira's empty stomach was full and happy with potatoes and roast as they got to know the priestesses. Even after the meal was complete, they remained in the hall. Eira and the other women made stars swirl in ribbons of darkness in a dance along with the songs a bard played. Cadeyrn became a bear once again and let the youngest acolytes take turns riding on his back, and played games. He shared a bright smile at Eira from across the room, and she couldn't help returning the gesture.

Eira finished showing some of the young girls a few tricks when Corvina came to her side, and they sat at an empty table.

"You fit in well here, even if it has only been a few hours."

"Yes, you have been more than welcoming," Eira said.

It was the most she'd felt at home in weeks—even when she'd been home in Farren Castle.

"It is good to have a few moments to relax for a bit."

"I remember Cynth once writing that it seemed as though you longed for the life of a priestess. Is this true?"

Eira considered how to answer the question, remembering how only days—or perhaps even a few weeks—ago, she was standing on her own balcony the day of the ceremony, and how envious she was of the priestesses below. How the idea of running away to the Paravian Mountains had been an appealing one. She was surprised Corvina had sensed it. Perhaps Eira wasn't as much of a closed book as she thought.

"Maybe I once did. More than anything, I envied them. I was treated as one of Luana's, and even as someone above the priestesses. Yet it seemed as though they had so much more freedom than I did."

Corvina tilted her head. "You would do well as a priestess, I'm sure. But there is more to it than you're sharing. You were placed in a unique position with limited options of which direction to take. It is one of privilege, though. You do know this, don't you?"

Eira folded her hands in her lap. This was part of why she was so conflicted.

"I am grateful for it. I do not wish to appear as though I am not."

There was a warm comfort when Corvina placed a hand on Eira's shoulder.

"Wanting your own life does not mean you are ungrateful. You can still choose how you use your position. But someday you need to be honest about what you want. Cynth wrote how, many times, she saw that your mind was elsewhere and something was troubling you, but she didn't know what. Let those who care for you in, Eira. Let them help you with these choices."

Eira blinked back a tear. "What if what I want isn't possible?"

"And why isn't it?"

The pre-dawn bells rang from a tower, not blaring but soft glistening notes floating to the temple.

"We should go to pre-dawn prayers." Eira stood and excused herself from the table.

Before going to her chambers to sleep for the day, Eira wrapped herself in a soft white robe and drifted to the baths. All the priestesses had gone to bed, so it would be quiet. The baths were in a large room on the top floor, with windows reaching from ceiling to floor, which overlooked the mountains, giving a perfect view the sky. It was so high there was no fear of anyone looking in on those enjoying the water.

She opened the doors, and when they shut again, they echoed through the room and she unwrapped her robe.

"Eira?"

She looked around, and Cadeyrn was reclining in the water against the side of the bath, legs outstretched. The bath was almost as long as the room itself. He lowered his legs and treaded water.

Eira pulled her robe to her body. "Sorry! Didn't know anyone was in here. I can come back later."

"No, no, it's fine." He swam to the edge and rested his arms on the marble tile. "I was letting my leg soak."

"How is it? Did you run it too hard today?"

"It's fine. Tired, but fine. I'll be fine."

The water gently sloshed against the sides of the large bath, and it echoed against the glass walls. Hints of Ray's sunrise peeked over the mountaintops in yellow beams.

Eira turned to leave. "I should let you finish. I can bathe this evening when I wake."

"No, don't leave. The bath is big enough for ten of us, if need be. I'll even turn around as you go in." He turned his back to her.

Eira clutched the robe closer to her body and bit her lip. It wasn't difficult to imagine what could happen if she joined him in the bath. Or what she wanted to happen.

Cadeyrn's confession at the Restoration House still rang through her mind, but he'd been with so many women. Was she simply what he couldn't have? She'd seen her ladies cry over heartbreaks such as those. When they'd been the object of a man's desire because they seemed out of reach. Then once they had gotten what they wanted, they discarded the women like an old shirt.

Cadeyrn didn't seem to behave that way. Maybe his feelings were true the way hers were. They could have another night together and never speak of it again. They could distract themselves from what they needed to do for one night. They'd come to such a wonderful place between them now, and Eira didn't want to ruin it. But maybe they owed each other this. Owed themselves.

Eira ran her fingers through her hair. Or maybe he only wanted her to join him so they could bathe and make plans for the next evening when they'd be traveling. The idea made her chest ache. He had still been recovering from his wound when they spoke at the Restoration House. There were so many different possible outcomes. She couldn't stand there wondering for forever. It was time she knew.

With a new sense of confidence, she took the robe off and placed it next to Cadeyrn's discarded clothing on the hooks on the wall. She stepped forward toward the massive pearl-white steps descending into the bath. She gasped when she looked across the room to the windows to see her reflection in the glass, and her gaze met Cadeyrn's in the window. A wave of shyness overcame her.

"Sorry. I hadn't accounted for the windows." Cadeyrn cleared his throat and busied himself with the levers on the side of the bath, allowing clouds of bubbles and oils into the water.

"It's fine."

Wasn't like he hadn't seen her naked before. Even if it was several years ago.

Eira submerged herself in the water, to her shoulders. There. That wasn't so difficult.

She took a deep breath. "We have a big day ahead of us tomorrow, don't we?"

Cadeyrn turned around and floated over to her side. "We do. High Priestess Atti gave me a map so we can find the correct mountain. From what I can tell, it won't take us long."

His arm brushed hers, and she nearly jumped out of her skin. She kicked her feet and swam to the storage on the side of the bath, where soaps were kept.

"There's also an armory on the lower floors," she said, "and we're permitted to borrow some since we had to leave some behind in the village."

Cadeyrn's gold gaze followed her movements, and he licked his lips.

"I'll be sure to take a look before we leave."

Eira flushed as she lathered the soap and scrubbed it into her hair. She almost sighed out of joy. She would never take a proper bath for granted again.

Eira dunked her head under the water and rinsed out her hair. Upon coming back to the surface, she flipped her hair back over her head and combed her fingers through it. *Glorious.*

A splash of water hit her arm. Then again. Two more times.

Cadeyrn was off to the side with his hands cupped to make a fountain of water, and aimed it toward her. She did the same, and they carried on, laughing and swimming and splashing, enjoying a calm moment where they were safe.

This time, when he splashed her, the water hit her eye. Eira returned the favor and drenched his head. Cadeyrn narrowed his eyes, a mischievous grin tugging at his lips.

"You shouldn't have done that." He swam toward her and enveloped her before dunking both of them under the water.

It happened so quickly, Eira barely had time to scream as he wrapped his arms around her, and they splashed beneath the surface. Underwater, Eira clung to him and let her legs tangle around his.

They burst back into the fresh air, panting and gasping for breath. Cadeyrn's arms remained around her waist, and she rested her hands on his shoulders. In spite of the water, Eira's skin burned as their bare chests pressed against one another, and…*oh.* He was hard against her legs. Eira couldn't help but lick her lips and pull closer to him, wanting to feel each inch.

Their gazes met, and she couldn't ignore the lust in his eyes. At least a part of her had been right. He did want her. For tonight, maybe longer. She didn't care either way.

"Cade…"

He blinked, breaking their stare, and released his grip on her waist. The places where his body had touched her turned cold in his absence.

"I'm sorry, Eira. I'm being too presumptuous. We never finished our conversation, and you didn't say anything…I assumed…I'm sorry…"

Damn Grandmother for being right. But damn being careful. All her life she was careful.

Before he could get too far away, and before she lost her nerve, Eira grabbed his arm and pulled herself to him. She held his face in her hands and kissed him.

Eira thought she'd made a mistake, because Cadeyrn did nothing. But after a moment, he wrapped his arms around her again and kissed her back.

It was real. All of it. And everything about him said he wanted her, from the way his soft lips sucked her own, to the gentle pressure of his fingers on the small of her back, to the press of his erection against her legs. The kiss was nothing like she remembered it being.

It was better.

They broke away only enough to breathe, and her nose bumped his.

"I didn't expect that," Cadeyrn breathed.

"I didn't plan it."

She'd planned the opposite. To never touch or kiss him again, if she could help it.

Apparently, she couldn't.

He ran his fingers through her soaked hair. "So does this mean you think about it as well?"

"I think of it all too often. Whenever I see you."

"You never said anything."

"Neither did you."

Cadeyrn threw his head back and groaned. "Eira, you are the heir. Betrothed to my brother. I couldn't say anything, even though I wanted to every moment of every single day. But it was always your choice. When you never said anything, I stepped away, although I wanted to be with you. Only you."

Eira almost laughed. They'd been such fools all this time.

She looped her arms around his neck as he squeezed closer to him. She tilted her head to meet his lips again, but paused. There was more to the story.

She sighed and rested her forehead against his, her eyes closed. Everything was perfect in that moment, and now she had to ruin it.

He tensed underneath her hands, but neither of them let go of the other. She hoped he never let go, even after what she had to say.

He said, "You don't want…"

She lifted her head and ran her fingers across his chest.

"I do. But you need to know, when we were together…something happened."

Cadeyrn's eyebrows pinched in concern, and he tucked a strand of hair behind Eira's ear.

"What do you mean, something happened? What's wrong? Did I hurt you?"

Eira leaned into Cadeyrn's touch as he stroked her hair. They weren't ever supposed to be in this position again. Now that they were, she couldn't keep it a secret any longer. It wouldn't be fair, and he needed to go in with all of the facts.

"Cadeyrn, I got pregnant."

His hand stopped, and she felt each muscle in him freeze. But he didn't pull away.

"You…what?"

"I didn't find out until after you left. It had been weeks. I couldn't decide if I should tell you or not, and then…" she tried to stop herself from shaking, "…it was gone. I don't know what happened. Maybe I was never pregnant at all and my cycle came late. I'm not sure."

"And you went through it on your own?" He grasped her shoulders and pulled them over to the steps that led into the bath, and they sat.

"I'm fine. It was so long ago now."

In those moments, she hadn't been all right, by any means. Now, while it was still painful, she'd come to peace with it.

They curled together, and Eira swung her legs over his lap.

"And I wasn't alone. Rose was there."

Cadeyrn held her hands and froze again. "Rose knows?"

"Yes…well, no. She didn't when we were together. She assumed the baby belonged to Alvis, and I didn't correct her. I only told her the truth after the festival. She knew I was hesitant about the wedding."

Cadeyrn's shoulders relaxed, and he rested his arms over her thighs. With his rough hand, he rubbed and squeezed her flesh in comforting movements.

"Eira, I'm so sorry. If I'd known, I'd have been there in an instant."

"I'm fine. At least, now I am. It was for the best. But before anything happened with us tonight, you needed to know."

He kissed her temple, and she rested her head on his shoulder, finally able to find solace in him, the person she wished to have shared this burden with years ago.

"Thank you for telling me. I'm sorry. Gods! My love, I'm so sorry."

They sat there for several long minutes, silently comforting one another and listening to the sloshing of the bath water.

Finally, after so much time, she didn't have something to hide from him anymore. She pulled herself closer to him and reveled in his strong arms around her, her head buried in his neck, and inhaled the scent of the fresh soap. He held her chin and kissed her softly. He took all of this so well, and it made her heart burst even more than it already had been. Yet there was still so much more. They couldn't ignore everything else outside of this wonderful moment.

Alvis. Their families. The alliance. Finding the chalice. Facing a dragon. Having an affair with her betrothed's brother should not be high on the priority list.

Except…

"What do we do now?" Cadeyrn said.

He must have been thinking the same thing she was.

"It's all complicated," she replied. "Although, maybe it isn't."

"What do you mean?"

He gazed at her with a look that was so familiar, but altogether new. As though before he'd only let her see parts of him, but now everything was out in the open and there was nothing to hide.

"I love you, Eira. I always have. I know so much is happening, but that fact has always been simple to me."

Tears could have rushed out from her. She'd never allowed herself to even consider him saying those words. But now they surrounded and filled her.

"I love you, too."

They poured all the love they had into another kiss. And it was as simple as that. He ignited something in her she never thought was possible—freedom.

Even in the confines of her name and title, this was what Cadeyrn always was. She was free to be who she wanted. The person she only dreamed she could be.

She couldn't give him up.

THE HALLS WERE EMPTY AS EIRA AND CADEYRN FOUND THEIR WAY TO her chambers. They'd been holding back from one another for so long, and now the gate was open and a tidal wave poured through. No telling what they would encounter in the coming days, and this could be their last chance to be together in some time. Eira intended to take advantage of each moment.

When they approached her room, Cadeyrn hoisted her into his arms and she locked her legs around his waist. He pushed the door open and kicked it closed once inside, while his tongue explored her mouth, and he clutched her rear so she was fully pressed against him.

He stumbled to the bed, and Eira fell onto her back on the mattress, her robe flying out of place. But any of the shyness she'd had in the bath was gone, and she didn't care what parts of her were being revealed to Cadeyrn.

Eira sank into the soft mattress. The deep blue comforter was so plush it could have enveloped her. She moaned.

Cadeyrn raised his brows. "I knew I was good, but I haven't done anything to you yet."

Eira ran her hands across the bedspread and rubbed her cheek against it.

"Been so long since I've been in a real bed."

Cadeyrn chuckled. "Should I leave you two alone?"

Eira propped herself on her elbows and curled her lip.

"Don't you dare."

With a swift tug, she grabbed his robe and pulled him on top of her, their arms wrapping around one another as though he was to be her blanket. A wave of peace swept over her as they breathed each other in, and she tugged him tighter against her body, her fingers tangling in his tousled hair. She kissed his temple with a contented sigh. They lay together, soaking one another in as if to memorize the moment and keep it forever.

She'd thought she remembered all the details of Cadeyrn's body, the way if felt pressed against hers, and the flutter of his soft lips pressed against her neck. She'd looked at him as much as she could in the bath, but she was getting to know him all over again.

A fire ignited in her as Cadeyrn's kisses trailed from her mouth to her neck, and he pulled her robe aside, letting it fall to the floor.

"You're so perfect." He kissed her, moving his fingers to cup her breast and rolled his thumb over her nipple. "I've had dreams about your perfect breasts. The way they fit in my palm. How soft your skin is." He traced his tongue over her tattoo. "I love you so much, Eira."

She'd dreamed about it, too. For too many lonely nights, she'd imagined him doing just this. Eira never felt more beautiful than she did in that moment.

"I love you, too."

He teased her nipple, rubbing his lips against that soft skin, then sucking, taking her so quickly she gasped at the sensation. Diar bless it. This man was going to make her orgasm before even getting to the place she wanted him.

"Do you know when I first knew?" Eira said when she eventually found her breath and they rolled onto their sides.

Cadeyrn only grunted in response, his mouth still busy with her breast.

"It was the day you talked about at the Restoration House. When you took me to your dance lesson and stepped on your instructor's toes."

Cadeyrn placed a soft kiss on her tender tip. "You were only ten."

Eira stroked his hair. "It didn't matter. I'd loved you before then, but it was the day I realized it."

Cadeyrn smiled and moved to her other breast. "Do you know when I knew?"

Eira shook her head and whimpered when he licked a circle around her nipple.

"When I was a young boy and we would come to visit. You were the one I was most happy to see, and I didn't care about anyone else." He trailed a hand between her legs, rubbing her. "Gods, you feel so good."

Eira couldn't even respond to his confession, except for a soft moan. He had no idea. Or maybe he did, as he must have remembered what she enjoyed.

Already she was wet for him and spread her legs further apart as he slid a finger inside her. Their mouths collided in a hungry kiss as she ground against his fingers, desperate to feel more.

Cadeyrn's lips caressed her bosom one last time, and he continued his journey downward.

"When I was a little older, I knew because I would do anything to be sure you never cried again." He trailed his tongue to her torso, licking her navel, and continued on, but stopped before her reaching where she most desired him.

She could have cursed him for stopping there.

Cadeyrn slid off the bed and onto his knees. "When I was a young man, I knew when I realized the women I sought out reminded me of you. But I was never satisfied because there is no one like you."

He grasped her behind the knees and pulled her toward the edge of the bed so her legs hung over. As he ran his hands up her legs and to her thighs, he slowly spread them apart, and Eira knew he could see how wet and trembling she was for him. He kissed the inside of her thigh, taking his time, and Eira's body went tense, then limp.

"There's no one like you." He looked at Eira with a raised brow. "Should we find out if I remember how to please you, my princess?"

Eira tensed and threw her head back. He'd always been such a tease.

"If you don't, I'm going to scream."

Cadeyrn chuckled. "Don't worry. I have every intention of making you scream."

Eira's toes curled at the words, and when his lips touched her core, she gasped.

He kissed her there, humming against her soft skin. "Gods, you taste even better than I remember."

Eira's hips buckled as he kissed and navigated her folds. Pleasing her. Worshiping her. He certainly did remember.

She dug her fingers into his hair and pressed him closer as she writhed and trembled. It only made him grip her thighs harder and kiss her stronger. She was going to have bruises from his hands the next day, but she didn't care. He didn't treat her like some delicate flower. Loving, yes, but not gentle. She was exhausted of people handling her delicately. Eira was strong and powerful.

He found her clit with his mouth and circled around it until Eira thought she would cry from the sensation.

"Oh, Gods, I've needed you," she said.

Cadeyrn raised himself onto his feet and ran a hand through his hair before removing his robe and letting it join Eira's on the floor.

"I've needed you, too."

It was her turn to take in his naked body and the way his cock was stiff and ready for her. She laced her arms around his neck and kissed him.

"Have me."

"Eira, especially after what you told me in the bath, I don't want you to be put in such a situation again." His voice was hoarse and tight, trying to control himself. "I don't have the—"

"Check the bedside table."

Cadeyrn furrowed his brows, but obeyed. Sure enough, in the drawer was a few bottles of the tonic to prevent pregnancy.

He picked one up and shook it. "The priestesses expected this. Or did you have a secret plan to seduce me all along?"

"Sex is an activity of the night, and Luana's priestesses and followers are encouraged to indulge as they please. Each bed chamber is replenished with tonics each day. I assure you, most of them likely already had a good rut even before we arrived."

"I always knew I liked the daughters of Luana." Cadeyrn uncorked the tiny bottle and gulped it down, then crawled onto the bed with a devilish smile. "So if we run out of them tonight, we can always go back to my room for more?"

His scruff tickled against Eira's neck as he nuzzled her, and she giggled.

"Yes. But as much as I want to be awake with you and never rest, we do need some sleep today. We have a journey ahead of us."

"I should be sure this is well worth it." He held her face in his hands and kissed her as they fell onto the mattress in a tangle of arms and legs.

When Cadeyrn tried to get Eira on her back, she pushed him and pulled herself on top.

"Now it's my turn."

The way he tensed encouraged her as she trailed kisses down Cadeyrn's body the way he did for hers. Every kiss on his cheek or lick of his hard muscle was her repayment for how he made her feel. He groaned beneath her, and she smiled.

She salivated when she reached for his perfect cock and softly ran her hand to it.

Cadeyrn shuddered at her touch. "Damn."

She lowered her head to kiss him at the base and left tiny kisses all the way to the tip, where she ended with a flick of her tongue. She'd dreamed of this, too.

Cadeyrn groaned loudly this time. "You are a cruel woman."

She loved making him finish when her mouth was wrapped around his hard cock. But not now. Eira straddled his hips and leaned forward, letting her breasts dangle over him.

"I need you to come inside me."

She captured his mouth in hers, and when they broke apart, he swatted her on the rear. She straightened on top of him, and Cadeyrn's eyes glazed over in pure lust.

"You ready?" he said.

Eira put her hand over his, and together they guided him inside of her wet and ready body. He was so tight and full inside of her she couldn't help but cry out. There was a glimmer of pain, but it was the most beautiful pain she'd ever known, and it subsided as she slid up and down him.

They were back where they belonged. Together. Not out of a sense of obligation, or because there was no one else to explore their desires with. This was out of equal love and want. This was how it was supposed to be. And it was as natural as the sun, which poured through the windows and over Cadeyrn's body to illuminate his tan skin.

"Gods," Cadeyrn groaned.

His hips moved in time with hers, and she ground against him. She braced herself by placing her hands on his abdomen, and arched her back while he cupped her heavy breasts.

"You're so soft and tight. I know we need to sleep, but I might have to take you again."

"Yes," Eira gasped.

She knew it wasn't logical, but she needed him even more, especially when he sucked on her nipple again. Cadeyrn's hand wandered lower, and he slid it between their bodies and pinched her sensitive clit.

"Gods, yes. Please, don't stop."

He sat straight as he rubbed and pulled Eira flat against him with his free hand, and kissed her roughly.

"Let me get you on your back. I need to fuck you."

Gods, she wanted him to do just that.

No sooner had Eira nodded, than Cadeyrn flipped her over. They lay there for a one sweet moment, his fingers caressing her cheek. Then he placed a soft kiss on her lips. Yet they couldn't wait any longer. They'd waited long enough.

He lifted her legs around his waist and thrusted himself deeper inside. A cry erupted from Eira, and she dug her fingers into his muscled shoulder. He gave her everything he had, and Eira let herself soak in all of his passion. She wanted to give him as much, and rocked her hips against his, following his lead, and fucked him back. Their kisses and hands were greedy, taking whatever ever piece of each other they were willing to give.

She grasped his rear and cried out as she went over the edge and he spilled himself inside of her. Cadeyrn shuddered and cried out at the same time Eira did, and collapsed on top of her.

Never in her dreams did she imagine she could have such pleasure.

At least, not since the last time they were together.

Cadeyrn stroked Eira's hair and kissed her. "Sorry, I got a little enthusiastic. Was it too much?"

She shook her head. "It was perfect."

"You're perfect."

He kissed her again and rolled to the side while keeping his arms around her, and she rolled to her side and nuzzled against his chest. His heart was pounding as fast as hers.

"Let's not wait another five years this time to do this again," Cadeyrn said into the top of her head, and kissed her hair.

Eira giggled. "I fully agree."

"So when this is all over…"

Eira propped onto his chest and looked at him. "I want this. Every night. Forever. We can discuss what we'll do later, but for now you must know it's what I want."

He held her face in his hand as though she were the most precious being in the world.

"I do. And it's what I want, too. Forever."

They kissed as though it was still brand new, and Cadeyrn made sure another bottle of tonic was prepared.

Chapter Seventeen

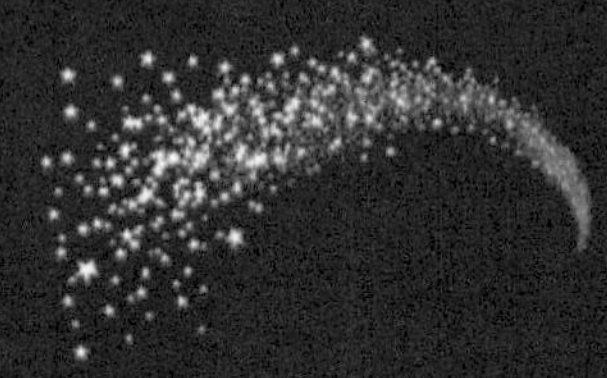

EIRA

According to Atti, the dragon kept the same hours as the priestesses, so Eira and Cadeyrn departed from the temple the next evening and planned to arrive late in the night. Thankfully, the temple provided them with winter clothes and boots, for while it was still autumn in the rest of Cresin, the higher into the mountains they went the more winter made its presence known.

The wind bit at their faces, and snow fell, making the paths slick. Eira slipped and stumbled more than she cared to, but didn't complain. If she slowed their pace, Cadeyrn didn't say a word, but only took her hand and helped guide the way.

The sky grew darker each hour as they climbed. Yet the mountains shimmered as though they were kissed by the stars. Perhaps they were, and this truly was where Luana used to dwell in the stories Eira knew so well. Luana could have placed stars on the peaks to twinkle and shine for those traveling through them.

"Eira, I think we're here."

The wind howled around the mountains, but Cadeyrn held the map the priestesses had given them, and pointed. If they'd followed it correctly, where they stood was the entrance, but the only thing there was a sliver of space between the rocks.

In her imagination, the entrance to a dragon lair would be a large skeletal mouth filled with the bones of their victims, with smoke and fire bursting through the wall and incinerating anyone in its path. Or something else as horrifying. She didn't expect a tiny crack between mountains, which appeared as though not even the smallest dwarf could slide through.

Cadeyrn drew his sword and tapped the tip of it on the crack as though it would burst open from the touch. Yet the only thing that happened was a few bits of stardust flew into the air and flurried around his head.

He looked at Eira's chest. "Perhaps it needs someone else's touch."

Eira followed his gaze to her breastbone to find that her tattoo was glowing through her fur vest and red cloak. Even though she hadn't willed her magic forward, the ice and darkness in her still stirred. The flurries of stardust beckoned to her like a siren's call.

The stone glowed white and silver, and more stardust flew when she stepped forward. She closed her eyes and focused, her hand on the mountain wall, making the stone hum at the contact. Behind her closed lids, stars floated through the darkness, and a bright light shone in the distance. The magic of the stone danced and sang with Eira's magic, but it was faded. There was something deeper in the mountain she wasn't reaching. She needed something more to make it stronger.

"I need help. Put your hand on mine."

Cadeyrn did as she asked. The mountain hummed even stronger now, as though it were feeding off of the two of them together. The stone bent at their touch, and Eira stepped forward, Cadeyrn following her lead. The stone pressed against them on all sides and molded around them, adjusting only enough with each step for them to pass through.

There was something odd about the walls on the inside of the mountain. While it was solid rock, it was also cool and soft. Eira's tattoo still glowed as bright as it had before, and she willed starlight to shine to brighten the space so they could see through the tight path. Once she did, the dark walls sparkled and shimmered.

Her hands were covered in silver dust. When she looked at the ground, the bottom of her red cloak was covered in the same dust.

"Moon rock," she said. "I didn't know it existed."

Another thing that was supposed to only be a legend. Luana used all the moon rock in the world to create a home for her and Ray to be together outside the confines of the hours of day and night. But the dream never came to fruition. No one knew why, and the story was not considered part of temple cannon because of it, similar to the tale of the crossroads for Stula's followers.

They moved for some time through the tight tunnel, not able to walk side by side, but still stayed hand in hand. The further they went, the more the air changed. It wasn't as cold as the outside, where the wind hit her face in an icy rage, and there was a gentle crispness in the atmosphere, like an autumn day with the sun shining on you. Cozy and comforting.

Ahead, a light shone, like a starlit lantern, and she and Cadeyrn stepped into a cavernous area. Eira gasped as she took in the open space before them. Stars filled their surroundings, and colorful galaxies danced on the night sky. The sun shone in the distance, creating a pink and purple hue around them, as though it was sunset. Tall towers loomed before them as a silver and gold castle in a sky paradise. It looked as though it were made of glass. A sparkling dark river wove around the towers, and silver grass and flowers grew beside it. The whole place was a beautiful combination of the sun and moon. Only when Eira looked closer did she notice the mountain walls still surrounded them.

A familiarity in the cavern made Eira's magic dance inside of it. She'd never seen this place before, but it was like coming home. She was certain now that this was where Luana had built a palace for her and Ray. She sensed it in the way one could sense when snow was about to fall.

Eira took a step onto a stone path, and the ground cracked beneath her feet. It was old and fragile, as though no one had stepped on it in years. Cadeyrn now stood next to Eira, and she placed a hand on his shoulder. His presence warmed her, and her magic danced again.

"Where are we?" he said.

"She wanted this to be their home."

The darkness and ice within Eira's veins swelled and swirled from being in a place Luana built with her own hands.

"This was where Ray and Luana were to live. But they were not able to. It has been abandoned."

Cadeyrn stepped forward, and his footfalls echoed through the space.

"Where is the dragon? Shouldn't we see more evidence of life if this is its lair?"

Eira looked to the darkened castle. There were no lights in the windows. She strained to listen for the batting of wings or a sizzling fire from the dragon's breath, but there was nothing.

"Perhaps he is dead," she replied, "or has left to live elsewhere."

The ground glowed, and moon dust floated around her steps when they approached the castle, as though it recognized Luana's Chosen. When they arrived at the castle door, Cadeyrn grasped the handle and tried to pull, but nothing happened.

"Perhaps it needs Luana's Chosen to open it," he said. "Worked the first time."

"It worked when the two of us tried."

Eira took Cadeyrn's hand, and together they placed them on the door.

What seemed to be solid glass, or perhaps even ice, rippled at their touch in dark waves. Swirls of black clouds seeped through the door, moving around their ankles. It was cold to the touch and sent shivers through Eira's body. The whole cavern turned black, and she could barely see inches in front of her.

Eira was frozen, her vision clouded, and Cadeyrn's breath fogged heavy and quick at her side. They tried to pry their hands away from the door, but found themselves stuck.

The ice and darkness had betrayed her. It had never betrayed her before. They were part of her magic, and ran in her veins. How could they turn on her in this way, where she couldn't see or move at all?

"Become one with the darkness."

Eira's darted about for the source of the voice. She didn't recognize it. Yet it was as familiar as it would be if Rose were there with her.

Eira ached at the thought of her sister. Rose would find a way to push through the dark and beat the door down with her bare hands if needed.

"Look through it. Use the darkness inside of you."

She closed her eyes and dug inside herself to search for the magic given to her when she was a young child. It swirled and rolled inside of her the way rumbling clouds would when they prepared for a storm. It called to the darkness in the cavern, and she pulled it toward herself. An invisible finger touched Eira's forehead, and she wanted to cry out, but nothing came.

In moments, it was as though wool had been lifted from her eyes, and she could see through the darkness. Ice spread over her and Cadeyrn's legs to their ankles, binding them to the ground.

Surely this could not be Luana's magic at work. Luana was full of grace and beauty, while this was terrifying and cruel. Yet these were Luana's elements. Someone had warped her magic into something dangerous.

"Eira, I can't see you. What's happening?" Cadeyrn tried to make his voice calm, but she could hear it breaking.

"I can see you. It's going to be fine. I'll free you." Eira lowered her free arm and stretched her hand toward the ice spreading at her feet.

It wasn't ice she had created herself, but perhaps she could still manipulate it.

She willed starlight from her fingers and toward the ice, and little by little it melted away. She pushed the starlight more and more as the ice melted around their feet, and she was able to wrench hers out of the curse. Yet the door still wouldn't open, and her hand was stuck.

"Clear your mind, my child. Sense it. Become one with it."

Eira closed her eyes once more and let herself fade into the darkness and cold. The glow of her tattoo warmed her, and the heat ran through her arm. The same siren call from the mountain beckoned her toward it, singing to her from inside the castle. The ice swirling within her veins stilled, and the darkness calmed into a smooth stream. It poured out of her to blend with the castle's magic, and the door pressed forward. A glimmer of black light shone through, and it summoned her. This darkness was part of who she was, and she leaned into it.

Her dark swirls turned into shades of purple and indigo and

continued to press the door forward until there was enough space to enter. With a final push from Cadeyrn, they burst into the castle and ripped their hands off the door. They hit the cold white floor with a thud as the door slammed shut.

"Eira, what happened back there?"

A dark shadow flew over the dimly lit foyer, and the shape of a wing floated across the far silver wall. Eira's mouth went dry as she stood, and she backed against Cadeyrn. The tattoo on his arm glowed as he tensed and grabbed his sword. Their hair blew in the breeze as the shadow flew around them in circles. Yet they couldn't tell where it came from. Couldn't even hear where the wings were.

"Well, well, well," a voice rumbled, which shook the walls. "Who has dared enter my home? I wasn't prepared for company. I should have tidied a bit."

The shadow continued to fly around them, but the dragon himself remained out of sight. It grew smaller with each turn around the castle foyer and flew lower to the ground. When it finally landed on the opposite side of the room, Eira and Cadeyrn huddled together, and he held his sword out in front of them. Eira gulped and tried to will her heart to calm itself.

The dragon approached, standing on two legs, with a long white tail trailing and folded wings on his back. He wore a pristine white jacket, had deep blue eyes and smooth white hair. On his face were white and silver scales which trailed across his neck, and his smile was eerily human. The skin not covered in scales was as translucent as ice.

Eira was not ready for was how human he appeared. She'd prepared herself to have to defeat—even kill, if needed—a creature or a monster. Not…this. Part man, part beast. She placed her hand on the hilt of her sword to keep it from trembling.

The dragon clapped his clawed hands. "Now, now. What is all this? You are afraid of me?" He placed a hand on his heart as though he were offended. "Those who break into my home, after centuries of those who have failed, I'm sure have great power and bravery, especially with such a leader as this."

He locked his gaze with Eira's, and she sensed swirls of piercing ice in his eyes. He bowed deeply, never losing eye contact with her.

"Welcome, little Luana."

She wanted to tear her eyes away but wouldn't give him the satisfaction of admitting her fear. There was something odd about the way he looked at her. It wasn't desire or attraction, but a possessiveness which made her want to curl into herself and hide.

"I am merely her servant," Eira said.

The dragon stood again, and a sly smile crept over his scaled face.

"Your power says you are her Chosen. Am I wrong? What brings you here to my humble abode, Princess? I have not been granted the gift of guests in all these centuries." His words were smooth and soft, as though he were still trying to comprehend her presence.

"We have come for Gallis's chalice." Eira raised her brows and kept her voice light.

Perhaps his knowledge of her connection to Luana would assist them in the matter, since he was also one of her servants.

He clapped his hands again. "I was afraid you would say so. But alas, it is something I will not grant. Even for Luana's Chosen."

"If you won't give it to us, we'll take it instead," Cadeyrn snarled.

The dragon laughed. Any of the awe he had for Eira vanished when addressing Cadeyrn.

"I would love to see you try."

Cadeyrn snarled again and lunged for the dragon. The dragon pushed him away with the wave of a hand and formed a circle with his lips, blowing an icy cloud. Cadeyrn cried out as it hit his face, and flew across the room and hit the wall, a veil of frost covering his skin. His leg buckled beneath him.

"Cade!" The cry ripped out of Eira's throat, and she moved to run to him, but was hit with a wall of the same icy cloud, which burned her skin.

"Well, isn't this interesting. He's not even Ray's Chosen, and yet you call after him like a lover would." The dragon looked between Eira and Cadeyrn while she tried to claw the ice off her skin. "I don't do well with attacks, as I'm sure you understand. Let me show you to your rooms before I fear for my life more than I already do."

He snapped his fingers, and Eira found herself no longer in the castle foyer but in a large bed chamber covered in blue and silver, not unlike her home in Farren Castle.

But Cadeyrn wasn't there.

She ran to the chamber door and pulled on the tarnished silver knob. It didn't budge. She pulled and pushed and slammed herself against the wooden door, but nothing happened. She darted to the other side of the room, toward the windows where balcony lay, but when she went to step out, she hit an invisible wall and fell flat on her back. With each window, the same happened over and over again.

Eira slammed her body against the chamber door. "Where is he?"

Her yell echoed and bounced off the walls, but silence was the only reply.

The dragon kept her prisoner. It was a beautiful prison, but a prison all the same. She could tolerate it if she only knew where Cadeyrn was.

She called his name. Screamed it through any crevice or hole she could find.

Nothing.

Eira's search for an escape went on for what seemed like hours, until her voice was hoarse and hands raw.

She screamed one last time before collapsing to the bed, and sobbed. They'd come so far. She knew it wasn't going to be easy, but Eira never considered being separated from Cade.

She curled up and closed her eyes and tried not to imagine the worst. In time, she let exhaustion overtake her.

A cold breeze graced her cheek, and she sat up from where she lay. The room was still dark, so she hadn't slept the whole night.

The breeze blew past again, and on the end of the bed lay a white gown lined with fur. She stood and examined the gown to find a note attached.

I may be able to forgive your little attack and intrusion. Join me for a midnight dinner, and we will discuss the matter further.

—Your humble host, Aytigin

He had a name.

Things were much more complicated when the monster had a name.

Chapter Eighteen

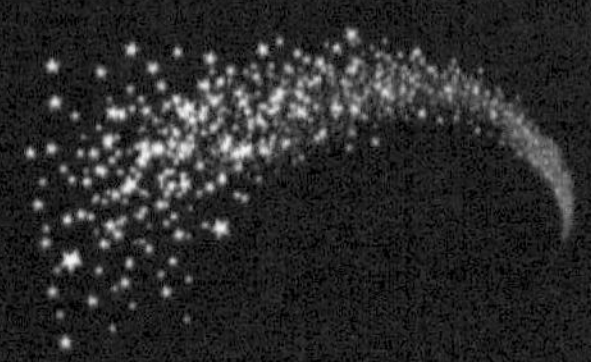

EIRA

When it was time for dinner, the bed chamber doors opened on their own. To appease the dragon, Eira donned the gown he'd provided. In all honesty, it was a relief to wear something other than her travel clothes for a change.

She had no idea where Aytigin had gotten such a garment, but it was as cool and soft as any silk Eira had ever worn at home. She'd learned long ago that beauty and elegance could be used as weapons as much as a sword. In this gown, Eira wasn't a naïve princess running away, she was a queen preparing to greet her fate.

A scared and confused princess traveling through the wilderness, while also on the run for her life, may not be able to negotiate with a dragon. But a future queen could.

Frost trailed the glass halls and stairs to the dining room, where starlit lamps and candles lined the walls and a long table made of ice. Cracked and faded glass plates and dishes were splayed over the blue tablecloth holding meats, fruits, and vegetables for dinner. Crystal goblets filled with wine sat before two place settings.

Aytigin sat on the chair at the head of the table, which was built to accommodate his wings and tail, and stood when Eira entered.

"You have decided to accept my invitation."

"It's the least I can do for your *generous* accommodations." Eira was tense as she sat in the chair that he pulled out for her.

"I am glad you like them." Aytigin sat in his own seat once again.

"Reminds me of the Paravian temple."

Aytigin smiled, something he surely thought appeared charming, but the look he gave her when they first met returned, and any positive impression he may have tried give was gone because of it.

"I would imagine so," he said. "It was built to honor Luana, and this castle was built by Luana herself."

Eira couldn't help but examine the room when she heard this. So this *was* the castle of the legend. The priestesses choosing Paravia as their place of worship hadn't been in vain.

Her pulse quickened. She was in Luana's home.

Aytigin gestured to the array of food before them. "Please, help yourself. You must be starving after such a long journey."

The momentary joy of realizing where she was vanished. She may have been in Luana's home, but Luana wasn't there. Aytigin was.

Eira pressed her lips into a thin line. "I hope my companion is also being taken care of."

"He's fine," the dragon bit out.

"Why am I not with him?" Eira attempted to be polite and focus on her food, which looked delicious, but she couldn't tell what the meat was. "I was the one who started this whole quest, and he is only here because of me. If he is receiving lesser treatment than me, I deserve to be there along with him. Perhaps even in worse conditions. I'm sure there's a dungeon perfectly suited for the situation."

Aytigin finished his bite of food. "The heir of Cresin and Luana's Chosen in a small room along with some simple servant of Aros? Do not insult me. I know how to be hospitable. With your position and power, I would do nothing less. Besides, there is no dungeon here. Luana never had one built. This was to be a peaceful and happy home."

An odd warmth filled Eira's chest. "My father always hated how our castle had one, and we never used it. He said it went against the ways of Luana."

"Your father sounds like a good man." Aytigin continued to eat, his gaze rarely leaving Eira's face.

She tried to ignore him as she ate the berries and bread on her plate but couldn't stop the chills running through her.

"He has his faults," she said, "as do we all. But yes, I've always considered him one."

"It's not poisoned, you know." Aytigin gestured to her uneaten meat. "I'm not your stepmother."

Eira raised her brows.

"I may be stuck in the mountains, but I still make a point to know what happens in Cresin."

From how empty this castle was, Eira doubted he had much contact with other people, even the priestesses.

She pushed the meat with a fork. "I'll have to admit, I'm not sure what this is. I can only imagine what a dragon considers a hospitable meal. I've only heard stories."

Aytigin leaned back in his chair with an amused smile. "I'm sure you have. What types of stories? I would love to hear them. And the meat on your plate is bear."

Eira paled.

Aytigin laughed. "Not your *friend*. And yes, I know all about him and his gift. What is on your plate is one I had hunted the other day and still had its meat in the storage. With your last-minute arrival, I did not have time to gather anything else."

It still seemed wrong to eat the slab on her plate. Eira swallowed the bile in her throat and instead focused on the potatoes and apples.

"Now, what stories have you heard?"

Eira glanced over at her host. "They say you terrorize the towns. Take their livestock. That those who journey to this mountain never return. People can hear screams coming from here."

Aytigin rested his chin on his fist. "Not entirely lies. I eat meat to survive, it is true. It's not my fault there are times when animals in the mountains are scarce and my presence frightens the people. Yes, there are occasions I hunt in the village. But I keep it to a minimum. I have been here longer than they have, and what am I supposed to do? Starve?"

"I suppose not," Eira said.

"As for people who come to my mountain and never return,

usually when someone pays me a visit it is not to be friends, I can assure you. They come to attack and steal, the way you had intended to. If someone were to invade Farren Castle, how would you react? Besides, it is my job. Luana herself commissioned me to protect Gallis's chalice. I am simply following my goddess. Surely you cannot fault me for it."

"Is it necessary to kill them?"

"Do you have any other solutions?" Aytigin raised his brows and stood.

He moved away from the table and stopped next to a window, looking out at the midnight sky and the stars shining there.

"Luana is peaceful, but people forget the other side of the night. The stars may shine bright, but there is still darkness. There is danger and ugliness. Snow is lovely, but ice is sharp and piercing. People have painted a pretty little picture of Luana and the stars, and erased the rest. Everything and everyone has two sides to them, even your precious goddess you claim you know so well."

Eira left the table and stood at his side. The view was stunning, and something within her stirred as she looked out. Stars were so close she could almost hold them in her hand. Silver clouds floated past the castle and shimmered in the light. Below was a black lake. Not black like the one from Stula's cave, but shining and sparkling with swirls of blue and indigo swimming in the water. Stars fell from the sky, and instead of igniting the ground when they landed, they scattered and sprayed light all around.

Starlight danced around Eira's fingers, and swirls of darkness danced along with it without her having to summon it, as though her body were reacting to her surroundings of its own will.

"But have you forgotten the beauty?" she said.

Aytigin looked at her out of the corner of his eye, the moon making his scaled skin shimmer in its light.

"It's possible. But perhaps you can remind me. I have also heard stories about you, you know. Your power, kindness, and beauty."

He took a step closer, and she sensed his blue-eyed gaze boring into her, from her face all the way to her chest. Her tattoo hadn't stopped glowing since she'd arrived at the lair, and the dress he'd chosen had a deep neckline to display it properly. She was used to such ensembles, but still had to fight the urge to cover herself.

He ran a clawed finger through her hair. "They say you're the most beautiful woman in all the kingdoms. I have to say, they may be right. The likeness to Luana is uncanny."

Obsession. That was the look he'd been giving her ever since they'd met.

She shivered. "What is it you want from me?"

He chuckled and pulled his hand away. "You like to cut to the chase."

Eira turned to face him with her arms crossed in front of her chest, though it did little to cover her skin.

"I have had a long several days," she said. "Pardon me if I am anxious to move things along."

Aytigin matched her stance but maintained his steady smile and piercing gaze.

"Stay here. Live with me. Be my queen."

Blood drained from her face, and she took a step back.

"Pardon?"

"You heard me."

Eira blinked and tried to clear her thoughts. Wasn't the answer she'd expected.

She tried to find a response but couldn't.

"But…I—I'm betrothed," she finally said. "You should know. As Luana's Chosen, I am to marry Ray's Chosen."

Aytigin laughed. "What a joke. First, the Chosen of Luana and Ray is a silly little tradition your people started centuries ago as something to cling to for peace. Second, do you believe it is mere friendship which made you and Cadeyrn able to come into this place?"

Eira dropped her arms and looked out the window. "I don't know what you mean."

Aytigin stepped toward her and breathed down her neck. "This was a place made for lovers, my little Luana. It needed the two of you to open the tunnel into the mountain. It needed both of your hands for the door to the castle. Surely you figured this out on your own." He took her hand and raised it and circled a claw around her bare wrist. "And you wear no betrothal band."

Eira's throat went dry, and she tried to swallow.

He took a step back, let go of her arm, and Eira was able to release the breath she'd been holding.

"I'm not asking you to marry me, if that's what you think. Your being Chosen could be useful, anyway. I noticed you journeying toward the mountain days ago. It didn't take me long to figure out what you needed. We could be useful to each other. I wouldn't have permitted you to enter this mountain otherwise."

"You let us in?" Eira covered her wrist with her other hand.

Already she'd grown used to not wearing the band and had forgotten about how she'd given it to the Stula priest.

"What about how the ice attacked us?"

"Some of the precautions are not easily removed. Besides, if things were too easy you would have suspected something. I will admit, perhaps I could have been more welcoming."

The starlight coming out of Eira's fingers turned cold.

"What can I offer you?" she said.

He stepped behind Eira and locked eyes with her through the reflection in the window. He ran his claw over her hair again, and she tried not to tremble.

"Haven't you been listening? I am stuck here in this mountain. There are times I do not have much to hunt for food. There are no others here with me other than those who wish to attack and pillage. I have been here for centuries, watching over a damn cup. Live here. Rule here. I'll have company, power, food, and support. I have jewels galore to fund whatever your kingdom needs. I'll let your...*friend*...take the chalice back to cure your father. You'll stay here with me, and the capital can return to your precious ancient temple. You'll live and rule in the home Luana herself built. Do you think a prince of Ray—or even Aros—will understand your connection to Luana the way I would? Look at how your magic is dancing simply by being here. Imagine what it could do if you lived here."

He gestured to Eira's hands. Darkness, stars, ice, and snow all swirled around them. Her skin had an iridescent glow, and in the window's reflection her hair shone like the night sky. Ever since Eira had come to the mountains, something had awoken in her, and she sensed Luana's presence more acutely than ever before.

"With me, you could be the greatest queen Cresin has seen since Isadore. You can cure your father, and all of this could be yours. Marrying me isn't a requirement for you to live here, but it could be helpful. I could be a good husband to you, if it is what you chose. I'm not terrible on the eyes, am I?"

He stepped to the side so she could take a good look, and when he stretched an arm out toward the window, the stars seemed to shine brighter than before. Underneath the scales, tail, and wings, a man was visible. A well-sculpted face, a fine physique, and perhaps even a welcoming smile.

But he wasn't Cadeyrn.

"Oxare is a fine kingdom, Eira. But what can your two princes offer you that I cannot? Or you can be your own woman. You only have to stay here with me and not go back to the kingdom."

This was not what Eira expected. Part of her wished for the grand and bloody battle she'd pictured and been preparing for.

Aytigin turned back to the window and stared out at the scene before them. His eyes grew distant and glazed over.

He pointed to the far wing of the castle. "The west portion of the castle has been destroyed. You need to fix it."

Eira blinked and set her hands on the windowsill. Yet another surprise.

"I'm not a building attendant. How can I help with fixing your castle?"

Aytigin gestured to where Eira's hands rested. The old and cracked marble material was turning smooth and shone beneath her touch.

Eira jerked her hands away. She'd never repaired anything with her magic before.

"What do you say, my little Luana?"

Eira tugged the long sleeves of the gown so it covered her bare wrists and hid that her betrothal band was no longer there.

"And if I don't?"

Aytigin's smile vanished, and he gave her a cold stare.

"That's for me to decide, when I so choose." He snapped his fingers, and the castle shook.

Eira grasped onto the windowsill to keep herself standing as a man screamed in the distance.

Eira snarled at the dragon. "Where is Cadeyrn? What did you do to him?"

He snapped his fingers again so the castle stood still once again, and the screaming stopped.

"Stay with me, and I'll let him go."

Eira let go of the windowsill and stepped in front of Aytigin so they stood nose to nose. He was much taller than she was, but Eira held her head high.

"I can never live and rule with someone like you. You claim you're a servant of Luana, but you know nothing of her ways."

Aytigin laughed, a loud and deep chuckle which made the castle shake again.

"And what do you know of it? I have personally met Luana. Have you?"

Eira clenched her jaw and narrowed her eyes at him.

"And how long has it been since she's graced your presence? Luana has abandoned you. Cast you off to punish you for something, surely so you could be out of her sight. Why do you think you could possibly be worthy of marrying me or even ruling by my side?"

Ice clouds poured out of Aytigin's nose, and he scowled at her.

"Is this your answer? You refuse to stay here? What will happen to your father and your kingdom? Do you believe you will be able to leave this place and steal the chalice on your own?"

Eira wanted to step back but refused to give him any indication that she was quitting or letting him win this argument. Yet she couldn't deny his point. She had no idea where the chalice was or how to get out of the lair. Especially since he'd withdrawn the barriers that would have prevented her and Cadeyrn from entering in the first place. Surely he wouldn't remove them for her to leave safely.

"I haven't decided yet," Eira finally said.

It wasn't what she wanted, and she'd never accept the offer, but she couldn't deny that some of his points were appealing.

"You need to show me that this truly is the best place for me to rule my kingdom."

Aytigin raised a brow. "And how would I be able to impress the mighty princess?"

"Don't lock me or Cadeyrn away. Let us be free to roam the castle on our own. If this is to be my home, and I need to repair it, I should be able to walk through it as I please and get to know it well. If the chalice is as safe as you claim, there should be no danger in my, or Cadeyrn's, doing so."

Eira held her breath while she waited for Aytigin's answer. If he let them wander freely, even if she couldn't find the chalice, she could at least speak with Cadeyrn and they could make a plan together.

Aytigin crossed his arms over his broad chest and strummed his claws.

"You can't have full reign of the castle. Never come to my chambers. And I'll be creating more precautions around the chalice. This castle is not like the one you call home. But I can't wait forever. I'll give you tomorrow to consider it. And when I rise the evening after, you'll tell me your choice."

He snapped his fingers again, and Eira stood in another hallway she'd never seen before. She spun and looked over her shoulder as though Aytigin may still be there watching her, even if she couldn't see him.

"Eira."

When Eira spun around again, Cadeyrn had emerged from one of the doors, and she launched into his arms. Cadeyrn squeezed her tight and spoke into her hair.

"I've been trying to get out for hours, but all of a sudden the door opened."

They parted enough so they could look at one another, and Eira bit her bottom lip.

"I have much to tell you."

Chapter Nineteen

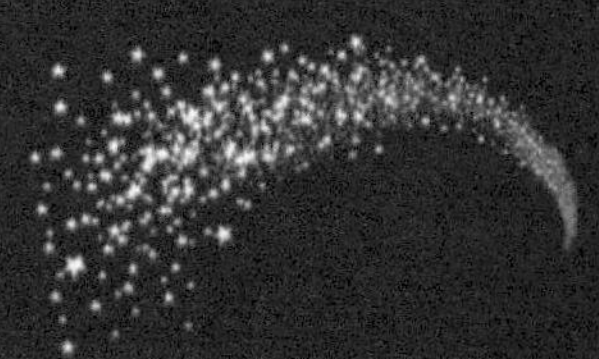

EIRA

Eira wandered the halls of the castle the next evening in search of anything that could help her make a decision. She shivered and rubbed her arms. A constant draft ran through the castle, and Eira was comfortable except when she tried to decide what to do next. She didn't want to walk away from her kingdom and risk her throne.

Only, they didn't have any other options.

A roar came from outside, and the walls shook as Aytigin's shadow soared past the windows. He stayed clear of Eira and Cadeyrn while he slept through the day, and Eira hadn't seen him all evening. No telling what would happen if he were to encounter Cadeyrn while he did his own exploring. He'd been furious when she told him of Aytigin's bargain, and replied, "Absolutely not!" which only made her more upset.

Eira frowned when she recalled their debate about the situation before going to sleep for the day. While Cadeyrn raised several good points about how they couldn't be sure Aytigin was being truthful, and they may not be able to convince the council to move court to the mountains, he didn't even consider the benefits of the situation.

Eira was in the west wing of the castle, which became more deteriorated with each step. A gray haze hovered in the space, and cracks like lightning splayed across the floor. Before her stood a set of doors made of ice and engraved with roses and images of snowflakes and the sky. The ceiling was taller than the trees of Eral. The air hummed around them, and a dark light glowed underneath the doors and illuminated the cracks along the floor.

While Eira's tattoo always glowed here, the color turned darker and it thumped to the same hum in the air. It called to her the way the mountain called to her when she wanted to find the entrance to the dragon's lair.

She stepped forward and tried to push one of the doors open. The ice turned black beneath her hand, and a sharp pain shot through her arm. She pulled it back, gasping.

Surely this could not be magic from Luana. And still, it called to her.

Eira backed away from the doors and held her hand close to her heart, and the dark light dimmed, making everything turn dank and gray. Many contradictions were present in this castle. It contained such beauty, and Eira's magic sang within her with each turn. Yet such darkness lurked in the corners, catching her off guard.

She wasn't sure what she was searching for, but there had to be something to help make the choice of whether to stay or go. There was the possibility of encountering the chalice—even though she doubted it. But being in Luana's home, she could find some sort of guidance or peace as to what her next move was.

There was another hall nearby, and the ground illuminated as Eira walked through, as though the castle knew Eira needed to get away from the doors and wanted to pave the way for where she needed to be.

Paintings lined the walls, and the images of queens gone by seemed to watch Eira as she wandered. The canvases were weathered and torn, and a sheen of dust covered the pictures, but each depicted the different Chosens of Luana through the centuries.

Isadore stood proud in her armor next to a silver steed, and Sanson was on the other side, his arm stretched out to her across a battlefield. The lines may have been crude and harsh, and the colors faded with age, but Isadore's beauty was still evident, and the ice circling her hands glimmered in Eira's light.

No matter where she turned, the castle called to her. Even these paintings made her believe she could reach out and touch the images they depicted as if doing so she would enter their world. How wonderful it would be if it were possible for the Chosens of the past to let her see their stories and show her what to do.

Isadore was Luana's first Chosen, so many centuries ago. She was strong and brave and powerful. What would she tell Eira to do?

She couldn't resist the urge to grace the paintings with her finger. Ice passed from her hand to the painting, and the image became clearer as the ice spread like it was cleaning off the dirt and grime of the past.

This was where it had all begun, with them seeing one another in battle, and eventually became a love that brought peace to the two kingdoms. The priestesses claimed Isadore's power was the strongest out of all of the daughters of Luana and none had matched her since.

The ice within Eira's veins stirred, and snowflakes floated from her hands. The paintings continued on through the never-ending hall, the art style evolving with each time period, and Eira's magic responded to each one in a different way. As she examined them, the layers of dust and grime melted away as her magic awakened and let each of Luana's Chosens shine in their glory.

She paused at the portrait of Malle. Dark swirls surrounded her in an embrace. The stars in the sky shone in her eyes, and a small smile played on her lips. In the distance stood a tall figure illuminated with light, which caught Malle's gaze. A vast contrast from any of the images and stories Eira had heard about Malle in her travels, where she was stripped of her crown and banished after her affair. Here, she was…happy.

Eira's own darkness swirled around her, and stars danced in the air and cleared the painting along with it. She touched her hand to her heart and found herself lost in the painting. Was the illuminated figure the man Malle had fallen in love with? The stories claimed he had been killed by a mob, and no one ever saw Malle again. Some claimed she died from grief.

This wasn't the message of the painting. It wasn't sad or full of dread and warning. Perhaps this was before all those tragic events happened, and Luana wanted to remember her this way.

A new hope filled Eira's chest. The stories may have been wrong. Maybe Malle was happy even through all of what happened to her and her lover.

The shadows, stars, and snow floated through the hall, and Eira waved her arms to let them complete their work of restoring the paintings. Each of these women, her ancestors, had their own power and stories, and someday Eira was to take her place on the throne along with them. All of them had helped their kingdom and made it a better place. Yet when she reached the end of the hall, there was no painting of herself.

She was so inadequate. Could she be strong like Isadore and face enemies and do what was needed to keep her kingdom safe and unified? Was she capable of being brave like Malle and follow her heart in spite of the consequences? They were only two of the stories of the leaders of Cresin, and there were countless more where they all had to make choices and sacrifices for the good of the kingdom.

Standing among them, or at least their paintings, she gained strength from them all.

The shadows coming from her were darker as she let them soar through the hall. The stars twinkled more brightly through the darkness and formed new constellations. The snowflakes had more intricate designs and fell from the ceiling, but never touched the ground. The ice was sharper and colder as it spread over the paintings and vanished while making the images clearer.

From the end of the hall, Cadeyrn appeared. His eyes grew wide at the sight of Eira's magic and all of the paintings.

"Wow!"

Eira outstretched her arms and marveled at the scene herself.

"I know."

Cadeyrn moved toward her. The snow landed in his dark hair, and the stars lit the path.

He arrived at her side and kissed her cheek. "What is this?"

"A gallery of all of Luana's Chosens." Eira took his hand.

"They're looking at you."

Eira glanced around the hall at the paintings. All of the queens were still facing the direction they always had, but their eyes seemed to have followed her to the end.

Eira held Cadeyrn's hand tighter. "Sometimes it seems like paintings do that."

"And what about this?" He outstretched his hand, and snowflakes fell into his palm. "It's incredible."

"They made my powers stronger." Eira waved her hand, and the snow stopped in midair. "And the paintings were old and faded when I arrived, and my magic fixed them. I didn't know that could happen without the help of an attendant or one of Efare's artists."

"Your power has been growing ever since we arrived in the mountains."

"Is it terrible that I'm fascinated by this place? If these were different circumstances, perhaps…"

As awful as Aytigin was, and as terrible at their situation was, there was a small part of her that wanted to explore it more. Perhaps she could help to restore the parts of the castle Aytigin wanted her to.

She and Cadeyrn linked arms and turned down the hall towards where their chambers were.

"It's natural," he replied. "Luana built this place, so I would only imagine you'd have a connection with it." He rubbed her arm as he strolled along. "Once, when I was with my men in the desert, we encountered one of Aros's oldest temples, and the priests there said Aros used to visit there. They let me visit one of the sacred rooms, and it held Aros's helmet." He shivered beneath her touch, and his voice grew distant. "I was stronger there than I'd ever been before. I could have stayed for days."

All that Eira loved and wanted kept going against what she should be doing. Being with Cadeyrn as they walked the halls of the castle was as natural to her as breathing, but doing so made her betray everything she—and Alvis—stood for. Using her magic and being close to Luana in this castle called to her soul. Yet staying here meant she couldn't be in her own kingdom, with her family, or Cadeyrn.

"Did you find anything?" Eira said. "Any hint of the chalice?"

She lay her head against Cadeyrn's shoulder and waved her free hand. Stars floated toward a torn curtain and held it upright.

"I did not. But I did find some excellent hunting and the most incredible armory."

A smile played on his lips, and Eira sensed excitement in his voice when he mentioned the armory.

"There's so much here that could be shared with the kingdom," he said, "or even the town of Paravia."

"Will you show me?"

A playful gleam sparked in his eye, and he took her hand and led her out of the hallway, past the doors of ice, and towards the armory.

"Wait." Eira tugged on his arm, and they paused.

With a tap of her foot, ice spread across the floor, and Eira wrapped her arms around his waist.

She whispered in his ear, "Hold on."

They slid through the hall, ice paving a path for them, and Eira shrieked in delight as they flew through the castle. Cadeyrn whooped and laughed and directed which way they should go. Eira's feet were steady as they whizzed through, and Cadeyrn's hands remained firm around her. When they arrived, both were crying with laughter, and Eira kissed his cheek.

"Now show me these weapons of yours."

Cadeyrn opened the door, and before them stood the largest armory Eira had ever seen. Item by item, Cadeyrn showed them off, explaining how they all worked, and helped her learn how to hold them properly. He talked about what he'd seen while exploring the castle in his bear form, and what he could do to help the mountain villages and the kingdom. It wasn't only about the weapons and battles. He had a vision for Cresin. What it could be. How he could fit into it.

Eira leaned on a club Cadeyrn had passed to her and stared at him. He was a king. She could see all of it. Him ruling at her side.

Her chest warmed when she pictured what it would be like to rule with him, side by side. They would have a peaceful, but strong, kingdom. He'd seen more sides of all the kingdoms than she and Alvis had been able to, with his work as a soldier. She didn't want to partner with anyone else. No matter what she chose, she would find a way for him to be with her.

"You've thought about all of this?" she said.

Cadeyrn swung a sword around as if it were a rope. "Of course I have. More in the last few days. But I do have my own estate, you know, and was raised around you and Alvis. It's not as though I'm new to the idea of how to govern. People assumed I wasn't paying attention, but I was. I wanted to have lands of my own and create my own name. Then I wouldn't have to worry about staying in the good graces of the royal family."

Yes. Eira had almost forgotten about what he'd told her when they found out he was a shapeshifter. It didn't matter to her one bit if he was royal or not, but it did to him. Wasn't anything she'd ever had to worry about, and it was naive of her to not realize Cadeyrn did.

"It's why you worked so hard in the military. You wanted to earn your own place. Do you have control over your estate? I know it's yours, but especially when you're away, do you still make all the decisions?"

Cadeyrn tapped the sword to the ground and did a turning bow, using it as support.

"Someone is sitting as regent at the moment. And obviously, for the last few weeks I haven't been able to maintain my correspondence. But yes." He stood upright and kicked the sword, then swung it once more with a flourish before sheathing it. "I'm not anyone, Eira. It's why I've worked for all I have, because if I were to fall out of favor… I know what you said the other night, but when all this is over, and if you decide to leave us in the past, I'll understand. I know what you'd be risking to be with me."

Eira set the club aside and crossed the room. Both of them were risking something. Lands, titles, reputations, and all they'd worked for.

She held his face and kissed him. "My whole life I've wanted nothing more than to be queen."

Cadeyrn rested his hands on her hips. "I know. Which is why, as much as I love you, I'll step aside if it's what you need."

Eira pulled closer to him. "But I want you at my side. I love you more each moment, Cadeyrn. I can't walk away, and I don't want to. Whether it's here or there—"

"There. It'll be there. In Farren Castle, with your sister and your people. We're going to find a way for you to be with your kingdom. I promise."

Eira pressed her forehead against his. “No matter where, you’re always going to be the one I want at my side.”

Their lips met again, and stars danced around them.

“We’re not going to figure out anything if you keep doing that.” Cadeyrn smiled but didn’t stop kissing her, and let his hands roam over her body.

“I want to have these moments while we can.”

Their hearts beat as one, united, as they were united in all of this. As they always had been and would be, moving forward.

How it would happen wasn’t clear, and when Cadeyrn carried her to the wall and made love to her against it, she didn’t receive any answers. Yet never had she been calmer and more confident.

When the top of her dress came undone and she was exposed, Eira arched back so Cadeyrn could appreciate it more.

“My queen,” he murmured into her neck as he cupped her breast, circling her nipple with his thumb.

“My king.” Eira guided his face back to hers.

Cadeyrn stopped for a half-moment before covering her mouth with his, and they let the rest fade away.

Chapter Twenty

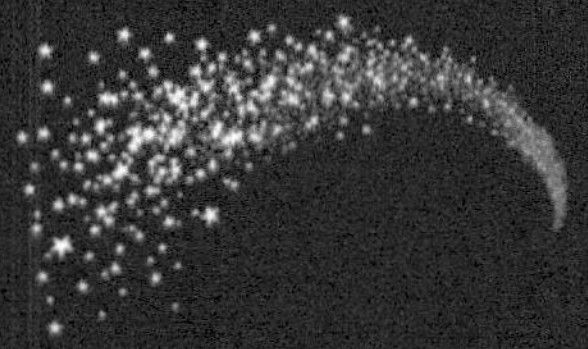

ALVIS

THE MARQUIS OF MARALLIS SWIRLED HIS GLASS OF WINE AND CROSSED his legs. His thin mustache wasn't as neatly trimmed as usual and his clothes were rumpled, but he still sat with a confident grace.

"I have the feeling you did not ask me here for a social call."

Alvis tossed aside the newest message from his family, which was in the same vein as all the others lately. Come home. There is no purpose for you to be in Cresin any longer. Nobles are approaching the family with alliance agreements if he marries their daughter, niece, granddaughter, or whoever they wanted to give to the highest bidder.

Even if he wanted to go home, which he didn't, for there was more he needed to learn from Cal and Nell, Queen Amelia wouldn't allow it. One by one, nobles had tried to leave the castle, only to mysteriously turn up missing or dead days later. She wasn't preventing people from leaving—yet—but they all knew these occurrences weren't as mysterious as she was leading others to believe.

A draft of his response was on the table, but he needed to finalize a few things. He needed to be sure it was clear that he wasn't coming home soon, without giving away anything that could harm them.

"You're right," Alvis replied. "As much as I enjoy your company, I have matters to discuss. I take it you heard the queen has sent away several of the attendants who have been helping the king?"

The marquis curled his fingers around his glass as though he were strangling the queen's neck.

"Yes. She claims it is because she wants only the best overseeing him."

"She's been letting you visit the king? A surprising mercy she lets his majesty's lover near him."

The marquis was calm as he placed his glass on the table. "Only because I own the largest lands, which provide grain for Farren and the other northern territories. Unless she wants an uprising due to her citizens starving, she needs me. Besides, we also have the same god."

Alvis raised his brows. "Your lands are in the plains near the southern mountains. I don't recall any large bodies of water there. Most of Colma's followers I know live near the coast or on islands, even near a lake or river."

He leaned in as the marquis pushed up his shirtsleeve to reveal a tattooed bracelet of waves around his wrist.

"It is because of me they are able to get water to all of their fields. I created a system so they would not need to be near a water source."

"Impressive."

The marquis lowered his sleeve.

"What if she did have an uprising?" Alvis said.

The marquis quirked the corner of his mouth and narrowed his eyes.

"The idea of an uprising sounds appealing, and almost inevitable if Queen Amelia continues as she is. The people won't stand this much longer. But…if I take away my grain, the people of Cresin could suffer, and Amelia won't be the one punished. It would be them."

"I don't want to starve the people of Cresin." Alvis waved his hand and took a seat.

It was an idea that had been churning in his mind over the last several days, and the dilemma the marquis mentioned was, too. But things could not continue as they were, and wherever Eira, Rose, and Cadeyrn were, it would be foolish to sit around hoping they would return.

"However, the queen needs to be reminded that her resources are not unlimited," Alvis said. "She only has what she does because those loyal to the crown give them to her."

The marquis leaned back in his seat and considered this. "The other nobles have been growing unhappy. They've tried to speak reason to her, but she does what she wants anyway."

Exactly. Amelia had become a tyrant who thought she had unlimited power, which wasn't the case. The kingdoms had councils for a reason—to keep the monarch in check.

Alvis rested his elbows on his knees. His voice grew faster and stronger.

"The only reason she is in power is because the council deemed she could be regent while we attempt to cure the king. The council can take her title away. She does not have any other claim to the throne. What if each of her strongest allies pulled back, only enough where she feels the pressure? What if the council put enough pressure on her that she has no choice but to listen?"

"And if she doesn't anyway?"

"Oxare has always cooperated with Cresin and promised their full partnership when I was betrothed to Eira. But my country is not happy with the current situation. I'm sure there are plenty of nobles in Cresin with legitimate claims to the throne who would be happy to find a way to gain power. And I'm sure Oxare will be more than happy to support one of them."

The duke chuckled and raised his glass. "Well, it's about time you arrived, Your Highness."

"STOP THE RAIDS." ALVIS SLAMMED THE NEWS REPORT PARCHMENT ON the table and gripped it with his fist. "Those are innocent citizens, and it is your duty to protect them, not slaughter them!"

Amelia ripped the parchment away, tore it in half, and threw it into the fire.

"Know your place, young prince. Cresin is no longer your concern.

What I choose to do in my kingdom is nothing you should be worrying about."

"It is not your kingdom," Alvis hissed. "It is King Brennan's kingdom. And Eira's. And Rose's."

The slap across his face happened so quickly he didn't see it coming.

Roaring waves splashed in Amelia's eyes. "It is mine."

From his pocket, Alvis revealed several letters, each of them from important nobles of Cresin and the neighboring kingdoms, including his own.

"Not for long if you keep behaving this way." He placed them on the table and pointed to each one. "Grain and stones from Marallis will lessen. Slania is cutting back their fish supply to you. Breasel won't send crops. Oxare is refusing trade."

Amelia grasped at the letters, her eyes frantic as she scanned the pages.

"Lies!"

"They're not lies. Your allies are refusing to work with you, one by one, and soon you won't have a kingdom. They'll rise against you, and no one will be at your side to stop them. After the year Cresin has had because of the fires, you can't afford to lose resources. You need the nobles and other kingdoms to support you."

He exited the room before she could argue.

She was nervous—maybe even panicked.

Good.

Alvis woke in the night to something hitting the window. He rose from the bed and saw people storming to the castle and throwing rocks. The people were already revolting.

A surge of water poured from the castle. From all sides a tide came roaring in, hitting the rebels. They screamed and cried as the water tried to drown them.

Where did it all come from?

No. This wasn't supposed to happen.

Alvis pushed the window open and sent pillars of fire to dry the water, but there was too much. Far too much for a single person to have created.

Some of the citizens escaped, but most didn't. Within minutes, the siege was over and the castle was now surrounded by water. Some tried to cross through, but the moment someone's foot touched the edge, the water surged forward and drowned them before they could even try to swim.

No one was getting in.

Chapter Twenty-One

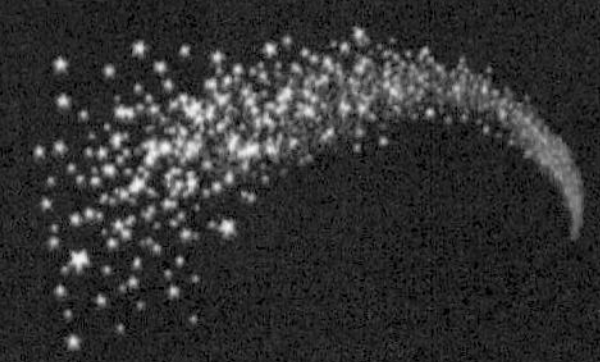

EIRA

Aytigin required Eira and Cadeyrn to eat each meal with him. If they didn't, they wouldn't eat at all.

Yet Eira found that she didn't dread the meals as much as she thought she would have. She hated the snarls aimed toward Cadeyrn and the penetrating stares in her direction. But when prompted, Aytigin told interesting stories. More often than not, she found herself leaning forward and engaging in his tales, entranced by what he had to say. It was obvious he was craving attention and the company of another, as his eyes sparkled when he told an exciting tale.

He also enjoyed listening to what Eira had to share about Cresin and even tolerated Cadeyrn's offerings to the conversation. Aytigin peppered them with questions about what the Moon Festival was like, Rose, the desert, and life outside the mountain. More than anything, he liked to hear about the temple and Eira's thoughts on various sacred texts. She couldn't help but oblige.

Yet Aytigin was cold. He was harsh in his judgments, and when they disagreed, he unleashed a temper. A few times, they had to dodge his icy breath when he was angry.

"I want to see more of the castle," Eira said when they finished eating.

Aytigin raised his brows and dabbed the corner of his mouth with a napkin.

"Didn't you explore today? I saw the work you did in the Chosen Gallery. It was remarkable."

"Of course it was remarkable," Cadeyrn said. "Everything Eira does always is." He leaned back in his seat and stared at the dragon.

Eira flicked her gaze toward the ceiling and pushed her plate aside. Cadeyrn treated each interaction with Aytigin as though it were a battle. Which, in a way, they were. Even so, it was exhausting.

"Thank you," Eira said. "But there is so much more to this castle, and if I'm to make a proper decision about staying, in such a limited amount of time, I need to get to know as much of it as possible."

Aytigin cocked his head. "Fine. It is a reasonable enough request. I can give you a tour if you like."

"We would be delighted." Eira forced a smile.

Spending more time with Aytigin wasn't something she wanted to do, but they could gain more clues as to where the chalice was hidden.

They stood, and she and Cadeyrn followed Aytigin out of the dining hall. In spite of its dilapidated state, it wasn't difficult to imagine her own court walking the halls and preparing for various events.

Aytigin spoke of the rooms and halls with a distant fondness and pride, and Eira almost pitied him. If she were in his place alone, perhaps she would have turned out the same way as he.

Eira lingered near a large painting of Luana and Ray dancing among the stars. She held Cadeyrn's hand, and he paused with her. It was one of the few things that did not appear to be shadowed by the passing of time. Luana's black hair cascaded over her shoulders, and her bright blue eyes shone with delight, a wide smile on her face. In most images of Luana, she was lovely, of course, but also regal and poised. In this image, she was relaxed and happy.

Aytigin noticed them looking at the image, and his features relaxed.

"Luana commissioned Efare to paint this one herself."

Just like in the Chosens Gallery, Eira wanted to touch it as though Luana were there in front of them instead of in a painting. She almost did, but restrained as if her touch would ruin the image.

"It's stunning," she said.

Aytigin stood at their side, hands clasped behind his back. "I'll admit, this is one of my favorites. Efare depicted Luana's likeness perfectly."

Eira tilted her head towards Aytigin. "Do you know her well? Luana?"

"A long time ago. It has been some time since I've seen the goddess." Aytigin looked at Eira.

His deep blue eyes softened as he gazed, and it was like galaxies swam in them how they did in other followers of Luana. Yet he remained dedicated to the goddess in spite the appearance of her abandoning him. He abused her power and warped it, but perhaps there was some sort of pure devotion still salvageable beneath those thick white scales.

Almost as soon as the pity and understanding darted through Eira's mind, they vanished when his lips parted as he stepped forward. Her face warmed, for this was not like when she met him the day before, where he was trying to intimidate her. It was as though he were transferring that devotion to her, like she was Luana, and she took a step toward Cadeyrn, grasping his hand in hers.

People looked at Eira in awe due to her title and place in court, and their faith. But never had they looked at her the way this dragon did. She could handle Aytigin on her own but was still grateful Cadeyrn was there.

He squeezed her hand back.

"You look like her, you know." Aytigin stood so close she could smell the snow and ice on him.

"So I've been told."

"It's remarkable."

At her side, Cadeyrn cleared his throat and tightened his grip on her hand.

"You seem to like that word."

Aytigin's attention toward her bothered Cadeyrn, she knew. He hadn't been quiet about it when they spoke in private. He wasn't jealous, but the way Aytigin looked at her was disturbing. She couldn't have the two of them at each other's throats, though.

Eira patted Cadeyrn's arm. "But not entirely uncommon. They say Queen Isadore also resembled Luana."

In an unusual act of insight and empathy for the situation, Aytigin took a step back and nodded. Even if he still looked at Eira.

"She did," he replied.

"You knew her also?" Cadeyrn rubbed the back of his neck. "Gods, you must be old."

Aytigin smirked. "I've known many queens, my little Luana and her bastard prince." He finally broke his gaze and turned to walk further down the hallway. "Come. I know what it is you truly wish to see."

Aytigin led them toward another painting and pressed his hand on it. Ice spread over the canvas, and the image dissolved, showing a dark entryway. Light glowed from the ground with each step, making the moon rock walls sparkle. It was dark, but Eira's eyes soon adjusted, far better than they would have even a day ago, and she easily found her way.

The hall wound about, had stairs going up, down, and up again. It was meant for anyone who wandered through to lose their way, but never once did Eira become disoriented.

They came to a door, and Aytigin placed his clawed hand on it the same way he did the painting. Ice mixed with darkness spread on the door, and it swung open. Dazzling stars filled the room before them, and their light was magnified by the jewels displayed all around.

Eira gasped at the sight. She had no idea such riches lay within the mountains.

"Luana's treasures." Aytigin stretched his arms out wide to show off the collection. "Things she gathered through the years that she found valuable, or simply liked. She commissioned me to keep them safe for her. But there is the one thing I need to protect above all others."

He strode through the room, and when he reached a pile of gold, he waved a hand over it. The gold spread apart in rustling metal waves, and a silver chalice rose, carried by a cloud of stardust. It floated, hovering at Eira's eye level.

Gallis's chalice.

She extended an arm, but when her hand passed through the stardust cloud, a searing pain shot through her. She cried out and collapsed, in spite of Cadeyrn's attempt to catch her, feeling like she were on fire. The room trembled and shook as though it were about to collapse in on them.

Cadeyrn knelt at her side, and she flinched at his touch. He looked as if he was about to attack Aytigin on the spot. Claws pierced through his fingers.

Aytigin waved a hand, and it all stopped. The pain vanished, and the chalice lowered back into its golden prison. Eira gasped, and Cadeyrn's claws shrank back into his skin.

Aytigin chuckled. "You didn't think I would let you grab the chalice, did you?"

Eira glared at him as Cadeyrn helped her to her feet.

"Why did you let me try?"

Aytigin leaned against a marble pillar and crossed his arms.

"This was only a taste of the protections the chalice has around it."

"Why show it to us at all?" Cadeyrn kept his arms around Eira and flared his nostrils.

She leaned into his embrace and let herself be comforted by his protection.

"To remind you of what I'm offering," Aytigin replied. "In case you thought you could capture the chalice without me, I had to show you cannot. I know you don't want to admit it, but you need me to save your father. Don't come searching for it on your own."

"You're despicable," Eira spat, appalled she'd started to get along with him, even sympathized and attempted to understand him.

He raised a brow and looked at her as though remembering her blush from before.

"I am simply doing my duty."

"Do you want to turn away Luana's Chosen?" Eira stepped between the two men, her face flushed now from anger instead of embarrassment. "To let her lose her place on the throne?"

Aytigin stepped forward and locked his gaze with her again. He stood so close his cool breath graced her skin.

"But are you truly her Chosen? Is there such a thing? Or is it simply something your people do to bring comfort?"

Eira opened her mouth, but couldn't find anything to say. Twice now, he'd challenged her title. She wouldn't say it out loud, but his questions rang true and shook Eira to her core.

If Luana didn't have a Chosen…who was Eira? What power did she truly hold?

There were things about Luana and magic he knew that Eira could only dream of. She wasn't sure if the thought frightened her or simply made her more curious.

Cadeyrn's claws were fighting to pry out of his hands again, and she could see the bear rumbling beneath his skin, but he kept his voice steady.

"Of course there is. And Eira is it. You said so yourself—her powers are remarkable."

Aytigin pushed off the pillar and continued to walk through the treasure room.

"There's something else I want you to see."

There had to be a way they could get to the chalice on their own. Maybe she needed to earn his trust more. Or maybe there was a way to endure the pain.

They could only learn more if they kept going, so Eira followed.

Cadeyrn caught her arm. "Eira, it might be a trap."

She loved him, but sometimes he was too protective for his own good.

She shook her head. "We need to know more."

After passing countless treasures, they approached a tiered platform, and a blue orb floated above it. Aytigin circled the orb and hovered his hand over it, making it cloud over and change colors to show snow-covered trees.

"This is how I can see beyond the mountains. Or at least, to those connected to Luana. It's one of the few mercies I was given when I received my punishment all those years ago."

An image of the temple at Farren Castle formed in the orb. Far away at first. Then it was as though they floated through the air, and the closer they got to the building, the larger it grew. The area surrounding the castle wasn't what it used to be, though. A wall of water surrounded the castle, as thick as a wall barring any entrance through the castle gates. It was as though the ocean had been transported to the castle and made into a wall to prohibit people from entering or exiting. Eira couldn't even make out where a door or entryway would be.

Sea creatures swam around the castle and jumped through the surface and back in again. Small groups of people were camped outside of the wall, and when they tried to enter, a serpent-like creature bolted out and ate them whole. The people around the castle screamed and scattered, leaving their belongings behind before they could become the next victim.

Eira gasped and shook her head. *No. This can't be.*

The castle gates were always open to those who needed them. Amelia was holding those inside captive and lashing out at the people of Cresin. Eira's people. The ones she should be protecting.

The image floated closer in and went inside the castle, where the priestesses were worshipping. Priestess Cynth and Lady Evony were there. Cynth tried turning the water to ice, but alone it didn't make any difference. The water was too strong and melted any of the ice Cynth created. Evony hugged Cynth in comfort and guided her back into the temple.

Worship was scantly attended. No surprise, considering no one could enter the castle grounds. It wasn't the usual evening prayers, but ones of mourning. They prayed and cried over the lives lost at the castle gate and those lost in raids.

But not the king.

Eira breathed a sigh of relief. It may have been selfish to be grateful that her father was still alive, but at least there was still hope. Yet there were so many names they chanted over. All who'd lost their lives because Queen Amelia still hunted Eira.

"You can save them, Eira," Aytigin said. "You have the power to save them if you stay here. Repair the castle, give Cadeyrn the chalice so your father can be awakened, and all of this will be over."

Eira stepped back from the orb. "I know what's at risk. There's no need to remind me. Stop with your poisonous words and visions."

Aytigin outstretched his hands in feigned innocence. "You claim you know, yet you haven't made a choice. I'm amazed it hasn't been an easy one for you to make."

Cadeyrn's body was tense, and he held her hand as though it was his only solace. So much so, she half-expected smoke to pour out of his ears.

"Or you could give us the chalice and be done with it," he said. "If there is a delay in progress being made, it is through no fault of Eira's, but yours."

Aytigin waved his hand over the orb, and it returned to its previous dark blue and clouded state.

His voice sounded bored. "It is the way of dragons. If you did not know this, it is no fault of mine. Your time is running shorter, little Luana. You don't want to wait much longer."

THE SUNRISE WAS BEAUTIFUL THAT DAY, AND EIRA STILL COULDN'T TELL if it was the real sun or one created inside of the cave to appear to be the real thing. Either way, it rose gloriously, with pink and yellow rays piercing through the sky.

This must be how Luana saw Ray. A grand tribute to the god she loved but could never see. A shame they couldn't enjoy this place together. What had happened? Why had this castle gone into such ruin, and its only use was to harbor ancient artifacts and a dragon?

"It's sad we aren't here under different circumstances." Eira rested her hands on the windowsill as she watched the sunrise.

Cadeyrn had finished preparing for bed, which consisted of him wearing only a white pair of lounge pants, giving Eira a wonderful view of his muscular arms and chest. He crossed the room and wrapped his arms around her waist.

"We finish this, and you can return whenever you wish."

"If we find a way to steal the chalice, I doubt Aytigin will let us return."

Cadeyrn kissed the top of her head. "I could eliminate Aytigin from the picture, if it's what you want."

"And if you don't succeed, I lose you and the chalice." Eira turned with his arms still around her so she could look in his eyes. "Do you find the idea of killing another appealing?"

Eira put her hand over his tattoo. It glowed faintly, and his muscles flexed at her touch.

"I'm a soldier, Eira. You know I've done it."

"But do you enjoy it? Is killing something you're eager to do?"

The tattoo faded, and his muscles relaxed again.

"No, but I'm also willing to do what's needed to save our families and Cresin. I'm especially willing to do what's needed to ensure you aren't trapped here the rest of your life."

Eira embraced him and rested her head against his chest. It was what she'd been afraid of, and what she was afraid of asking herself. She'd always thought she would be willing to do anything to ensure her kingdom and crown, but now she wasn't sure. For each option, she lost something. Removing Aytigin from the picture could be the easiest and most logical option—if Cadeyrn succeeded. Besides, it wouldn't mean there still wasn't a painful curse on the chalice when they touched it.

Beyond that, as painful as it was to admit, she pitied Aytigin. He was cruel, temperamental, and despicable. Yet there was something incredibly sad about the whole thing.

Eira stood on her tiptoes and kissed Cadeyrn. "A last resort. If it comes to it, I'll tell you. For now…"

"We don't have time for *for now*." Cadeyrn was melting as she continued to kiss him along the strong line of his jaw and across to his neck. "Tomorrow evening, we'll be awake early, before Aytigin, and capture the chalice. We'll be gone before he has the chance to ask you what your choice is."

Eira continued to kiss him and led him to the bed. She fell onto the mattress, with Cadeyrn on top of her, and wrapped her leg around his.

She wanted to be with him one last time before it all changed.

Chapter Twenty-Two

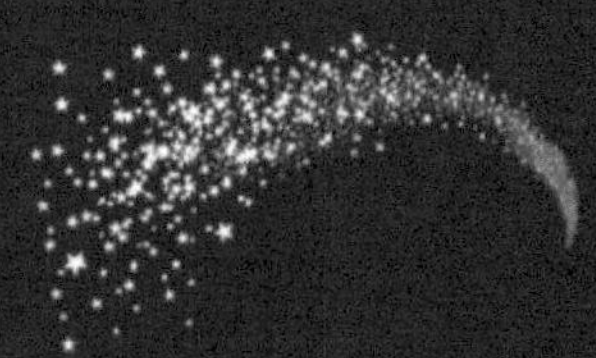

EIRA

Eira's heart stopped the next evening when she saw the space next to her in bed was empty. Maybe Cadeyrn had gone in search of the chalice without her.

This didn't bring her any comfort, and she changed into the dress Aytigin had provided her for the day and went to the dining hall to see if he'd gone to eat, or if Aytigin had seen him. But their evening breakfast was not laid out the way it had been the previous nights. Instead, the chalice stood in the center of the table, and the dark blue orb glowed next to it.

Eira's heart lurched into her throat at the sight of Cadeyrn beside the stable, struggling to free himself from what must have been invisible bonds tying his arms together.

Aytigin casually stood from where he sat at the end of the table in his usual chair, as though this were a leisurely gathering.

Eira strode towards Aytigin, her eyes narrowed to mere slits.

"What is this?"

"Let's get this done, shall we, little Luana?"

"What do you mean?"

Aytigin circled his claw around the edge of the chalice.

"I knew when I showed you the chalice, you and your lover would devise a plan to steal it in spite of my warnings."

Eira gaped, and her chest tightened.

Aytigin sighed and rested against the table, arms crossed.

"Don't be so worried. I didn't spy on you. But by the way you're blushing, I can assume what may have happened after you devised your plans." He gazed over her and grinned. "And since you refused my offer, I can only assume you still plan on stealing it. So I made sure your prince was taken care of, and instead of our usual meal with us arguing, I have a proposition for you."

Cadeyrn fought against his invisible bonds. "We won't accept anything from you."

Aytigin waved him off. "It's not your choice, servant of Aros. It's our little Luana's."

Something about the way he said the nickname made Eira shiver and want to recoil away. It rolled off his tongue as though he were salivating over a good meal.

"I've already told you," she said. "I won't stay."

Aytigin snapped his fingers, and Cadeyrn collapsed to his knees with a grunt. Eira tried to go to his side, but Aytigin outstretched his arm and she was prevented from doing so.

"Eira, don't," Cadeyrn said through clenched teeth.

His body trembled with pain, but he didn't cry out.

She glared at the dragon, not caring how strong the frost was forming across the ground from her anger.

"You can only threaten him so long. If you were to harm him, you would no longer have anything to bargain with."

With another snap of his fingers, Aytigin released whatever pain he was inflicting on Cadeyrn, who gasped with relief.

The dragon cocked his head. "And what about Rose? I can make her incredibly miserable."

The black clouds on the orb cleared to show the outside of the castle. Giants made from snow and ice were raised from the ground and carried weapons as tall as a door. The scene changed to show Rose huddled in a dark empty room. In the distance, the cries of the queen's soldiers echoed, and Rose hid herself deeper in the shadows. Aytigin blew over the orb, and an icy wind blew through her hiding place. She gasped and coughed, and her skin turned blue.

"Stop!" Eira threw her hands to her mouth.

He couldn't hurt Rose. She wouldn't let him.

Aytigin obeyed, and with a wave of his hand, Rose's skin returned to its usual soft and freckled state, and she slumped where she sat. Although, frozen tears remained on her cheeks.

"We don't know if what he's showing us is real," Cadeyrn growled.

Cadeyrn could be right. But what if he isn't? Eira could never live with herself.

She turned away from Cadeyrn, to Aytigin. "What is your proposition?"

He passed the chalice from hand to hand. "I will give Cadeyrn your precious chalice so he can wake your father. You will stay here and live with me."

"I've already refused."

Aytigin raised a finger and waved it back and forth as though scolding a small child.

"You do not need to stay forever. You only need to complete the task of restoring the portion of the castle I told you about. And once the restoration is done, you may go free."

Eira and Cadeyrn exchanged a look. It seemed too easy.

Cadeyrn shook his head. "Eira, you do not stay here a minute longer than necessary."

Aytigin slammed the chalice on the table, making them both jump.

"Don't you see how ridiculous this is? You claim you're Luana's Chosen and have your kingdoms best interest at heart, but you refuse this one small thing. What does it matter if you are here or there as long as your father and kingdom are saved? Besides, you have all the texts and powers of Luana here at your fingertips. What else could you possibly want?"

She couldn't deny the point he was making. The whole purpose of this quest was to save her father and Cresin. Naturally, she'd assumed she would also be there and would be able to continue to live in Farren Castle and become queen someday. But who was to say she couldn't do it from this castle? Especially if she didn't have to stay forever.

Cadeyrn was pleading to her with his eyes to not accept the bargain. She shouldn't trust this dragon, and it surely must have been a trick. Yet perhaps this only had to be a temporary solution.

"Tell me more about the task."

"The west wing of the castle is in complete disrepair, and it contains the temple. I can't imagine anyone more suited for the task than Luana's Chosen. Make it the most beautiful temple you've ever seen, and you will be free to go."

Fix one of Luana's temples? It would be difficult, surely, but not impossible. She would find a way to fix it. Or a way to escape. She was running out of options.

Eira pulled her shoulders back and met Aytigin's gaze.

"Agreed."

"Eira, no!" Cadeyrn was freed from his invisible bonds, and he ran to her, held her face in his hands and kissed her. "Eira, what are you thinking?"

"I'll return to you, I promise."

Aytigin latched a claw to Cadeyrn's collar, pulled him back, and thrust the chalice into his hands. As Eira went to embrace him one last time, an icy band formed around her wrist and burned her skin. It reminded her of the betrothal band to Alvis, only instead of engravings of Isadore and Sanson, there was a dragon flying through the stars.

"Yes, we'll miss you dearly. But I fear you've outstayed your welcome." Aytigin's voice was light and airy as he pushed Cadeyrn away.

With a clap, Cadeyrn was gone.

He couldn't be gone. Not yet.

She cried out, and spun and searched until she faced Aytigin.

"You could have let me say goodbye!"

Aytigin grabbed Eira's wrist, his face so close to hers she could see each glimmer of the scales on his skin.

He smirked. "You have no time to waste, do you?"

In a moment, they were in the west wing, with the tall doors and the Gallery of Chosens. The doors Eira had found painful and impossible to push opened with Aytigin's swift kick, while still holding Eira's wrist, and they went inside.

To say the temple was in shambles would have been an understatement. It was as though someone had taken a hammer and thrashed it about the space, demolishing each item in its path. There were hardly even two pieces of items to put together to make a whole. She wouldn't be able to walk a step without tripping on debris.

Aytigin finally released her wrist and walked around the room. An air of sadness surrounded him as he looked around.

"I'm sure you'll want to get started straight away. This used to be beautiful. With your powers coming into their own these past few days, surely Luana will guide your hands to make it glorious once again."

Eira rubbed the new icy band around her wrist and followed his gaze.

"Surely even the best of the building attendants would not be able to repair this room on their own."

He turned on one heel and went back to the door. "I'm sure you'll manage. I'll have lunch and dinner brought here for you, and I'll see you at breakfast tomorrow. Feel free to retire to your chambers once you are ready to sleep. You now have full access to the castle. Have a good day."

The doors slammed when he left, and Eira jumped. She stepped through the temple and pushed aside pieces of rubble with her foot to make a path. The temple seemed to go on for ages. Far larger than any temple she'd ever seen.

One piece on the ground caught her eye. It glimmered in the moonlight, and she knelt to look closer. It was the piece of a blade, but appeared to have been made of ice. She lifted it, and as soon as she did, the room went dark. A scream pierced through the room, and Eira threw the blade to the ground again.

Something of this nature should never enter the realm of Luana. She would never allow it. Would she?

Eira ran back to the door and pounded on it, yelling Aytigin's name, but he never replied. He wouldn't let her go until this task was complete, and now she was alone. Cadeyrn was gone.

She sank to the ground and let the tears fall.

What have I done?

Chapter Twenty-Three

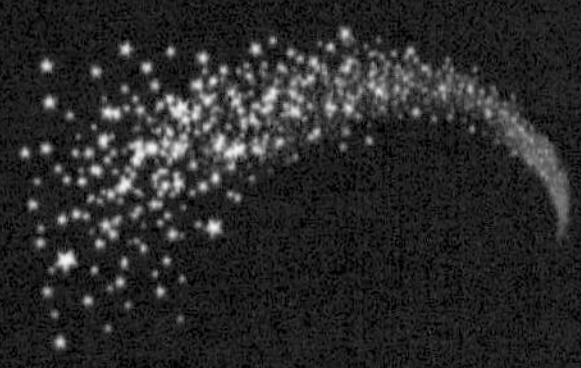

EIRA

THE SCREAMING CAME FIRST, AS USUAL, AND THE WORLD TURNED BLACK. Images flashed before Eira's eyes. Pools of blood. Blots of ice flying. A woman writhing in pain on the table.

But the screaming. All the screaming.

Eira jerked her hand away from the shattered stone table and held it close, as if she'd been burned, as she cried. It was the piece she'd been focusing on the last few days—weeks? She wasn't sure anymore, for there were large enough pieces where she could figure out where they went and meld them together. But the screams were the worst here.

Eira didn't bother wiping away the tears anymore as she cowered over the table. They were constant now.

How could she possibly do all this when she had to hear the pain all through the process and it continued to haunt her in her dreams? But others had experienced similar things and pushed through. Cadeyrn, who'd been in battles and saw and heard people suffering all the time. Rose, who had her own pain each day.

Eira tried to bear her burden the way they bore theirs.

Maybe she should forget the whole thing. She could make a life here. Grow her powers. Maybe even someday convince Aytigin to let others in and build a court there. Besides, Rose could take care of

Cresin. She would have been able to solve all of this ages ago. What kingdom would want a queen who couldn't come and save them herself?

It wasn't as though life in the mountains was terrible—when she wasn't working on the task, anyway. Outside the temple, Aytigin treated her like royalty. Almost as if she were Luana herself. Lavish meals, gorgeous gowns, and nearly anything she wanted at her fingertips. When she wasn't working, he discussed sacred texts with her and the growth of her powers. At first, it'd been enough to help her get through this task.

Not anymore.

At least Cadeyrn could move on. There wasn't a lack of women seeking his attention.

Eira shook her head. No. She'd promised him, and herself. She was going to complete this and see him again. She'd see them all again.

She had to keep going.

Eira rolled her stiff shoulders and placed her hands back on the table. The screams rang through the temple, shaking the debris and walls. She covered her ears and collapsed to her knees, sobbing, but the images wouldn't leave her. Men with cuts all over their arms. Pools of icy water, and people crashing into them. A woman writhed and cried on the table. She had long brown hair and blue eyes, and wore a thin white gown that may as well not have even been present for what little it covered. All over her pale body were what seemed to be tattoos, but were inscriptions made of ice seared into her skin like brands. Across her arms. Her legs. Breasts. Hands. Neck.

Traitor. Whore. Adulteress. Heretic.

"Let me go, please." Tears poured from the woman's eyes as she sobbed and begged.

Her wish would not be granted, though, as Gallis's chalice was thrust toward her and she was forced to drink its contents.

Eira curled onto the ground in a heap and let the tears fall. The visions had never shown this before, and she didn't need to be told the woman was Malle. She recognized her from the paintings. This wasn't a place worship. It was a torture chamber. And now it was her own torture chamber as she had to relive its events.

There had to be another way to get home. She couldn't do this anymore.

Eira slammed her wrist over and over, until it was trembling in pain. But the band didn't receive even a dent.

She wouldn't do it.

Eira crawled back to the doors and scrambled to her feet to open them again. She slammed the doors behind her and sank to the ground once again, unable to control her tears. This wasn't how it was supposed to be. There had to be another way.

Forcing herself to stand, Eira rose and traipsed through the castle to find Aytigin. Her footsteps echoed against the ice-covered walls, and she could hear another person's steps behind her. The remnants of her visions haunted her, and she resisted the temptation to look over her shoulder after each step.

She'd never been in his apartments but knew the direction he went each morning when the night was over. By now, she'd done enough exploring to have gotten an idea of the ways the castle tricked you. She'd learned to predict when a hall would turn, or a staircase vanish and reappear in a new location.

Near the top is where he would sleep, surely. It was the closest to the stars.

The higher she went, the darker the space became, and Eira had to adjust her eyes, even with a stardust lantern to guide her feet.

It was becoming easier to see in the dark now. When she got closer to the top, there were distant voices. One of them Aytigin's.

"She won't be leaving any time soon."

"But she could leave? Someday?"

The second voice was a woman's, and a chill ran down Eira's spine.

She tiptoed near a door.

"It's not likely," Aytigin replied.

Eira nudged the door open enough to see a sliver inside. Aytigin stood before a floor-length silver mirror, with his back to the door. His white tail swished across the ground, back and forth, like a metronome.

"This wasn't part of the deal," the woman said.

Her voice was cool and flowing, and Eira knew it was Amelia.

She curled into herself and wanted to run. But she couldn't. If

Aytigin was working with Amelia, there was more to this than Eira thought.

She leaned forward to listen.

"There was to be no chance of her leaving. Ever. You got to have your precious *little Luana* for the rest of time, and she was out of my hair."

If Amelia was speaking with Aytigin…what did it mean for the others?

Eira ran back to her chambers. Echoes of footsteps rang through her ears. Were they hers? Someone else's? Or was it just her imagination from the paranoia and the visions still haunting her?

Once in her room, she changed into her traveling clothes from the Paravian temple and gathered as many things as she could carry. There had to be a way out of this place. It had been part of her plan all along, anyway—to escape if the task was taking too much time. She shouldn't have waited this long.

However long it had been.

Clothes, a blanket, a cloak, daggers—thankfully, Aytigin hadn't disposed of all her weapons. A tray of food was prepared on the table, and Eira nabbed a red apple. She strummed her fingers on the fruit as she considered what else she should try to bring. This food should fit in the bag and would be something to tide her over, at least until she found Priestess Corvina and the other priestesses at the temple. That had to be her first stop. Maybe they knew about Cadeyrn and Rose's whereabouts.

Eira took a bite into the apple and gathered the rest of the fruit. But while it was sweet at first, the apple became bitter, soft, and sour all at once, causing Eira to gag and drop it to the ground with a soft thump.

The room turned fuzzy, and her head was light. She fell to her knees and coughed. Everything turned frigid.

A figure appeared before her and knelt. Amelia's blue eyes and golden hair filled Eira's vision. She tried to gasp but couldn't. Her throat was closing in.

"If I want something done right, I need to do it myself." Amelia held Eira's chin and jerked her hand away. "I knew you were listening. You spoiled creature. You and your family ruined me. Did you know that? Your father took me from my home in the Dravian Islands. Took me from my lover. My daughter."

Eira could only blink as she fell to the side and attempted to gasp for breath.

"Oh, yes, there's much you don't know. I didn't want to be queen. But the longer I watched you, the more I wanted to take it all away from you. Now it's my turn to tell people how to run their lives. You won't get in my way any longer." Amelia pushed Eira onto her back with her foot and sat in a chair, where she crossed her legs and stared at Eira. "Watching you suffer is the most wonderful part of it. And I'll be here until the bitter end."

Darkness closed in on Eira. Not Luana's darkness, which brought peace and comfort. This was cold and empty.

Eira shuddered as the world turned black and silent, until there was nothing.

Chapter Twenty-Four

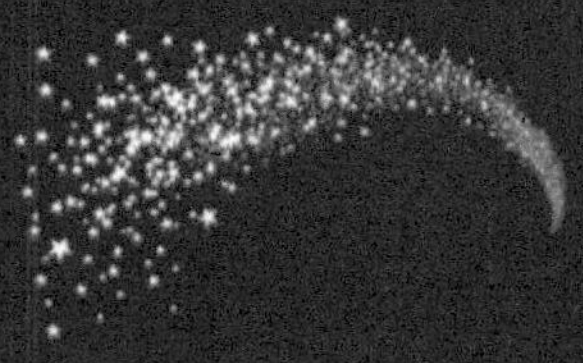

EIRA

Eira walked along a deserted path but couldn't remember where she had come from or where she was going. The world was empty save for snow and ice, with the night sky looming over her head. She'd been walking for so long her legs were growing numb. But when had she begun?

Eira blinked. She couldn't remember.

But she wasn't walking any longer.

When had that happened?

She looked about to see two paths in front of her. One was dark. Snow-covered trees crowded the path, and where it led was impossible to see. The other path glowed with starlight, destination also unclear.

Images of the people she knew floated around and away from her. Rose. Cadeyrn. Alvis. Grandmother. Father. Aytigin. Cynth. Corvina. Cal.

Amelia's face appeared and smiled. The queen grew larger and larger until it appeared as though she was going to eat Eira. Then she disappeared.

Eira tried to lift her foot to move forward, but nothing happened. No matter what she did, Eira couldn't move.

She was frozen.

Chapter Twenty-Five

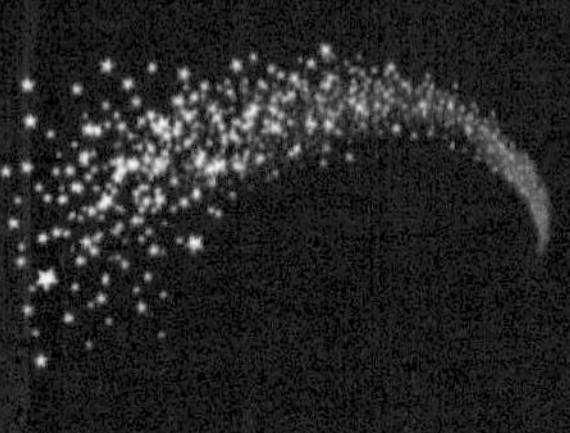

EIRA

Eira lay on the snow-covered ground and watched the stars. There was no sun or moon. Only endless night. In spite of the snow, Eira wasn't cold. Instead, it was like lying on a soft blanket and floating through the sky.

She took in a deep breath of the scentless air.

Nothing was real here. Nothing to grasp or hold on to.

Eira rocked her head against the snow, letting the flakes tangle in her hair. She should stand and pick a path, but it was no use. Any time she made a decision, her feet weren't able to move. Not as though it mattered which path she chose, anyway.

There was so much more she should have done. She should have seen Amelia's threat sooner. Should have listened to the priest. There should have been another way to get the chalice.

Eira closed her eyes and bit her lip. No wonder she was here. She couldn't save her family from Amelia or escape the castle. So how could she protect and take care of her kingdom?

At least in this place she had the stars and the snow. The only things which ever made sense to her. The pretty stars and snow. Maybe it's all she ever was. A pretty thing who could do tricks with elements that sparkled so people could feel better, while others handled the serious matters. The dirty and difficult things.

Eira wasn't dirty and difficult. She was beautiful and delicate and obedient.

"Rise, my child."

Eira blinked at the sound of the voice, which echoed through the air. She'd heard this voice once before, when she and Cadeyrn were stuck in the ice by the castle. It was the same voice who taught her to see through the darkness.

She sat and looked around. "Luana?"

From between the two paths, a figure formed in the darkness. Her long dress flowed around her as though it were made of air, and Eira could scarcely tell where the dress ended and the rest of the world began. The figure didn't leave any footprints in the snow, but a trail of ice followed in her wake, while clouds of stars danced around her head. Her pale skin glowed, and light shone from her long black hair. The goddess was almost too beautiful to look at, but Eira couldn't tear her eyes away.

"Rise."

Luana extended a hand to Eira, and she took it, hoisting herself to her feet until she was standing in line with Luana's indigo eyes, where galaxies danced in their depths.

Eira had imagined many times what it would be like to meet Luana face to face. All of it vanished from her mind, and all she could do was stand in awe.

Until the tears came.

She couldn't stop them. For all of her failures. Her heartbreak. Cadeyrn. Alvis. Her family. Her kingdom. Whoever was being tortured in the castle. Even Aytigin, for all the harm he'd done and whatever had caused him to be what he was now. In spite of all of the tears Eira had shed over the past weeks, there were still more she'd bottled away inside that needed to be let out.

Luana welcomed Eira in a warm embrace the way a mother would her distraught child. She took in all of Eira's emotions as though she could soak and melt them away with the snow. They stood there for ages while Eira released all of it, until they finally stepped away from one another.

Eira wiped her eyes, then looked up at Luana. "What are you doing here?"

"Guiding you."

Eira looked toward the two paths. "You have the ingredients to break the curse?"

Luana gently smiled and guided Eira's face to look back at her with a soft touch of her fingertips, wiping a stray tear from Eira's eye.

"Not in that way. Let's go somewhere we're more comfortable."

The goddess flicked her wrist, and they were now standing on the moon. The world was far below, floating in a sea of stars. In the distance was the faint glow of Ray surrounding the world in a heavenly ring.

Luana led Eira to a resting place with large pillows and blankets spread over the ground, with a tray filled with fruit, cheese, bread, and a drink Eira was unfamiliar with. The cushions were like a cloud when sat on, and Eira marveled at where she was and the company she was with. Luana gestured to the food, and they nibbled on the berries.

"You have done well, my daughter."

The goddess radiated elegance and beauty. When she moved, it was as though she floated, or even danced.

"How you have grown and learned of your powers these past weeks has made me proud. But I know you have doubts and questions."

Eira looked at the food in her hand, trying to decide what to say. She didn't want to appear weak or unfaithful in Luana's eyes. But perhaps this was the time and place to receive answers.

"I'm lost, Luana. I always thought I was prepared to be your Chosen and to rule Cresin. I've wanted nothing more than to follow you and dedicate my life to you. Am I truly your Chosen? I'm not sure what it means. Am I able to fill the role?"

Luana chuckled and took a sip from her glass. "I wondered if this was to be your question. It was never my intention to have a chosen one. It was never Ray's, either. The tradition began with Queen Isadore and King Sanson. She was the firstborn heir for Cresin, he for Oxare."

Eira relaxed and listened, even though it was a story she was familiar with.

"At their birth, the kingdoms were at war with one another. Together, they fought for peace. They married as a way for their two kingdoms to become allies. It took much time, but eventually peace was achieved. Thus, the tradition began centuries ago by our followers, as a way to remind the people of where they came from. Both of the world's origin, but also how the kingdoms came to be in the peaceful place they are now. It is a lovely idea. But not something either Ray or I ordained. You are Chosen because the people have made you so."

Eira's shoulders sank at the answer, and she tried to absorb it. Her whole life had been based on being Luana's Chosen. But it wasn't real. She was simply another royal who happened to be dedicated to the goddess. Given more power than others, yes, but nothing unique. Like so many other things that had happened and been discovered over the past days, it changed everything yet nothing at all.

"Isadore knew she needed assistance to achieve the peace she and Sanson dreamed of. She sought me out and convinced Sanson to do the same of Ray. It is how they gained the magic which you all now consider legendary. You do not need to step into this role if you do not wish. Perhaps being the heir, which you were born into, is not your choice. But how your dedication to me plays into your role *is* your decision."

"What about the magic I have?" Eira said.

Hers was nothing compared to what had been told of Queen Isadore, but it was more than even the high priestesses.

"Because you were believed to be Chosen, the high priestess performed a more powerful and potent dedication ceremony for you. Your training was more intense than it was for the priestesses and others dedicated to me. Therefore, you have more abilities than the others."

Eira took a drink and leaned back into the pillows. All she knew about her life fell to pieces in one conversation.

"What about my relationship with Alvis?"

Luana leaned over with a conspiratorial grin. "Or perhaps you are asking about Cadeyrn? It appears as though you have already chosen your way in that matter."

Eira took another drink to hide how her face flushed.

"I did not plan it this way."

"What way did you plan it?"

Eira did not have an answer, ashamed of her behavior.

"Will Alvis be hurt when we tell him?"

"I imagine so. But he is a good man, and an intelligent one. I believe, in time, he will see what was always before him in plain sight and know it is for the best." Luana placed a hand on Eira's arm. "What you and Cadeyrn have is true. It reminds me much of Ray and I. We never would have created and built what we have if we didn't have the love and passion for one another that we do. If you are my Chosen, you need to be with someone you truly love. Not out of obligation or duty, no matter how good of a man he is. You need to be with someone who speaks to your heart the way Ray speaks to mine. Perhaps it did not happen in the most ideal manner, and you will have to deal with the repercussions. However, I believe Cadeyrn is good for you and you for him."

"You said there was no *Luana's Chosen*."

"Not unless you want there to be."

"What would I do?"

Luana stood and walked ahead to look over the universe before them.

"The night is an interesting time. There are those who fear it, for it is dark, many times cold, mysterious, a time for dark deeds, and strange creatures roam about. At least, strange to them. But they do not see what we do. The quietness, the beauty, elegance, and comfort. There's something lovely about a quiet night with only the stars around you." Luana wrapped her arms around herself.

The peacefulness of night was always what Eira loved about being dedicated to Luana.

"And the moon and stars bring light to the darkness," Luana said. "If I have a Chosen, I need her to bring light while also embracing the darkness. Isadore was willing to do so to bring peace to the kingdoms."

Eira stood beside Luana and looked out at the vast sky. Never had she seen it without obstruction of trees, or the castle, or birds flying overhead. Nothing separated her from the stars standing here. She felt both incredibly small and as though she could conquer anything.

"But the kingdoms are still in a time of peace," Eira said. "Until recent events, at least."

"There may not be any large battles between kingdoms and nations, but it doesn't mean people are not at war with one another. As you have learned, people hold grudges and do terrible things to one another. Not all wars are visible."

"Has my father not been taking care of his people?"

Luana shook her head and covered her face with her hands.

"No, that is not what I meant. He is a fair and kind king. But no matter how great of a ruler someone is, it does not mean everything, and everyone, is perfect. Even you will not be perfect all of the time, Eira."

This was a truth Eira could not deny, as much as she wanted to. The weight of being heir and Chosen was always there. It was a constant pressure to be strong, responsible, and perfect. Someone was always wanting something, and a brave face was put on no matter the circumstance.

Now, some of these weights were lifted. She didn't have to be the Chosen. She was not going to be perfect all the time.

"I need someone who is not afraid of the darkness and is willing to go into it. Isadore knew perfect peace for all of time was not an achievable goal, but she was willing to dive into those dark moments. We can bring comfort to people and bring them through it. But it will have a price. When you gain my power, you will also gain control of this castle. It will heed to your will and recognize you as its mistress. This means Aytigin will also be bound to you, due to his curse."

"What do you mean? Couldn't I erase it?"

"You may have many of my powers, but it does not mean you *are* me. The temple here still needs to be restored before he can no longer be bound to you."

Eira had to pause at the phrasing. Bound to *her*, not the castle. All this time, she thought Aytigin was trapped to the castle itself.

"What do you mean by *bound to me*?"

"Aytigin is trapped here as punishment for past crimes. If I still walked among people, he would be bound to *me*. As I do not, it is my castle. Since the castle will see you as mistress, his punishment is connected to you. If you leave the mountains, he will be able to also, as long as he is near you. You may be separated to an extent, but if you go too far, you'll find it won't be pleasant."

Eira's stomach lurched at this additional revelation. The idea of being bound to Aytigin was not one she relished. Yet if they were able to complete the restoration…

"What do you say?"

The world was not perfect. It was a difficult lesson. Life had been sheltered until now, and it was not going to change any time soon. It would be easy to deny what Luana was offering and turn back to life before.

It should not have been something to second guess, as it was a title given to her from birth. There was something different about now, though. It was right, in spite of the additional strings with Aytigin.

"What do I need to do?"

Luana clasped Eira's hand, and they were thrown into pitch darkness.

Chapter Twenty-Six

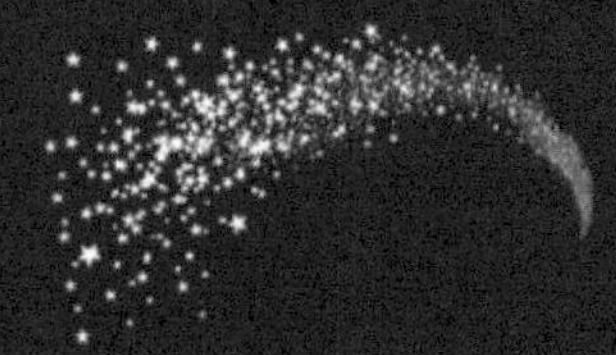

EIRA

Eira couldn't breathe when she opened her eyes to pitch darkness. She was naked. And encased in ice. The world was colder than Stula's cave. Colder than the mountain. Colder than anything. It was worse than her dedication ceremony as a child. Worse than when they were trapped outside of Luana's castle.

Shooting stars zoomed toward her in blinding light, overtaking the darkness, and crashed into her body. It all happened so quickly she couldn't even cry out.

It went on like this, repeating itself. Each time, Eira's body withstood more. The ice, the darkness, and the stars absorbing into her skin until they were one and the same. Her essence glowed and shimmered with it.

Eira closed her eyes and tried to will the pain away.

"Are you ready?" Luana's voice echoed all around.

Eira opened her eyes.

She stood on the balcony and looked toward her love, Ray, who stood on the balcony of their master suite and watched the artificial sunset. Luana had done such a marvelous job creating it, one would never know it wasn't real. Except for Ray, of course, considering he was the one who made the real one rise and set each day and evening.

No. That wasn't right. She wasn't Eira. She was…Luana. She sensed the power coursing through her veins and heard Luana's thoughts. The overpowering love she had for Ray. Devotion, passion… but her heart was also breaking. Things were broken in the world as they'd been living her in the castle. The weight of it all pressed on Luana like she was being crushed by a boulder.

"This isn't working." Ray gripped the balcony railing with his tan hands as though he were about to crush it.

Instead, they turned pink and the rail melted at his touch. With a deep breath, he loosened his grip and the stone returned to its firm form. He was so powerful, yet gentle, even in their distress.

"I know." Luana rubbed his muscular arm in comfort.

She couldn't stand to see him this way. They'd been trying this for months, him staying with her and her staying with him. It was supposed to be the perfect plan so they could each be in their own realms but also together. Confessing it hadn't worked was painful. The repercussions of the world staying in daylight at all hours for weeks at a time and switching to night for the next several weeks had devastated this new world they'd created. They needed to make it right again.

"We'll still see one another." Ray's voice strained, but he remained calm. "Twice a day. Sunrise and sunset. Twice a day for all eternity. Would you be able to live with it?"

In theory, it was plenty. Even in this short age the world had existed, Luana could tell it was more than many would have in their quick lifetime. These humans who walked among them had such fleeting lives. Yet the reality seemed much starker. Sunrise and sunset went by in such a short time. Hardly enough to have a conversation.

But they'd grown to love these humans and this world. The one which exploded into being when they came together. After everything, they couldn't let it go to waste.

"We can live with it. We have to."

Luana—no, now Eira again—closed her eyes and the scene faded. The images before her dissolved into the stars and flew toward her, crashing through the ice and pouring into her tattoo. It shone brighter than the sun, and the light spread from her chest all the way to her arms and fingers.

The hope of a new world.

She opened her eyes at the sound of a scream. Smoke filled the air, and she blinked to stop her eyes from watering. Soldiers walked among shabby tents and sat on the muddy grass, not caring if their blood-soaked clothing became even dirtier. She lifted her arm to see leather armor strapped around her body.

She was Queen Isadore now.

Another scream came from the attendant's tent. Isadore cringed and walked away. Not as though there was much to walk away to. Only more tents filled with wounded soldiers. Or a cart taking the dead away. Their rotting stench offended her nostrils, a smell she'd never grown used to. It was a reminder of the people she'd failed. The ones who'd risked and lost everything for a cause she wasn't sure was worth it anymore. Especially if they didn't succeed.

She couldn't be there anymore. Listening to their cries of pain as the attendants attempted to piece soldiers back together after another failed battle against the Oxarian army was growing to be too much. Each day, she sat at their sides, encouraging them, speaking words of comfort, bringing comforting darkness and bright stars to the tents. But it wasn't enough.

She broke into a sprint and ran away from it all. She was supposed to be their leader and ruler. With her remarkable likeness to Luana, she'd been dedicated to the goddess at a young age, and her affinity for ice was beyond compare. Yet she still felt inadequate.

The ground was icy and slick, but she never slid. Each step only made the ice thicker, and snow formed all around. She stopped at the edge of a riverbank and collapsed to her knees. Dirt and dried blood flaked off her fighting leathers, sprinkling across the snow and ice like the blood sprayed across the battlefield. She slammed her hands to the ground and screamed.

"Queen Isadore?" a man said.

On the other side of the river, the grass was green, without a single shred of ice or snow. A tall man stood on the edge in his military uniform. It was dirty and covered in blood the way hers was, but pieces of its ornaments still glimmered in the moonlight.

"King Sanson."

She'd seen him from a distance, and in portraits, of course. It was widely known that the Oxarian king was handsome. In person, even after battle, he was breathtaking.

This was ridiculous. He was her enemy. He shouldn't be breathtaking.

Isadore stood as gracefully as she could. She could kill him on the spot. One blast of ice and he'd be frozen, and this whole thing could be over. Surely he must have been thinking the same thing of her. Only, he could send a pillar of fire her way and she'd burn to a crisp. Yet there they stood, staring at one another.

When he called her name, it hadn't been angry or accusatory. Instead, it was gentle and filled with concern. Perhaps he was trying to catch her off guard or lead her into a false sense of security. But he didn't move.

Isadore took a step forward into the river water, and it turned to ice. The whole river turned solid as stone, and she stepped on it. Sanson did the same on his side. Step by step, they walked until they met in the middle.

"How does this end?" Sanson turned to his side and propped his head in his hand.

Firelight flickered over his face, illuminating his dark skin and gentle eyes. For weeks, they'd been meeting in secret like this ever since they met across the river after battle. Hiding in the forest, in caves, or even once in an abandoned barn. They talked and made love and planned.

"We'll negotiate with each of our councils." Isadore ran her fingers through his long hair and memorized the planes of his face. "And we'll unite our kingdoms."

"They're going to need more than negotiations."

Isadore rose from her reclined position and sat straight.

"What did you have in mind?"

Sanson took her hands in his. "We both know our kingdoms will be stronger united, and you and I are stronger together. Both our powers are stronger than most who are dedicated to the same deities. What's more, is you're dedicated to Luana, and I to Ray."

Isadore rubbed the back of her neck and rolled it. So much sleeping on the ground during war and spending the night in caves with Sanson made her body stiff.

"Yes. And?"

"Luana and Ray is the greatest love story of all time. Both of our kingdoms value it over all the others. How often is it where the king of Oxare, the firstborn in the line to the throne, is dedicated to Ray, and in the same generation the queen of Cresin, the first in line for the throne, is dedicated to Luana? What if we use it?"

Isadore smiled. "Go on."

The scene dissolved again, and Eira looked around. The ancient king and queen faded into the ice encasing Eira, and it caved in on her. She pressed her hands and feet against the ice walls, but no matter how hard she pushed, it kept closing in, molding itself around Eira's body like a second skin. Her tattoo glowed again, and the light spread across her body and the ice. With a flash, the ice squeezed around her limbs until she thought her bones would snap. She wanted to scream, but no sound came out. The ice sank into her skin, and her muscles expanded and contracted.

"Your strength."

Eira closed her eyes once again.

She now stood at the city gate of Farren. Only a robe covered her body, and she clung to it as though there was nothing left. Which, there wasn't. All of it was gone. Malle's name, title, home, family…she had nothing. She *was* nothing. At least, not to the people of Cresin anymore. She'd barely had the chance to make herself decent before being dragged before the council.

Malle stood at the city gates with nothing but the robe on her back, yet she'd never been more satisfied. She should have been devastated, but she was…relieved. She'd never handled well the pressure of being the Chosen, and after she married that…monster…each day had been bleaker than the last. Now she was finally free. She could go wherever she wanted.

With him.

He was waiting, and they no longer had to hide their relationship. They could go off and live their lives how they pleased.

The cries and screams coming from the city square took Malle out of her joyous haze. Her heart plummeted into her stomach. Surely news of her banishment and excommunication hadn't spread so far yet.

In spite of how fast Malle ran, when she arrived in the city square it was too late. The mob was scattering, and in the center was Aytigin in a crumpled heap. Streams of ice stretched out around him, and shadows hovered above. One of his wings hung at an odd angle. He wasn't breathing.

The world around Malle froze, and her breath left along with his.

No. This wasn't how it was supposed to happen. They were supposed to be free to go about and live their lives. No more obligations or abusive husbands or secrecy. This was their time to be together. He couldn't be…

Malle fell to her knees at his side and shook his icy shoulder.

He didn't budge.

No.

No. No. No. No. No.

She couldn't control her sobs as she collapsed into him. How could they do this? How could they…

Malle paused when she leaned against his chest. His heartbeat was weak and faint, but it was there. He wasn't dead.

It took weeks, but they'd finally arrived. Getting to the Paravian Mountains hadn't been easy with Aytigin in his state. But when they did, the priestesses were gracious enough to let them stay and had their attendants assist Aytigin as long as necessary. Gallis herself had given them permission to guard her enchanted chalice and were able to use it for Aytigin to return to his full strength.

The priestesses hadn't been so keen on their plan to seek out the legendary castle of Luana and Ray, but once he was on his feet—or wings, rather—they were determined. Their mutual devotion to Luana had brought them together, and with Aytigin's history with the goddess, they surely were the ones to finally find the castle.

There it was. Their new home. And they were going to restore it to all of its former glory.

Together.

Aytigin and the priests had all gathered in the temple again. They were coming more frequently these days once word spread about how Malle and Aytigin had found Luana's legendary castle. There weren't many male priests of Luana anymore, but the remaining few still loved to experiment with new ways to come closer to the goddess.

Malle had observed their rituals many times. It was horrifying. Freezing themselves and submitting to the darkness, and being revived by the chalice. Toeing the line between life and death in a way one would imagine Stula's followers would experiment with—not Luana's. Even then, it would have been followers of Stula who warped her magic.

Aytigin promised he never experienced Luana's presence in such a way since he'd walked by her side so long ago.

The sounds which came from the temple sent chills across her skin. But she had to admit she was curious.

The magnificent doors opened, and the priests all waited inside. They were lined along the sides leading to a table where Aytigin stood like a groom waiting for his bride. The room was cold—colder than any other places in the mountain—and the sheer gown she wore did little to shelter her.

Aytigin caressed her face with a gentle claw and gazed into her eyes as though no one else in the world existed.

"Are you sure you want to?"

Malle nodded. "If you can do it, I can, yes? I want to at least try."

"I'll do it with you."

They climbed onto the table together and lay side by side while the priests chanted. Aytigin turned over and kissed her as he had so many times before, and it still made her weak at the knees. The room grew darker and colder with each passing moment, and the priests surrounded the table. She knew it was going to be this way, for Aytigin had told her as much.

The priests drew in closer, and as they chanted, their faces grew more sinister.

"Traitor," one said.

Malle cried out, and the word was etched into her arm, in ice.

Aytigin never told her anything about this.

"Whore," spoke another, and the word was etched across her breast, covering her crescent moon tattoo.

"Wait…stop…what are you doing?" Aytigin sat up and tried to cover Malle with his body to protect her from their curses.

"Adulteress."

The pain started, and it was all Malle knew.

Eira was Luana once again and glared at Aytigin.

"What have you done?" Luana shouted as the room shook and pieces of marble from the walls fell and crumbled to the ground.

It was already ruined when she arrived, for Aytigin in his anguish had destroyed all that lay in his path, including the priests who'd been with him.

She pointed at the table in the center of this so-called temple, where a dead girl lay.

"Malle is dead! How could you have let this happen? I trusted you!"

Aytigin knelt before her, eyes bloodshot and puffy from his weeping. He was a broken man, but Luana couldn't find it in herself to pity or care. Because of his foolishness and obsession, Malle, one of her own, was gone. This poor young woman, who'd endured so much and hoped for so much, was led to such a tragic end. And all in the name of Luana. Her name.

"The…the chalice…" he said,"…it was supposed to…"

Luana extended her hands, and bolts of ice shot out of them, smashing more of the room to bits.

"The chalice," she said. "A gift my friend Gallis entrusted me and my followers with, and you abused it. Gallis's chalice is meant to heal people, not for some sick act of claimed devotion."

"Luana, your grace. I loved her. If I knew they would… I didn't know the priests were going to…I trusted them—"

"Do not speak to me of love, for clearly you don't know what it is. You have destroyed this place and all it was to stand for. You've warped the gifts I've given my followers into something disgusting and torturous. Your lover is dead. You are to remain here the rest of your days. Or at least until someone worthy can come and bring this room of worship back to its former glory. Then, and only then, will you be able to leave."

A band of ice formed around Aytigin's wrist. He didn't bother to try and remove it.

"You will also guard Gallis's chalice. No one is to use it ever again, since it appears as though everyone has forgotten its purpose. Until someone intends to use it for good and not their own personal gain, it will remain here. I will know if you've abused its power again."

Luana went to the table and scooped Malle's body into her arms with the tenderness of a mother carrying her sleeping child. Without saying another word, or even looking at Aytigin, she took Malle out of the castle.

Aytigin's roars echoed across the mountains as Luana buried her. It wasn't the royal and honorable burial the princess deserved, but it was high in the mountains. As close to the sky as Luana could find.

There, she wept.

Darkness rolled over the scene in dark clouds until Eira was herself once again. It drew in around her and crept over her body, making it vanish. The darkness wasn't cold. It didn't hurt. It merely existed. Eira didn't resist it the way she had with the stars and ice. She let it all consume her. Not only her body, but her soul.

"The reality and beauty of the darkness."

Eira saw all of their stories through their eyes. Each Chosen of Luana. Stories of triumph and tragedy, and all they did to serve their kingdoms and goddess. Their powers poured into Eira one by one, and she grew stronger. Not only her magic, but her knowledge and understanding of what was expected. She was now stronger because of them and all they'd done. Because they were now part of her.

Streams of ice flew toward Eira as she floated in the darkness. Instead of shattering, the ice seared into her skin. Cold consumed her. So much so, Eira couldn't even cry out. From her hair, to her skin, to the blood running through her veins, was ice.

Darkness enveloped Eira again, and she couldn't see anything until dots of stars appeared. Soon, they zoomed past her and there was a bright light. Then darkness again.

Eira opened her eyes.

Chapter Twenty-Seven

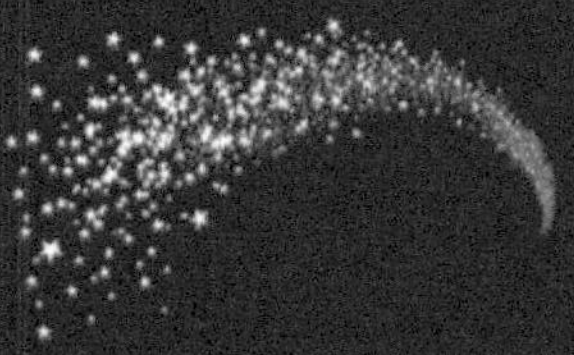

EIRA

The crossroads lay before Eira with two paths. Down one was bright light. Down the other was pitch black. Clouds of stars swirled around her hands, and the tattoo on her heart glowed. She took a step forward and paused. Then changed directions.

No.

That wasn't right, either.

Both were wrong.

She chose another way. A third path. One she would forge herself.

A patch of ice stretched before her with each step. Ribbons of darkness flew ahead, leaving stardust in their wake, and a tunnel opened, filled with stars.

Eira didn't even have to try to make it do her bidding.

She went forward.

Chapter Twenty-Eight

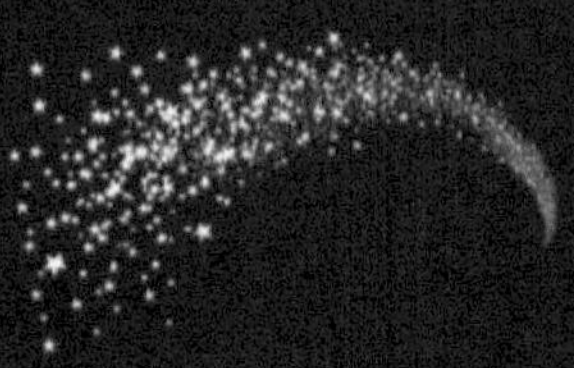

EIRA

Eira gasped when she awoke. She lay on the bed in her chambers in Luana's castle. A ring of ice surrounded it, and soft snow fell from the ceiling. But beyond this, nothing else was different.

Except for Eira. She'd changed.

The world was brighter and sharper now. The shadows in the corners and behind furniture were darker and deeper than they'd been before. She sat up and looked around. From the window, the night sky had a new depth to it. Stars she'd never seen before filled in the gaps, and the darkness was in layers before her.

Eira was alive, and Luana had bestowed on her more power than any other Chosen could have ever dreamed of. She needed to use it to save her kingdom.

She climbed out of the bed, and when her feet touched the icy ground, it was as though it were an early spring day. The snow melted the moment it fell on Eira, and it was barely a whisper on her skin. She was immune to the cold now, instead of merely having a higher tolerance for it.

How long had she been asleep? Had Cadeyrn already brought the chalice to the castle? Maybe Father was already awake. But what of the queen and Rose?

Regardless of what state the situation was in, Eira needed to return home as quickly as possible.

With a dragon at her side.

Out of the corner of her eye, Eira caught her reflection in the mirror. Streaks of sparkling silver stars ran through her dark hair, and her skin was luminous.

The mirror. She needed to find the mirror Aytigin had used. From what she'd been able to tell, it was how Amelia had gotten there to poison her. It surely was the fastest path to the castle. If it was where Cadeyrn and the chalice were.

The orb first. It could tell her where to find her lover and sister.

The castle seemed to part way for Eira as she stormed through the halls, the walls themselves making space for her. A path of ice and stars followed in her wake, and she didn't pause until she found the entrance to the treasure room. The painting moved to the side with only Eira raising her hand, obeying her thoughts.

This castle was hers now.

She didn't bother to resist a smile at the realization. Luana had said as much, but to see it at work was more satisfying than she'd imagined.

Her steps grew stronger and surer, and she imagined this must be how Rose felt approaching her men in the Guard, prepared to give them orders.

Aytigin stood hunched over the orb. His wings were lax behind him, and the tips dragged the ground like a heavy weight. He looked sad—the way he did in her visions. It didn't excuse all he did, but if what happened to Malle happed to Cadeyrn, Eira would have torn the world apart. She would have been as cursed as he was.

"Show me where Cadeyrn is."

Aytigin raised his head and stared at Eira, his eyes wide and unblinking.

"I'm dreaming."

"Hardly." Eira climbed the steps leading to the orb, and she gazed into its clouds.

"But you were—" Aytigin raised his hand to touch her, as though that would convince him she wasn't a figment of his imagination.

"And now I'm not."

Eira swatted his hand away, and it must have been enough to convince him, for he shook his head and blinked.

Aytigin focused on her and narrowed his brows. "How are you awake? What's happened to you? You're…different."

"Luana happened. Now show me Cadeyrn. Has he returned the chalice to the castle yet?"

Aytigin tapped the orb, and the clouds thinned away.

"It's only been a few days, so Cadeyrn has not returned to the castle. He is with the priestesses in the Paravian temple."

The image cleared to show that Cadeyrn and the priestesses weren't alone. Villagers filled the great hall, and he was handing weapons out to anyone who could hold them. Some were wounded and being cared for by the priestesses.

"What's happened?"

"Another raid. Refugees have been able to make it to the temple, but Queen Amelia's soldiers are barricading the doors, and no one can escape." Aytigin's voice was grave.

So much so, she thought he was concerned.

Amelia must have feared Eira wouldn't stay asleep forever, or else she wouldn't have sent out more raids. Or she knew Cadeyrn had the chalice. If he were to leave the temple, even more raids and violence would follow him until he was caught.

"We'll take him ourselves," Eira said.

"We?"

Eira was already walking to the steps. They didn't have time to lose if they wanted to help the refugees and save Cadeyrn.

"I'll explain on the way there."

Aytigin followed her. "Do you not recall the tiny detail of how neither of us can leave the mountains?"

Eira raised a brow. "We'll see about that."

There was an old saddle in one of the storerooms, and Eira worked at strapping it on Aytigin's enormous back when he shifted into his full dragon form. Luana never mentioned what it would be like to ride on the back of a dragon, and Eira imagined it was far different than on a horse. But if she was bound to Aytigin, surely no harm would come to her.

"What is your connection to Amelia?" Eira said.

"The mirror is a relic that was found in the castle years ago. I don't know how it got there. In recent months, Amelia started speaking to me through it." He crossed one of his white scaled arms over and showed Eira where to strap the saddle. "Not long ago, she promised me you'd come and that you were my key to breaking the curse. As long as I kept you here, she would keep you alive."

Eira had gathered as much. At least, the part about the curse.

She buckled the strap and tightened it. "And the poison?"

"I didn't know she was going to harm you. When I approached her, she claimed she kept her end of the bargain because you weren't technically dead."

In spite of herself, Eira believed him. The darkness inside her swirled at his words, and it reassured her of his truthfulness.

She hoisted herself onto the saddle after climbing a short rope ladder that led to the seat. Her head spun for a moment. He was much taller than any horse.

"Now are you going to tell me how you expect me to be able to deliver you, Cadeyrn, and the chalice to Farren Castle? The Paravian temple is the furthest I'm able to go."

Eira gripped the reigns and wrapped them around her wrists. This better help her hold on, because she didn't look forward to falling. Particularly once they were in flight.

"Out of anyone," she replied, "you'll appreciate this tale the most. I'll tell you as we fly."

Flying on the back of Aytigin was one of the most terrifying things Eira had ever done. Her arms and legs strained as she clung to the saddle, and her stomach twisted at the flapping of his wings. In time, though, she grew used to the movement. She leaned into his magic with her own. There was a bond between them she couldn't have explained if it hadn't been for what Luana told her about it.

They moved as one through the sky, and before long they arrived at the temple as she finished telling him her tale.

The temple door was barricaded by soldiers, and bodies of people who'd tried to escape were all around. Cadeyrn stood at the front, fighting off the soldiers and defending the victims, with others at his side who barely knew how to wield a sword.

Madness.

They hid on the cliff of a nearby mountain and watched the scene.

"We can't leave them here like this," Eira said.

"Aren't you eager to get to your father? You don't have time for a battle."

Perhaps not. But she couldn't leave them to fend for themselves while she whisked Cadeyrn and the chalice away.

Eira looked over Aytigin's broad shoulder. "You can see in the dark, correct?"

He huffed, and a puff of white ice clouds came from his nose.

"Of course."

"Good."

It was time she put these new powers to the test.

They swooped out from their post and toward the temple. When they were near, Eira spread her arms and gathered all the shadows she could find and dug deep inside herself for all the darkness she held. As they circled the temple, a blanket of darkness followed, covering all in their presence. People shouted as they were blinded, and the sounds of swords clashing came to a halt. Aytigin blew an arctic wind over the fighting crowd, and they shivered.

Once everything was darker than night, Eira found ice, and she and Aytigin aimed it toward the soldiers. One by one, shrieks of pain rose from their lips as ice encased their feet and ankles and crawled over their legs.

Aytigin swooped far enough for Eira to jump to the ground to search for Cadeyrn.

He was in the middle of the fray and trying to see through the darkness. His sword and clothing were torn and bloody, but he was uninjured.

Eira stepped in front of him as quiet as night. He must have sensed her presence, for he tensed as she came nearer.

She held her lips next to his ear. "Cade."

He jumped at the sound of her voice. "Eir—"

She pressed her fingertips to his mouth. "Shh. We need to get the chalice and take it to Farren. Aytigin and I have slowed the soldiers, but we need to go. Where is the chalice? Does anyone else know about it?"

Cadeyrn blinked as though he were still trying to comprehend her presence. But he didn't question her.

It warmed her to know that in spite of how impossible it may seem that she was there, he still trusted her.

"My chambers," he replied. "No one else knows."

"Good. Follow me."

She took him by the hand, and they wove through the people, who were encased in darkness. The queen's soldiers were still frozen, the ice spreading across their bodies. Some were already covered head to foot, their faces permanently in frozen terror.

She'd done this. She and Aytigin, together.

Eira didn't feel anything as she passed them. No sympathy, anger, or regret. This alone made her more uneasy than anything.

Those who'd been battling against them were all scattering, unsure of where to go or how to get there. Some were attempting to get back inside, while others went back to the village. Yet they all were blind.

Eira cast a few small clouds of stardust into the space to help illuminate their way, but not enough to reveal her and Aytigin's presence.

The darkness extended through the temple, and Cadeyrn never let go of Eira's hand as she guided him, and the number of people they encountered reduced to a few until there was no one else.

"Eira, how did you get here?" Cadeyrn said when they were alone.

She told him the story as they climbed the stairs and entered his chamber.

After Eira cast a cloud of stardust, the room was illuminated, and Cadeyrn dug through a trunk that held the chalice.

"And we can trust Aytigin now?" He also gathered weapons, in addition to the sword at his hip.

A bow and tube of quivers were strapped to his back, and he gave Eira her own sword. She attached the holster to her belt and ran her thumb over the hilt. Her magic may have been stronger, but it didn't mean she could wield a sword any better. She would have to try, though.

"He has no choice but to help us," she replied.

"I don't like the idea of you being bound to him." Cadeyrn pulled the chalice out of the bottom of the trunk and closed the lid.

From the window, a pair of white leathery wings flew past, and Eira went to it.

"We don't have a choice, either. Now let's get this done."

Chapter Twenty-Nine

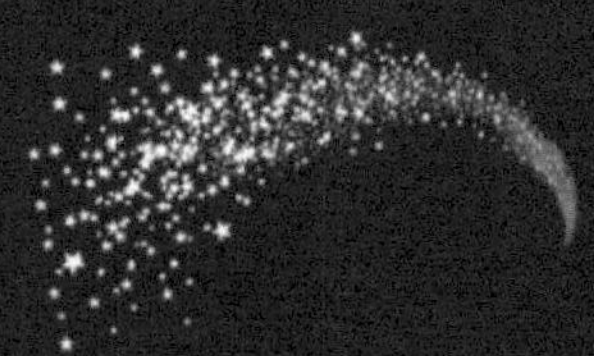

EIRA

The first thing they needed was the water from Stula's pond to create the cure. The rest they could get at the castle. They didn't have a phoenix feather as the bards had suggested, but surely some of Alvis's magic would suffice.

Flying on the dragon shortened the journey to a few of hours instead of the days it had taken Eira and Cadeyrn on their own. They stood at the edge of the pond, and Eira knelt with a vial they'd taken from the temple. She dipped it into the black water, but when she lifted it, nothing was inside.

The water rippled and waved, and the priest rose from the center. His arms were crossed, with hands hidden within the sleeves.

"You can't merely take it." The priest's quiet voice made the cave walls shutter. "What is your offering?"

Another offering. Of course. In their haste, Eira hadn't considered what they should bring.

Aytigin stepped forward past Eira and Cadeyrn. From his pocket, he drew a small piece of cloth. He almost didn't let it go when handing it to the priest. But after a long moment, he did and stepped away.

"It is a piece of the dress Malle wore when she died."

A tiny part of Eira broke. There was so little of Malle left, if anything. The simple act of Aytigin keeping even the smallest piece of her clothing after all these years was nothing short of a miracle. She wanted to grab it back from the priest, if not for Aytigin, herself. But she didn't. She wouldn't cheapen his offering in such a way.

"This will suffice." The priest dropped the cloth into the pond, and it disintegrated in the water. He cocked his head and looked at Eira. "You've been touched by death. How did you awake?"

Eira straightened her shoulders and gazed at where she assumed his eyes would be. The fear she'd had the first time they'd met was gone. Her blood no longer ran cold at the sound of his voice.

"I found my own path."

His shoulders relaxed, and while there was no sign of his face, Eira could sense a smile coming from the priest. In a moment, the slight change in his stance disappeared, and he was stiff and cold again.

"Do you have all you need?" he said.

From the back of the group, Cadeyrn huffed. "Almost. The remaining items are at the castle. Can we have the water now?"

"Don't you want to know how to kill a sorceress?"

The priest's suggestion hung heavy in the air.

"Will it take another offering?" Cadeyrn said.

This whole thing could be another disaster, as it had been the first time they'd tried to save Father. Only now, Eira had all Luana had given her. They also had Aytigin, who could do more than any of them. Even with all these things, Eira didn't relish the idea of killing Amelia. Not the way she had before. Many lives had been lost already.

Eira gripped the glass vial until her knuckles turned white.

"We'll figure it out. I take it Aytigin's offering was enough to receive what we need for the water?"

The priest nodded and extended an arm. "Only take what you need."

Eira knelt again and dipped the vial back into the water. This time, it remained full.

She stood and looked out at the priest. "Thank you."

He bowed his head. "Remember us when you take the throne, Princess."

His vote of confidence lifted her spirits, and Eira clasped the vial to her chest.

"I will."

THEY HID AT THE EDGE OF ERAL FOREST AS THEY CALCULATED THEIR plan to break into the castle. Aytigin's orb hadn't lied, for it was a different place than when they'd left it mere weeks ago. While the ground where rebels had made their camps was covered with a thin layer of snow, waves of water as tall as the castle walls crashed around it, and periodically the razor-sharp fin of a serpent appeared over the surface. Guards stood at the top of each tower, with spears glistening in the sun.

Here they were, more prepared than Eira had been the last time. They had a plan now, but they still did not know how to kill a sorceress. Eira prayed to Luana it wouldn't come to that.

She raised an arm and glided her hand back and forth in front of Cadeyrn. Shadows fell around his body, helping him blend with the darkness. Aytigin was going to keep watch outside of the castle while Eira and Cadeyrn went inside. It would be too conspicuous if he were to fly them inside. They would climb the rose tree outside Eira's window to gather the petals needed for the cure and enter the castle through there.

Weapons prepared, the pair stalked closer to the castle like wraiths, hiding in the darkness without any of the guards knowing they were about to be seized. Shadows danced over the snow, faint outlines of who they were. When they were close enough, Eira crouched to the ground and touched it with her finger. A thin stream of ice crawled over the grass, toward the water. The wave broke apart as an icy path formed, leading to Eira's bedroom. The path was thin enough that, without careful attention, the small break in the water would go unnoticed, but still wide enough for a person to walk through.

They tiptoed between the walls of water so as not to slip, in spite of their sturdy boots. Sea serpents with pointed teeth swam on the edges of the walls of water around them. Their long fins scratched the surface here and there, splashing on them. It would only take a simple stretch, and Eira could grace their scales with her fingertips. Fish swam around them, seemingly oblivious to the treacherous beasts.

A roar rang through the air, and a serpent jumped out from one side of the water and toward the other, snatching a fish in its teeth, flying so close to Eira it almost knocked her over. A flashing of one of Cadeyrn's arrows flew into its neck, and the body crashed onto the ice. He caught Eira with his arm. It all happened so quickly she didn't even see him move.

"Are you all right?"

Eira nodded. "I'm fine."

They kept their weapons prepared, shooting and slicing at the other serpents that tried to cross their path, until the rose tree stood before them in full white blooms in spite of being surrounded by water and being so close to winter.

They sheathed their weapons and climbed. Thankfully, the ice didn't get to the tree, which made it easy to grip. Eira grabbed a strong branch and hoisted herself over it, then crawled toward the roses. She straddled the branch and pulled out the dagger from her belt. With a whack, she sliced off a stem with a perfect white rose attached, along with the sharp thorns. One pierced her thumb, and she sucked at it as she handed the flower to Cadeyrn, who held open a small pouch and dropped it inside.

They continued to climb, and when they reached the window, it was locked. Cadeyrn used the handle of his dagger to break through the glass, and they climbed through.

Eira was finally home.

Chapter Thirty

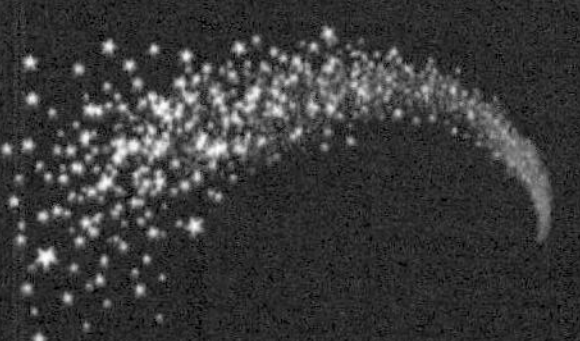

ALVIS

Alvis shivered as a draft wafted through his chamber. Winter was rapidly approaching, and even in the confines of the castle walls, no one was immune. Nor were they immune from the constant moisture in the air now that Amelia was in charge of things.

If they were in a castle by the seaside, it would have been refreshing. But they were in the north, surrounded by forests and mountains, which only made Alvis's southern blood colder.

The door burst open, with a pair of shadowed figures stalking through. Alvis rose from his seat, and flames surrounded his hands. When the shadows faded, so did his flames from the shock of what appeared before him.

Eira and Cadeyrn.

He stumbled a few steps back and dropped the letter he'd been drafting to his family. He'd dreamed of seeing them again, but it was never true. Only when Eira spoke did he let himself believe they were there.

"Alvis." Eira stepped toward him.

She wore a dazzling silver gown, which had been torn and dirtied, but it didn't make her look any less radiant. There was something different about her. The way her pale skin glowed against the starlit lanterns. Her black hair shimmered with stardust. In her eyes was a depth filled with the light and darkness of galaxies he'd never seen, even in the high priestesses of Luana. If he didn't know better, he'd think she was Luana herself, and he had to resist the part of him that wanted to bow at her feet.

They all stared at each other in silence as Alvis tried to wrap his mind around their presence. Both of them were here and unharmed. The castle was barricaded, and it should have been impossible for them to enter. Yet…it didn't matter. They were home, and they were safe.

A smile broke out across Alvis's face, and forgetting himself, he threw his arms around his brother, who returned the gesture with all the strength he had, nearly suffocating him.

"How?" Alvis breathed and tried to reach out to Eira to be sure she was real, but Cadeyrn grabbed his arm before he could.

"It's a long story," Cadeyrn said.

He was different, too. But not in the same physical sense Eira was. There was something in his demeanor and stance that Alvis didn't recognize. Had it only been a few weeks since they'd seen one another?

"But we have a way to save the king," Cadeyrn said, "and we need your help."

Alvis perked at the suggestion. A way to save the king. After all this time? The attendants claimed there was nothing they could do for him but wait. Surely he *was* dreaming. All this time, Alvis imagined they were dead or worse, but now they had returned, and this is the first thing they mention to him. If it were anyone else, he may have questioned what was going on.

Having been gone for weeks without any word or not, these were the two people in the world he trusted the most.

"Anything," Alvis replied.

Eira beamed, and from her pockets she revealed a golden chalice, along with a vial filled with black water.

It can't be. "Eira…that's not…"

"Gallis's chalice, yes." She cradled it in her soft and shimmering palms as though it were as fragile as glass.

Alvis moved forward again and gazed at the item. He'd heard of it, of course. But…

"It's only a legend."

"We've learned otherwise, and it is the key to awakening my father. We also need to save Rose. Do you know where she is?"

The idea of disappointing her when she was so happy sent a stab of guilt through Alvis. But he shook his head, unable to lie either. He never saw Rose, and a spark of hope faded within him. He'd thought she had been with them this whole time.

The light from Eira's face faded, but she nodded. "We'll find her."

Alvis cleared his throat, and they all looked at him. They weren't the only ones with news to share. As much as he wanted to throw Amelia off the throne, things were more complicated than Eira or Cadeyrn realized.

"There's a couple other things we need to address."

"Such as?" Cadeyrn said.

"Cal and his sister Myra. He's been in the dungeon ever since you ran away, and Amelia has been mistreating Myra. I've tried to help as much as I can…" Alvis lowered his head, embarrassed he hadn't been able to do more.

Here they were, prepared to reclaim the kingdom and save Eira's father, and he'd barely done anything.

Eira's face fell, but she nodded again. "We'll help them, and we could use Cal's strength, I'm sure. What else do we need to know?"

Alvis raised his gaze to Eira again, grateful there wasn't any disappointment in her face. Only curiosity and confidence.

"The mirror. There's a child who lives inside of it. Nell. She's Amelia's daughter and has been living here the whole time Amelia has been married to King Brennan. I'm almost certain there's someone living with her, but I haven't been able to see, and there must be other ways it's being used. There's an odd power from it I've never witnessed before."

A glimmer of recognition flickered in Eira's eyes, and the corners of her mouth turned up.

"Aytigin also had a mirror. It was how he was able to communicate with Amelia. You're saying there might be more to it? Can we get to it?"

"Who's Aytigin?"

After a few minutes of discussion, they devised a plan, and Eira and

Cadeyrn told Alvis a tale about traveling, mountains, and a dragon. Alvis could scarcely believe his ears as they talked about the chalice and a curse Eira needed to break. It was even more unbelievable to hear there was a dragon—Aytigin—outside keeping watch over the castle. There was something missing, though, that they weren't telling him. Parts of the story they dodged around and stumbled over. Something wasn't adding up, but he wasn't sure what.

Eira held out the vial of black water, and Cadeyrn opened his sack with the rose petals and thorns. They disintegrated the moment they touched the water. She waved a hand over the water, stardust falling from her palm into the concoction, and more smoke wafted from the liquid. All the ingredients stirred themselves in until the black water turned silver.

Eira brought the vial to Alvis and held it out. "Now the last piece."

Alvis's jaw was stiff and shoulders tight, but he nodded. "Will it suffice?"

"We have to take the risk."

Alvis rolled his sleeves to his elbows and summoned flames around his hand. As he rubbed his palms together, ashes fell into the silver water. It burst into flames and vanished. The water turned white as milk, and still as an icy pond.

Now it was time for them to part ways.

After sending a quick message, Alvis remained in his chambers while Eira clouded him, Cadeyrn, and herself in shadows, making them invisible, so Eira could go to the king's chambers, Cadeyrn to the queen's, and Alvis to the dungeon.

ALVIS CALMED HIS BREATH AS HE NAVIGATED THE HALLS WITH THE shadows Eira had concealed him with.

Cal had been correct when he warned that the queen had eyes and ears everywhere. Amelia kept a close eye on him these days, but he could still roam the castle. If only he'd had Eira's shadows sooner, he could have helped Cal escape ages ago.

Alvis paused behind a corner to wait and rubbed his hands against his trousers. For years, Cadeyrn had told him tales of daring escapes and rescues, but never once had Alvis been invited to join on the adventure. While the stories were entertaining, Alvis knew he would have been out of his element. Yet here he was helping a prisoner escape from the dungeons. He wasn't sure if he should be thrilled or terrified. It didn't matter, though, as long as the task was successful.

The patter of footsteps followed Alvis, and from around the corner, Myra's soft face appeared. She narrowed her eyes and examined the shadows.

"Your Highness?"

Alvis tilted his head. "You can see me? Are you dedicated to Luana?"

He'd never seen a dedication tattoo on her in all his visits to Cal.

Myra lifted her arm and gathered more shadows so she was hidden along with him.

"Not exactly. It's a long story. Besides, the shadows don't make you invisible. Since I know what I'm looking for, I can find you easily."

Of course she could. He should have known as much. But she could manipulate shadows—and wasn't exactly dedicated to Luana. Every time Alvis thought he was making sense of the world, it continued to surprise him. Instead of being discouraged by it, it only made his sense of curiosity heighten. If they didn't have a mission to complete, he would have pressed her further.

"Have you been able to use the shadows all this time?" he said.

Myra wavered her hand in front of her. "Not well. Having these to assist makes it easier. Otherwise, I would have been able to help Cal escape sooner. Princess Eira has really returned?"

The shadows shifted around them as they crept around the corners to the dungeon.

"I can scarcely believe it myself, and wouldn't have if I hadn't seen her and Cadeyrn with my own eyes."

There wouldn't be any bothering with convincing the guard on duty to let him down to Cal's cell, or time constraints. The unlikely pair blended into the wall's shadows until they were at his side. The guard barely had time to notice two dark figures appear before him when Alvis slammed a rock into his head. The man fell to the floor, and when Myra swiped the keys from his belt, they hurried down the stairs. Cal was slumped in his usual place in his cell, shaking as he coughed. The ball of fire Alvis had given him had faded, and Cal looked worse.

Alvis crouched so his gaze met Cal's. He grasped the iron bars and made his hands warm.

"Are you ready?" he said.

Cal coughed again. "Ready for what?"

"To leave." Myra unlocked the cell door and swung it open.

Cal didn't move, his gaze darting between Alvis and Myra.

"But…how. Why?"

Alvis extended an arm and helped Cal get to his feet. He was healing from his wounds, but not as quickly as he should have been. There were new cuts and bruises on him. Amelia must have continued her questioning. He moved better than he had been the first time Alvis had visited, though.

"Eira and Cadeyrn are back."

Something lit in Cal. "And Rose?"

Alvis grasped his arm. "We'll find her. But they need you with the rebels. Eira expects Amelia will put up a fight, and there isn't much time."

The siblings embraced before she led the two men to a back wall in the dungeon, which Alvis had never paid attention to before. Myra held a hand to the wall and closed her eyes, feeling for the entrance. Swirls of shadows circled her hand, and she clutched it in her fist. Alvis stared at her in awe as she opened her eyes and smiled, delighted she was able to figure it out. She pulled at the shadows and revealed an opening where a cool wind blew through. Alvis summoned a small ball of fire and let it light their path.

Before them, when they reached the end, stood a wall of ice so thick you couldn't see how deep it went. Someone must have sealed the exit.

"Shit!" Alvis said.

They'd knocked out the guard, and Alvis wasn't sure how long he'd be out. For all they knew, he could have summoned the others by now, or Eira and Cadeyrn had been caught.

"Do you have anything to pick at it with?" he said to Myra.

The words were barely out of his mouth and she had already pulled a knife out of each boot and handed one to Cal. Together they stabbed at the wall, chipping the ice away. The two of them barely even needed him. Although…Alvis wasn't completely useless. He was Ray's Chosen, after all.

He placed a hand upon the ice wall and summoned the fire burning beneath his skin. It bubbled and seethed toward the ice, and the wall began to melt, but only a bit at a time. A strong follower of Luana must have built this wall, but it wasn't immune to Alvis's magic.

Footsteps echoed through the tunnel, and they exchanged a look. It was Cal and Myra's turn to swear now. The ice wall was melting, but Alvis wasn't sure if it was enough to weaken it so they could push through. Still, they had to try.

All three pushed against the melting wall with their shoulders as the footsteps drew nearer. It cracked through the middle, but didn't break. If Eira had been there, she would have been able to command the ice to disappear.

"Hey!" the guard called. "Who's there? You get back here!"

They pushed some more, and ice chipped away, falling upon them. More cracks grew by the moment, until finally a large piece fell away. Mustering more of his power, and with his tattoo glowing in the darkness, Cal punched through it and the ice crashed around them.

"Stop!" the guard yelled when he reached the trio.

They ran through the tunnel, with Alvis throwing balls of fire behind them, forcing the guard to dodge and duck them. The hem of his uniform singed from one of the flames, and he yelled out as he swatted at the garment to put it out. A short distraction, at least.

They reached the end of the tunnel, and Myra fumbled to grab for more shadows. The guard was still following them, crying out from where the fire had burned him.

"Please, please, please," Myra whispered as she grasped for the shadows.

They wrapped around her hand, and she whipped them away to reveal an exit. They burst through the shadows as Priestess Cynth rode by on the horse she'd been told to meet them with.

Myra let go of Cal's arm as she tried to gather the shadows again to close the tunnel exit, and Alvis led Cal to the horse. Cynth jumped off and handed Cal the reigns, and once he was on, he lifted Myra to join him.

"There's a dragon flying around the castle, protecting the rebels," Cynth said. "Go to them and help." She raised an arm and froze the tunnel exit closed again before the guard caught them, then shook her head when she saw the confused looks on Myra and Cal's faces. "I wish I could explain, but I can't. We'll have to wait for Eira and Cadeyrn when this is all over."

"Where will you go?" Myra looked at Alvis, her brown eyes deep with concern.

"I'll see you on the other side. I have to go speak with Amelia."

Chapter Thirty-One

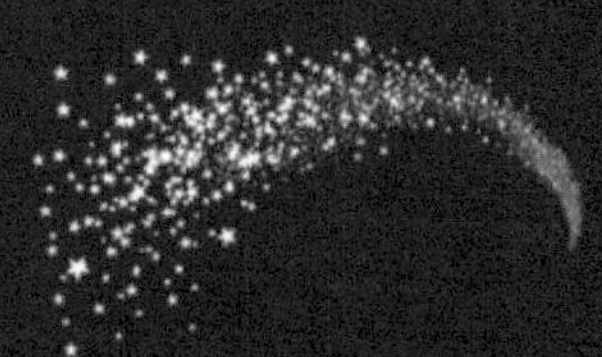

EIRA

The halls were littered with guards, but none of them noticed Eira and Cadeyrn passing through in the shadows.

Eira rubbed the vile and tapped her fingers around the glass when they arrived at the king's chamber doors. They didn't need to go together, as Cadeyrn had his own task to perform, but she was glad to have him at her side, even if only for a few more moments.

"It's time," she said.

Cadeyrn gave Eira one last kiss before he left to seek out Amelia's chambers.

"It'll all be over soon," he said.

She looked behind her and watched as the shadows of the castle covered him. She didn't need to be as close anymore for her magic to spread to others.

Wasn't the first time she'd watched him leave to go somewhere dangerous, and it wouldn't be the last. Nevertheless, it was something she would never get used to.

Eira closed her eyes and took a deep breath. They would be brave for each other.

She straightened her spine and crept past the guards standing on either side of the door, then opened and shut it before they noticed anything.

On the bed lay Father, as still as he had been before, with the Marquis of Marallis at his side. While he kept the same ornate velvet clothing he always wore, it was wrinkled and worn. How often had he sat at Father's side? Every day? Eira couldn't remember the last time one of Father's lovers had been so dedicated and concerned.

She gripped the chalice and vile even tighter. Father needed to wake not only for the kingdom, but for himself. To be able to experience the care the marquis felt for him.

Eira removed her shadows, and the marquis jumped out of his seat.

He bowed. "Your Highness…you…you're…how?"

Eira gestured for him to stand straight again. He looked at her the way Alvis did when they'd reunited—awestruck.

People had always been respectful and reverent around her, but her physical changes made them afraid of her. Yet another change she wasn't sure she could get used to. The list was growing longer by the moment.

"There's no time to explain now. But I'm here to awaken the king."

The marquis looked like he was about to weep.

"Praise Gallis." He bowed and led Eira to the bed.

Not a single hair on the king's head, or piece of clothing, had moved from when Eira last saw him. It was as though no time had passed.

A chill ran up her arms. "Perhaps you should prop him to sit. It would make it easier for him to drink."

The marquis nodded. "Of course."

They lifted the king so he was partially sitting. He didn't move or do anything to indicate he was awake.

The marquis held the king up while Eira transferred the liquid from the vial to the chalice. This needed to work. The priest said it would, but inklings of doubt cracked in her mind like a spider web. She needed to have faith that the deities had led her on the proper course.

Eira lifted the chalice and pressed it against her father's lips. The first couple tries, the white liquid only dribbled onto his beard. The next time, a few drops fell into his mouth, and his lips twitched. Little by little, they formed around the lip of the chalice, and the potion poured into his throat. He guzzled it down until the last drop was gone. Yet his eyes were still closed.

They lay him back onto the mattress again and watched.

"Maybe we didn't do it right." The marquis stroked his usually well-kept beard, which had grown unruly.

Eira worried the same thing. She'd imagined that once he drank the cure, he would simply…awaken.

She sank back and leaned against the headboard. They'd followed the tale the way the priest told them, hadn't they?

The marquis gasped.

The king coughed. His eyes popped open. He blinked a few times and looked back and forth.

"Eira? Phillip? What…what happened? I was at the ball, and all of the sudden I remember walking and standing at a crossroads for the longest time…"

He was truly there and not simply a body in a bed. They hadn't failed, after all.

A sob escaped her lips as he sat.

"Oh, my darling girl, it's all right. I'm here now."

Father's voice was thin and hoarse from not being used for so long, but it was his voice. Eira hadn't realized how much she'd missed the sound.

She laughed, not because it was funny, but because she had no other way to react. She threw her arms around him and cried into his shoulder the way she would have as a child after a bad dream.

"Now," Father said, once they all had calmed, and sat as straight and proud as he would be on his throne. "Does someone want to tell me what's going on here?"

A scream rang through the castle, and all three of them looked toward the source of the sound. The ceiling trembled above them going along on with the next portion of their plan.

"Your wife has taken over the kingdom and has been destroying everything," Eira said, "along with trying to take our lives for the past several weeks."

Father furrowed his brows and blinked a few times as though he were trying to absorb the information. He looked to the marquis, who nodded.

"I'm afraid that's the short version, Brennan."

"Shit. Damnable woman. I knew she was unhappy. But this? At least in the past she took care of Cresin when I was gone."

Another roar came from outside, along with shouts and cries. From outside the window a hawk flew past and cawed. Eira prayed Alvis had been successful in freeing him. She swallowed the lump in her throat and slid off the bed. Their mission was far from over.

"Rose is also missing," she said.

Father moved to get off the bed, but his limbs were too stiff to rush out.

"Shit! Rose is missing? Get me to Amelia. No one threatens my daughters and gets away with it."

He tried again to get himself from the bed, but groaned when his legs creaked at the movement. Eira hesitated. She'd only now gotten him back and didn't want to leave him.

The marquis wrapped his arm around Father's waist to assist.

"Do what you must, Your Highness. I'll be sure he's safe."

Yes, she had to keep going. Seeing the tenderness in Father's eyes, Eira knew he was in safe hands.

She grasped the hilt of her sword and ran out of the room.

Chapter Thirty-Two

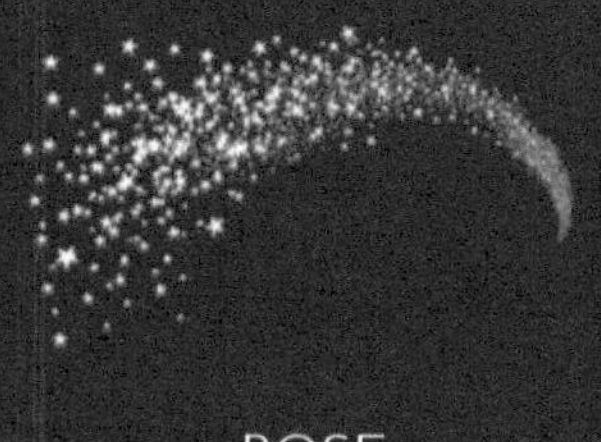

ROSE

Something was happening. Rose could sense it in the pit of her stomach.

First, Amelia was far too happy when she got a message to visit Alvis in his chamber only minutes before. Whenever Amelia was happy, it meant everyone else was going to be miserable soon. Rose had learned as much being stuck inside Amelia's mirror all these weeks.

Second, if Alvis was desperate enough to do something that would make Amelia happy, it must mean things had taken a turn for the worse. Or maybe he finally had a plan.

Took him long enough.

Rose had tried to catch Alvis's attention each time he was in the room and spoke with Nell, but any time she'd gotten close they were almost caught by Amelia. Alvis suspected there was someone else hiding in the glass, though. Rose could tell. He was smart. Maybe he'd put the pieces together himself.

Rose limped back and forth in front of the glass and tried to think of what must have been happening, while the little girl sat on the bed and watched her with wide eyes. This small, strange child with hair wilder than Rose's had been her only companion all this time, beyond Amelia questioning Rose about Eira's whereabouts. Truth was, Rose had no idea. This didn't stop Amelia, though. And each time she questioned Rose, she insisted Rose was lying.

The only thing Rose could imagine was that Eira was out searching for the cure, but Rose didn't know where she would do such a thing. The other option would be that Eira was at their grandmother's home in Eral. Eira wouldn't still be sitting there, though, after all this time.

Being trapped in a mirror, the questioning, the torture—yes, all those things were awful. But the uncertainty of what was happening with her sister, and being powerless to help, that was the worst part. Rose hated being powerless.

Now the feeling was even worse. If only she'd been able to catch Alvis's attention, maybe she could have helped him. She could know what was happening out there.

"You're making me dizzy." Nell sat on the bed with her legs crossed beneath her and twirled a wild strand of curly hair round her finger, tangling it in knots.

Rose stopped and put a hand on her hip. "Don't you want to know what's going on?"

Nell tossed her hair to the side and lay on the bed, waving her feet back and forth.

"Something is always going on. If I need to worry, Mother will tell us."

Rose rubbed her face and grasped at her own hair. Each word Amelia told the child was a lie, and Rose could see right through all of them. But whenever she'd argued, she almost drowned from the inside out.

The chamber door opened, and someone rushed in.

Cadeyrn! Rose yelped in delight.

How was he here? If he was here, it meant Eira had to be near. But she wasn't there.

His gaze went to the mirror, and he smiled from ear to ear as they locked eyes.

Locked eyes. Rose's heart stopped. Amelia forgot to enchant the mirror again in her haste to leave.

Cadeyrn whooped and placed his palms on the glass. "Rose! How… you're here! I didn't know what I was going to find, but I never thought it would be you. Eira is going to be so happy to see you." He blinked a few times as Nell peered around Rose's waist. "Now you, I've heard about."

Rose patted Nell's head. "This is Amelia's daughter, Nell. How did you know?"

Cadeyrn's smile vanished, and his eyes grew wide.

"Alvis told me."

Nell walked around Rose and stared at Cadeyrn with a wide smile.

"I recognize you. Sometimes when Mother lets me into her mirror necklace, I see other people. Even if you don't see me. You've been to many balls."

Cadeyrn chuckled and crouched so he was at eye level with Nell.

"You're right, I have been. I'm sorry I haven't had the pleasure to meet you until now. How old are you, my dear?"

Nell's tan face blushed. His charms even worked on children. No wonder Eira hadn't been able to resist him.

"Eleven."

"And how long have you lived here?"

"My whole life."

Cadeyrn glanced at Rose, who nodded. She and Nell had nothing to do but talk, and she'd heard all about Nell's life in the mirror. Nell had been living in this mirror the entire time Amelia had been married to King Brennan. Considering her darker skin and mix of blond and brown curls looked nothing like Amelia or the king, it was safe to assume she was a child from another man.

"Mother said the king was mean and wouldn't let me come to the castle. So I'm here." Nell continued to twirl her hair around a finger. "It was the only way we could be together. Mother says everything she's doing is for me. But I wish she wouldn't."

"That makes two of us," Rose muttered.

It was sad, really, the lies Amelia fed Nell. Maybe once upon a time, Amelia wanted what was best for her daughter, but there was nothing but selfishness and power in her heart now.

"Would you like to see something other than this room for once?" Cadeyrn flashed a sly grin. "I imagine it must get boring."

Nell looked back and forth between them. "Do you think I can? Will you be able to take my mirror somewhere else?

Cadeyrn smiled gently. "That, and get you out of there. For good. How do you like the sound of that?"

"And Rose can come, too? I don't think she likes it here."

Rose laughed. What an understatement.

"I imagine that could be arranged." Cadeyrn looked at all of Nell's hair, which filled the space. "But...we might have to do something about your hair."

Chapter Thirty-Three

EIRA

A scream echoed against the walls, and the stone floors shook. Their party all paused and placed hands on the hilts of their swords, ready to attack and defend. Eira's breath caught, and she glanced around the hall as though Amelia would appear at any moment. She needed more time to prepare.

"It would appear Amelia knows we're here."

The words had barely come out of her mouth, when water trickled out of the walls. Then it grew stronger and pooled on the ground to form a roaring stream.

Water splashed under Eira's feet as she hurried to the temple to meet the others, the faint struggles of Father and Phillip behind her.

"Over here." Cadeyrn revealed himself from behind a tapestry.

Behind it was another entrance to a secret passage, and he ushered Eira through. They waited in the darkness until they could hear Father and the marquis, then helped them in. It was a struggle for Father to walk, and he leaned on the marquis. But he could get from place to place, even if it was slow.

Cynth and Evony welcomed them into the temple, and as much as Eira wanted an appropriate reunion, there wasn't time.

They shut the door. Outside, the sound of rushing water pounding against the temple walls.

"It won't get through as long as we keep the doors shut," Cynth said. "Luana's magic won't let it."

A large mirror stood in the center of the room, and in its reflection stood a young girl with the longest hair Eira had ever seen. It was wild and curly and went all the way to the floor, and trailed behind her. She was barefoot and peered at all the people around her with wide brown eyes. Tears formed in Eira's eyes when she saw who was with her.

Rose.

Eira and Father rushed to the glass and pressed their hands against it as though they could grab her. Rose placed her hands over theirs on the other side, and a rare tear escaped her eye as well. They'd found her. She was alive and well. She didn't have her crutch, and there were bruises on her arms, but Rose was alive.

"You're here," Rose repeated over and over.

Behind them, Cynth and Evony held hands with happy tears in their eyes.

Then there was the girl. Alvis had told them about Nell and her connection to Amelia, but it was difficult to believe until one was staring right at her. All this time, Amelia had a daughter.

Father kneeled to the ground as Nell looked at him with wondering eyes.

"I knew Amelia had a child, but she told me she'd left you in the care of her mother on the island. I've been sending funds there all these years to ensure you were taken care of. My girl, I am so sorry. Can you ever forgive me?"

"Can you get me out?" the girl said. "Not to Mother's necklace. But…out?"

"I can try."

"Or perhaps I can." The marquis stepped forward and raised his sleeves to show his glowing Colma tattoo. "If Amelia's magic placed her inside, perhaps I can use my skills to release her." He placed a hand on the glass, and it wavered like water.

Father put his arm through the water and grabbed the girl's hand, and she stepped through. She gasped when her foot touched the marble floor.

"It's cold."

They all chuckled.

Rose came next, and she and Eira threw themselves into a strong hug. Eira clung to her sister and wept, never wanting to let go of her again.

"I'm so sorry I couldn't get you. I wanted to come, I swear."

Rose stroked her hair, and Eira swore she was crying, too.

"I know, I know. We're here now. It's going to be okay."

The temple walls shook, and water pounded against them, forcing the sisters to part. A sea serpent cried, and the temple altar trembled. Cadeyrn and Father unsheathed their swords and stepped in front of the group. Clouds of ice circled Eira's hands.

Rose reached for her dagger. "We can't stay in here forever. How long are we to wait out Amelia? She knows we have the mirror."

A cry sounded from outside. Through the window, they could see a crowd had gathered, and Aytigin's wings flapped, sounding like thunder as he rallied the rebels together. It wasn't long before the battle cries of the people and guards surrounded them, along with the slicing and attacking of the serpents. They could stay in the temple and be protected, but…

Eira looked to Cadeyrn, who nodded. These were their people, and they needed to help.

Eira turned to Cynth. "Open the doors. Don't let Amelia get to Nell or the mirror. Alvis is on his way to get Nell and take her somewhere safe."

Evony grabbed Nell's arm and pulled her close. Eira gathered shadows and hid them away as Cynth opened the temple doors. Before them was a sea of guards, warriors, and serpents battling one another. Eira knelt to the ground and placed a hand on the marble, a path of ice forging through the water.

With a cry, Cadeyrn and Rose led the charge as they ran out into the fight. But Eira grabbed Cadeyrn before he got too far.

"We're going to the roof." She looked at Rose and nodded. "I'll see you on the other side."

They took off, Cadeyrn tearing down anyone who crossed their path and Eira shooting ice at any he missed.

Chapter Thirty-Four

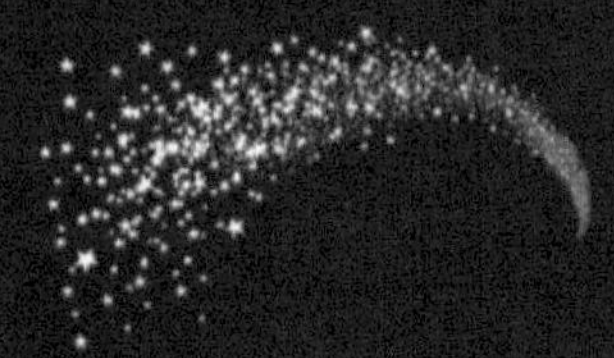

ALVIS

ALVIS'S HEART POUNDED AS HE LOOKED OUT HIS CHAMBER WINDOW. CAL and Myra had escaped, but that didn't promise they were out of danger. And there was more to be done.

Out of the window, Alvis saw nothing. All was quiet beyond the wall of water that surrounded the castle. He knew he wouldn't see anything. The sun was setting, and if Eira's plan went right, she and Cadeyrn would be covered in shadows. It was comforting, but also unsettling, because there was no way for him to know all was going according to plan. They wouldn't succeed, though, if he didn't do his part.

Finally, it was all coming to an end. He hadn't been able to do much until this point, but he could do this.

Alvis stared through the window, toward the rebels. He needed to distract Amelia as long as possible. They could discuss plans for a future however long she wanted. Or at least, as long as Eira and Cadeyrn needed.

"I've been thinking…I'm not much use as a prisoner."

Amelia chuckled from behind him, lounging on his couch with a glass of wine in her hand. He turned to face her, and she crossed her legs, putting the Colma tattoo on her ankle in full sight. The queen's pregnant belly was visible and only made her more beautiful.

"What made you finally come to this conclusion?" she replied.

"You need Oxare, and my kingdom is not happy about how our original plan of ruling alongside Cresin has fallen through." Alvis moved to the chair beside the couch and sat on the edge so his knee could bump hers.

He'd never been good at this—flirting and seduction. That had always been Cadeyrn's forte. Being betrothed to Eira his whole life, he never needed to. Although, he'd seen Cadeyrn with women often enough. Surely he had picked up on a few things.

"You and I have our differences," Alvis said, "but perhaps we can find a way to work together."

"Well, it's about time you listened to reason." There was an edge to her voice, in spite of her effort to appear as confident and calm as she usually was.

The weeks of rebels defying her were finally taking their toll, and the desperation was forming behind her eyes.

She leaned forward, allowing him to have a clear view of her figure. He let her believe he welcomed the advance.

"Are you prepared to move on from Princess Eira? I don't share well. Even with memories."

Alvis straightened his tunic and let his gaze wander over Amelia. Her shoulders relaxed, and she swung her leg.

"Eira and I were an arrangement. One neither of us had a choice in. We got along, of course, but there was no love there between us."

He paused after the confession. It was supposed to be a lie, yet the words flowed far too easily. He and Eira cared for one another, but when he thought about the times they'd been together…had it been love? Even when they were supposedly making love, he'd assumed that's what it was. Maybe they only came together out of there being no one else to explore such things with, and out of habit. There hadn't been passion or desire. Never had he tried to gaze at Eira from across the room, or go out of his way to be with her outside of what was expected. Not the way…

Oh.

This was what Eira and Cadeyrn had been keeping from him as they told their tale. Memories from all their time together flashed through his mind like flickering flames. The shared laughter, stolen glances, and excuses to spend time together—Alvis had been blind to it all. Until now. Even the way, only moments before, Cadeyrn stopped Alvis from touching Eira at their reunion.

Cadeyrn had been in love with Eira this whole time, and he'd had no idea. Whether or not he'd acted on it—at least, until now—Alvis wasn't sure. But if his suspicion was correct, he'd be shocked if they hadn't these past few weeks.

A flare of anger surged through him at the revelation. Surprisingly enough, not at the notion that Eira wasn't in love with Alvis, but at how neither of them had told him and had went behind his back. Anger at himself for not noticing.

He couldn't worry about that now. Once Amelia was gone, he'd deal with it.

Alvis cleared his throat and hoped his face hadn't betrayed his thoughts.

"I need to consider what's best for my people, and yours," he said. "Don't you agree?"

"Hmm."

Amelia raised her glass, and Alvis clinked his against it.

She paused and tensed, then furrowed her brow and looked about the room. The miniature mirror around her neck flashed.

"Something is happening."

Alvis tried to keep his face from going pale. "I'm not sure what you mean?"

Her gaze turned cold, and crashing waves formed in her eyes.

"Liar." She threw her glass on the floor, and it shattered to pieces as she stormed out of the room.

Alvis chased her. *Please let them be gone already.*

She tore through the castle and into her chamber, then burst back out into the hall again.

"Where is my daughter?"

Chapter Thirty-Five

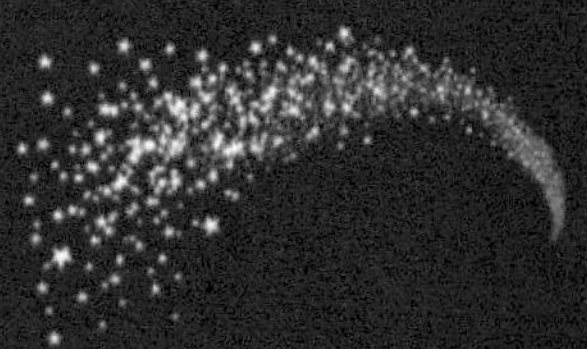

ALVIS

Amelia's rage was immeasurable. Water poured into Alvis's chamber from all sides, and with a cry, all of her guards went into action. People battled all around them, or drowned in the waves.

Amelia's skin turned to light blue-green scales, and her eyes flashed silver. The water parted as she stormed through the castle in search of Nell.

Alvis had to stop her.

Balls of fire formed in his hands, and he threw them toward the queen. She screamed as her scaly skin sizzled under the impact, and she fell. Alvis jumped over her and ran to the temple, throwing more fire over his shoulder. The flames erupted around them, blocking Amelia's path. He had no idea if she'd survive the attack, but if anything, it would slow her pace.

Flames followed Alvis wherever he went, drying the water that flooded the castle as he hustled to the meeting point. Cynth was guarding the temple door, using her ice and snow to ward off anyone who wished to intrude.

She rushed Alvis inside, and he searched about.

Where is everyone?

Shadows waved before him, and Evony revealed herself and Nell.

He breathed a sigh of relief. Nell was out of the mirror, which stood empty in the middle of the temple.

But what about the rest of them?

"We need to get her out," he said.

"But where can we go?" Evony replied. "We're surrounded."

Alvis looked around. The temple was the safest place for now. But what if Amelia found a way to break in?

"Eral Forest," he said. "Kutlaous will protect us, and if needed, I'll search for the minister's cottage. I'll burn our way through."

Nell's eyes were wide, and she cowered next to Evony as the battle raged beyond the temple walls.

"I don't want to go out there," she whimpered.

Alvis knelt before her. "I know. I don't either. But we need to be brave, and you need to get to safety. Can you be brave with me?"

Nell nodded and placed her hand in his.

He stood and spoke to Evony. "Will Eira's shadows cover us enough?"

"I don't know how far her powers can go, but we can try."

"It's all right. People are distracted with fighting, anyway. We only need a small amount to hide us until we get through."

Evony pulled the shadows and covered them.

With a blaze of fire, Alvis led the way.

Chapter Thirty-Six

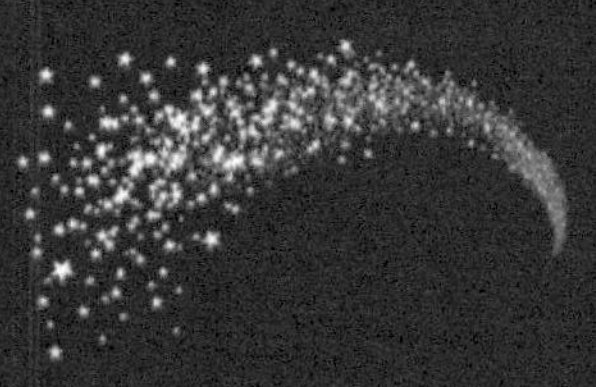

EIRA

Ice spread through the castle and the surrounding area, making paths for people to get through. But the waves still roared as people battled. Eira and Cadeyrn fought their way outside and around to the back of the temple. As much as she guided their path with ice, they were still both soaked. Cadeyrn shivered at her side, but Eira barely felt it.

She looked at the wall. Overhead, the snow clouds parted to reveal how the full moon shone over the peak of the temple.

"Can you climb?" she said.

Cadeyrn assessed the wall's terrain. "I can give it a shot."

At their feet, vines rose and came to life, crawling up the wall. Eira's skills for Luana may have been stronger than ever, but they hadn't erased her gifts from Grandmother's Fae lineage.

Eira climbed on his back, and he grasped at the vines as they scaled the wall. He moved with impossible speed, and the world went by in a blur. When they reached the top, Eira stood and looked over the scene. Water crashed all around, with serpents jumping out from the waves and destroying those in their path, and Aytigin flew overhead, breathing icy clouds on them all. So much violence and devastation. Because of her.

Cadeyrn must have sense Eira's distress. He softened his warrior stance.

"We can end it."

His words pulled Eira out of her stunned trance.

"Where is my daughter!" Amelia shrieked from below.

Water crashed around her and carried her toward the temple roof. The waves built higher and higher until Eira could see her stepmother clearly for the first time in weeks. Her scaled face and grand clothes… and pregnant belly.

Eira blinked. She hadn't expected that.

She planted her feet and looked to the night sky and the full moon. She closed her eyes and raised her hands, summoning all of its power over her. The darkness and ice within her danced and swelled as she gathered it.

She opened her eyes, and they turned gray like the surface of the moon. Starlight radiated from her skin, and everything glowed around her. Ahead, Amelia's wave grew larger and carried her toward Eira. Cadeyrn drew his sword and prepared for an attack.

Eira blinked, and the world was covered in darkness. For a brief moment, the fighting stopped. She'd never covered such a large expanse before.

Below, starlight danced and glowed. Father was there with Rose, sword drawn, and glaring at Amelia. Behind them, Cal was fighting off guards.

"Don't you touch her," he growled, and the three of them grabbed the vines to climb.

Eira lowered her arms and gathered ice and snow around her hands. She shoved them forward, and the ice and snow flew over the space, hitting Amelia in the chest, and filled the darkness. All the water froze, and the serpents along with it.

Amelia cried out and jumped from her frozen wave to Eira on the roof.

"Your family has taken everything from me." She sneered. "My daughter, my freedom. Snatching me from my home and forcing me to be here. While you have it all."

Cadeyrn swung his sword at her. "You made your own choices."

Amelia blocked it with a wave and kept moving toward Eira.

Father and Rose finally arrived and pulled themselves onto the roof, weapons drawn and pointed at the queen.

She laughed. "Your weapons can't harm me."

Perhaps not. But…

Frost emerged from Eira's foot and spread over the roof, turning into ice. They all slid and tried to regain their balance. Cadeyrn stomped on the ice, his tattoo glowing. *Crack!*

Cracks spread across the ice, and the vines spread across the space as a hold formed. The roof caved in, and while gripping a vine, Cadeyrn grabbed Eira and they fell through.

The roof of the temple crumbled as they all fell. Father and Rose followed Cadeyrn's lead and found vines to hold onto. But Amelia fell straight to the ground. She landed with *thud!* as stones fell around her.

Eira landed on her feet and approached the queen. "I'm truly sorry you were brought here. I know what it is to feel as though you don't have a choice in your fate. It was wrong for you to become queen."

Amelia struggled as she propped herself up. Her blue and gray skin was bruised and cut, but she was able to stand. If she'd been human, the fall may have killed her and her unborn child.

Eira was relieved. She wouldn't have forgiven herself if the baby hadn't survived.

"Sorry isn't enough," Amelia said.

It wasn't. There was nothing Eira could do or say to change the course of Amelia's life or the choices Father had made. Eira didn't excuse Amelia for what she'd done in response, but she still pitied the queen.

"I know," Eira said. "But you didn't have to do this. All that has happened is because you willed it to be."

"Where is my daughter?" Water gathered around Amelia's feet and lifted the stones nearby.

"Away, safe," Eira replied. "Not with you."

Amelia yelled and lifted her arms, making the waves push rocks toward Eira. She raised a hand, but before she could summon ice to freeze everything, someone jumped in front of her.

Cadeyrn took the hit and fell to the ground. Eira's ear-piercing scream filled the room as she lunged toward him. But it was too late. He lay on the floor, blood pouring from his head. She scrambled to his side and held his head in her lap, not caring how much blood got on her.

"No, no, please. Cadeyrn, please. Why did you do that?"

His eyelids fluttered.

Praise Gallis. He was alive.

"As much as I love you being all over me, darling, I fear you should have your focus on other things."

Eira laughed and kissed him, and he groaned in pain.

Amelia applauded as she stalked toward them and released a dark chuckle.

"Oh, my, I did not expect this. Luana's perfect Chosen one, in love with another. Her betrothed's brother, no less. Perhaps your people will prefer me as queen, after all."

For those brief moments, Eira had forgotten the other people in the room and found they were all staring at them, dumbfounded. Rose had grown pale, and while she didn't appear surprised, she was disappointed. The others, especially Father, were in shock.

There was never going to be a good way to tell them about their relationship, but this hadn't been what Eira had in mind.

Amelia continued toward Eira, water pouring from her hands. Shadows gathered around Eira, and Father ran to Amelia. He grabbed the queen and shoved her toward the mirror, which stood behind Eira. The glass turned to water, and Amelia was thrown inside. A surge of ice poured out from Eira and covered the glass, encasing the queen. She yelled and pounded against the mirror and tried to summon her magic to turn the glass into water again, but it was no use.

While they all had been battling, Cynth was enchanting the mirror with ice and night magic. The ice seal from Eira was the final touch.

The queen and her unborn child were not coming out.

Chapter Thirty-Seven

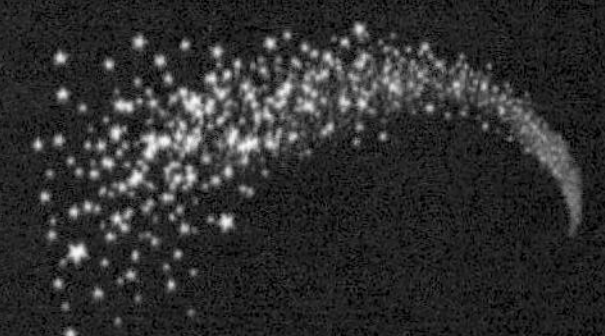

EIRA

The days following the defeat of Amelia were a whirlwind of meetings with the council and Luana's priestesses, restoring the castle, and helping the villages recover. They had only begun returning to their feet after last year's forest fires, and it was going to be another long journey after all of Amelia's raids.

Rose returned to the Guard, and Captain Avarett was removed from his position, which was offered to Rose, but she passed it to Cal, and the two of them started weeding out all those who'd been loyal to Amelia. It was as though she'd never been captured inside of a mirror for several weeks.

Those who were found trustworthy rotated shifts guarding the mirror to be sure Amelia didn't find a way out, and only allowed attendants and servants in and out. Otherwise, the mirror had been quiet.

A couple of the gentler guards were assigned to Amelia's daughter, Nell. She seemed harmless, but they were there to be sure she didn't help Amelia escape, along with protecting her from anyone who may want revenge and take it out on her. She may have been Amelia's daughter, but she was still an innocent child.

Meanwhile, Eira went out to help the villages. For once, she was grateful that Aytigin was there, for he could fly her and Cadeyrn to various locations. They tried to get Alvis to join them, but after everything, he visited other villages on his own and prepared for his journey home. Eira didn't blame him.

Eira and Cadeyrn each spoke to him—tearfully, on her part—and his reaction was worse than Eira had imagined. He didn't say a word. Just stared blankly at them as they spoke.

When they were done, he said, "It seems your mind is made up. I wish you happiness."

In spite of his few words, Eira knew the betrayal cut him deep.

Father was similar. They worked together each day on reclaiming the kingdom and regaining his strength, but whenever her relationship with Cadeyrn arose, he was silent.

Eira knew people's reactions were going to be varied, but the reality was still difficult to bear.

"They'll get used to it eventually," Rose said as they strolled through the gardens.

Winter was undoubtedly on its way, and Rose wore their mother's red cloak. Eira didn't need it anymore. She found that Rose looked better in it, anyway. The red stunningly complimented Rose's hair and fighting leathers.

They sat on a bench, and Aytigin flew overhead. He'd been flying further each day, testing how far the bond would let him go. So far, Eira had only felt a slight tug in the pit of her stomach when he pushed the bounds too much, while Aytigin claimed a sharp pain would radiate through every nerve in his body. But otherwise, he seemed to be enjoying his newfound freedom.

Besides, the residents of Farren Castle only tolerated his presence, so she could understand his need to get away. Especially since it wasn't only Alvis and Father, but also the council and High Priestess Nyx, who'd been avoiding Eira and her entourage. They spoke to her when necessary, but she couldn't ignore the looks mixed with awe and wonder at her new powers from Luana. There was wariness, too. More than even before, Eira felt out of place in her own home.

"I know the council and the priestesses will need time," she said.

"Some may never fully accept us. But there was a part of me that hoped it would be easier."

Eira tried to let her sister console her, and leaned into her hand while Rose rubbed her back.

"It's only been a few days," Rose said. "Give it time. No one can deny your dedication to Luana or to Cresin, in spite of who shares your bed. I'm proud of you. You've always done what you've been told. Now you finally did something for yourself. It's wonderful. Besides, I see how happy you and Cade make each other. How can anyone deny you such happiness? Did you know he spoke to me the other day?"

Eira blinked and turned to face her sister. "He did?"

A mischievous smile crept onto Rose's face, one of the few genuine smiles Eira had seen in what seemed like forever.

"He asked my permission for your hand. Assuming how Father would react, he said I was the best to ask."

A giggle bubbled out of Eira. Cadeyrn had asked Rose if he could have her hand. They'd talked about marriage and their future, but this made it all the more real.

"What did you say?"

Rose looked at her out of the corner of her eye and smirked.

"Yes, of course. Not as though you need anyone's permission. You'd go and get married anyway. But I was glad to."

Eira spread her arms wide and squeezed Rose in a hug.

"I'm sorry I didn't come to save you sooner."

Rose waved it off, as though it had been a mere blip in the plan.

"I knew you would come eventually, and we needed the cure more than anything else."

Alvis stood at the end of the walking path. "We've been summoned to the great hall. Your father, the council, and the high priests and priestess need to see us."

Something dark and hesitant in his voice made Eira pause. She knew what this was about—the council must have finally decided how they were going to respond to her and Cadeyrn's relationship. All the waiting and anticipation was going to be over, and Eira could move forward with her life. No matter what the decision was.

Alvis avoided her eyes and turned on his heel to go back inside. Eira and Rose stood and followed him into the grand hall, where everyone was waiting. The council sat on the left side of the room in two rows. On the right were representatives of Luana's priestesses, led by High Priestess Nyx, along with representatives of Ray's priests, led by High Priest Cyrus. Father sat in the center, on his throne, elevated over them all.

Cadeyrn was also there, standing in front of them, and Aytigin was in the back, leaning against the wall with the guards, Cal, and Myra. Rose and Alvis stood along with Cadeyrn, and Eira joined him, clasping her hand in his.

Cadeyrn leaned over and whispered into her ear, "You haven't changed your mind?"

Countless times over the last few days, they'd discussed and argued over what they would do with whatever choice the council made, but they finally came to a conclusion together.

Eira looked over the group who had gathered in the grand hall, and straightened her shoulders with a deep sigh. It was time to move forward.

"No, I haven't," she replied. "Have you?"

"I'm with you, no matter what. Whatever you need."

Eira swallowed the lump in her throat. None of this was going to be easy, regardless of the outcome. But she wasn't in it alone, and she not only had Cadeyrn's love, but the blessing of Luana. Eira knew what she needed to do.

"Well, I suppose there's no need for my first question," Father said to the room, staring at Eira and Cadeyrn's hands. He gripped the edge of the armrest with white knuckles and stood. "I'm sure you know why you were all called here."

"Eira, is it your intention to reject your betrothal to Prince Alvis?" A shred of hope glimmered in Father's eyes.

Hope that she would say no and do what she was meant to do. What they all expected her to do. They all knew the risk if she didn't.

"My heart belongs to another. I will not marry Prince Alvis." She looked at her former betrothed in hope that she'd catch his gaze.

But he remained stoic and wouldn't look at her.

"I'm sorry."

And she was. Sorry she'd hurt her friend.

Father's shoulders sagged, and a line formed on the skin between his eyes. No one would ever call King Brennan old, and Eira never saw him as such. But here, she could see the age in his face, and he was tired. It was all she needed to determine what was going to happen next.

Deep down, she knew this was going to be the end result, and she wasn't as bothered by it as she'd imagined she would be.

"After much debate, the council, with the encouragement of the Temple, has decided that since Princess Eira has turned her back on the most sacred of duties as Luana's Chosen, and an integral alliance with the kingdom of Oxare, to remove her from the line to the throne." King Brennan's voice was heavy and slow, as though someone were pulling the words out of his mouth, one by one.

The room erupted at the announcement, a cacophony of sound as priestesses spoke out—Priestess Cynth the most prominent—and several guards standing with Cal shouted in shock. Yet there was a clear divide. A majority of the council remained silent with determined smiles on their faces, while the few who disagreed clenched their jaws and fists. On the side of the religious leaders, High Priestess Nyx smirked, and her acolytes held their heads high. No matter what evidence lay before them, going against one of their most sacred and powerful traditions was not to be accepted easily. Even with some of them supporting her.

At Eira's side, Rose's face turned red and her knuckles white from her grasping her crutch.

"What?" she said. "You can't do that! She's the rightful heir! After all she's done—"

High Priestess Nyx stood. "Everything our kingdoms value and hold dear is symbolized in the stations of Luana and Ray's Chosen. It has been instituted since the time of Isadore and Sanson. Princess Eira turning her back on her gods-given duty is turning her back on her kingdom."

"She *saved* our kingdom! She is blessed by Luana. Do you not see her power?" Rose's pale and freckled face turned redder with each moment and almost matched her hair.

Priestess Cynth shook her head, and the Marquis of Marallis was seething in his seat. Yet the majority were nodding and speaking their approval.

Eira turned to Rose and outstretched an arm to encourage her to remain calm, even if she did appreciate her sister coming to her defense.

"Beliefs cannot be changed overnight," Eira said. "Prince Cadeyrn and I understand this. But we do ask you to reconsider."

One of the council members, an elderly gentleman from Slania, stood and raised his voice.

"She has also broken our alliance with Oxare, when our kingdom needs them more than ever. If we cannot trust her with decisions such as this, how can she be trusted to rule? Her choices are determined by the whims of her fancy. We do not know what she's been doing all this time while Queen Amelia was raiding our villages. Building power, having affairs, making alliances with dangerous dragons. If she truly cared, she would have revealed herself sooner."

Alvis raised a hand, and the voices quieted. "My family harbors no ill will against Cresin. We have not been enemies in some time, and we have no intention of starting now."

King Brennan crossed his arms. "If Eira were to change her mind, would you agree to return to the previous arrangement?"

For the first time in days, Alvis looked at Eira, his golden eyes hard and set.

"No. I would not. I have no desire to be someone's second choice. If she doesn't want to be with me, so be it. I wish them both happiness. Now if you'll excuse me. If there is nothing else you need from me, I need to attend to packing my things. It's time I planned my journey home. I've been away from Oxare too long."

Alvis nodded at Eira and turned to walk out of the room, not looking at his brother, who tried to catch his attention. The way Cadeyrn's face crumpled tore Eira into pieces. She hated what this did to him.

"Cade, if you want—"

He shook his head. "We knew he would be hurt." Cadeyrn tightened his grip on her hand. "I'm not turning away from you now."

And she wasn't turning her back on him, either.

King Brennan descended the steps toward Eira, using a cane, as his limbs were still stiff from lying in bed for such a long time. He looked so tall by the throne, towering over them all. The closer to Eira he came, the smaller he was in her eyes. This man, the one who'd raised her and loved her. He taught her everything he knew, and groomed her to be the perfect future queen. His face was pained now. Brokenhearted over the way these events had turned.

Eira had done all she could to save him. He might have fought with the council for her, but he hadn't fought hard enough. Not the way she had. It was the one element of this result Eira couldn't shake off. A part of her hoped he would find a way to sway their decision.

Ice and darkness swirled in Eira's veins as she looked at him, and she fought to keep them under control. Yet she couldn't help the thin sheet of ice spreading at her feet, or how her hands were being covered shadows. All of this had been her choice, but the betrayal from her father was the most devastating blow.

King Brennan eyed the ice spreading on the ground and took a step away. High Priestess Nyx clenched her hands as fear clouded her eyes. The others in the room had similar reactions, and tense silence spread through the crowd.

It wasn't only doubt at her words and turning away from tradition that made them dethrone her. They were afraid. A glimpse at Eira's new power sent fear through them.

A smirk pulled at her lips. *Good.* Let them be afraid. It showed that they knew there was truth to what she said about her encounter with Luana.

She could show them right there all the power she held. Prove to them Luana had touched her and that she could throw away this *important* tradition if she wanted. It wouldn't be the way to earn back her crown, though. Fear would help, and it could give her the status she deserved for the moment. But she needed more than their fear if she was going to be the queen she wanted to become.

Eira took a deep breath, and the ice and shadows calmed. This was her lot, and she was prepared for it, even if it broke her heart. All of this wasn't over yet, and she would gain their trust back. She would get her kingdom back. For now, something else needed her attention.

"If there is nothing else," she said, "I must be going. It appears as though my presence in Farren is no longer necessary, and I have tasks to attend to elsewhere. Allow me the night to prepare my things, and I will be on my way."

King Brennan tried to reach to her, to stroke her face the way he did when she was a child in need of comfort. But Eira gave a deep curtsey, and Cadeyrn bowed next to her.

"Goodbye, Your Majesty."

As Eira and Cadeyrn left the court, Rose jogged behind.

"Eira, wait!"

In their wake, those in the grand hall bowed. Not to Eira, but to Rose.

The future queen of Cresin.

Chapter Thirty-Eight

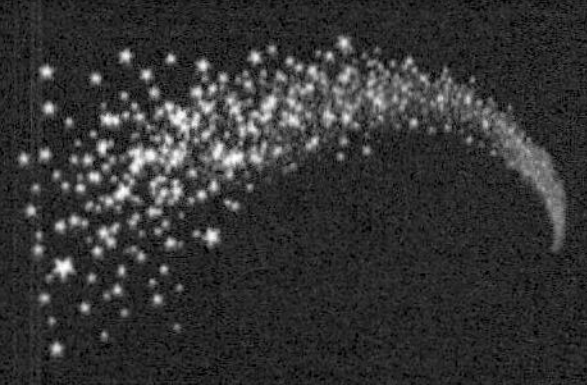

ALVIS

Alvis tapped on the chamber door, and after a soft voice told him to come in, he stepped inside.

Nell sat in the middle of the massive bed, an island in a sea of sheets and pillows. The curtains were drawn, and the late autumn sun shone into the room. She ran her fingers through her now short hair.

They'd never made it all the way to the cottage during the battle, but Alvis was able to get her far enough away until it was safe to return to the castle. His visits to her mirror may have been brief and far between, but he felt a strange kinship toward the girl. He'd only been held captive by Amelia for a few weeks and was still able to wander the castle, but Nell had been in the mirror her entire life.

Once things calmed over the last few days, Evony and Cynth had sat with the young girl and styled her hair for her. They showed her different ointments so the curls lay softly.

Nell grabbed a curl, pulled it in front of her face, and let it go. The curl bounced back like a spring.

"How do you like your room?" Alvis said.

She was quiet and strange, but in many ways, Alvis was, too.

She bit her lip and glanced around. "It's big."

"Indeed it is." Alvis dragged a stool closer to the bed and sat. "Have you looked around anywhere else in the castle at all? I'm sure there is much you haven't seen yet."

Nell fidgeted with her dress. "A little. But…it's so big. I was afraid I'd get lost."

Yes, this was going to be a major transition for her. A detail that hadn't occurred to Alvis when he'd planned to help her escape from the mirror. Living in a world outside of the mirror would be overwhelming. So many scents, sounds, sights, and the sheer space of it all. There were moments when Nell looked wistfully out the window, and he could tell she wanted to explore. But she was scared.

"We can help you, if you like," Alvis said. "We're always here if you want or need anything."

"Yes, everyone has been quite kind."

"Good. I'm glad." Alvis rested his elbows on his knees, unsure of how to go about this next topic. "I need to return to Oxare soon. My kingdom. There is some business I need to attend to."

He also needed to get away from Farren Castle. He'd done what he could to help, but…it was time. Seeing how happy Eira and Cadeyrn were together made him understand why she made the choice she did. Yet he needed time and space away from it. They were respectful and didn't do anything to intentionally make him uncomfortable. Yet…he couldn't stay here any longer.

Nell's focus was torn from her dress, and panic splashed across her face.

"You're leaving?"

"I'll come back."

For political reasons, he would, and even to visit his brother. In time.

"But I've been neglecting my kingdom for too long. I was wondering, though…would you like to join me?"

Nell bit her lip again. "Go with you?"

It was an idea he'd been ruminating on for some time now. Nell needed a new start even more than Alvis did. Being in Farren Castle would only remind her of her mother and the past. It would be difficult, for Oxare was so different from Cresin, but perhaps they could heal together. Besides, he was taking the mirror with him. Many of Colma's followers in Oxare would be able to ensure Amelia never escaped, and attendants could still help her, at least until the child was born. It only made sense for Nell to join them.

He'd researched Nell's family, and her grandmother had passed a few years ago. No one knew who her father was. There was nowhere for her to go. Surely Eira and Rose would not let Nell be neglected if she were to choose to stay. But Alvis wanted to extend the offer. It was the right thing to do.

"You would come as my ward," he said. "You would have whatever you want, and people to help you. I could introduce you to other children your age, give you a tutor, show you around the kingdom. The sun shines all the time. I think you would like it."

Nell gazed out the window as though she could see all the way to Oxare through it.

"How would we get there?"

"On a boat and sail along the river. You would see the Eastern kingdom of Marallis on our way."

The boat could be a good transition for her. It was small enough where she wouldn't be lost, but she could grow used to the open air. As long as she could control water sickness.

"I've never been on a boat!" Nell said. "There's so much I haven't seen. The world is big."

"Yes, it is. But you'll like it. Would you like me to help you explore?"

Nell sat in silence for a few moments, gazing out toward the sky.

Then she turned her head and smiled.

Preparations to leave went quickly. They needed to set sail before the heavy winter in Cresin fell, making travel more difficult. At least the further south they sailed, the warmer it would become. The heat was high on Alvis's list of things he was looking forward to.

A few days later, Alvis and Nell gathered in the great hall to say goodbye. Cynth and Evony had grown attached to Nell and were helping her tie her travel cloak and boots. Nell had spent most of her life barefoot and was still growing accustomed to how footwear worked.

"We'll miss you," Rose told him as the servants carried Alvis's trunks out to the carriage.

He had asked Rose if she would like Nell to stay in Cresin, as they'd grown close in their time in captivity. But with Rose's new role as the future queen of Cresin, she needed to focus on her duties and not raising a child.

"I know," Alvis replied. "But it's time."

Cal clapped a hand on Alvis's shoulder. "Thank you for all you did for Myra, and all of us."

"It was my pleasure."

Alvis hugged both of them and headed toward the door where Nell was waiting. She fidgeted with her travel clothes as Alvis said goodbye to Cynth and Evony, two people who, surprisingly, had become good friends.

Eira and Cadeyrn met Alvis and Nell at the carriage outside, standing a respectable distance apart. In spite of himself, a pang of guilt hit Alvis. It was because of him they were treading carefully around one another.

Yet another reason it was time to leave.

He was preventing them from moving on with the next part of their lives, along with his own.

"Are you sure you need to go?" Eira said as Nell stepped into the carriage. "You're welcome to stay as long as you like. We could use some of your guidance."

Alvis smiled. "You may always write, and I'll be sure Oxare comes to your aid whenever you need it. But I need to leave."

As though unable to stop herself, Eira launched into a warm embrace, and Alvis couldn't help but return it. He knew she was regretful of how she'd hurt him. The edge of it had worn off, and Alvis was making his peace. The more he saw Eira and Cadeyrn together, the more he saw that perhaps it was more of the idea of Eira he missed. He cared for her deeply, and she would always be a friend. But it was the future he'd seen with her that he missed. Now, for the first time, he wasn't sure what lay ahead, and he didn't know what to do with that.

When they broke apart, Eira gave Cadeyrn a pointed look and went back into the castle, leaving the brothers alone. In a way, Cadeyrn's betrayal was the one that stung the most. This was the first he'd been able to bear being in Cadeyrn's presence.

Alvis wasn't sure what to do as he bid farewell to his brother. He set his hands on the hilt of his sword.

"It's strange to be returning home without you."

It was the truth. They'd always taken these journeys between the two kingdoms together. But it would take the world's end for Cadeyrn to leave Eira's side. Even then, Alvis doubted they would ever part.

Cadeyrn stood with a noble confidence these days that he didn't possess in the past. He looked comfortable in the furs and winter outdoor wear as though he were a Cresin native. Maybe it was because it was similar to his bear fur. He looked at home because he *was* at home, which was now wherever Eira was.

Maybe it always had been.

The realization lifted a weight on Alvis's shoulders he hadn't realized had been there. Cadeyrn had found his place, and the one he'd always wanted. The person who brought out the best in him. Alvis was now free to do the same.

"It will be odd seeing you go," Cadeyrn replied. "I've barely seen you."

This might have been on purpose, which was cowardly, Alvis knew. He should have done more to reach out to his brother these last days.

Alvis clasped his hand and pulled him in for a hug.

"She's good for you. But if she doesn't take care of you, she has me to answer to."

Cadeyrn let out a hearty laugh. "I'll be sure to let her know. We'll see you soon. And if you need me, I'll be there."

Alvis nodded. He knew this, but it was reassuring to hear Cadeyrn say it.

As Alvis prepared to step into the carriage, a young woman ran toward him, carrying a small bag.

Myra. He smiled as she caught up to him and dropped her bag.

"Where are you off to in such a hurry?" Alvis said. "Not avoiding saying goodbye, are you?"

"I'm coming with you." Myra tucked a stray strand of hair behind her ear. "There's nothing for me here, and I've decided it's time I return home. If there is room on the ship."

Alvis grabbed her bag and tossed it into the back of the carriage with the rest of their luggage.

"Nell will be delighted to know you're joining us."

"I'm sure she will be." Myra smiled as Alvis let her step into the carriage before him.

Time to go home, indeed.

Chapter Thirty-Nine

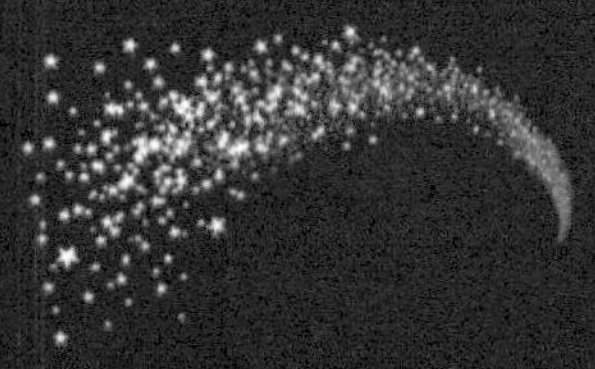

EIRA

Eira stood on the balcony of her room and looked past the budding rose tree, towards Eral forest. The sun was setting behind the trees, and the sky turned bright pink and yellow. She'd never noticed before, but in the distance twinkling stars were making their appearance. The coming of night was welcome, and it brought Eira strength. Peace and grace swept over her as she enjoyed the scene one last time.

A knock came to the door.

"Come in," Eira called.

Rose crutched into the room and stood beside her to look out at Eral.

"Do you have to go? Father never said you had to leave. He's devastated you are. Perhaps if you stay, Father—"

"It's for the best, Rose. I have other things I need to do now."

Rose turned so she leaned against the balcony rail and propped herself on one arm.

"You're determined to restore Luana's castle?" she said. "You believe you can do it?"

"I'll be able to recruit help, of course. After all Luana has done for me, and all that Malle went through, and Aytigin, I want to make it right for them. As best as I can, at least. Besides…I like it there."

It was the first Eira had admitted it to anyone. Cadeyrn suspected, of course, and Eira wondered if, deep down, Rose did too.

The prospect of returning to the Paravian Mountains and living in Luana's castle thrilled Eira like not much else had. There, she could learn more about Luana, live and love the way she wanted, and build a life for herself. Not governed by anyone else.

"You'll visit me there, won't you?" Eira said.

She'd been away from her sister so often, and their time to reunite had been cut short. Eira couldn't imagine living a life without her sister in it at all.

"I'll have to, won't I?" Rose said. "To see what all the fuss is about. Who knows? Maybe I'll want to live there with you."

She strummed her fingers on the top of her crutch, and even though no one else was around, she lowered her voice.

"The crown, it's yours, you know. I don't want it."

Eira took deep breath. "I know. I had no intentions of letting you keep it. Do you hate me?"

Rose let out a sigh of relief. "Praise the gods. I'd hoped you had a plan. I don't want to be queen. I would be terrible at it."

Eira chuckled and helped Rose stand straight again so they could go inside as Eira completed her preparations to leave.

"You would have been fine," she said. "But it's still my right, no matter what the council says. I also know that while you would have learned how to rule, you would have been miserable."

Rose perched herself on the vanity stool and set her crutch aside.

"Why didn't you fight for it with the council? You let them strip you of everything, and didn't say a word. You could have decided to marry Alvis, and all of this would be over."

"I knew what was going to happen when Cadeyrn and I announced our intentions. But I needed to do it for myself so I could raise my court and rule the way I want it to be. Not according to old traditions which shouldn't stand any longer, forcing people to be what they aren't. I did it for me, but also for Cadeyrn, and Malle, and Isadore, and Luana. All of us who have had positions and titles we never asked for and were forced to do what we didn't want to. I want to create a new court, Rose. New traditions."

"A new world."

Eira nodded. "Yes, you could say that."

She folded a dress and placed it inside the bag she was going to carry back to the mountains. Rose found their mother's red cloak and handed it to her.

Eira shook her head. "You take it. Mother's cloak assisted me on my journey. Now it's your turn. I don't need it anymore."

Rose held it close to her and smiled. "What are you going to do about Father?"

Eira closed the pack and pursed her lips. "Nothing. He will do a fine job helping the kingdom rise again, and I'll do my part on my own. I have no intentions of overthrowing him. Besides, he isn't old yet. It'll give me plenty of time to win the people's trust again."

As angry and hurt as she was by him, she couldn't deny he was a good ruler. She couldn't turn her back on him after all she'd done to save him.

"You have more of their trust than you know," Rose said.

"I hope you're right."

"I know I am."

THERE WAS NO GRAND PROCESSION OR LARGE GATHERING FOR EIRA AND Cadeyrn's parting. They'd said their goodbyes to the ones they chose, and while the rest of the castle was sleeping, the two of them left to meet Aytigin at the gate.

"You don't have to go with me," Eira said.

It was something she'd mentioned several times during their conversations the last several days as they made their plans.

"You can return to your estate in Oxare, and we'll visit one another. Aytigin can fly me anywhere I choose."

Cadeyrn lifted her hand and kissed it tenderly. "I know I don't, but I want to. Oddly enough, the place grew on me a bit. Besides, I never want to be parted from you again."

"Nor I you."

Cadeyrn fished for something in his pocket and held out a small box. He opened the lid, and inside sat a delicate silver band. All around it were carved images of the stars, moon, snow, a bear, a dragon, and a castle. It was their story.

"I know I'm only a bastard prince with a sword and have nothing to offer you. But—"

"Yes!" Eira threw her arms around his neck and pulled him into a kiss.

He picked her up by the waist so her feet hovered as he kissed her.

He still sent thrills through her, and she could have lost herself in him right then and there.

"I didn't have the chance to ask you yet. I had a speech planned," Cadeyrn said when they gasped for air.

"Then ask me, you fool."

He set her back on the ground, but they remained pressed against one another, his forehead resting on hers.

"Eira, will you marry me?"

"Yes. Forever yes."

He clasped the band around her wrist and kissed her again, his lips welcoming her into a lifetime of happiness. In the distance, Aytigin swooped out of sky and stood tall and proud in front of the gate. Even in his dragon form, he sneered.

"Are you done yet? I want to be home before the sun rises."

Home. In only a matter of hours, the three of them would be away from Farren and back in Luana's castle. The notion of it being home settled on Eira like a warm blanket.

She grasped Cadeyrn's hand and looked into his gold eyes. The location didn't matter. When Cadeyrn was there, she was already home.

"Are you ready?" she said.

"I've been ready my whole life."

With only a few bags in hand, they climbed onto Aytigin's back. Eira wrapped her arms around Cadeyrn's waist, and they dashed into the night's sky.

The stars danced as they flew, and Eira embraced their comforting light, ready for whatever was to come next.

Thank you for reading! Did you enjoy? Please add your review because nothing helps an author more and encourages readers to take a chance on a book than a review.

And don't miss book two, THE SHADOW'S HEIR, available now. Turn the page for a sneak peek!

You can also sign up for the City Owl Press newsletter to receive notice of all book releases!

Sneak Peek of The Shadow's Heir

Myra wasn't sure if she was nauseated from excitement or dread. The shore of Cyre had grown larger and more distinct each day during their trip down the Lotus River. At her side, Alvis, the crowned prince of Oxare, stood tall and proud as he surveyed his home city. He rested his hands on the rail of the riverboat, tapping his fingers against the wood as though they were keys on a musical instrument.

It was a habit Myra noticed he employed when excitement swam over him. When in such close proximity to people for a week, it was easy to pick up on little things like that. Alvis had been more than generous and hospitable when Myra invited herself along with his entourage to return to her home kingdom. She assumed the boat would be large enough for her to squeeze in.

It was large, and Myra only had to share a room with one other woman, who was friendly enough. But she was surprised at how often she still ran into the prince. He liked to spend as much time on the deck under the sun as possible, and the farther south they came, the more often he was there lounging on his cushions, a small bowl of nuts at his side, and tunic loosened at the collar. Usually reading a book. He finished at least two during the trip.

Myra rocked when the boat docked at the shore, and it was only a matter of minutes before the workers tied the riverboat so it wouldn't float away, and they unloaded all the travelers' luggage.

Everyone called the beautiful structure in the distance the Golden Palace, though its proper name was Cyre Palace, after the capital city.

"It's beautiful, isn't it?" Alvis gazed in the direction of the Golden Palace.

The roof was white with gold engravings of the sun, moon, and stars etched in. The palace reflected the light from the god Ray's sunbeams, making the whole building appear to be made of gold. It had been years since Myra had been to the capital city of Oxare, but she remembered clearly the way it looked like a miniature sun when night turned into day, and how if one looked directly at it, 'they'd think 'they'd gone blind.

Now, as the sun set, there was merely a warm pink glow around the rounded tops of the palace, and if she focused enough, she could almost see the intricate engravings and paintings around the pillars. The Golden Palace was a grand mountain among the small hills of buildings surrounding it. Some of them mansions, others shacks, and everything in between.

"It is impressive," Myra admitted. She'd worked in Farren Castle in the northern kingdoms of Cresin for years, and it was stunning with its tall towers and spires. Maybe it was the Oxarian blood and pride in her, but there was something about the Golden Palace that stirred awe. The shining metals and luxurious engravings surpassed most—if not all—other buildings Myra had seen or worked in.

"They built it several centuries ago to honor Ray and his love for Luana. The roof was designed to show his majesty and glory during the day, but also so Luana could see it during the night and remember their love was still there, even if they were apart." Alvis inhaled deeply, and the remaining sunbeams of the day shone on his brown hair and dark skin. It was good he was dedicated to the sun god, as he looked as though he was born to lie out in the sand for days on end and never grow tired of its warmth.

Only a couple of months ago, he'd been painted in gold and performed the ceremony to welcome the changing of the seasons with his then betrothed, Princess Eira. Myra had sneaked into the ballroom to watch and could have sworn he was the god himself. Alvis's left wrist twitched where his betrothal band used to be.

Myra's heart sank. Princess Eira had chosen instead to be with someone else and broken off their betrothal. With his brother no less. Myra had been betrayed by family in her past as well and could imagine the hurt he must have felt. He never mentioned it or acted as though he was angry or brokenhearted. But Myra knew about hiding feelings and locking them deep inside to put on a brave face. She knew about keeping secrets and needing to get away.

It was how she'd survived her whole life. Now she needed to be away more than ever after the events of this past autumn season in Cresin.

"That's a lovely story," Myra told him with a smile. Even if she'd heard it before, he was so proud of his god and kingdom, she couldn't help but indulge him. Over the past week, she'd often sat with him on the deck of the riverboat and listened to him read passages of books or tell his favorite tales of the deities. In those moments, he didn't seem like the next king of Oxare, but a normal man who was passionate about knowledge and heritage. Sometimes, she would think of a tale and tell him one, which he always listened to with interest.

Alvis nodded, and his gaze darted toward her and then to the shore. "The Golden Palace is large, and we're always in need of extra help. We have more space than we know what to do with. I don't know what your plans are now that we have returned to Oxare, but if you need employment or a place to stay while you decide what to do next, you'd be more than welcome to stay. And I know Nell will miss you."

Myra's breath caught, and she blinked. She hadn't expected Alvis to make such an offer. Least of all, minutes before they were to depart the boat and go their separate ways. It would be easy to go with him. She'd been a servant in Farren Castle, and she was sure working in the Golden Palace wasn't much different. She could do well there, and it was an opportunity many people would jump for, and it was being handed to her on a silver platter. Besides, Myra had grown close to Nell, Amelia's daughter, who she'd helped free from the enchanted mirror. Alvis was taking the young girl in as his ward.

Myra's shoulders sank. But what happened when the generosity ran out? What if he found out the truth of how those events came to be and her involvement in it? Too many times she'd had to rely on the whims of others for her future, and in the end, either she or someone else paid the price. No. She needed to leave everything of Farren Castle behind her.

She faced the kind prince and leaned against the boat rail. "I'm going to miss Nell, and your offer is generous, but one I must decline. I have other business to attend to upon my return. Thank you though."

Something that reminded Myra of disappointment and regret flashed in Alvis's desert-gold eyes, but it was gone in a moment after it appeared. "Of course. I understand. But please remember, the invitation is always open. If you are ever in need of something, do not hesitate to come to me."

The flush of her cheeks had Myra looking away from the prince. "You are far too generous. I'm only a servant."

Alvis held her chin between soft fingers and raised her gaze to meet his. A chill ran through Myra, and she knew it wasn't from the breeze. "You are a wonderful and strong woman, and it is the least I can do after all your help in Cresin. I, and the kingdoms, am indebted to you."

The heat warming Myra's cheeks surely turned them deep red by then, and she tried to find words. She'd hardly done anything in comparison to the rest of them. If it weren't for her, none of it would have happened in the first place. He was being far too kind. And if he knew who she was, who she really was, he wouldn't be saying these things. She took a step back out of his reach, and his arm fell to his side. There were too many people around, and as innocent as his gesture was, to spying eyes, it could be taken the wrong way. Myra wouldn't let her be attached to his name, especially now when he needed to be home after being gone for so long. And without the princess of Cresin at his side.

"My small effort was for the sake of the kingdoms."

Alvis clasped his hands behind his back and smiled. "Myra, please, let me give you a compliment."

She chuckled. "Very well. Thank you, your highness."

On land, a herd of white horses with red-and-gold caparisons along with richly ornamented carts with all the luggage arrived, ready for the prince and his entourage to return to the palace. A servant attempted to assist Nell onto one of the horses, but the girl seemed like she was afraid to go on. She shook her head, her brown-and-blond curls bouncing around her shoulders. Her chin quivered, and Myra knew tears were to come next. The poor girl had lived inside a mirror her whole life and was still adjusting to the outside world.

Alvis's jaw stiffened as he watched the scene. "I should go help Nell. Maybe if she sees I'm on a horse too, she'll get on, or I can get them to let her ride on a cart instead. A palanquin could do well…"

"Good idea."

They stood facing each other for a moment, and Myra knew it was time to say good-bye. It would be best to get it done and move on. She had other places to be, and before long, Alvis would only remember in faint memories the servant girl who helped him a bit. Taking care of Nell certainly would keep him busy.

She grasped the edges of her plain skirt and knelt in a small curtsy. "Thank you for everything, your highness."

Alvis bowed to her. "It was my pleasure, Myra." The sound of Nell yelling at the servants echoed up to the deck of the boat, and his focus shifted to his ward and the scene on land. The servants struggled to get Nell onto the horse still, and tears ran down her cheeks in earnest now. Alvis placed a hand on Myra's shoulder. "I must go. Take care of yourself, and please remember my offer."

Myra could only nod as he rushed past her and raced down the plank to land. She would remember his offer, but it didn't change anything. He was a prince with a job to do, and Myra was a servant girl who needed to make her way in the world. Against her chest, the necklace kept hidden beneath her tunic, and the memories and history it held hovered on her like a dense fog. An ever-present reminder of who she was and who she never could be.

A warm breeze embraced Myra and blew a strand of hair across her face. After living in Cresin for so long, it was hard to believe it was almost the winter solstice and she didn't need to wear any furs or wool scarfs. The kingdom of Oxare did turn cool in the winter, but it wasn't anything close to the harsh and snowy winters Myra had grown used to.

Some new clothes, Myra decided, was the first thing she would need to purchase. She had money saved, and tucked away in her bag were a few pieces of clothes and jewelry she'd made and intended to sell. The other servants in Farren Castle loved her wares, and she hoped she would have the same luck in Oxare. She only had enough to fill the couple bags she carried, and it might not be enough to pay for a cart or donkey, so she would need to make her travels on foot, but she didn't mind.

On land, Alvis was at Nell's side. He knelt to her and held her hands. Myra couldn't hear what he was saying, but whatever it was had Nell wiping her tears away. He stood again and showed the young girl how to get on top of the horse. When she saw he was safe, the servants helped her climb on too, so she was sitting in front of Alvis. Her brown eyes grew big as she looked around beneath them as though the ground was a few hundred and not a few feet below them. Myra smiled. They would be just fine. Both Alvis and Nell needed a fresh start, and Myra had a feeling they'd be good for one another.

"Hey!"

Myra's attention was pulled from the scene toward the sailor who'd called to her. He pointed to the plank, and his brows were pinched together in anger. "'Get a move on, girl! We can't have you on this boat forever!"

Myra waved him off and picked up the two bags she'd brought with her few belongings. She needed to have a fresh start too. When she got to the dock, Alvis and his entourage were already on their way to the palace. Alvis's white horse faced away like a cloud blowing across the sky.

It was time to move on.

Don't stop now. Keep reading with your copy of THE SHADOW'S HEIR.

And find more from E. E. Hornburg at www.emilyhornburg.com

A Guide to the Deities

Luana, goddess of the moon
Other influences: stars, darkness, winter, ice, night
Color: blue
Common Symbols: moon in various stages, stars, snowflakes
High Temple Location: Farren Castle in Cresin
Appearance: slender woman with long dark hair and pale skin

Ray, god of the sun
Other influences: clouds, light, summer, fire, day
Color: yellow
Common Symbols: sun, fire, sand, cloud, phoenix, dragon
High Temple Location: Cyre Palace—the Golden Palace—in Oxare
Appearance: large, muscular man with golden skin and flaming hair

Kutlaous, god of nature
Other influences: forest, jungle, agriculture, animals, plants
Color: green
Common Symbols: vine, stag, horns, leaves, flowers, animals
High Temple Location: Eral Forest
Appearance: human man with horns on his head and hooves for feet, green skin with vines wrapped around his body

Aros, god of war
Other influences: hunting, fitness, athletes
Color: red
Common Symbols: sword, arrow, snake, lion
High Temple Location: Khadi Desert

Appearance: tall, almost giant man with white skin, red eyes, and shaved head

Colma, god of water
Other influences: water creatures, other liquids, drinks
Color: blue or green
Common Symbols: waves, fish, pitcher, ship, mermaid tail
High Temple Location: Dravian Islands
Appearance: lanky yet muscular man with translucent skin, long blue hair, often wearing blue robes

Stula, goddess of death
Other influences: sickness, disability, change, maturity
Color: purple
Common Symbols: skull, bones, rose, clock, raven
High Temple Location: Underworld
Appearance: woman with dark skin, purple hair, and black robes

Yla, deity of birth
Other influences: fertility, childhood
Color: pink
Common Symbols: footprints, lotus flower, baby animals, egg
High Temple Location: Oxare Coast
Appearance: no one knows their "true" appearance, as they come as they are needed. A middle-aged woman to be a midwife; a young man preparing for fatherhood; a pregnant woman; a grandparent, etc. The commonalities are brown hair and a tattoo of the lotus flower.

Diar, deity of love
Other influences: beauty, desire, charity
Color: red or pink
Common Symbols: rose, heart, ribbons intertwined or tied together, doves
High Temple Location: Belovian Islands
Appearance: a nonbinary being containing anatomy of both male and female, long and flowing pink hair and light-brown skin

Efarae, goddess of inspiration
Other influences: the arts, keepers of the deities' tales
Color: Lavender
Common Symbols: music notes, a quill, paint brush, owl, scroll
High Temple Location: Kingdom of Marali
Appearance: petite woman with blond hair, purple eyes, and often wearing glasses

Gallis, goddess of restoration
Other influences: healing, health, fitness, building
Color: gold
Common Symbols: a chalice, building tools, bandages, tonic bottles, hands
High Temple Location: Kingdom of Imare
Appearance: a round and plump yet strong woman with brown hair and golden robes

Read book two, THE SHADOW'S HEIR, available now, and find more from E. E. Hornburg at www.emilyhornburg.com

---

Myra has spent years hiding—in servitude of the now imprisoned Queen Amelia, and from a lineage she never wanted.

Now that she is freed from Amelia's clutches, Myra is ready for a new start, but the echoes of the past, and the truth of who she is—a direct descendant of Stula, the goddess of death—will only disrupt the peace she wants to find in the kingdom of Oxare.

The kingdom is beautiful, as is the handsome prince Alvis and though his offer to join him at the Golden Palace is tempting, Myra is determined to make her own way.

But when a life on her own becomes too difficult, Myra is forced to accept Alvis' offer and lands in the thick of a plot to free Queen Amelia. To keep the entire realm and her people safe, Myra and Alvis must find out who among the Golden Palace court is the betrayer before Amelia escapes.

But with each passing day Myra feels her connection to Alvis growing stronger, and her past continues to haunt her. Can they protect the kingdom and each other, before Amelia takes her revenge and Alvis finds out the truth?

All reviews are **welcome** and **appreciated**. Please consider leaving one on your favorite social media and book buying sites.

For books in the world of romance and speculative fiction that embody Innovation, Creativity, and Affordability, check out City Owl Press at www.cityowlpress.com.

Acknowledgments

Publishing my first book has been a lifelong dream, and there are so many people to thank who have supported and helped me through this journey.

First, I want to thank God for all of the people and gifts he's given me. The path he's led me on has been winding, unusual, and not what I expected, but I know he's been there each step bringing me through.

Tee Tate my editor, thank you for all of your patience, kindness, and all of the work you've put into helping me make this book as amazing as it could possibly be. You've been able to see my vision for this book and help it come to life.

Tina, Yelena, and the rest of the City Owl team, you have been such an amazing press to work with. I couldn't have had a better experience.

All of the other authors with City Owl, thank you for welcoming me into your flock and being so open with all of my questions and comments. I'm honored to be part of such a talented and amazing group of authors.

The talented team at MiblArt, this cover is gorgeous! I'm blown away each time I look at it.

Paris Wynters, this book would not be where it is today without you taking me under your wing when you didn't have to, believing in my writing, and being such a great friend. I can never thank you enough.

Kim and Piera, you are the best writing group I could ever ask for! I don't know where I would be without our writing dates and chats and retreats. Thank you for being such amazing friends.

Ginny, my plot whisperer, where would I be without our hours long phone conversations when you help me figure out all of the knots and holes and curveballs in my book? You've been the best.

Raul, Michelle, Brooke, Ted, and Caitlin. Thank you for reading early versions of this book (and others!) and being such a great cheer squad.

All of my teachers, managers, supervisors, and co-worker's past and present who have been more than supportive of my writing dreams and over the moon over this book, thank you.

Julie, Jen, Jo, Emily, Sam, Kristen, Erin, Lauri, Sarah, and Trina. I am so blessed to have such fantastic and supportive friends! You know how long this has been a dream of mine you all have been there for me every step of the way.

Dale, thank you for being the best support system during all of this. You never miss an opportunity to tell me how proud you are. Every day has been happy.

The whole Kleeman crew – ever since I was a kid making up stories and devouring books you've encouraged me and been there through all of the ups and downs. I am so blessed to have such an amazing family.

Mom, Dad, Natalie, Tim, and Elsie, you all are my rocks and I don't know where I'd be without you. No one could have a more caring, dedicated, patient, and loving family. I would be nothing without you at my side.

About the Author

E. E. HORNBURG is a Chicago South-sider, consumer of nachos, dog mom, aunt to the greatest niece ever, and owner of far too many mugs and travel cups which hold her coffee. When not creating or devouring books you can find her pretending she can rap along with the *Hamilton* cast and plotting how she can get to Disney World (again). *The Night's Chosen* is the first in the *Cursed Queens* series and her debut novel.

You can follow along and get free stories by signing up for her newsletter at

www.emilyhornburg.com

 x.com/eehornburg

instagram.com/eehornburg

facebook.com/EmilyEHornburg

About the Publisher

City Owl Press is a cutting edge indie publishing company, bringing the world of romance and speculative fiction to discerning readers.

Escape Your World. Get Lost in Ours!

www.cityowlpress.com

facebook.com/CityOwlPress
x.com/cityowlpress
instagram.com/cityowlbooks
pinterest.com/cityowlpress
tiktok.com/@cityowlpress

www.ingramcontent.com/pod-product-compliance
Lightning Source LLC
Chambersburg PA
CBHW030624310726
48979CB00003B/863

* 9 7 8 1 6 4 8 9 8 4 2 6 6 *